Raves for the previous Valdemar Anthologies

"Fans of Lackey's epic Valdemar series will devour this superb anthology. Of the thirteen stories included, there is no weak link—an attribute exceedingly rare in collections of this sort. Highly recommended." —The Barnes and Noble Review

"This high-quality anthology mixes pieces by experienced authors and enthusiastic fans of editor Lackey's Valdemar. Valdemar fandom, especially, will revel in this sterling example of what such a mixture of fans' and pros' work can be. Engrossing even for newcomers to Valdemar." —*Booklist*

"Josepha Sherman, Tanya Huff, Mickey Zucker Reichert, and Michelle West have quite good stories, and there's another by Lackey herself. Familiarity with the series helps but is not a prerequisite to enjoying this book." —*Science Fiction Chronicle*

"Each tale adheres to the Lackey laws of the realm yet provides each author's personal stamp on the story. Well written and fun, Valdemarites will especially appreciate the magic of this book." —*The Midwest Book Review*

"The sixth collection set in Lackey's world of Valdemar presents stories of Heralds and their telepathic horselike Companions and of Bards and Healers, and provides glimpses of the many other aspects of a setting that has a large and avid readership. The fifteen original tales in this volume will appeal to series fans." —*Library Journal*

Bounda

DAW BOOKS BY MERCEDES LACKEY:

THE NOVELS OF VALDEMAR:

THE HERALDS OF VALDEMAR
ARROWS OF THE QUEEN
ARROW'S FLIGHT
ARROW'S FALL

THE LAST HERALD-MAGE
MAGIC'S PAWN
MAGIC'S PROMISE
MAGIC'S PRICE

THE MAGE WINDS
WINDS OF FATE
WINDS OF CHANGE
WINDS OF FURY

THE MAGE STORMS
STORM WARNING
STORM RISING
STORM BREAKING

VOWS AND HONOR
THE OATHBOUND
OATHBREAKERS
OATHBLOOD

THE COLLEGIUM CHRONICLES
FOUNDATION
INTRIGUES
CHANGES
REDOUBT
BASTION

THE HERALD SPY
CLOSER TO HOME
CLOSER TO THE HEART
CLOSER TO THE CHEST

FAMILY SPIES
THE HILLS HAVE SPIES
EYE SPY
SPY, SPY AGAIN

THE FOUNDING OF VALDEMAR
BEYOND
INTO THE WEST*

BY THE SWORD
BRIGHTLY BURNING
TAKE A THIEF

EXILE'S HONOR
EXILE'S VALOR

VALDEMAR ANTHOLOGIES:
SWORD OF ICE
SUN IN GLORY
CROSSROADS
MOVING TARGETS
CHANGING THE WORLD
FINDING THE WAY
UNDER THE VALE
CRUCIBLE
TEMPEST
CHOICES
SEASONS
PASSAGES
BOUNDARIES

Written with **LARRY DIXON:**

THE MAGE WARS
THE BLACK GRYPHON
THE WHITE GRYPHON
THE SILVER GRYPHON

DARIAN'S TALE
OWLFLIGHT
OWLSIGHT
OWLKNIGHT

OTHER NOVELS:

GWENHWYFAR
THE BLACK SWAN

THE DRAGON JOUSTERS
JOUST
ALTA
SANCTUARY
AERIE

THE ELEMENTAL MASTERS
THE SERPENT'S SHADOW
THE GATES OF SLEEP
PHOENIX AND ASHES
THE WIZARD OF LONDON
RESERVED FOR THE CAT
UNNATURAL ISSUE
HOME FROM THE SEA
STEADFAST
BLOOD RED
FROM A HIGH TOWER
A STUDY IN SABLE
A SCANDAL IN BATTERSEA
THE BARTERED BRIDES
THE CASE OF THE SPELLBOUND CHILD
JOLENE
THE SILVER BULLETS OF ANNIE OAKLEY

Anthologies:
ELEMENTAL MAGIC
ELEMENTARY

*Coming soon from DAW Books

Boundaries

All-New Tales of Valdemar

Edited by Mercedes Lackey

DAW BOOKS, INC.
DONALD A. WOLLHEIM, FOUNDER
1745 Broadway, New York, NY 10019
ELIZABETH R. WOLLHEIM
SHEILA E. GILBERT
PUBLISHERS
www.dawbooks.com

Cover art by Jody A. Lee.

Cover design by Adam Auerbach.

DAW Book Collectors No. 1899.

Published by DAW Books, Inc.
1745 Broadway, New York, NY 10019.

First Printing, December 2021
2nd Printing

DAW TRADEMARK REGISTERED
U.S. PAT. AND TM. OFF. AND FOREIGN COUNTRIES
—MARCA REGISTRADA
HECHO EN U.S.A.

PRINTED IN THE U.S.A.

Contents

Tides of War
Dylan Birtolo

"Are you ready?" Taelor asked, swinging her sword in arcs small enough to not rip the top of the tent as she brought the blade around. "I bet I'll get more of those Karsite bastards than you will."

Eranel shook his head and rolled his eyes, his hands moving over his weapon's edge in smooth, practiced motions. He had been through the routine enough that he didn't need to watch where his fingers went to keep from nicking them on the sharpened metal.

"You're a fool," he said.

Taelor stopped at the end of her swing, tip of the weapon pointed toward the tent flap. Despite her recent exercise, the blade didn't waver. Her strength would last through hours of training, and it had carved her athletic form out of stone. "You think I'm a fool? You're the one sharpening your sword for something like the twentieth time this week. Here's a tip: for it to get dull, it actually needs to cut something."

"'Taking care of one's gear is of critical importance—'"

Taelor jumped in with the second half of the quote. "—'Lest you be caught unawares on the battlefield.' I swear, it's like you don't remember we had the same tutors, were in the same bloody classes! But the time for study is over! We're finally going to get our chance to make our parents proud. Our first battle."

She twirled the blade, rolling her wrist as she pivoted on the ball of her front foot, swinging around to point the weapon at her companion. The tip of it hovered less than a hand's width away from his nose. She looked down the edge of it and smirked. Until the top of her dark hair fell in front of her face and she huffed at it to blow the straight strands back.

In that moment, Eranel leaned back and flicked his sharpening stone at Taelor. She jerked to the side, moving her hand to protect herself from the projectile, bringing her weapon off target. With a smooth but powerful motion, Eranel brought his sword around in a full arc, smacking the flat of it against Taelor's blade, knocking it out of her loose grip and into the dirt. Eranel stepped on it without so much as getting up. He had a strength and frame to match hers, as if they were both carved from the same marble.

"What was that about being caught unawares?" he asked, a grin teasing the corner of his mouth.

"This isn't a battlefield," Taelor said as she crouched down to snatch her weapon. He let her have it without a fight. She stood up and tucked it away. "But I'll give you that one. That was good. Luckily I don't think the Karsite army'll be chucking whetstones."

"You never know. They are savages, after all."

The friends shared a brief laugh before Taelor left the tent. Eranel gave his blade a final examination after wiping it down with an oiled rag. It shined enough like a mirror that he could see his blue eyes in the flawless surface. His own light hair was trimmed short in the front to keep it out of the way.

His mind wandered back to the stories of what Karse had done, of the slaughter of his people, of how they had grown bolder and more violent over his lifetime. All those moments, even before he was born, leading up to this, his chance to exact some vengeance from those who dared to attack Valdemar. The skin around his eyes tightened for a moment before he slammed the blade into its scabbard hard enough to make the fittings rattle.

No, the Karsite army was unlikely to throw stones their way, but Eranel wouldn't put anything beyond them. He'd seen the cruelty they were capable of firsthand, having seen the refugees coming to his home.

With quick jerks, he pulled his hair into a tight braid behind his head. It wasn't fashionable, but it would keep it out of his face. The attention he paid to it was a minuscule fraction of that which he paid to his gear. Standing up, he made sure everything was in its proper position, giving his armored shirt a tug to make sure it was tied firmly in place.

Moving to the tent flap, he pulled it aside and stood at the opening, looking out on the campground near the edge of what would soon be a glorious battle. Lines of small tents stretched across the ground, most of them for one or two people, like his own. Farther in the distance stood the medical tent, its green banners flapping in the breeze to help it stand out from the others. Healers would be there, prepping for the work they would have to do for those unfortunate enough to fall but still fortunate enough to survive. He did not envy the work they would have without the opportunity to experience the glory of the battle itself.

Turning to the south, he marched to where his company had been ordered to gather. Taelor was already there, joking with some of the other soldiers and taking bets over how successful they would be. Most of their company was fresh and had yet to see a real battle. Sure, they had taken part in war games as a company, but that was different.

Eranel heard the voice of his tutor in his head. "*When the real battle starts, when that blood flows, many will find that the first scream of pain will freeze their knees. This is where true warriors are born, those who rise above this fear and conquer it. You will be afraid, and anyone who says they're not is either a liar or has never seen battle before. Accept this now, or no amount of training shall save your hide.*"

Eranel clenched his jaw at the memory, and his hand went to the hilt of his sword, tightening around it hard enough to make the leather creak. He nodded to the other members of his company, staying on the edge, with his attention focused inward rather than on those around him. He recited the litany of Karsite crimes in his head. He deliberately forced himself to remember those who had lost their homes and family to these barbaric invaders. With those memories rushing through his body, it took a deliberate act of will to force himself to unclench his hand from his weapon. He longed for his chance to strike back at these beasts that could not even be considered human.

The trumpet blasts jerked him out of his mental wandering, pulling him back into the moment with razor-sharp clarity. The company gathered themselves, standing shoulder-to-shoulder three lines deep. They were part of the left flank, forming up and waiting for the moment to be called into battle.

The sun beat down with unrelenting force, despite only being a few fingers above the horizon. Across the field, the Karsite army stood in their own formation. They marched across the ground, and the steady beat of their drums could be heard, sounding like the heartbeat of some monstrous beast.

The commander shouted orders, but the words barely registered in Eranel's mind. He marched forward, joining the pace and cadence of the brothers and sisters to his side. They maintained a steady pace, attempting to maneuver around the Karsite army's flank.

A host of arrows flew out from the Karsite army, looking like a flock of birds as they arced over and dropped into the center of the Valdemar forces. Screams echoed across the field, merging into battle screams as both forces charged toward each other. More clouds of sleek, deadly birds flew through the sky in both directions, each met with its own collection of shouts. One of the soldiers beside Eranel faltered, and he picked the man up by the armpit, helping him stay in formation. Their company picked up the pace, jogging across the field and attempting to reach the area where the two forces met in a mad frenzy.

The din of the shouting and the clash of the weapons drowned out any hope of hearing any more orders. Eranel found his voice joining the wordless scream of fury as the company charged toward the battle. They crashed forward like a wave and, like water, broke up and scattered as they struck the shields of the Karsite line that turned to face them.

Eranel swatted a blade aside and drove his shoulder into a shield, attempting to pass through the guard and make room for his companions. He brought his blade up in time to deflect a blow that left his arms trembling from the force. Rather than hold his ground, he ducked forward and rolled, coming around and springing up without hesitation.

"Only a corpse rests on the ground."

His weapon snaked out, the heavy blade slicing through a spear shaft, disarming the Karsite warrior. Before he had a chance to follow up the blow, Eranel had to pull his shoulder back to keep it from being sliced open by one of the curved blades of the savages. He glanced to his right and saw only Karsite colors—the rest of his company had failed to penetrate the shield line.

"The waiting blade cannot strike that which does not stand still."

Eranel moved like a whirlwind, spinning round and swatting away blades whenever he saw them. He danced across the ground, staying on the balls of his feet and never keeping in one place for the space of a breath. His movements flowed from one stance to the next, staying just ahead of those who attempted to strike him. True, he didn't manage to land more than a couple of small scratches, but that was also all he received. In that moment, survival was more important than attacking.

Despite his best efforts, when he glanced back, his company and the shield line appeared at least as far away as before. They couldn't possibly be pushed back, could they? He redoubled his efforts, sweat pouring down his face from the effort and the sun that cared little for his movements. One Karsite warrior got too close, and he slammed his pommel into the man's ribs, forcing him away but not before he found a gap in Eranel's armored shirt.

"Your wounds shall not give you pain in the battle, but they will bring you down. Be aware of them, always."

As he forced a Karsite back with a sweeping cut, Eranel paid attention to the scratch. He registered the blood wetting his side, but he could still take a deep breath. It would slow him down if he wasn't careful, but for now it was survivable.

As someone lunged at him, Eranel defended against the thrust and snapped his armored foot into the soldier's knee. Metal struck bone with a sickening crunch and the soldier fell, his shrill cry piercing the sound around Eranel and making him stumble as he danced away.

His foot snagged on something, and he fell backward, rolling over his shoulder as his teacher's words reminded him that his death awaited him if he stopped moving. As he came around, he recognized the face of the man he had helped in the first charge. Blood coated his slashed throat, and his eyes were open wide and blank.

Eranel's knees wobbled, and his legs moved as if they were swirling through ankle-deep mud. His arm shook as he reached up to deflect a blow, not giving it enough distance to clear his body. The sword edge bit into his arm, and he hissed as he pulled back, trying to retreat to the rest of his company. He didn't dare look back and pull his attention away from those around him.

One of the Karsite soldiers attacking him stumbled over another corpse, and Eranel took advantage of the opening to jump back, taking several quick steps toward his companions. In that brief moment of respite, he became painfully aware of the sheer number of people lying around him, most of them unmoving. It felt like a matter of seconds, but so many had already fallen. And in that moment of awareness, the screams and cries of those who still clung to life, often in vain, pierced through his adrenaline-induced focus.

The soldier in front of him scrambled up and thrust before he had his full weight underneath him. Eranel's instincts kicked in, and he circled his blade over, smacking the weapon to the ground and disarming the soldier. He shifted his weight and brought his pommel around, striking the soldier's helmet hard enough to make his arm reverberate with the impact.

The blow knocked the Karsite to the ground, lying on his back with his elbows in the churned mud to prop himself up. Eranel brought his weapon around and moved forward to thrust, the tip of his weapon even with the soldier's exposed throat.

He froze, the weapon trembling in his hand, the tip almost touching the soldier's bare skin. When the Karsite swallowed, he grazed himself.

Eranel looked the Karsite in the eyes, unable to move forward. These were barbarians, evil creatures that brought chaos and death wherever they went. They needed to be stopped.

But he recognized that fear in those eyes. This was not the look of a beast or a demon. This was a man, hurt and afraid. A man, like him.

"Not every warrior is a killer."

A scream sounded from behind him, and he whipped around. He recognized Taelor in a small clump of members from his company. They were all but surrounded by Karsite soldiers. Eranel sprinted forward, charging into the line from the back, yanking a Karsite off-balance. Another soldier turned to face him, and Eranel acted without thinking, driving his blade into the soldier's gut.

The Karsite released his weapon, moving to grip Eranel's wrist in both hands as he fell back. The two men had their faces almost touching as they dropped to the ground, the Karsite's grip too strong for Eranel to pull away. The stranger stared at him in horror as tears streamed from his wide eyes and he shook with shuddering breaths. Eranel tugged on the sword, his brow creased as he yanked at it. It made a sickening, sucking sound as it came free, only matched by the man's gurgle as he struggled to breathe.

Eranel stumbled back, his sword tip dragging through the dirt as he backpedaled from the corpse. He couldn't stop staring at the body. He never saw the attack, just felt the blade slide through his side and get wrenched out with a force that jerked him to the ground. Warmth spread through his midsection, and the trumpet blasts and shouting voices grew ever more distant as darkness closed in on all sides.

* * *

Eranel woke with a start and screamed, reaching out to ward off the weapons falling all around him. He kicked and flailed wildly as strong hands gripped his wrists and ankles and forced him down onto the bed. He continued to jerk against the restraints, knowing he needed to move. If he didn't move, he would die. He couldn't just lie there.

It took a few moments before he realized he wasn't on the battlefield anymore. The coarse mattress biting into his back wasn't the dirt of the blood-washed ground. He relaxed and ceased his struggles. As he did, the people holding him down relented, their hands hovering over him for a bit, hesitant to move too far out of range.

Looking around, he saw several beds around him, most of them occupied with Valdemar soldiers in various states of injury and rest. A Healer stood over him, smiling softly when he met her gaze. The lines around her face gave her a weathered look. She held up a sponge over his mouth and squeezed it, dripping water into his mouth. He licked his lips and drank it eagerly, gulping down anything she provided him.

After she treated him for a few moments, she moved on, tending to other wounded in the medical tent. Eranel tried to push himself up on his elbows, but his entire side burned when he attempted to move. He collapsed back into the bed and closed his eyes, taking several deep breaths in an attempt to keep the pain at bay.

"Damn near got stuck like a wild boar and you're already trying to get up and move about. And you think I'm the fool?"

Eranel smiled. "Taelor. Guess you managed to make it out of that mess."

He turned to face his friend and saw her crouched on the ground beside his bed. Her armor was stained with a mixture of mud, dirt, and blood. The scabbard at her side was empty, her hair was matted against her head, and she had either a rag or an incredibly dirty bandage tied around her upper arm. But her eyes still had the sparkle he had seen since their youth. He reached out with a hand, and she grabbed it in both of hers. He gave as strong a squeeze as he could manage, realizing it felt weak even to him.

"It was quite a mess. The Karsite shield line turned to face us and didn't go down like we hoped. Lost damn near a third of our company in the first charge alone. I thought we were goners until you crashed into the line from out of nowhere. Even still, we lost you shortly after that, and I thought we had lost you for good."

She tightened her grip for a moment before continuing. "Shield line pushed us back, tried to circle around and attack the main forces. Then the trumpets sounded, and not a moment too soon. Cavalry came rushing in and chased off those Karsite bastards. Sent them running back to their rocks."

"So we won?"

"Not quite. Most of their army's still camped out a short way away, and we have no idea if they're going to turn tail and run or if we'll have to square up with them in the morning. Either way, fighting's done for the day. Commanders figured we had some time to tend to our wounded and take care of ourselves before picking it back up tomorrow. Figure you won't be in much shape to do more than come along for the ride though. Even with the Healers' help, we almost lost you."

"Yeah, my entire side's on fire, and it's a struggle just to breathe."

"I'll let you be and get some rest then." Taelor took Eranel's hand and placed it on the bed beside him. "Just one last question before I go. How many'd you get? I'm up to five of those animals."

Eranel's mind flashed back to the soldier staring at him as the light faded from his gaze. He shuddered, and his hands clenched tight around the sheet covering his body. ". . . One."

Taelor barked a harsh laugh but cut it short. She reached out and squeezed his shoulder. "Plenty of time for you catch up to me later, I'm sure."

She left, leaving Eranel to his own churning thoughts, causing a discomfort that ran deeper than the hole in his side. He drifted off to sleep, listening to the soft moans of those around him in too much pain to have a restful slumber. The Healers moved about, tending to the worst of the injured as best as they could. Their ministrations stretched through all hours of the night.

When he fell asleep, visions of the battlefield rushed through his mind, moving so fast that they blurred, until the moment the Karsite grabbed his hands. They were wet, the man's blood gushing out over them both. That singular moment paused, all while the screams and sounds of anguish echoed in his ears on repeat. The hands of the dead soldiers reached up and tugged at the armor on his legs, dragging him down while his weapon sank deeper into the Karsite. Eranel found himself sinking below the man, growing smaller as the soldier somehow continued to hold onto his hands, locking him in place. He looked up into the face of the giant soldier, blood pouring out around his sword and coming up to his knees, then his waist. It continued to rise, threatening to drown him, all while those hands dug into his, all while those eyes continued to stare at him with the heart-stopping mixture of terror and accusation.

Eranel screamed, but his voice was lost among the screams of those around him. He wasn't sure if they mocked him or drowned him out because their pain was that much greater. He screamed louder, hoping to be heard, asking for someone to save him. Blood came up to his chin and he thrashed, needing to be free.

He woke in his bed, strong hands holding his shoulders down while a Healer's hand hovered over his chest. This was a different Healer, but his face had the same weathered expression and a tired sadness in his eyes. When Eranel realized where he was, he gulped down a few breaths of air. The hands holding him down locked him in position for a bit longer before finally releasing him and applying a cool rag to his forehead.

Someone propped him up and placed a warm cup in his still-shaking hands. The assistant put her fingers under the edge of the cup, guiding it to Eranel's lips. He sipped, and it tasted sweet. He drank the entire contents and then dropped back down, noticing the world grow indistinct in his vision before he faded into a dreamless sleep.

* * *

Several days passed before Eranel was given leave of the medical encampment. The army had moved a couple of times since then, but he traveled with the medical camp until his injury had healed enough that he was capable of walking on his own. Taelor escorted him back to their tent, and he hesitated while standing outside the front of it.

"I know the beds aren't as comfy as those in the medical camp, but at least this way you'll be able to get back into the fighting. You didn't want to have to stay on your back the entire time while I ran away with an unstoppable lead, did you? I've even kept your gear maintained, in case you're ready to fully rejoin us."

She lifted the tent flap and stepped inside, gesturing for her to join him. He did so, his knees trembling despite the absence of a fight.

"Not all of the battles we must fight are faced with sword in hand."

Once inside, he saw Taelor had been true to her word. Not only had she carted his gear along with hers, she had taken the time to arrange the inside of the tent so it was exactly the way it had been on that fateful day. She had even laid out his armor on his bed the same way he had every morning before donning it. His fingers traced the side, dancing across the stitching that covered the hole pierced in the side. The work lacked the professional touch of a seamstress or an armorer, with ugly knots that formed a ridge where the two edges met. That just told him Taelor had taken the time to mend it herself rather than take it to the quartermaster.

He smiled at the gesture, knowing she was watching him while he did so. His fingers drifted to the pommel of his sword, and he jerked his hand back with a sharp intake of breath, as if it burned. He saw the blade covered in blood, the handle sticky and red. He squeezed his eyes shut and shook his head, forcing the image away and telling himself it was not real. When he opened his eyes, he fixated on the blade. He needed to know.

"Steel tells a story, if you listen."

It was true, this weapon had a story to tell—and it was not one he wished to hear. But it was one he needed to face. As he reached out to grab the scabbard, his hand trembled. Gripping the sheath to steady his hand, he pulled the weapon free. It had been sharpened and polished once again to a mirror shine, unsoiled from its legacy. Would that his own spirit could be cleansed as easily. When he looked at his reflection, he saw the eyes of the man dying on the weapon.

Eranel slammed the weapon back into the scabbard, putting it down on the floor at the edge of his bed with as much composure as he could manage.

Taelor stared at him, her head tilted to the side, her eyes narrowed a bit in what looked like puzzlement. "Did I miss something?"

"No . . . it's fine. Thank you for taking care of it. It's my injury, I think. It will probably still take some time to recover from that."

"Of course," Taelor said, moving over to her bed. "Best rest up. I'm sure the commander will want to see you in the morning."

"Right."

It was all Eranel could manage to say as he struggled to control his visions. He took the armor and folded it with care at the edge of his bed, placing it over his sword in an attempt to hide it from view. It didn't help. He could still see the weapon in his imagination, lying there in a pool of blood.

As he drifted off to sleep, the same nightmare plagued him. He woke up with a strangled scream, his hands tangled in the bedding at his sides. He panted for breath and forced himself to calm down, reminding himself where he was.

Glancing over at Taelor, he saw that her back was turned to him. She took long, slow, deep breaths, but he knew her well enough to know she was pretending to be asleep. When she was actually asleep, her breathing was much shallower.

He got up and left the tent, knowing sleep was a lost cause. Without the drugs from the Healers to chase away his dreams, there was no chance of him returning to slumber. Instead, he walked through the camp, enjoying the moments of quiet before sunrise.

His feet brought him back to the medical tent. The Healers continued their work, moving among the wounded and tending to their injuries. They worked in shifts, some of them always working through every hour of the day and night. There were always more injured to take care of. He watched them move about the injured, observing their actions with a fascination normally reserved for a dance.

"Every man and woman on the battlefield must serve their purpose. Only if each does their part, will the army be victorious."

As the sun crested the horizon, Eranel marched to the commander's tent. He knew she would already be up, reviewing battle plans, scout reports, and planning for the day's actions. He waited outside until one of the guards announced his presence and told him to enter.

"Young Eranel, it's good to see you up and about. It will be good to have your sword on the line again. Are you fit enough to wield it in Valdemar's name?"

Eranel swallowed, hesitating a moment before speaking. "Actually, I don't think I'll be able to return to the front lines."

Commander Faras put both hands on the desk in front of her, keeping the papers there pinned to the surface as she straightened up and stared at Eranel, one eyebrow raised. Her face looked hard enough to stop a spear with her gaze alone. "I gather from your tone that this is unrelated to your injury. Is that correct?"

"Yes, Commander."

"I understand. Despite your skills with the blade, you don't have the strength of will to do what must be done. It's a shame, but I'll not have you on the front lines putting others in danger. You are dismissed."

Eranel coughed, catching the commander's attention as she had turned her attention back to the papers in front of her. She looked up, and her previous countenance was gentle compared to the gaze she fixed on him now.

"I was hoping I could still serve—perhaps in the medical tent?"

"Very well. Consider yourself transferred. Perhaps if you can stomach that work, you will still be of some use."

She waved him toward the tent entrance as she turned her attention back to the desk, making it clear there was nothing more to discuss. Eranel bowed and left, returning to his tent to retrieve his gear.

When he got there, Taelor was sitting on her bed, looking toward the flap. She jumped up as he entered. "So? What did the commander say? Will you be rejoining the front lines? I'll feel safer having you at my side. Although you'll have to see if you can keep up."

Eranel smiled and walked over to his gear, picking up his sword despite the urge to jerk back when he touched it. He walked over to his friend and presented it to her.

"I'm afraid I won't be joining you on the front lines today or ever. It's not something I can do. Please, take this, and may it protect you when I could not."

"I don't understand . . ." Taelor took the sword, but her brow knit together as her eyes dropped to the sheathed blade, then rose back up to Eranel's face.

"It's like our tutor said. 'Every man and woman on the battlefield must do their part.' I don't think my part is swinging a sword . . . I just don't have it in me. I'm heading to the medical tent, to see if I can serve my purpose there."

After a moment of silence, Taelor nodded. "I still don't understand, but if you think it's what you have to do, I've got your back. I'll come by regularly to give you a hard time. Of course, now I've got plenty of motivation not to get hurt. Otherwise, you might be stitching me up, and that's not something either of us wants!"

The two of them shared a nervous laugh before Eranel took his leave and headed to the medical tent.

"We're running low on Valerian root, we need more."

Eranel shook his head. "Please, let me try."

The other Healers gave him dubious looks but allowed him to

pass as he approached the bedside of one of the soldiers. She was still coated in sweat after waking up in the middle of a fever dream, screaming herself awake and rousing half the patients in the medical tent. Her eyes were clenched shut and she murmured to herself.

Eranel crouched by her side and placed a hand near her own, waiting for her to recognize his presence before he held out his hand with the palm down.

"May I?" he asked.

She nodded, and he placed his hand on her shoulder. It quaked underneath his touch at first, and he gave some gentle massages.

"You're here now," he whispered, keeping his voice soft to avoid startling her. "The dreams can't hurt you."

"But they're so real. Whenever I close my eyes, I see . . ." her words trailed off as she looked around with wide eyes.

"I know. I see it, too."

Eranel's calm statement of fact cut through her panic and made her take a few deep breaths. She stopped looking around and focused on him, reaching up to grab his hand with her good arm. Her other one was mangled from getting caught behind a shield as she'd been trampled.

"You do?"

"Yes."

"Why can't they leave me alone?" Her eyes closed, and fresh tears welled up and ran down her cheeks.

"They won't. They will keep coming, and you're holding onto false hope if you think this is something that can be cured. This is something that you have to face, that you must accept as a burden you carry."

He gave her shoulder another squeeze. "But I can promise you that we will watch over you and give you the strength you need to face these terrors. They may not go away, but we will keep you safe until you have the tools to face them on your own."

He kept his voice soft, letting it grow softer with each word until it was barely a whisper. The tension eased from her brow, and he continued speaking, reassuring her of her safety all while admitting the reality of the terrors she faced. He continued speaking even after her hand grew limp and her chest rose and fell in deep breaths. When he finished, he dropped back, sitting on the ground with a weary sigh.

One of the Healers came up behind him, approaching until he could feel her presence just behind his back. He looked up and saw the weathered face of Healer Aelyn, the one who first healed him of his injury. He offered her a weary smile.

"I've seen you toil with the most injured every day, easing their rest in a way that no one else can. At this rate, you'll have more wrinkles than I do in just a few years."

"If that happens, I'll view it as a badge of honor. Helping to ease their pain helps ease my own."

She came around to his side and offered a hand to help him rise. He took it, clambering to his feet with a small stumble. When she offered more assistance, he gestured that he was fine. Once he recovered his balance, she reached into her robe and produced a sealed scroll, handing it over to him.

"What is this?"

"A letter signed by all the senior Healers here. When this is over, we want you to take it and go to the Healer's Collegium. Present them with this, and they will see if you have the Gift."

"That's impossible. There's no way I could have the Gift. I can't do what you do."

"Not yet, but you can do things that none of us can. Perhaps you have more talent than you realize, and have found your true calling."

Eranel took the scroll, clutching it to his chest.

"We have no way to predict where the tides of war will send us. We must have faith that our skills will carry us to where we are meant to be."

A Time for Prayer

Kristin Schwengel

"I assure you, Father Derigal, there has been no word from Sunhame. And there is no other priest of the Sunlord near enough to serve two villages, even for a short time."

Fidesa rubbed her forehead, pinching the bridge of her nose in a vain attempt to forestall her incipient headache. She hated being so stern with him, but they both knew he would not be here for the Midsummer rituals. If no replacement was sent by the Son of the Sun, what were the villagers to do?

"And I assure you, my young acolyte, there will be no interruption to the worship of the Sunlord in Waldhang." The frail priest smiled slightly at her ill-concealed snort when he called her young. "All shall be well, and all shall be well, and all manner of thing shall be well." The words had the ring of a quotation, but even Fidesa's sharp memory could bring up nothing from the Writ of Vkandis that matched. The priest's pale hand, knobby and veined, continued to stroke the large orange cat that had plastered itself next to his blanketed thigh.

"For the villagers' sake, I hope you're right, Father," Fidesa muttered, although hope was far from her mind. She glanced at the shadows spilling through the small window across the room, blinking as she realized how time had flown as they spoke. "But it is time and past for me to tend the Flame as best I can."

"Our best is all the Sunlord asks of us, and all we have to offer

Him," was the old red-robe's reply, and Fidesa took it as a dismissal, hurrying from the tiny bedchamber into the barely larger main room that served as the temple for Waldhang.

There, a familiar peace washed over her, cleansing her worry for her family and friends as she moved back and forth from the storage cabinet to the altar, gathering the few tools of the Sunpriest's trade. The blessed candle to hold the Sunlord's fire, the knife to trim the Flame's wick, the salver to catch the trimmings and keep them from fouling the Flame's basin, the oil to refill the Flame, and the cup for blessed water to douse the candle after it had rekindled the Flame.

With measured steps, reciting the sequence of blessings as she circled the altar, Fidesa felt the rhythm of the prayer take her outside of herself, to a place where she was not Fidesa, not a woman attempting to fill a man's role, but an anonymous vessel, a channel whereby the blessings of the Sunlord came to Waldhang. Here, as she murmured and measured and precisely cut, it was easier to find Derigal's confidence that all should be well. Vkandis' warmth filled her, the cold flagstones unheeded beneath her feet.

When the Flame was once again lit, when she had cleansed and purified and stored the ritual articles, she took a deep breath, the smell of the beeswax and the tiny pinch of incense tingling at the back of her nose. It had always been thus for her, that peace and solace was to be found within the walls of the Temple. Widowed after a bandit raid, she had not chosen to remarry but had taken her brother's offer of a home with his family, raising her infant daughter with his children.

Eight—no, nine years ago now—she had begun helping Father Derigal teach the village children the Writ and the Rule, preparing them for the periodic visits from a black-robed Voice of the Sunlord. Despite the fact that a woman could never be a priest of Vkandis, no one in the village had expressed surprise or offense at her filling the role of Father Derigal's acolyte, taking on more and more of his duties as he aged, and now ailed.

She glanced at the door to the priest's bedchamber and suppressed a sigh. His faith in the Sunlord was great, a faith she shared, but she placed far less confidence in the high and powerful priests in Sunhame. So far removed from their tiny village tucked away in a region of woods and small farm plots in the northern reaches of Karse, how much attention could the Archpriests give to their concerns? She tamped down the critical thought that the small and lowly were every bit as important to the Sunlord Himself as were the great and powerful. Such thoughts could perhaps be voiced by Father Derigal, a venerable priest himself, but not by a mere acolyte—and most especially not by a woman.

Rather than start another argument with her mentor, she moved out of the Temple and into the tiny garden plot behind it, taking advantage of the fading light after SunDescending to finish the weeding and harvest a few of the ripest berries to tempt Derigal's waning appetite.

The funerary observations were simple, as Derigal wanted. The villagers buried him in the tiny grave plot in the space nearest the Temple reserved for the priests of Waldhang. His orange cat had stayed by his side to the end and now sat near the stone that was all the marker they used. The cat watched Fidesa with an uncanny gaze as she recited the prayers for Derigal's spirit, that he might find himself welcomed into the warm and loving gaze of the Sunlord and feel not His flames of wrath. To Fidesa, the cat seemed to be waiting for something, or someone.

Fidesa, in turn, waited dry-eyed in the doorway until all the villagers drifted away from the Temple, back to the tasks of field and forest. She had wept out her grief for her mentor during the long watches of the last nights of his life. Her thoughts now were for those villagers. No one seemed as concerned as she about the coming Midsummer rituals and who would lead them.

As she had feared, no word had come from Sunhame regarding the future priest of Waldhang, though Fidesa had promptly sent her unsigned notice of Derigal's final passing. As the last of her friends and neighbors left the graveyard, Fidesa turned back into the Temple, to review more closely all of Derigal's correspondence with Sunhame, even his copies of those written before she had taken over writing out his dictations for him to sign.

Late that evening, Fidesa pushed the last pile of letters away and pressed her fingers to the tender points at the bridge of her nose that usually helped her headaches. Tonight, there was no relief from the pulse that pounded inside her skull.

"If you weren't already in Vkandis' arms, Derigal, I swear I would put you there myself," she muttered. *What* had he been thinking? Closing her eyes, she pressed more firmly up against her brow ridges. If she was honest with herself, she knew what he had been thinking, the solution he had perceived, had engineered.

In all of his correspondence, Father Derigal had rarely used her name, only the initial "F" to refer to his acolyte among the villagers. The one time she saw her name, the ending letters were blurred together enough that one could read it as "Fides." Which meant no one in Sunhame knew she was a woman. Which meant the Archpriests probably assumed the acolyte would take over leading worship in Waldhang until a black-robed Voice visited them and could confirm the acolyte as priest-in-full.

She sighed, then stood to return to her brother's home. She needed to call the town heads together. Derigal's plan could lead to the destruction of the whole village if she followed it and failed.

Fidesa resisted the urge to pinch the bridge of her nose. *Why* did no one else see the dangers? She looked around the room. Gathered in the common room of the village tavern were the half-dozen individuals that passed for Waldhang's town council: the tavern-keep, the oldest and most prosperous landowners, including her brother Rellin, and herself. She had described Derigal's "solution" and the risks it encompassed as clearly as she could, but the blank looks from all of them meant they had failed to take her seriously.

"You've been acting for Derigal for the last six moons or more, and the Sunlord has not taken His blessing from Waldhang for it," Rocast the tavern-keep finally said. The others nodded.

"If He had not seen you as suitable, surely He would have withdrawn His favor, but the Flame has stayed lit, the people have been healthy, the crops are flourishing," Tivreen added. He was the oldest one present, and he had been close friends with Father Derigal since their boyhood. "He must approve of you and your service."

"It is not the Sunlord I'm truly worried about," Fidesa replied. "If the Archpriests in Sunhame find out, the whole village would be razed by the black-robes and the Sunsguard and the ground salted behind them. A woman serving the Sunlord is anathema, proscribed, impossible."

Her brother eyed her, then raised one brow slightly. "And yet you serve, and the Sunlord hears your prayers. So we make sure they don't find out."

She blinked at him.

"Instead of Fidesa, what if you became Fides, as Father Derigal must have intended?"

The other elders nodded while Fidesa stared at Rellin. "What on earth are you talking about?"

"Your daughter is already living in my household, so she can remain there while you live in the Temple. You've always been tall and lean, your voice low; if you cut your hair, in robes you'd pass as a thin, frail sort of man. Especially if the rest of the villagers support it, there's no reason you'd be looked at twice."

The others nodded even more enthusiastically.

"In no time at all, the people will forget Fidesa ever existed," Tivreen said. "There will only be Brother Fides."

Fidesa did not like it, but she found herself overruled at every corner, every objection she raised smoothed over by the blind determination of the elders. In the end, she bent to that obstinate resolve. Her time as a wife had ended years ago, and now it seemed her time as a mother would end as well. The needs of Waldhang and the Sunlord meant that now she would be—what, exactly, she was not sure, but it was clearly a new time, a new season in the cycle of her life.

At long last, she capitulated, and went with her brother to explain to her daughter and retrieve from his home what few personal things she would need. Her ten-year-old daughter, with one of the flashes of uncanny insight she sometimes had, grasped the situation at once, accepting the "loss" of her mother with greater grace than her mother herself.

That night, in Father Derigal's tiny bedroom—now hers—Fidesa sat in front of the polished metal mirror, staring for long minutes at the narrow face that looked back at her. Finally, she took one of her long brown braids in her hand and neatly sliced through it with her knife, cropping her hair short around her head. Without taking a breath, she repeated the process with the other braid, then allowed herself to look once more at her reflection.

Despite the imperfections of the mirror's surface, she was surprised to see that she did, in fact, look passably male. The few streaks of gray that had been mostly hidden in her braids now became more pronounced, lending gravity to her still-youthful face. In a last step, she drew on one of Father Derigal's robes, which she had already shortened to match her own height. With her frame concealed, her hair short, the mirror showed her that the subterfuge was possible.

"You've won this bout, Derigal," she murmured. "I just hope Waldhang won't have cause to regret this."

A flicker of movement caught the corner of her eye, and she saw Father Derigal's large orange cat standing at the doorway from the bedroom to the Temple area. He gave her a long, measuring look—how had she never noticed that his eyes were bright blue?—then twitched his tail, turned, and walked out of the Temple, vanishing into the night.

To Fidesa's great relief (and her brother's secret satisfaction), the Midsummer rituals were flawless. The Flame of Vkandis set the village bonfire alight without pause.

As summer waned into autumn and the harvest rituals neared, Fidesa began to think her subterfuge might just be successful. The elders had abjured the villagers strongly that she was now Brother Fides, her daughter now her brother's child, and all seemed to understand what was necessary.

A handful of traders, tinker-peddlers and the like, had come and gone through Waldhang, and none had given Brother Fides a second glance.

Then had come the messenger, with the crest of the Sunsguard on his cloak. He had delivered his letter to her without comment, with no sign of suspicion, and had left almost immediately to get to the next village on his route before nightfall. Ullenheim was a larger town with a more appealing tavern, and Fidesa could hardly blame the messenger for moving quickly.

After watching him ride out of the village, Fidesa stared at the folded missive in her hand, the wax marked with the seal of the Son of the Sun, then set it aside. *After SunDescending*, she told herself. Whatever command from Sunhame could wait until after she had completed the service to the Sunlord. After all, the messenger himself had not waited, so clearly there was no response necessary.

Later, in the quiet of the evening, she slit the seal and read, holding her breath while she scanned the spare lines. There was no salutation, no signature.

A Voice of the Sunlord will be traveling north in two weeks' time. All children between the ages of six and ten years should be prepared to be presented to the Voice for his approval.

Fidesa let out her breath in a slow sigh, her mind scattering in a thousand directions. This was the moment she had feared most of all: to face a Voice in her disguise, to hold her ruse before his questioning eye. If he was to examine the village children, surely he would also be looking sharply at all around him. Especially if, as she presumed, he intended to confirm Derigal's acolyte as priest-in-full for Waldhang.

Two weeks. She had two weeks to prepare. To prepare herself, to prepare the villagers, and to prepare the children. And protect them. She thought of Father Derigal, of the secrets he had taught her, and what he had told her to do when the Voices came to examine the children. He had even told her which children to keep special watch over—and her own daughter was one of these, for she had been too young to be examined when last a Voice came to Waldhang.

"Remember," he had said, *"that what the Voices call evil is not always so, but it too comes from the Sunlord. But it does not do the bidding of those in Sunhame, and so they fear it. Your daughter has potential only for those Gifts that the Archpriests fear, but they wish to stamp out the potential as well as the actual. Tamilan you can protect with the herbs to numb her mind, but her cousin Bikahn should be sent to the North, to those who can teach him properly, before the Voice visits."*

Two weeks. She had two weeks to get Bikahn out of the village and across the border, and to come up with a reasonable explanation for the disappearance of a child who was on the birth-and-childhood rolls sent to Sunhame each year. She had two weeks to teach her daughter what would be expected of her.

Two weeks. She prayed to Vkandis Sunlord it would be enough.

One week. She had one week to prepare. The day after the letter had arrived, her sister-in-marriage had fled with Bikahn on the family's stoutest pony, taking him north to the Valdemaran border by a circuitous route, to reduce the odds they would be seen. The daughter of a merchant in Ullenheim, Gianni spoke enough of the common Trade tongue that she could ask for assistance for her eight-year-old son, and she would leave him there. She should be returning to Waldhang today, to throw herself into mourning for the son who had supposedly been lost to a febrile infection.

"Better Rellin and I lose our son but know he lives than watch him die in the Fires of Cleansing," she had said to Fidesa before she left.

A small grave had been dug and filled in, a marker-stone placed, and Fidesa had carefully annotated the village's rolls to be sent to Sunhame with the duration of his illness and the date of his supposed death. *It is ironic*, she thought, *that the birth rolls are so carefully kept, but once the children have the approval of the Voice, Sunhame seems not to care what happens to them, or to the adults in the village.* Presumably the name of Fidesa, not Fides, was on a roll somewhere in Sunhame, lost in some archive or another that no one ever thought twice about.

One day. Two days at most, Fidesa thought, before the Voice would come to Waldhang. She had done all she could to prepare the children for their examination and had begun to dose Tamilan with the herbs as Father Derigal had directed. They made her a little sleepy, her speech slow, but Fidesa didn't think that would be a bad thing; after all, if her younger "brother" had just died of a fever, it would be assumed that she too had been ill and was still recovering.

A sharp whistle from the woods echoed toward the village, and she took a deep breath. The older lad she had sent out to keep watch for the Voice came scurrying down the lane.

"They're just turning off the Trade Road to the side track, Brother," he gasped, and she nodded.

"A quarter-mark, then," she replied. "Bring the elders and the children to the square." He nodded and scampered off, although she was sure everyone in the village must have heard his warning whistle.

Indeed, by the time she reached the center of the village, where the bonfire lay ready to be kindled, nearly everyone who wasn't out in the fields was already gathered. Rellin and Gianni stood to one side, Tamilan leaning heavily against Gianni's legs. There were three other young ones of an age to be examined, and each stood with his or her parents, nervousness clear in their fidgeting.

Fidesa took another breath and began the mental exercise Derigal had taught her, clearing her mind of everything but the Sunlord's name. By the time the horses of the Sunsguard and the Voice had entered the village, her thoughts were carefully reined in, her worries deeply buried beneath a shield of the Sunlord.

"Greetings of Vkandis Sunlord be with you, people of Waldhang," boomed the first rider of the Sunsguard.

"And with you, honored visitors," Fidesa replied, pitching her voice to her lowest range.

The Sunsguard nodded and dismounted as one, followed by the black-robed Voice, who came forward to stand in front of her.

"I was grieved to hear of Father Derigal's passing," he said to her, "for he and I had long been friends."

Fidesa blinked, then recognition dawned. "You must be Master Fawlen, then, for he often spoke of your studies together." If Father Derigal's longtime friend shared even some of his views, perhaps this wouldn't be so hard after all.

"Indeed. I trust he did not suffer overly?"

"His passing was gentle at the last; may the Sunlord hold him in His arms."

The Voice nodded. "You are Fides, the acolyte who served with Derigal?" His brown eyes sharpened a little as he studied the acolyte.

Fidesa inclined her head, careful not to speak anything that was not precise truth, in case the Voice could sense spoken falsehood. "Father Derigal was kind to mentor me and guide me in the service of His Light." She couldn't help but feel she was engaged in some sort of bizarre dance, where Master Fawlen stepped and she tried to follow. Or a sparring exercise, full of feints and counterfeints. She kept her thoughts focused on blankness and the

Sunlord, a wall of faith in her mind, as Father Derigal had taught her.

"If time permits, I should like to talk more of his teachings later, but for now let us attend to the task for which I am here, that the people of Waldhang need not be longer kept from their daily tasks." The Voice turned to the assembled crowd. "Bring the eligible children forward."

The parents led the four little ones out from the gathering to stand in front of Master Fawlen. He frowned. "Were there not five children in this village of age?"

Gianni burst into tears and buried her face against Rellin's chest, her fingers clutching Tamilan's shoulder.

"Our youngest, our son Bikahn, took a fever not three weeks ago and is gone, and our daughter is still not well," Rellin said, his voice gruff with emotion. Fidesa held her breath. If Master Fawlen suspected an untruth, this would be the moment.

But the Voice only nodded. "I will question the children now."

It was a strange sort of questioning, jumping from one aspect to another of the Sunlord's teachings, and Fidesa got the impression Master Fawlen was listening to more than just the answers. Each time he addressed Tamilan, she couldn't help but tense a little, but the girl's words were clear, if faint, and always correct. If there was one thing Father Derigal—and now Fidesa—took pride in, it was that in Waldhang, the Writ and the Rule were taught and followed thoroughly.

At last, the black-robe straightened and stepped back from the children. "I find that Father Derigal and Brother Fides have done well in teaching these little ones. Let us light the fire to celebrate the Sunlord's kindness."

Fidesa picked up the oil and tinderstick from the bench at the Temple entrance and moved to hand them to the Voice, but he shook his head.

"Brother Fides, I ask you to offer the rite and prayer to the Sunlord so that I may observe and confirm your authority."

Fidesa struggled to keep her mind in its blank mask. This was not what she had expected. The senior priest was always the one who led, who took precedence, and who was entrusted to call the Flame of Vkandis. What if she failed to light the fire? What if the Voice intended to expose her after all? What if Tamilan's potential had somehow revealed itself to him, and he would be consigning her to be Cleansed?

She nodded, her face betraying nothing of her thoughts, and turned to the pile of branches in the center of the square. Despite the warm late summer air, a chill of nerves rippled down her spine. It was a test, clearly. As the Voice had examined the children, so now he would examine her and her performance of the ritual.

Murmuring the supplications, she prepared just as she had for the Midsummer rites. She held the tinderstick at the ready, but as she fell into the rhythm of the prayer, she knew she would not need it. As it had at Midsummer, as it had at Father Derigal's funerary service, as it had on the countless days before and since, she felt the warm embrace of the Sunlord's affection surrounding and filling her. And just as it had at Midsummer, the oil-sprinkled branches leaped to flame effortlessly at the moment she finished the words.

She dared a glance at the Voice. His eyes were wide with surprise, but there was no anger in them. He paced forward, joining her in measured steps as she circled the fire, ensuring the whole of the pile was burning cleanly.

"It is well, Brother Fides," he declared, his voice pitched to carry to the gathered villagers. "Long may you serve the Sunlord and the people of Waldhang."

A restless stamping and snorting from one of the Sunsguard's horses drew his attention, and he glanced up at the sky, reading the sun's position.

He sighed, and suddenly he seemed to Fidesa to be less the Voice and more the man Father Derigal would have called friend. "I would have liked to stay longer and talk more of Father Derigal, Brother Fides, but the horse recalls me to my duty."

"Our duty is always to the Sunlord and the Son of the Sun," she replied without pause. "Father Derigal was fond of saying that all He asks is that we do our best, and that our best is all we have to offer Him."

"May He not find our service wanting."

Fidesa inclined her head once more, not trusting her voice as Master Fawlen turned back to rejoin the Sunsguard, who had all remounted except the one who held the Master's horse for him.

"I do not know if I shall travel this road again, Brother Fides, but I am glad to see that Father Derigal's spirit will not be forgotten."

"As long as I serve the Sunlord in Waldhang, it shall not be."

Fidesa and the villagers watched as the black-robed Voice mounted and he and the Sunsguard trotted back out to the track that would take them back to the Trade Road. The children and their parents and the rest of the gathered villagers returned to their interrupted daily tasks, but still Fidesa stood looking down the road. It was long after the sounds of the horses had faded when she allowed herself to exhale a deep sigh of relief, her shoulders slumping beneath her red robes.

Turning back to the small Temple as the bonfire burned down, its heat dwindling, she saw a flicker of orange over the low wall around the Waldhang graveyard, a thick, bushy tail held at a jaunty angle before it vanished into the undergrowth.

And as she stood there, Derigal's voice echoed in Fidesa's mind.

"All shall be well, and all shall be well, and all manner of thing shall be well."

The Ghost of the High Hills

Stephanie Shaver

Herald Challen was somewhere in the High Hills when she Sensed a startled mind's burst of panic.

Her head snapped toward the "sound." She couldn't pick out distinct thoughts, just a flurried blurt—

And then nothing.

She sat perfectly still on her Companion, Lukas, as the breeze ruffled both her chin-length brown hair and the leaves sprouting on the towering trees.

Minutes passed in silence.

:Are you sure you Sensed someone?*:* Lukas asked.

"Yes," she said firmly. "West."

He strode in that direction, but nothing more came to her.

"Odd," she muttered.

:Maybe they shielded?:

"Maybe they died," she said, ominously.

They'd been patrolling all day and hadn't picked up a single thought for candlemarks. Lukas continued to weave north and south as Challen listened. Nothing further surfaced, and eventually she admitted defeat.

:Home?: he asked.

"For me," she said. "The dogs need feeding. Can you check in on Aesha? Let her know things are safe."

:"Safe.":

Challen frowned, looking westward.

"Relatively," she said, the wind tugging the words out of her mouth and scattering them to the Hills.

Aesha leaned her forearms on the wagon's rear gate and looked over the young Northerners, bound with rope. Their ringleader sat alone in his own wagon.

"Well," she said, "I know you have no idea what I'm saying, but if you did, I'd tell you that you picked the worst possible day for a jailbreak."

From his lonely wagon, the ringleader spat at her. "*Sheka*!" she yelled, dodging the glob easily. She pointed a finger at him. "Be good!"

Slapping the wagon's side, Aesha called to the driver. "All ready!"

The wagons rolled south down the road, away from Sweetbark.

A Guard walked up to stand beside her. Like most Valdemarans, he stood nearly a full head shorter than her. Hands on his hips, he looked up at her and said, "You're lucky we got into town today."

Aesha cracked her knuckles. "My militia would have taken them. Might've just broken a few bones in the process."

"Those barbarians—"

She dropped a finger on his lips and shook her head warningly. "We don't use the 'b'-word around here."

The Guard's eyes *darted*, his mind processing why the woman with forearms like oak limbs had deigned to shove her finger in his face. Usually at this point people noticed Aesha's cropped black hair and tan skin and realized *who* they were talking to, and suddenly their speech took a turn toward the *polite* and *agreeable.*

If they didn't, she showed them why she felt confident she could take a pack of five Northern youths hellbent on raising a ruckus on their way south into Valdemar.

As the Guard no doubt contemplated this, a flicker of white

along the forest line surrounding Sweetbark caught Aesha's eye. A voice whispered in her mind, :*Meet me at the Hollow.*:

"C'mon," she said, releasing the Guard's mouth and draping an arm around his shoulder. "Let's get you a tankard of Kael's finest ale." She deliberately propelled him toward a nearby building. "He mixes tree sap into it."

"He *what*—"

"You'll *love it.* I'm buying."

Once she'd turned the Guard's attention toward the novelty of Kael's maplebeer, she slipped out again. A few of the Guards had stayed behind, ostensibly because there might be more invaders coming, but Aesha knew there'd be none. These five had been outliers . . . unless Challen's patrol had turned up something else.

Aesha followed a trail out of the village, away from the cheerfully painted houses, vegetable gardens, chicken coops, and goats standing on whatever they could find. She zig-zagged through the trees, down to a trickling stream and a hollowed-out oak stump. A cleverly woven mat of mosses and grass flopped over it to keep out wildlife and weather. Challen's work, that. You had to know to find any of it.

Lukas waited for her.

"Good to see you, Sparkles," she said. "Bit of excitement today, glad you missed it."

The Companion bowed his head in greeting. :*Saw the Guards. They got here early. What happened?*:

"Jailbreak attempt by the five we rounded up earlier," she said. "It didn't work out. We're sending the poor babies on their way to Kelmskeep now."

:*And was that it? Just this—jailbreak?*:

"All the excitement I need in a day, thanks."

Lukas pawed the earth.

Aesha cocked a brow. "What?"

:*I don't know. She swears she Sensed . . . something, but we couldn't find it.*:

"Something to do with what happened in town?"

:I don't think so. Damned wild Talent.: Lukas kicked up a clump of sod with his back leg.

Aesha grunted. "Well. Tell her to take care of herself—" She wagged a finger. "—or else."

The Companion lowered his lashes. :*What?*:

She threw her hands into the air. "I'll write poetry again?"

The Companion shook his mane. :*No one wants* that, *Aesha.*:

"Then give her my love. And maybe if you check the Hollow tomorrow, there'll be a bottle of mead waiting. And some pears." She stroked his ears. "Sorry I failed you today. The Guards ask a lot of questions."

:*Questions about . . . ?*:

Aesha screwed up her face and crossed her eyes, affecting a voice. "Is it true," she said, half an octave higher than her normally husky voice, "that you used to be a Skybolt? Oh! Oh! Didn't you marry a *Herald*? Did she—" She slapped a hand over her mouth. "Oh, I'm *so sorry*! I didn't mean to *pry!*" She relaxed her features.

:*That's terrible.*:

"Ehh, I'm used to it."

:*That doesn't make it okay!*:

Aesha knocked her skull with her fist. "Head's too thick to be bothered by it."

:*Yes . . . but . . .* : He seemed flustered.

"I've told you before, Lukas: You and Challen are the best thing that ever happened to me. We're together for the long haul, no matter what."

The Companion shuffled his hooves, perhaps not sure what to say to this. Finally, :*Well, next time . . .* :

"Yes?"

:*Don't forget the pears.*:

She gestured. "Begone, Sparkles."

:*Look,* I'm *the one carrying her around. I deserve a treat.*:

"I've been thinking. A new 'Sun and Shadow' stanza."

:*Havens, no! Away!*:

He wheeled and cantered off into the forest, following no clear track, toward a person very few knew still lived.

Challen paced on the porch, sipping tea and peering at her maps, rubbing the silvery scar that ran from the top of her hairline down to her chin.

Spring meant the days were warmer—and a little longer. Light yet remained in the sky as Lukas approached, coming off the ridge with the unearthly grace only a Companion could muster.

"I want to go back," she said.

:*What?*:

"We didn't check the Obsidian Glade or the abandoned mine," she said. "Hellfires, we didn't check any of the shepherd huts, either."

He held still, and she could tell her Companion wanted to shove her into the cabin and brace himself against the door.

:*It's all hinterland,*: he said. :*No one should be out there. Especially the Glade.*:

"And we shouldn't have Northern youths cutting around Sorrows to slink into Valdemar!" she blurted at him. "Something's off. I don't like it."

His nostrils flared.

"I'll go myself if you don't—"

:*Get on,*: he said, tossing his head at the empty saddle.

And just like that, her determination did a bellyflop over into guilt. Okay, so maybe they *didn't* need to go now, so close to sunset. Maybe it *could* wait. Maybe—

:*It's just—I was* really *looking forward to a nice rub down,*: he said, wistfully.

"Oh, love, you shall have one," she assured him. "I promise."

She kissed the smooth line of his cheek and hauled herself into the saddle.

The mine didn't show signs of disturbance, nor did any of the little stone huts shepherds used when storms sprung up. In the past, Challen's broad-ranging Gift had rescued Sweetbark denizens huddled away in these shelters, but not today.

By the time they entered the Glade the moon had risen, and Challen had begun to realize that whatever she'd heard would never be explained. Maybe another Herald or other Gifted person nearby had opened their mind up and then just as quickly shut it? Or possibly a death, causing a burst of thought, and whoever it was had already been dragged off and hidden. Which, yes, was *very* worrisome, but the High Hills were *vast*, and she didn't have Farsight or Foresight, just a broken wild Talent that never wound down. She and Lukas could only cover so much ground. She'd done her best. She'd—

"What's that?" she said, and Lukas froze.

The Glade had an uneasy history in the Hills. No one liked it. The grass here grew darker. It felt out of place.

The giant stone woman in the middle of it didn't help.

The statue had been carved of smooth snowflake obsidian—except for her eyes, which sparkled from some rough material in the moonlight. Looking at her made Challen feel *extremely* uneasy. It felt like—walking in on someone you *liked* but weren't yet romantic with while they were getting undressed. *Awkward*.

But the statue wasn't what had called her attention. The horse browsing in front of the statue *was*.

The mare lifted her head as Challen dismounted. No one had bred this beast for looks. Her squat, boxy head had plenty of room for brains and biting teeth. She also had a saddle, bridle, and a bedroll.

"Do you see a rider?" Challen asked.

:*Look down,*: Lukas said.

Curled at the foot of the statue, half-buried in the tall grass, lay a woman.

The Herald's whole body seized up with unexpected terror, as if a mortal poison had appeared in front of her. Her skin prickled and her head swam. Even sleeping, people were a threat to her wellbeing. Thoughts just—*leaked*.

But she couldn't Sense this person *at all.* Cautiously, Challen bent down, the mare's eyes tracking her every movement. She instantly recognized the designs of the woman's midnight blue clothing as Shin'a'in. She reached past the long black braids to touch her neck, seeking a pulse—

"She's alive," she said to Lukas.

"That's a relief," a voice said, sounding wryly amused. "I was starting to think I'd died."

Lukas wheeled around, a move that would have impressed Challen if she hadn't been so utterly stricken with terror.

She tried, tried to protect herself. Even now, knowing it to be futile, Challen raised shields around her mind, as Teren had taught her back when she'd been a Trainee, as she'd once been able to do like any other fully trained Gifted Herald. She imagined the wall around her mind—but it collapsed as if she'd attempted to lay bricks on a fast-moving river.

All her efforts ended this way—and had since the war.

Lukas, bless him, snapped shields down over her mind as they both faced the unknown woman—

A woman in midnight blue, with long black braids. *The same person Challen knelt over.*

"Please," the stranger said, hands up. "I'm not a ghost."

"You're—" Challen said. "What?"

"Something happened here," the woman went on. "And I seem to be . . . temporarily out of bounds. *Not* of my own volition."

Challen shook her head. "What are you—I don't—"

:*She's out of her body.*:

Challen looked at Lukas, who stared intently at the woman. "She's *what*?"

:*Look closer.*:

She squinted at the stranger and realized that she . . . blurred around the edges a little. Her feet were even faintly transparent. Challen picked up a pebble and tossed it—and it flew *through* her, landing with a muffled thump beyond.

"Rude," the woman said, with a whiff of amusement. "Satisfied?"

Lukas lifted the shields around Challen's mind, and, as before, she Sensed no thoughts. Challen straightened, mystified—and also relieved.

"Are you—Swordsworn?" she asked.

"I am *Scrollsworn,*" the Shin'a'in said. "You know of the people of the Plains?"

"My wife," Challen said. "She—well, she *came* from there."

The woman's eyebrows rose. "Then you are of the people, too."

"Not exactly," Challen replied, with some humor. "I am firmly a daughter of Valdemar, and Aesha—well, it's complicated."

"Even so. I need help, as you can see."

"We should get you shelter." She regarded the mare. "Will she bite my face off?"

"Tch. Toecrusher won't—"

"*Toecrusher?*"

"Her sister is Nosebiter." The woman chuckled. "She will not hurt you. While we are naming things, I am Khaari shena Pretera'sedrin."

"Herald Challen. This is Lukas." She patted her Companion's neck. "Let's get your . . . body . . . onto his saddle. We'll figure out the rest from there."

Khaari's spirit flickered in and out of the patches of moonlight as they walked. She tried to talk but then gave up, as the inconsistent light made conversation impossible. They did not speak again until Challen had her body off the Companion and inside the cabin. She heaped Khaari in front of the hearth, onto a woolen pad. Her two hounds, Maple and Birch, curled up around the body as she prepared tea and then went out to sit on the porch.

Khaari stood in a pool of moonlight.

"You seem to be where the moon is," Challen observed. "Kal'enedral . . . you're a kind of priest, right?"

"Yes. I'm riding the Moonpaths."

Challen shook her head. "I don't know what that is."

"Your wife will," Khaari replied. "Where—is she?"

"Oh." Challen sunk in her chair. "Back at the nearby village, Sweetbark."

"I'm sorry. Are you two—separated?"

Not like you think, Challen thought. "That's neither here nor there," she said instead. "Why are you in the High Hills? In Valdemar? It's a long way from home."

"I'm tracking prey," Khaari said. "I was asked to take care of something my—ah—*teachers* felt needed to be addressed. That statue—"

Challen involuntarily shuddered.

"I see you know of it," Khaari said. "*What* do you know of it?"

"It's been here—well, forever, far as I know. Everyone avoids it."

"Tch. Well, it makes no sense. Shin'a'in don't make statues of the Star-Eyed. Our shrines are made for portability."

"The Star-Eyed? Is that Who that is?" She pursed her lips. Privately, she thought, *I wonder why* Aesha *dislikes it so much, though?*

"I touched it," Khaari said. "While examining it. And this happened."

"Did you scream?"

Khaari lifted her chin. "I gave a *very* dignified yalp."

Challen hid a smile. "I have this Talent. I can Sense *everyone* within a broad radius. *Very* broad."

Khaari nodded.

"And I *think* I Sensed the moment when you touched the statue. But I didn't Sense you before that."

"Well, I have—you call them shields?"

Challen wrapped her hands around her mug, the warmth seeping into her joints, and nodded.

"I have *something* like that. As a Scrollsworn—as Shin'a'in—I am shielded. But I could see them getting disrupted if I were, say, abruptly ripped from my body."

Challen nodded. "I could see that, too." She pursed her lips. "So how do we fix you? Touch the statue again?"

"That would require taking me *back* to the glade."

Challen sipped her tea. "It was worth getting you out of the cold for a night. Exposure is nothing to trifle with."

"You would have to be careful not to touch the statue either, lest you also wind up on the Moonpaths."

"Oh, that might not be so bad," Challen said, absently running a finger down her scar. "If it meant I wouldn't have to worry about my Gift going wild . . ."

Khaari cocked her head. "There is something more here. The reason you are alone at this cabin with your Companion."

Challen nodded.

"Will you tell me?"

Challen gazed off toward the stars. *How I've missed uncomplicated conversations with another two-legged being,* she thought, and started to open her mouth to respond.

A cloud slid over the moon, and Khaari vanished.

"So much for uncomplicated," she said, and laughed to herself.

Challen rolled Khaari's body onto her back or side every few candlemarks. They would need to take Khaari to a Healer if any more time passed. Kelmskeep, maybe.

How did you put someone back in their body? None of this was Challen's area of expertise. She didn't even know what her area of expertise *was.* Stopping invaders from getting into Valdemar, mostly, and the vast number of those were just half-starved youngsters trying not to get murdered by whatever lived in Sorrows.

Maybe Aesha would *know,* she thought. *We should talk anyway. That statue has to have something to do with it. We all knew to avoid it except Khaari, and that is what Aesha would call an* exception, *and an exception is where you start to solve a problem.*

Khaari's spirit still hadn't returned by morning, and emerging outside with her morning sausage roll, Challen said to her Companion, "I need Aesha."

:I expected as much, Chosen.:

"I can get Khaari to the Glade on Toecrusher. Can you and Aesha meet us there?"

Lukas blew lightly. *:Take the dogs.:*

"Those lazy lumps'll chase lizards and get burrs in their coats."

:Oh, it'll do them good. And Aesha and I will feel better knowing they're with you.:

"Fine, fine." She patted his withers. "Thank you, Lukas."

He turned and trotted off up the ridge, vanishing into the woods.

On the Moonpaths, Khaari *tried* to practice curiosity for her new state, because otherwise she'd go mad.

She'd never spent so long here. Her visits had always been in training, the tapestry room that housed the Webs of Time, and meditation.

In fact, the statue of the Kal'enel in the glade had felt like being back in the tapestry room. That beautiful snowflake obsidian statue, with gleaming and wide-open arms, had *hummed* with ancient power. Even Toecrusher had sensed a difference—the grass growing in the glade had been more like Dhorisha Plains grass than Valdemaran.

For Khaari, being so far from Kata'shin'a'in, from the work of protecting the artifacts of destruction buried in the Dhorisha Plains for *so long*, that moment she'd entered the glade had stirred her to tears. All she could think as she'd stepped toward the statue was—

Home.

In retrospect, that moment of lowered guard was what had trapped her.

On the Moonpaths, she had visits from one of her teachers, the *leshya'e Kal'enedral*, who seemed amused by it all.

"I'm too old for this," she groused at him.

"Well, then," he replied, his eyes crinkling with humor above his black veil, "let me take you directly to the Kal'enel and have you fitted for a veil."

"*No*," she replied, heavily. "But you *could* give me some hints."

"'Whatever it is you seek, won't come in the form you expect.'"

"A proverb? Really?"

He laughed. "It's my way of saying I don't have any," he said. "It's a magic older than us. But you have all the tools you need to fix this. I have been assured of this."

That was all he would—or could—tell her.

Annoyed with the interminable waiting, she tried to seek out her kinswoman—Aesha, Challen had named her—but strangely couldn't place her on the Moonpaths.

Perhaps she is not Shin'a'in after all? Maybe she's boasting of a heritage she doesn't have.

After that, she had no choice but to wait for moonrise.

Aesha could tell Lukas had his entire focus bent on two things: transporting her, and keeping his Chosen shielded. He'd come to her saying Challen wanted to talk, somewhere deep in the High Hills, but he hadn't said *where.*

So she *almost* couldn't be mad at him when she realized he'd brought her to the Obsidian Glade.

"Ugh, this place," she muttered. Followed immediately by a flying dismount and shout of, "*Li'ha'eer!* Did you murder a Swordsworn, beloved?"

"*What?*" Challen said, half-squeaking from where she sat by what looked like a Kal'enedral warrior sprawled in the grass next to a Shin'a'in battlemare. "*No*!"

Aesha inspected the body. "Why's she wearing blue?" she muttered.

"She said she's a Scrollsworn."

"At least she's breathing. What—"

Challen flung her arms around Aesha in a fierce embrace. Aesha reflexively put her face in her wife's hair, inhaling the smell of pine soap and thyme. They clung to each other, stretching out the moment as long as they dared—

And like a fragile soap bubble popping, it ended. Challen darted away, her smile strained, as though she'd been dancing but stepped on broken glass. Physical contact amplified the talent. Even Lukas couldn't help that.

"Okay," Aesha said, "explain."

As she did, the mare cropped greedily at the grass while the dogs snapped at lizards they would never, ever catch.

"Ideas?" Challen asked, finishing.

Aesha looked up at the statue. "If this is the Star-Eyed, I guess now I know why I always felt like She was judging me."

Challen's brow furrowed with concern. "Dearest—"

Birch suddenly barked excitedly and launched himself at the foot of the statue. Maple joined in. Challen whistled, but they ignored her.

"What've you found, hm?" she asked. The dogs kept digging down, ripping up the turf.

Both women approached to see what centuries of growth had obscured: stone at the statue's base. The battle steed had eaten a fair bit of it, but much yet remained.

"Something's extending from the base," Challen said, peering as close as she dared.

"Good thing I brought a shovel," Aesha said.

"You *did*?"

"Lunch, too." She gave her a confused look. "We're in the middle of nowhere. You gotta be able to dig a hole. And eat."

"You *do?*"

Aesha wagged a finger at her. "*You* are not an ex-merc, and it shows." She took a bundle off Lukas' back, through which she'd threaded her shovel. "Normally I use this for cat holes."

"Cat h—*oh*."

"When you gotta go, you gotta go." Aesha grinned and stripped off her shirt, down to the bandeau around her breasts. "Time to work."

It took two candlemarks to dig out the area around the statue, but slowly she revealed its secrets: a circle of smooth glass with two additional circles inset around it and what looked like words in a language neither of them read.

When she finished, sweat dripping freely down her chest and brow, Challen posed the obvious. "Any ideas?"

Aesha took a long drink of water before answering. "If I had to guess, and I'm giving you my *professional* opinion as an ex-merc—"

"Yes?"

"Looks like cursed mage shit to me."

Challen rubbed her forehead. "Aesha."

"Sorry."

The Herald had a calculating look in her eyes. "Can you—walk the Moonpaths?"

Aesha grimaced, remembering a midnight lesson, an impatient shaman, raised voices, and sprinting out of a tent into the cold night. "No. I signed up for the Skybolts and left the Plains before . . ." Her heart panged. "I'm sorry. If I could, I'd visit you every full moon."

Challen's lips lifted in a gentle smile. "Well, I guess we wait for moonrise and hope Khaari reappears. Trouble is—"

She looked over toward Lukas, head bent, sweat dripping down his sides.

"Go." Aesha shooed her. "Give Sparkles a break. Take the dogs, too. I'll stay with these two." She walked over to take the battle steed's reins.

"Careful," Challen said, "she might bite your face off."

"Oh, she wouldn't do that." Aesha stroked the mare's neck. "Who're you? Corpsebreath? Heartburster?"

"What is *wrong* with—okay, fine, *you* have fun with Toecrusher."

"What a *wonderful* name. Toecrusher." The mare flicked her ears at the sound of it. "Aren't you beautiful, *jel'sutho'edrin?*"

Challen rolled her eyes. "We'll be back."

Aesha winked. "We'll be waiting."

* * *

Aesha hunched on a rock and chipped away at a tree branch with her knife, her back to the statue.

"Greetings, kinswoman."

She startled. The woman had appeared out of nothing in front of her. She spoke with the same accent Aesha had carefully schooled out of her mouth two decades ago.

Aesha looked skyward. The moon had risen—but sunlight still lit the horizon.

"You must be Khaari." Aesha sheathed her knife.

"And you, Aesha." One crows-wing brow lifted. "You *are* Shin'a'in."

"*Yes*," Aesha said, scowling. "Half by my wastrel father, not that he wanted me. Why?"

"I sought you on the Moonpaths last night so we could talk, but could not find you."

Aesha folded her arms. "I don't—*do* that."

A faint furrow creased her brow. "The Moonpaths are open to all Her children."

Aesha set her jaw. "Maybe there's a reason I don't live on the Plains anymore."

"It hurts my heart to hear that," Khaari said. She approached the exposed circles. "This makes more sense now. The writing tells the tale. This is *not* Shin'a'in. It's Kaled'a'in. The Clans before our Clan. The west circle says: 'Eyes-that-are-open'. The eastern one: 'Eyes-that-are-shut'. And the Star-Eyed to the north." Khaari stood in thought. "Can we try touching my hand to Her?"

Aesha dutifully hauled Khaari's body over and flopped her hand on the statue's base, being *very* careful to steer clear of it, then looked to spirit-Khaari.

"*Sheka*," the still-visibly-out-of-her-body Scrollsworn muttered. "Put me in the western circle? I think I accidentally stood there when I touched Her."

Aesha grabbed her ankles and dragged her—

The air *tingled*. Aesha sneezed. Khaari's form rippled.

"Progress!" Khaari said.

Aesha's eyes darted to the empty circle. She slowly retreated back to her rock before Khaari could make any suggestions.

I am not *touching that statue,* she thought.

Instead, time passed until Khaari finally cleared her throat. "May I ask something?"

"Sure."

"Your wife—"

Aesha's shoulders tightened. "What about her?"

Khaari's eyes were soft, her questioning gentle. "Why *don't* you live together?"

The former Skybolt burst out laughing. "You're worse than the Guards."

Khaari frowned. "I'm what?"

From across the glade, Challen said, "I can explain."

Aesha turned to see her wife dismounting and slowly crossing the glade. "You don't have to do this."

Challen had a smile on her face as she approached. She put a hand on Aesha's cheek and her mouth went dry. "My protector. Like I haven't relived it in my head nearly every night since," the Herald whispered. "I can tell her. It's okay."

She turned to Khaari, her smile fading.

"We were under assault by a Mage we called the Levinbug."

The Levinbug's bolts sizzled out of the blue, literally. They were hopelessly pinned down by a random pattern of lightning arcs that ripped their battalion to pieces. It tore up the forest, exploding trees and stones, and kicking up great clouds of dirt.

"She's got a shield around her," their battalion's Mage, Zerof, had said. "But she opens it every time she strikes. So you need to get in *then*. And it can be anything. A sword, an arrow. Mind-magic, too."

And then, while Aesha and Challen had been drawing up plans, the bold fool had thrown himself in plain sight to try and distract the Adept, with predictable lethal results.

They'd decided on an assault only slightly less insane: Aesha's team would distract, Challen would come in from behind with arrows and a brute force Mindspeech scream.

On her mental cue, Aesha and twelve of her bravest had burst out on horseback. The Hardorn Mage, one of Ancar's darlings, had stood there under her pearlescent dome on the road, the smell of ozone ripening around her—

The dome split, and Challen had screamed into the Adept's mind, simultaneously releasing the tension on her bowstring.

Challen's arrow sunk squarely between the Mage's shoulder blades as Aesha and her team followed up with a volley of their own, so that the Levinbug looked like a many-feathered thing, reeling and arcing electricity.

The mental scream had prevented her lightning from flying, but not from discharging—and in that instant something—*something*—had happened. Maybe Challen's mind had connected with the Mage's. No one knew. But *something* arced at Challen. It whiplashed her in the saddle. A brightness enfolded her—

"It felt like the top of my head ripped off," Challen said.

Aesha wanted to put her arm around her shoulders, but she couldn't.

"After," Challen said, "I couldn't shut out the voices anymore."

No Healer could figure out how to repair her broken mind. Fellow Heralds and Companions took turns, but they couldn't maintain shields forever. The voices were everywhere. She couldn't sleep. She couldn't think. Just voices, voices, random, endless, *droning* voices. They bombarded her, wave after wave of thoughts.

The Healers fed her something to keep her drugged and out of her mind until someone figured something out.

"Aesha found Sweetbark, as far out of the way as she could get us," Challen said, looking over at her partner. "If it weren't for her, I . . . I don't think I'd still be alive. The Heraldic Circle pretends I died in the war, so no one comes looking for me." Challen spread her hands. "If someone has *very* good shields, I can tolerate them, but thoughts leak. And I hear *all* of them."

"*I* know she's here," Aesha added. "As does most everyone in Sweetbark, but they keep mum. Otherwise . . ."

"Is there *no* cure?" Khaari said.

"None our Healers know," Challen said.

"Perhaps a different approach—maybe someone knows something you do not?"

"Skybolt Mages tried something," Aesha said. "But it wasn't the right *kind* of shielding. We *tried*, Khaari."

"It can be useful," Challen added. "It's excellent for search and rescue. And we've no problem with raiders sneaking in because of me. With Lukas' help, Aesha and I steal time together." The two exchanged a look. "But it'll never be the same." She exhaled. "Like I said, talking to you the other night was amazing. There's just—" She gestured toward Khaari. "—nothing there."

Khaari laughed.

"I mean it in the nicest way possible." Challen smiled. "I wish you *could* teach Aesha to do that."

Khaari's head snapped in her direction. "Say that again."

"If you could teach Aesha—"

Khaari pointed to her, then looked at Aesha. "That's it."

"That's what?" Aesha said.

"The circle, the circles within. 'Eyes-that-are-open' is the teacher. 'Eyes-that-are-shut'—someone who cannot yet walk the Moonpaths. *That's* why it's familiar. This circle *is* like the Webs of Time. It's a teaching instrument." She started pacing back and forth. "We have shamans to teach us all this now. Did the Kaled'a'in Mage who made this?"

The Scrollsworn abruptly spun and faced Aesha—a doubly strange movement because of its total soundlessness. "Kinswoman, *it's why you're here.* I need you to go stand in that circle over there."

"Wait—*what*?" Challen said.

Aesha felt like she'd been hit in the head. For the first time since she'd finished digging out the circle, she looked at the statue.

"Is it?" she said to Her. "Is this why we're here?"

During the time when Challen had been seizing and screaming, when her mind had been under relentless assault, the greatest agony for Aesha had been the realization that she *was not special.*

That, except Lukas, the only mind Challen could have near her from now on would have to be dumb animals—or none at all.

She'd alternately screamed at and bargained with the Healers, begged them for something—some solution. They'd tried to teach her to shield, but at the end of the day she was just a thickheaded merc.

Aesha didn't pray. She'd been wary of the gods since she'd watched her mother's lips turn blue and her father cough up chunks of his lungs. The blowout with the shamans had been the final straw. She'd joined the Skybolts rather than give her heart to the Plains. Leaving had just been easier.

But to find Challen. To lose her. To know she still walked and breathed, but without her.

"No," she'd whispered in the darkness. "No, I won't. I won't let her go alone into exile."

Desperation had burned her up. Alone in a tent, she'd done what every Shin'a'in was entitled to: she'd invoked her Goddess.

She'd cut off her braids and burned incense to ash. She'd wept and begged until dawn broke.

The silence had crushed her heart.

The next day, she had found Sweetbark on a map.

Aesha could hear the panic in Challen's voice as she said, "Absolutely *not.*"

But Aesha suddenly couldn't tear her gaze from the statue.

Somehow, in the last few minutes, the statue had stopped being a source of antipathy. She saw it now, the beauty in the curves, the awe and the agelessness—and the absolute horror it could contain if improperly harnessed.

Her heart swelled with an old pain and a memory: her own words in her ears, a prayer whispered over and over in perfumed darkness.

Please, I'll do anything. Just let me go back to her someday.

And the *next day,* staring at the maps of this country she'd decided to call home—she just happened to pick the one place with a rogue statue of the Star-Eyed.

"I'd have appreciated more *direct* guidance, but this is fine, I guess," she said to the statue, marching over. She jumped lightly over Khaari's outstretched body and turned back to her beloved. "If it doesn't work," she said, "I just want you to know—"

"Aesha!" the Herald screamed.

"—I love you."

She stepped into the east circle, closed her eyes, and touched the statue.

A Voice said: *Open your eyes.*

Aesha saw—shifting silver mists.

Directly across from her stood the Scrollsworn, looking startled—but also excited.

"You made it!" Khaari said.

"I better not be dead," Aesha said.

"You're not dead," someone said, to her left, and she looked to see a man in black with a veil around his face. "But you do have a choice to make."

He put his hand out. His other one already held Khaari's.

"Is it really a choice?" Aesha asked.

He hesitated. "It has always been so, kinswoman. If it weren't, you'd never have been able to leave the Plains in the first place."

Aesha reached out with her free hand. Her other arm still connected to the statue—except here, on the Moonpaths, it wasn't a *statue*. It was something vast and starlit and cosmic, and her mind didn't want to put a name or form to it. She knew the Voice had come from it, and the less she thought about it, the better.

"We've been watching the Hills this long," Aesha said. "What's a little longer?"

The circle completed. She and Khaari snapped back into their bodies, in the last dying light of day.

Sometime later, with Challen safe at her cabin, Aesha took the Scrollsworn to her favorite place to get a drink, which coincidentally was the *only* place to get a drink in Sweetbark: Kael's inn.

"How many people do you think that statue has left to die of starvation?" Aesha asked, taking a seat and signaling to Kael that she wanted two mugs.

"Who knows?" Khaari replied. "Just make sure it never happens again. Treat it like any of the things buried under the Plains. In the meantime, I'll see if any Tayledras nearby can help."

Aesha grunted.

"I do not know what all you have been through, Aesha shena Tale'sedrin—"

"Mutt," Aesha said.

"Excuse me?"

"The shaman called me a mutt," she said, half under her breath. "He got mad and impatient with me. He called me a mutt." She shrugged. "My parents didn't raise me on the Plains. They treated me with indifference. When they died, I got fostered into Tale'sedrin because no one else wanted me. I wasn't an easy child to love." She thought of the Northerners and their ringleader, glaring daggers at her. "I had to break my fists a few times before I got the violence out of me. I'm lucky I lived to find Challen. I'm lucky—" Her throat caught, and her vision grew misty. "She's *everything*."

Khaari reached out and took her hand. "You are not to blame."

Aesha wiped her eyes. "Tell that to younger me."

"I wish I could."

She sniffed.

Khaari cleared her throat. "Do me a favor. I know you will want to seek them tonight, but—the Moonpaths. Wait."

"*Wait?*"

"One month."

"*Why?*"

"Yours is not the only choice to make."

The ale showed up, and Aesha sat in contemplation as Khaari raised her cup. They clinked, and Khaari took a sip, then made a face.

"Bah!" she exclaimed. "*Why* is this ale *sweet*?"

As asked, Aesha waited until the moon had grown full before she gave it a try. Then she threw open the window to her one-room cottage and let the moonlight bathe her.

Her stomach flip-flopped. She thought she might puke. She took a deep breath and stilled her mind, ready to walk to the cabin—

Someone knocked on the door.

Aesha rolled out of bed, ready to murder the interruption.

The door cracked and then opened fully, and Challen peered inside.

"Are you asleep?" she asked.

"*What?*" Aesha yelled.

Her wife grinned. "Khaari—"

The Scrollsworn had appeared in the flesh on Toecrusher, and Challen *still* hadn't Sensed her coming.

"So you are shielded," she said.

"You call it shielding, but it is not taught the same, and it is done with the blessing of the Star-Eyed." Khaari dismounted. "I am Shin'a'in, and by right of marriage to Aesha, you are also of the Plains."

She stepped onto the porch. "Aesha took up the work of protecting the relic the Kaled'a'in left in these Hills until we can find a way to make it safe. As a daughter of Valdemar, you are already doing this work. What do you say here? 'There is no one true way.'

"You can no longer protect your mind from the thoughts of others. But what if it's not your mind, but the *method* you are trying to force over it? Perhaps all you need is . . . a different way. I believe She sent me to help Aesha, but Aesha's love for you means She also sent me for you." She inhaled a deep breath. "You are *both* Her daughters. I can try to teach you as I was taught, and if I fail—"

A Scrollsworn appeared behind her in the moonlight, wearing a veil. Off to the side, still another. And more. So many like her, most in her midnight blue. Each regarding Challen with curiosity, compassion, and warmth.

"We are all teachers," Khaari said. "We all know ways. Maybe one knows a way that can help."

Tears filled Challen's eyes. "What if it doesn't work?"

Khaari cocked her head. "What if it does?"

It would be impossible to tell which threw herself at the other the fastest, or the fiercest.

Bathed in moonlight, in full view of the endless field of stars, they kissed passionately and wept with mingled joy, without any boundaries to keep them apart.

Unsavory
Jennifer Brozek

Tressa pulled the six tartlets from the oven and frowned. Instead of the expected savory scent of hot onions and cheese, a sour smell arose from the tray. Still grimacing at them in puzzlement, she put the batch on the kitchen window to cool. Already, the sun was peeking over the horizon. Soon Heralds and Trainees alike would be heading in her direction.

"What is that?" Marley asked. "New experiment?"

Tressa nodded to her more senior peer. "Yes, but I'm not certain it worked."

The other baker took a sniff and wrinkled her nose. "Too much of *something*. What spices did you use?"

"The new one from Rethwellan. I thought it would go with . . ." Her voice faded as Marley's rose.

"Sweeper! Get out of here, you mangy mutt!" She pushed the dog with her foot in Tressa's direction with an annoyed, "Dammit, Tressa."

The "mangy mutt" in question was a beautiful, medium-sized dog with a moderately long, silky, chestnut-colored coat. His tail swept the floor whenever he sat. It banged against legs, tables, and chairs when he stood. The dog belonged to Herald Arden and was forever getting underfoot since the Herald often visited the kitchens, looking for a snack.

"I'm sorry. I'm sorry." Tressa pulled Sweeper by the collar and escorted him to the back door, then shoved him out. Sweeper, lovable goof that he was, went willingly enough, but he turned around and sat up to beg for a treat.

"No. You know you aren't supposed to be here. Go home. Go on." Tressa turned back to the kitchen and saw several people lurking near the kitchen window. Since she'd been working in the Palace kitchens and started her bakery experiments, lovers of baked goods had learned they could come to the back window and have a good chance of scoring something new and interesting to eat from the newest Palace baker. Her cheese biscuits and moonberry scones were already legendary.

Herald Vidar appeared in the window with his usual grin and asked, "These good to go?"

"Yes . . . but . . ." Tressa shrugged with a weak smile.

"I know. Experiment. 'May not be the best.'"

Tressa cut each tartlet into four pieces. Some mornings there were more people than usual. Word-of-mouth was almost as fast as gossip in the Palace, and a free treat was always in vogue. At least, her experiments were usually a treat.

The Herald picked up a quarter piece of tartlet and balanced it on his fingertips. "Hot hot hot."

Marley reappeared with a tray of bread loaves. "Careful. You don't know what you're playing with there."

"I'm always careful," Herald Vidar said, then nodded to the side, at the kitchen's back courtyard. "Babysitting again?"

Tressa looked out the window. Sweeper was there, nosing over the ground, still looking for something to eat. She huffed impatiently. "Yes. Sweeper! Go home!"

Sweeper didn't even bother to look at her.

Herald Vidar laughed, then took a generous bite of the experimental tartlet. He chewed twice and stopped, grimacing. Without chewing anymore, he swallowed his bite and tried to school his face into something more neutral and failed.

Tressa put a hand to her mouth. "Oh, dear. That bad?"

Herald Vidar coughed and gave her a weak smile. "'Fraid so. What *was* that?"

"Rethwellan chervil with onion in a cheese custard. It should've been great." Tressa picked up a piece of the tartlet, paused as the sour scent hit her again, then pushed on and took a bite. She regretted it, but she still chewed well, trying to figure out what happened. The sour taste overcame even the cheese. It was not pleasant.

Laughing at her expression, Herald Vidar leaned over and fed the rest of the tartlet to Sweeper, who gobbled it up. As he did so, the other lurking pastry lovers backed off. "Rethwellan chervil reacts badly with onion from any country. Even its own. It's a chemical thing. All Heralds that head that way are warned in advance. Some Rethwellan people like to prank strangers with the concoction. Though Sweeper doesn't seem to mind."

The dog wagged his tail and looked for more treats.

"And now I know." Tressa put the rest of the tartlets down. "These are not even fit for dogs. Especially ones that will eat absolutely anything."

"I don't know. I might take a couple and use them as punishment for my Trainees . . ."

"You do that, and I cut you off from all future experiments."

Marley, who had watched the conversation from the other side of the kitchen, shook her head. "Can't do it, Herald. Not allowed to poison the Trainees. No matter how much they upset you."

"Spoilsports." Herald Vidar waved and left.

Tressa took the tray from the window and dumped the remaining tartlets into the slop bucket. If the dog would eat them, so would the hogs. Waste not, want not. It was too bad she hadn't known about the weird reaction between Rethwellan chervil and onion. She had hoped to use the ambassador's gift for the upcoming ambassadorial meals. Perhaps she should talk to Landon, the Rethwellan ambassadorial assistant, about what goes well with the herb. It had been a while since she'd talked with him.

In the meantime, she had other baked goods to get done, and the sun continued to rise.

As Tressa finished her baker's duties, the kitchen filled up with the next wave of cooks, cleaners, and other staff. Used to having the kitchen mostly to herself and the other three bakers in the wee hours of the morning, she hurried along before the clamor that came with the arrival of the breakfast shift rose into its usual horrifyingly loud din.

Heading out the back door after almost being run over by a distracted page, Tressa paused as she saw Marley talking with a man she didn't know. Something about the way the two of them leaned in together for their conversation itched at the back of her mind.

They talked like friends with a secret. The man had a basket of *something* he handed over with a nod. Marley took it with a smile. She looked around and saw Tressa watching. She had another quick word with the man then turned away with a wave and headed toward Tressa.

The way Marley walked toward her made Tressa feel as though she'd seen something she wasn't supposed to see. It was in the woman's careful steps and straightened shoulders. Part of her wanted to run. The rest of her waited to see what would happen.

"All done with everything?" Marley asked.

"Yes. Who was that?" She tried to keep her voice light. "And what's in the basket?"

Marley didn't lose her smile. "Mushrooms from Yesslin. He's a mushroom farmer and an old friend."

Tressa nodded, looking at the still covered basket. "What are they for?"

"Eating, silly."

"But . . ." Tressa stopped at the flash in Marley's eyes.

"But what?"

She heard the hard tone in the other baker's voice. It heralded one of her infamous biting comments. Tressa pushed onward.

"Just . . . we aren't supposed to accept food for the kitchen that Jala or Enri haven't approved . . . ?"

Marley scoffed. "This is for my own experiments. You know, like you do most mornings. I'll cook something interesting with them and have the chefs taste it. When they say they like it, I'll let them know about Yesslin."

Tressa's stomach rolled uncertainly at the idea. "I thought we weren't supposed to give preference to anyone? All produce and livestock farmers are supposed to go through the same vetting process."

"Like you did?"

Surprised and a little hurt, she asked, "What's that mean?"

Marley gave a little hmph. "Didn't *you* walk into the kitchens with a letter from your beloved *Mariah* that put you to the head of the class? You only had to bake one thing for Jala and Enri. I remember when I applied, I was quizzed within an inch of my life and had to bake for an entire day before I was accepted."

"That's not a fair comparison. I—"

"I think it is." Marley leaned closer. "I'm not the only one who's noticed the preferential treatment you get from Jala and Enri. None of us get to experiment with pastries to give out at first light to those brave enough to taste them, wasting food that could be used elsewhere. Why do you get to do that, I wonder?"

Tressa pressed her lips together. "Because I asked, and I'm not wasting food. I'm creating new things for the menu."

Shrugging, Marley turned away with a last retort, "You certainly wasted food this morning. Favorite or not, you've only been here three months. You're still on probation, learning how to work in the Palace kitchen. Troublemakers don't last long. Remember that."

Watching her go, Tressa had the sinking suspicion she'd made a serious mistake. She didn't want to be known as the favorite *or* as a troublemaker. Who was she to question Marley? Unfortunately, the woman was right. She *had* walked in and gotten the job at Mariah's urging. It had been almost too easy.

Still, as the meeting between Yesslin and Marley played over in her head, she couldn't shake the idea that something was wrong. It reminded her too much of something she'd seen before she worked at the Palace. Something that went against everything she'd learned as a baker back at the Rise & Shine, and everything she was learning as a Palace baker.

Tressa looked at herself in the mirror. She was put together enough to feel that she could walk through the Palace back corridors without someone stopping her. With a wag of her finger, she told Sweeper's reflection, "You stay here. I don't know how you keep getting out, but the kitchen is no place for a dog. Don't get me in any more trouble."

He sat there with an unrepentant grin on his face, wagging his tail furiously, sweeping the floor clean.

Turning, she gave Sweeper a quick pet, then made sure he was inside before closing her door. She lived in the same building as many of the other unmarried Palace workers. A clean, warm, safe roof over your head was one of the perks of working for Haven's Palace. Not required but available to those who didn't mind the dormlike accommodations.

The Palace itself was a series of outbuildings surrounding the main structure. Every building had its primary focus—Herald Training, the different Collegia, barracks, the stables, the kitchens, the Healers' Hall. Some buildings she was used to. Others were as foreign as a distant land.

Most of her time was spent in the kitchen or helping the staff to deliver food. She didn't have to clean the kitchen from top to bottom every day. That job belonged to those who specialized in it. Her main focus was the baking of breads, pies, biscuits, cakes, and other such pastries. Her secondary focus involved bringing some of those fresh-baked goods to important people in the Palace when requested.

It was how she'd met Landon in the first place. As an assistant to the Rethwellan ambassador, he was the person she interacted with most. The Rethwellan ambassador had a particular love of fresh, hot bread most days, and if one of the other bakers couldn't make the delivery, she would.

Peeking into the office where Landon guarded the ambassador's schedule and privacy with appropriate zeal, Tressa smiled at the young man and waved when she saw that he was alone.

"Oh, hello." Landon waved her in and gestured to the chair opposite his small desk. "What can I do for you? The ambassador is out right now, so . . . ?"

Tressa entered and sat in the chair Landon indicated. "I came to ask you about Rethwellan chervil and what it goes with, but there's something else . . ."

"Yes?"

She paused, unsure of how to begin, then blurted the question. "Do you accept gifts from people for the ambassador in order to have the gifter seen in a better light?"

Landon sat back. "Well. That's unexpected. I mean . . . ambassadors are given gifts all the time. So, yes? Why do you ask?"

Tressa hesitated then explained her encounter with Marley from earlier. She ended with, ". . . and I don't know if she's breaking a rule or not. Nor do I know what I should do about it."

He shrugged. "If it was me, I wouldn't worry about it. Sometimes such gifts are needed to smooth the way for negotiations. Just like our ambassador gifting your monarch with goods from Rethwellan. Then again, there are many differences between the Palace kitchens and the customs of those in diplomacy. So I can't help you there."

She nodded. "Two very different situations and allowed behaviors."

"But what about the chervil?"

Accepting that she needed to figure out the problem on her own, Tressa pushed it aside and asked, "What goes with Rethwellan chervil? I've discovered that onion does not."

Landon grimaced. "It most certainly does not. Let me look in our records. I'm sure we have recipes you can have. One of the diplomatic exchanges is always the trading of recipes—whether or not the recipient actually intends to use them. In the meantime, you must tell me the gossip from the kitchens. Did Sarah and Troy ever make up?"

Tressa grinned. "Yes, but it took a bit." She settled in for a good gossip session with her friend and put the problem of Yesslin, Marley, and the mushrooms out of her head.

On the way back to her rooms, Tressa saw Sweeper lying in the grass next to the walkway. "Sweeper! How in Haven . . . ?" She stopped in mid-sentence as she realized that Sweeper wasn't sleeping or resting. The dog lay on his side and trembled, and white flecks of foam dotted his mouth as his eyes rolled in his head.

Concern drove all other thoughts out of her mind. She knelt by the dog and touched his side. Sweeper yelped in pain, then groaned. He tried to raise his head and failed. She'd never seen an animal this kind of sick before. Fear gave her strength as she scooped Sweeper up and put him half over her shoulder. She all but ran to the Healers' Hall, trying not to jostle Sweeper too much. To his credit, he only yelped and growled but did not bite or snap at her.

A Healer Trainee standing at the door took one look at Tressa's face and didn't bother with niceties. He pointed to the left. "Animal Healer's entrance is around the side."

"Thank you," Tressa gasped, her fear-born strength failing. Hurrying around the side of the building, she rushed to the door just in time for Sweeper to start convulsing. "Please," was all she managed to get out before the green-clad Healers on staff moved and caught Sweeper before she dropped him.

"Trauma room," one of them said. As Sweeper disappeared into the back, another Healer said, "Wait here."

Tressa all but collapsed into one of the waiting chairs. Only then did she realize she wasn't alone in the waiting room. She looked around and saw two other people. Both held animals—an older woman holding a snowy white cat and a boy holding a cage with a colorful bird. "I'm sorry," she said and dropped her eyes.

"It's all right," the woman said. "Just a checkup here. Emergencies take precedence. What happened?"

Tressa shook her head. "I don't know. I think he ate something bad."

"Well, Healer Betin will get to the bottom of it. He's got Animal Mindspeech. All of the Healers on this side of the Healers' Hall do. It helps keep the animals calm, even if they're in pain."

"I don't know what I'll do if he dies."

The older woman shook her head. "He won't. He's in good hands . . . ."

A Trainee in pale green popped out of the door the staff had disappeared through and waved at Tressa. "Miss? Miss? Healer Betin would like to see you."

Tressa rose and followed him. As they ducked into the working part of the Animal Healer Hall, she saw numerous animals in cages resting, eating, or sleeping. Most of them did not seem to be in pain. On one of the main tables Sweeper lay; a man in dark green was touching the dog's head and hip. Sweeper was no longer convulsing, but he whimpered and drooled. Sweat beaded on the man's forehead.

"She's here," the Trainee said.

Healer Betin opened his eyes. "I need to know what you fed him and where you got it." His voice was stern and direct.

"I—" Tressa shook her head. "I didn't feed him anything. I found him like this, lying on his side. He must've eaten something. He's always getting out. He's Herald Arden's dog."

The Healer nodded, then frowned. "I'm aware of this dog's proclivity for eating anything and everything. You are not the 'loud one?'"

Tressa shook her head again, eyes wide. "I don't know what you mean."

Taking a deep breath, Healer Betin tried again. "He was in the place of good smells and treats. I assume that is a kitchen?"

Grateful she could answer something, Tressa nodded. "Yes. When I babysit him, he breaks out of my room and invariably makes it to the kitchens."

"Who yells at him?"

"Well, we all do . . ." Tressa didn't know she could feel any worse than she did now, but dread compounded the feelings. "But mostly it's Marley."

"And what is a meaty flower?"

"Meaty flower?" She felt like she was taking the final exam for a class she'd never attended.

He took another breath. "One moment." Closing his eyes, Healer Betin concentrated on Sweeper who was, thankfully, no longer convulsing, yelping in pain, or even whimpering. When the Healer opened his eyes again, he seemed calmer. "I am paraphrasing what I believe Sweeper is trying to tell me: He was in the kitchen, nosing around. He was yelled at by a number of kitchen staff, but none kicked or hit him. Then 'the loud one' offered a 'meaty flower' that smelled new and different. She waggled it like a treat, then threw it out the back door. He chased it down and ate it. The kitchen door closed again, he wandered off. Very soon after he felt burning in his stomach and throat. So, again, I ask . . . meaty flower?"

Tressa swallowed hard. "It's a mushroom. It has to be. Will he live?"

"Working on it. Those mushrooms are deadly. I need samples as soon as possible. No one should touch them with bare hands, much less eat them. Handle them with care."

She nodded. "I'll get them." Without waiting for an answer, Tressa took off running. She didn't stop for anyone or anything. She knew she had to get to the kitchen before anyone used the mushrooms for anything. As she ran, she wondered whether Marley knew about the mushrooms, and, if she did, what she was going to use them for—or, rather, who she was going to use them against.

By the time she got to the kitchens, she was out of breath and panting. She threw open the back door and charged in, almost knocking someone over. “Sorry,” she breathed and bolted into the pantry where fruits and vegetables were stored. Shelf after shelf, she scanned for the covered basket Marley had taken from Yesslin.

Nothing. There were mushrooms, but not the basket, and she recognized the ones that were there. Stepping out of the pantry, she asked, “Mushrooms? Where are they? Who took them?”

No one answered her in the bustle of the lunch rush.

Grabbing Alisa, one of the staff holding a tray of plates filled with steaming dumplings, she demanded, “Mushrooms! They were in a covered basket. Where are they?” She peered at the dumplings with suspicion.

Alisa pulled herself out of Tressa’s grip. “I don’t know. I didn’t use any mushrooms.” She shifted away from Tressa’s questing hand. “I have to go serve this. There’s an important ambassadorial lunch on. Nothing can go wrong.” Alisa slipped away, down the back hall towards one of the smaller formal meeting rooms.

Colin, an older daytime cook, walked over. “What about the mushrooms? Marley said there was a special request. And what’s with you? You look like something the cat would decline to drag in.”

Tressa didn’t care that she was sweaty, covered in dirt, dog hair, and probably Sweeper’s vomit from when she carried him. All she cared about now was stopping whatever it was Marley intended to do. “They’re poison.”

Without any more explanation, she sprinted down the back hallway and saw which room Alisa ducked into. Tressa didn’t stop. She rushed to and through the doorway, slamming into Alisa’s back, causing her to up-end the tray of plates the woman had been carrying as she burst into the room.

The room itself was one of the smaller, more intimate meeting rooms. An oval table sat in the middle with eight chairs around it. Five of those chairs were occupied. A small feast sat in the middle of everyone. On both sides of the room, ambassadorial assistants and guards stood. The room was already tense from whatever the negotiations were going on between the rival countries.

That didn't stop Tressa. "Poison!" she shouted as the dropped plates crashed to the floor and ambassadorial guards from both sides of the room moved. "The mushrooms! Don't eat—"

Then she was hit from the side as one of the guards slammed her to the ground. A great clatter and din of shouts, scraping chairs, plates being crushed by hasty feet, and metal against metal rose around her and Alisa, who had also been brought to the ground by another overzealous guard. People pushed away from the table. The only things she recognized was Landon's concerned face and Herald Whites coming into view.

Again, she said, desperate to get the message across, "The mushrooms are poison. Don't eat them." As she tried to get up, reaching for the Herald, struggling against the guard, he punched her in the side of the face before the Herald could stop him.

Tressa prodded the side of her face with a cautious finger. Despite her care, the merest touch hurt, and she pulled her hand away from her bruised cheek.

"You look . . . ah . . . fine," Landon said.

"I look and feel terrible."

He stood in the doorway of a small room off to the side of a larger meeting room. Alisa, she was sure, was in another small room, with another guard. Landon was allowed in here because he'd vouched for her, and he tried to tell everyone that she'd been investigating the mushrooms since that morning. Of course, no one had believed her or him or even Alisa until they all had been put under the truth spell and questioned by Herald Nuala.

"They didn't find her."

Tressa wished there were a window to look out of. "Marley?"

He shrugged. "She hasn't been seen since she served the savory bread pudding that had the mushrooms in it."

"What was she trying to do?"

Landon moved into the room and took a seat. "More to the point, who was she trying to kill and why? My ambassador? The ambassador from Karse? Herald Nuala?"

"I wish I knew. I just . . ." Tressa sat next to him then stopped. "Oh! Sweeper . . ."

"He's fine. A Healer Trainee reported to the kitchens for the mushrooms. Apparently, you weren't fast enough for Healer Betin's liking."

She smiled. "Blame it on the Rethwellan guard who punched me."

"Draven was just doing his job, and he had no idea if you were magical or not."

"Really?"

Landon nodded. "Really. You did just crash a delicate meeting between ambassadors, shouting about poison, and then you tried to make a motion towards the Herald."

She shook her head. "No good deed goes unpunished."

"That is where you are wrong," a new voice said from the doorway. As Herald Nuala stepped into the room, both Tressa and Landon jumped to their feet.

The Herald waved a calming hand. "Baker Tressa, I am here to tell you that you are not at fault for anything that has happened. You did put yourself at risk to save the ambassadors. The crown thanks you for your efforts, and you may go. You may be required to attend another meeting or two, as there are still a few questions you might be able to help with. We'll let you know." She gestured at Landon as she said this last bit.

Herald Nuala focused in on Tressa, allowing a bit of a smile to show. "You did good work. Perhaps even saved more than one life. Though, Chef Jala would like a word with you tomorrow about the incident. As a personal aside, thank you for taking care of Sweeper. I know he's a pain, but he's a lovable one. I'm sure Herald Arden will appreciate it when he finds out."

Tressa returned the smile, despite her aching cheek. "Thank you, Herald. Ah, can I go?"

"Yes. And Tressa?"

Her stomach roiled. “Yes?”

“I don’t suppose you’ll be experimenting with a new cheese biscuit soon, will you?”

Relief washed over her. “I probably will. As soon as I’m allowed back in the kitchen, that is.”

Herald Nuala winked. “Good.” She turned and left.

Landon tilted his head to her. “Miss Tressa, would you allow me to escort you back to your room? Better that someone come with you to stop the many, many questions I’m sure you’re going to get.”

“I would like that, good sir.”

He offered her his arm. “You know, you’re going to be the subject of a lot of gossip—and not all of it for your baking.”

She smiled. “Got any pointers?”

“Well, as we’ve discovered, there’s a big difference between our specialties. But I think I can come up with some equivalents.”

“Good. I look forward to learning the different ways of managing diplomatic gossip rather than kitchen gossip.”

Final Consequences

Elizabeth Vaughan

To Lady Cera of Sandbriar, in the Kingdom of Valdemar,

Greetings,

Once again, I must express the thanks of the Healers' Collegium and The Crown, as well as my own personal thanks, for the supply of wild kandace. My hands suffer from stiffness, and the oil is a marvelous remedy, one I had been without for some time due to the shortages. It is a great relief to have a reliable source for the herb and its by-products.

Master Jebren writes that a number of your young people have been trained in the creation and production of the oils and syrups that can be made from the plant and that you yourself have taken an interest in his methods.

Master Xenos does not write, which, to be honest, is odd, since he is usually complaining bitterly about something by now.

However, I must inform you that I am recalling both Master Jebren and Master Xenos to their duties here at the Collegium and have done so under separate letter. We wish to have them return before the worst of winter sets in. The Herald Helgara has been instructed to escort them back to the Collegium.

I know that you might wish to continue to have their expertise at hand, but they will always be available to answer any correspondence from you.

In any event, please accept our grateful thanks for all of your assistance.

Naritha,
Assistant Dean, Healers' Collegium, Haven,
in the Kingdom of Valdemar

Lady Cera of Sandbriar walked toward Jebren's . . . to the still house, the letter from the Collegium still clutched in her hand.

The sun was still rising, and the cool air felt good on her hot cheeks. Fall was here in all its glory, and she'd been so busy with harvests and the herds, she hadn't thought of the passage of time, or what that might mean for . . . for Sandbriar, of course.

Had it only been midsummer that Jebren and Xenos had arrived? It didn't feel that way, it felt as though he—they—had been at Sandbriar for years.

Of course, it also felt as though she'd been here for years. She'd come to love Sandbriar and its people. She'd never dreamed, on the day Queen Selenay had confirmed her in her late husband's land, that she would come so far, achieve so much. Master Jebren had aided her in this, helping her develop a trade in wild kandace that brought such benefit to her people.

Why hadn't she thought they'd be leaving? They were masters of their crafts, and their services would be needed back in Haven.

Cera bit her lip as she knocked on the open door of the still house, a shed really, the scent of drying herbs and bubbling elixirs tickling her nose. Master Jebren stood within, by his worktable, clutching a letter, looking as lost as she felt.

He looked up, a sad welcome blooming when he saw it was her. "My Lady . . ." he said. "I thought you were meeting with Athelnor all morning about the petitions."

"Yes, but," Cera stepped closer, holding up her letter. "Did you get . . ." her voice trailed off.

Jebren looked down at the letter in his hand. "Yes," he sighed. "Herald Helgara brought it."

Cera looked down at the parchment in her hand. "She brought mine as well. I sent her to the kitchens to get warm and eat something." She could hear herself babbling and took a breath. "Did she say when you would be leaving?"

"She wanted to," he said. "But there are some things I should finish before—" he stopped. "I will miss you," he said sadly. "This place, I mean, the people."

"The sheep?" Cera said, feeling sharp edges form in her chest, trying to lift the moment with a soft laugh at the memory.

Jebren puffed up. "I will have you know Old Meron said I 'would do' for the next shearing."

"High praise," Cera said as they exchanged smiles.

"And one I will cherish." Jebren deflated. "Sandbriar, it feels . . . well, never mind." He smiled at her ruefully. "I have enjoyed my time here."

"I—we have enjoyed having you here." Cera looked into his warm brown eyes until she flushed at the silence and forced herself to look away. "I should go," she stepped back to the door. "There are people waiting."

"Of course, My Lady," Jebren said.

She left him, disquieted and upset and feeling awkward and foolish.

Cera took a breath and headed to the kitchens, since that was where they always found Xenos these days. The scent of yeast and sweet spices wrapped around her as she opened the door.

"I can't believe they really expected you to cure their sniffles," Bella snorted as she kneaded dough at the large table in the center of the room. "Not when a hot cup of tea and a few days rest would set them right."

Xenos heaved a very put-upon sigh. "Happens all the time," he grumbled as he rolled out dough on his side of the table. He made an odd picture, with a flowered apron over his green Healer's garb.

Herald Helgara had wedged herself in a corner, away from the work. She sat close to the ovens, with a biscuit in one hand, tea in the other, clearly enjoying the warmth.

They all looked over as Cera entered. Bella's face split in a wide smile. "Lady," she grabbed a towel and threw it over the dough. "What can I do for you?"

"Nothing, thank you." Cera smiled at Helgara. "Just getting food?"

She'd caught the poor Herald in midbite. Helgara covered her mouth as she tried to swallow, but Xenos spoke up. "I had to check my handiwork. See that she hadn't put any more dents in that thick skull."

Helgara rolled her eyes at Cera, but Cera noticed Xenos hadn't looked up from the dough in front of him.

"Xenos." She moved closer. "Did you get a letter from Assistant Dean Naritha?"

"Yes," he said, still not looking up.

Bella darted a glance from Cera to him and back. "Was that what you threw in the fire?"

Cera bit her lip. "I got one as well," she explained. "I just wanted to say that you will be missed. You did a great service in healing Herald Helgara and aiding my people and—"

"I am not going," Xenos snapped.

"What?" Cera almost took a step back from his harsh tone.

"Going where?" Bella demanded.

"I am recalled," Xenos took up a biscuit cutter and started stamping out shapes in his dough with more force than was necessary. "I am not going."

Bella looked at him, her face filled with pain, and eyes filling with tears. "But—"

"The Collegium—" Cera started.

"I will write." Xenos's lips were tight, his face drawn. "These need to get in the oven. Lady Cera, you impede our work." He hefted the baking sheet, still avoiding her eyes.

Cera opened her mouth, but nothing coherent came out. She darted a glance to the Herald, who looked just as uncomfortable as she felt.

Helgara stood, biscuit in hand. "I should see to Stonas." She was out the door with swift steps.

Retreat did seem the wisest course. "I need to return to Athelnor," Cera said, making for the door to the back stairs. "We will talk later."

"There is nothing more to be said." Xenos moved toward the oven. "I will include a note for the Head Cooks in the Collegium," he continued. "Their biscuits are atrocious. Leaden lumps of despair. I will tell them that Bella's are better by far."

"You could send them my recipe . . ." Bella's voice wavered, watery and weak.

Cera closed the door behind her, cutting off Xenos's reply. She was late and took the stairs two at a time to Steward Athelnor's office.

Her Chatelaine, Athelnor's wife, Marga, was waiting by the door. She huffed a sigh of relief when she saw Cera. "I'll give you a minute, then start bringing them in."

"Come inside first," Cera said. She pulled her in, and quickly shared Xenos's reaction with both of them.

"That explains that," Athelnor looked back at his own papers. "Important enough to send a Circuit rider with word." He sighed. "A pity, I have enjoyed Jebren's company, and the man knows his craft." He gave her a sly grin. "Xenos, on the other hand . . ." he chuckled. "None to mourn that departure."

Marga was flabbergasted. "One does not ignore a summons from the Collegium," she said. "Whatever is the man thinking?"

Cera just shrugged, as puzzled as the two of them.

"Let's get started," Athelnor settled himself behind his desk.

Normally interviews of this nature were in the Great Hall, but given Athelnor's health, Cera wanted to avoid the drafts. Gareth knelt by the fireplace, adding wood. He'd been conscripted to take notes by his grandfather, protesting mightily. Now he grinned at her, clearly not as upset as he had pretended to be.

A knock at the door. "Come," Cera called, pleased when Ager

and Alaina were the first to walk in. Ager seemed nervous as he settled a pregnant Alaina into her chair.

"A spring baby," Cera smiled. "Perhaps we will have enough *chirra* wool by then for a proper baby blanket."

Alaina started to protest, blushing, but Cera just laughed. "No better use," she said. "Now, please tell me I am not losing my *chirra* herder."

"No, Lady," Ager sat himself. "We are not asking for land. We were thinking more of chambers within the manor. I'd ask to tend the *chirras*."

"And I can tend to you, Lady," Alaina said.

"I suspect you will have enough on your hands with the little one." Cera laughed. "But you are both most welcome."

The next hour was filled with all kinds of trade and craftspeople, petitions in hand. Cera had the experience of her father's mercantile and her mother's wool trade, but there were so many other things to take into consideration. Taxes, land rights, apprenticeships, leaseholds, some old arguments over boundaries coming to the fore.

"Now, no worrying about the boundary dispute," Athelnor said as the door closed behind that quarrel. He snorted. "They've been carrying on for years, and we can look at the old records and finally set that to rest."

"Are you sure?" Cera asked.

"Of course," Athelnor said. "You are the Lady of Sandbriar."

Thankfully, she had Athelnor at her side, well familiar with the laws of Valdemar and the traditions of Sandbriar. Gareth took notes, but he'd also remind his grandfather of facts, and he was amazing at adding up columns of figures.

And the assortment of people, such a variety. Athelnor chortled with glee over a cordwainer (making new shoes, if you please, Lady) and a cobbler (repairing badly made shoes, if you please, Lady), each glaring at the other and bickering over the definitions of their trades.

Headman Odon ushered in a stout, weary widow with six massive sons who filled the office, all staring at her with desperate eyes.

"She be wanting to start a brewery," Odon announced. "But afraid to approach your ladyship. I told her, no such thing, you'd hear her out and consider her fairly," he said, looking rather pleased with himself.

"Of course," Cera gave them all a smile as they towered over her. "What is your experience?"

Hope bloomed in those tired, desperate eyes. Cera was suddenly caught in the flash of memory. Of kneeling before the Queen in her garden, placing her hands between Her Majesty's and swearing fealty. Had the Queen seen the same hope in her eyes?

Then the woman started talking, her sons chiming in, their voices as massive as their bodies. Their words and excitement spilled out and over each other and, underneath, a rising sense of the possibilities.

"I think we can discuss a leasehold on the old brewery," Cera said, after they all finally ran out of breath.

Headman Odon helped usher them all out. "We saw Ager and his missus on the way in," he said. "He's promised to give advice and share his recipe for cider. I'll just take them to the old brewery," he said as the last of them disappeared through the door, still talking among themselves. "And we'll have a look around."

"No final decisions have been made yet," Athelnor reminded him.

Odon looked over his shoulder and lowered his voice. "Cider," he whispered loudly, and winked at them before closing the door behind him.

Cera chuckled as Athelnor huffed and shook his head.

"But that's good, right?" Gareth asked. "Ager can't deal with drink anymore, but we don't want to lose his knowledge, right?" He tilted his head thoughtfully. "And this'd be a way to get us a trade item and save that skill. Sandbriar benefits from its people, and its people benefit from Sandbriar."

Athelnor beamed at the lad. "Been thinking on that, have you?"

Gareth ducked his head and then shrugged.

The door opened and Marga put her head in. "I want in on this one," she said with an impish smile.

She threw the door wide, and there stood Withrin Ashkevron and, slightly behind him, Emerson, the Tapestry Weaver, holding hands.

"Does this mean what I think it does?" Cera stood, her excitement growing.

Withrin limped in, tugging a blushing Emerson to stand beside him. "Emerson has honored me with his hand," he said simply, yet beaming like the sun.

"Finally." Gareth rolled his eyes even as he grinned.

They all laughed, and in the midst of the laughter and congratulations Cera hugged them both hard, so pleased for them.

Yet, as she stepped back, she had the odd feeling of . . . envy. A lump deep inside that her heart fluttered against. But she shook herself and folded her arms over her chest. "Emerson," she asked teasingly, "do your parents know?" She gave him a pointed look. "Lady Parissa, especially."

They both paled a bit, but then Emerson straightened. "I will write Mother," he said firmly. "Once our petition is heard and settled."

"Very well." Cera gestured them to the chairs. "What did you have in mind?"

"This area." Withrin leaned over and pointed to an area on the map. "There's already a small house there that needs repair. I'll have a barn rearing, for both a barn and a weaving mill for Emerson."

Athelnor frowned. "That's a lot of scrub and gorse, if I remember right. Back-breaking work to clear."

"But perfect graze for donkeys." Withrin smiled. "I've a mind to breed for mules. I'll ask my family for some breeding stock as a wedding gift. There's always a demand for good, steady, well-trained animals. The army is always in need."

"But Valdemar is at peace," Cera protested.

Withrin gave her a shaded look, and she was reminded that he'd been injured in the last conflict with Karse. "War always comes, Lady."

Cera sighed, and then she leaned in to discuss acreage.

When they left, Marga brought in tea. The mug warmed Cera's cold fingers. "Is that true? Does war always come?" she asked.

Athelnor sighed. "Perhaps not war, Lady, but conflict and trouble? That always arises. And it must be faced when it does." He took a mug of tea from Marga with a grateful smile. "So we plan for the worst and hope for the best, yes?"

Glumly, Cera sipped her tea and added that thought to her list of future worries.

"You've a few more that we can get in before lunch," Marga said. "Sooner started, sooner done."

The time flew, with some tradespeople wanting to dicker over terms and times and costs. Cera kept an eye on Athelnor, since his energy seemed to be waning. But Gareth stepped up, writing down their requests and assuring everyone that their proposals would be considered, making sure that Cera didn't agree to anything too quickly. He even snorted at a few figures, and the people making the offer just smiled and shrugged, as if aware he knew the game they were playing.

"I saved the best for last." Marga grinned, and the office flooded with dogs and kids and Old Meron, Young Meron, and Katarina.

"Well, here now," Athelnor's face lit up at the sight of the little ones. "I wonder if maybe there is a bit of sugar candy in my desk?"

Lukas and Greta, Katarina's brother and sister, squealed and scurried over to help him look, over Katarina's protests. Young Meron settled his dad in a chair and stood behind him as the dogs flopped down around the chair.

"So, been all over ya like burrs in a fleece, have they?" Old Meron asked. The effects of his stroke hadn't dulled his sharp tongue.

Cera looked at Young Meron, who opened his mouth to speak.

"Come to ask for provision for my son," Old Meron started in. "He'll take over for me when the time comes." He paused, squinting at Cera. "With yerself approving."

"Perfect," Cera said, knowing full well that Old Meron's role was already limited to supervising these days.

Young Meron tried again, but his father continued on. "He'll be needing a bit of a homestead close," Old Meron said firmly. "I suspect there'll be a handfasting soon enough, once he works up the nerve."

"Da," Young Meron protested.

Katarina blushed and covered her smile with her hand.

The children had found the rock candy and giggled as Athelnor pretended to protect it from them. They each ended up with a piece, cramming it in their mouths with wide smiles. Even Gareth had managed to sneak a piece amid the chaos.

"And what to the Steward do we say?" Katarina asked the children, her words clear but strongly accented. She'd made great progress, but her sentences still showed her Karsite origins.

Both children turned to Athelnor and bobbed their heads. *"Thank you, kind sir,"* they chorused.

"You've been helping with the smaller children, haven't you?" Cera asked.

Katarina looked at her, startled, then looked to Young Meron for reassurance. "Yes, Lady," her voice tentative. "All is well with this?"

"Yes," Cera said firmly. The tensions of the Tedral Wars still lingered, and there were still hard feelings toward Karse. But they shared a border with her lands, remote and desolate. Who knew what the future might hold?

"I think we should make that official," Cera said. "I want you to teach Karsite to them."

There was surprise at that, but it was Old Meron who spoke up. "Might not be a liked thing," he said gruffly.

"I will require it," Cera said firmly. "And I will announce that

I will be taking lessons from her as well. For good or ill, Karse is our neighbor. Best to know how to talk to them before the need arrives." She lifted an eyebrow. "Besides, who am I to ignore potential markets?"

Katarina's smile lit up the room.

"Well then, if that is settled," Marga stood and started to herd them out. "Steward Athelnor needs his lunch." She waited at the door as everyone, including the dogs, cleared out. "I'll be back with a tray."

Gareth leaped up. "I'll help," he grinned as he followed her out.

"You two had best clear that desk." Marga nodded at the maps and papers strewn over the surface.

"Yes, ma'am," Cera said with mock meekness, and proceeded to do just that, trying to keep everything organized.

"You'll need more help," Athelnor said carefully as he worked with her. "Keeping all this straight will be a task in and of itself."

Cera nodded, setting one stack aside and starting to clear the maps. "I can see that now."

Athelnor opened his mouth, but the door opened and Marga and Gareth both entered, carrying trays filled with food and drink. Gareth had a cookie in his mouth, his hands full.

"Here now," Marga said. "No more work until you've eaten."

Except it never quite worked out that way. Gareth had a question before he swallowed his first bite. "What's a barn rearing?"

"The community gathers and works together to frame a barn or other structures." Athelnor said. "That way, a lot of work gets done in a day. Of course, that also means you go to the aid of your neighbors when they have a need."

"Huh," Gareth pulled over one of the maps and studied it as he chewed. "But they need wood for framing too, don't they?"

"Yes, well, that's why the Old Lord set aside woodlands and pasture areas for common use." Athelnor pulled over another map. "Since the war, they haven't been cut, so we will have what we need. But still, we'll have to watch how much is taken, so the woods and fields stay viable."

Cera leaned over, her mug in hand. "How much did he set aside?"

They ate as they talked, and she learned more about common spaces, overgrazing, and maintenance. "No fears, Lady," Athelnor chuckled. "Each knows what is permitted, and each knows his neighbor will come running if he uses more than his fair share."

"All the more reason to keep our records in good order," Cera said, shaking her head. "You are right. I am going to need help."

"As to that," Marga said, giving her husband a meaningful look.

"As to that, Lady," Athelnor cleared his throat. "Before we continue this afternoon, I'd ask you to consider Gareth's future."

Gareth went still.

"If possible, I'd ask that we discuss his future position. He could replace me, or if you are not inclined that way, perhaps set some land aside for him." Athelnor cleared his throat again. "I know he's not yet coming of age, but Marga and I would like to see him settled."

"We won't be here forever," Marga chimed in.

"Grandma—" Gareth protested.

"It's never too early to consider these things," Marga said firmly. "We want you to have every opportunity, young man."

"He is a hard worker," Athelnor said. "And I know he would serve you well."

"Athelnor," Cera said gently. "I know all of Gareth's qualities, good and bad."

"Bad?" Gareth protested.

"Boar spears," Cera and Marga said together, and they laughed as Gareth protested while Athelnor scolded his grandson once again for hunting feral boars without a proper weapon.

"Never gonna live that down," Gareth grumbled.

Cera glanced up at the portrait of the Old Lord and his family that hung above the fireplace. "I've given a lot of thought to Gareth's future, and Sandbriar's," she said. "You were a cousin to the Old Lord, yes? So of the bloodline?"

"Well, yes . . ." Athelnor frowned. "But not in the line of succession. Besides, with the death of all of that side of the family, the Queen was within her rights to award these lands to you."

"Yes." Cera smiled. She took a breath, having given her next words a great deal of thought. "I am willing to talk about whatever you want for Gareth." she said. "But I have my own proposal I would like you to consider." She drew another breath. "I would like to adopt Gareth as my son and heir."

All three stared at her.

Cera plunged on. "Gareth knows the people of Sandbriar, and they know him. They are owed the sense of security that would come if he is my son."

"But . . . if you marry—" Marga's voice was a dry whisper.

Cera had already made this argument in her head a million times. "Any husband I choose—if I marry at all—would understand that Gareth is my heir," she said. "Besides, any child I bear in the future—again, if I have any—well, it would be years before we knew if that child could or would want to hold the Lordship of the land." Cera smiled. "Gareth, adopted as my son and heir, boar spear and all, would offer this land so very much."

She hesitated, then forged on again. "It would also mean that the pressure would be off me to marry and breed," she said bluntly.

The silence that greeted her proposal was so profound, Cera started to worry. "Be assured that I mean no insult to his parents or to you, but I've come to care deeply for him, and only want what is best for him and Sandbriar."

Athelnor struggled to his feet.

Marga had her hands to her face, weeping.

Gareth sat up straight, staring at her. "You know I'd do my best for you," he said, his voice trembling.

Athelnor walked over and leaned down to embrace Cera. "I thank all the Gods that the Crown sent you to us, Lady."

Cera smiled, wrapped in his arms as Gareth lunged over, knelt at her feet and wrapped his arms around her waist, burying his face in her lap. She placed her hand on his head and offered her own thanks to the Trine for her blessings.

"Well," Marga stood, wiping her face. "We best be finishing these interviews."

"Let's not make an announcement regarding this just yet," Cera said. "I need to have the adoption formalized first and then present my will and testament to the Crown and Council for approval, yes?"

"Yes," Athelnor straightened, his hand on her shoulder. "I can help you draft the documents, of course."

"I'll ask Herald Helgara to delay her departure," Cera said. "She can take the papers to Haven with—" she cut herself off from saying it out loud. She didn't want to think about who would be traveling with the Herald.

"Then let's get to work," Athelnor said, with a new strength in his voice.

"Can I finish my sandwich first?" Gareth asked, his voice muffled in her skirts. He lifted his head as Cera laughed and ruffled his hair.

The remaining interviews went quickly after that, and they had the notes and requests well organized before they called a halt.

Cera headed out into the late afternoon sun, knowing full well she'd find the Herald in the barns or close thereto. Sure enough, she was sitting on top of the fence, watching her Companion romp in the field with the *chirras*.

Cera leaned up against the fence next to her, enjoying the sight of the bright white Companion dancing like a colt, mock-charging the *chirras*, who scattered and then turned to give chase. Tail cocked high, Stonas galloped quickly out of reach, then circled back for the game to begin again.

Helgara laughed, and to Cera's pleasure looked healthy and well, fully recovered from her encounter with the bandits the previous summer. Dressed in Whites, she gleamed as bright as her Companion.

"The herd looks good," Helgara said, smiling down at Cera. "They did well with the heat?"

"Better than expected," Cera said as she climbed up on the fence and sat next to her. "They should go into season in the next few weeks, and with the blessing of the Trine the fields will be filled with baby . . ." Cera stopped, puzzled. "What do you call a baby *chirra*?"

Helgara shrugged. "I have no idea."

"A *chir*?" Cera asked. "A *chirp? A cheep*?"

Helgara snorted. "It's your herd, Lady of Sandbriar. You can call them whatever you wish."

"I can, can't I?" Cera said. She took a breath, reveling in the moment, of her lands, her fields, her animals.

"I've come to ask that you delay your return to Haven," she said. "I am going to adopt Gareth as my son and heir. Athelnor and I will be drafting the adoption papers and my will and testament, and I want you to take them to the Queen and Council, if you would." Cera set her shoulders. "I am hoping they approve my decision."

Helgara gave Cera a steady look. "It should not be an issue. You are the Lady of Sandbriar and able to make your own choices. I doubt there will be any objections." She paused. "Not many would make this choice."

"It is the best choice," Cera said. "And as you said, mine to make."

"So it is," Helgara said.

Stonas left off his games, trotting over in front of them, only to drop and start rolling in the field. A small cloud of dust and horsehair rose around him.

Cera snort-laughed; such a majestic creature, rolling in the dirt with such glee.

Stonas came back to his feet, and shook himself all over.

Helgara gave him a disgusted look. "Yes, I know you were itchy, but who has to groom that all off you, now? The one with hands, eh?"

Stonas snorted. Cera swore the Companion was grinning at both of them.

"I'm sure you can find some children to help," she suggested. "Of course, they'll want to braid ribbons and flowers in his mane."

Stonas hung his head. But then he tossed it high and danced over to Helgara, head butting her.

"Fine, fine." Helgara scratched him between his ears. "I'll tell her."

"Tell me what?"

"Xenos and Bella are Lifebonded."

"What?" Cera blinked.

"Stonas insists," Helgara said. "He is rarely—"

Her Companion snorted indignantly.

"—all right, *never*—wrong about these sorts of things."

"But . . ." Cera stumbled over her thoughts. "Oh, dear Trine, what do we do?"

"Nothing," Helgara said. "They need to work that out for themselves. As all couples do." She chuckled. "I can't wait to see their faces at the Collegium when they find out. Such a mix of joy and pain. Pain for the loss of his skills and joy for the loss of his personality."

"If Withrin and Emerson are any example, they will take forever," Cera complained. "Dancing around the situation, neither one willing to say anything, take the risk, make a decision . . ." She trailed off, hearing her own words as if for the first time.

It was so odd to listen to herself, her own advice, and realize the truth of it. She was the Lady of Sandbriar, wasn't she? Her life was hers, her decisions, her own. Free to make choices, take risks, set boundaries—

Or ignore them.

Her heart started to beat faster.

"Cera?" Helgara gave her a worried look. "Something wrong?"

"No," Cera said firmly. "No. I just realized that Xenos was right. Sometimes I really am rather dense." She dropped from the fence and brushed dust and grass from her clothes.

Helgara turned. "Cera?"

"I need to go talk to someone." She started off, hope and terror rising in her like a wind, her steps speeding up as she crossed the yard. With a roaring in her ears, she pushed open the door of the stillroom.

Jebren was still within, working at the table.

"Lady," he said, and there was that sad tone in his voice again. She hadn't imagined it. "I thought I would make up a last batch of wild kandace oil. I don't know when the Herald will want to depart, but I hope there is time before—"

"Jebren," Cera interrupted, determined, but then she faltered, her nerves setting her hands shaking. She licked her dry lips. "In Rethwellan," she started again, blurting out the words "if a young woman took a fancy to a young man, she would not approach him. She would go to her father and see what he thought. And if her father thought the match was suitable, he would approach the young man's father, and arrangements would be made."

Jebren stared at her, puzzled and confused.

She took a step forward. "How is it in Valdemar?"

He lowered his eyes and shrugged. "In Valdemar, a young man who is interested in a young woman can approach her and express his admiration and feelings, unless she is of the nobility, in which case it really isn't suitable—"

Cera flung herself at him, rattling the bottles and bowls, grabbed his tunic, and kissed him.

A frozen moment of terror, then his arms came up and wrapped around her, and his lips warmed and moved, and it was all so wonderful, warm, bright . . . and she needed air.

They broke the kiss, his arms still wonderfully wrapped around her. Jebren looked into her eyes, and they both burst out laughing.

"I was so afraid," Cera gasped.

"So was I," he admitted. "You are wonderful and amazing, and I didn't dare—"

Cera tightened her grip on his tunic. "You are not going back to the Collegium, and if they come for you, I will steal Gareth's boar spear and run them off."

Jebren laughed again, his entire body shaking as he held her tight.

Dearest Father,

My adoption of Gareth has been approved by the Crown and announced to all of Sandbriar. The formal documents arrived just yesterday.

But I am really writing to confirm all of your suspicions.

Beyond all hope and all expectation, I have found my place, my people, and my purpose. But I have also been graced with my heart's prize. And yes, he is the man that I have mentioned occasionally (not every letter, Father, surely), and yes, I do seem to have more interest in him than in anything or anyone else. You can stop your subtle probing, for I am enclosing the invitation to our wedding.

I cannot wait for you to meet my Sandbriar family, to see the wild kandace in bloom, and the chirras *with their* chirps *in the fields. By the time you arrive, I will have even more to show you, for we seem to be growing by leaps and bounds. Emerson's tapestry might even be completed by then, or so he claims.*

I will not pretend that all of our struggles are over, Father. You and I know full well that life is not like that.

But oh, my Father, the joy I have found.

Your loving daughter,
Lady Cera of Sandbriar,
in the Kingdom of Valdemar.

Hearts Are Made for Mending

Dayle A. Dermatis

A resounding boom shook the stables.

Jolted into wakefulness, Maglia choked back a scream and curled into a fetal position, hands clasped over her ears.

:Just a thunderstorm. You're safe.:

The soothing words from her Companion, Elyth, penetrated Maglia's terror.

Just a thunderstorm. Not battle. No fiery death raining down, no stench of blood, no screams of pain. *Safe.*

Maglia breathed in the scents of sweet hay and horsey Companion, in and out again, and though her heartbeat didn't entirely stop racing, it slowed to closer to normal.

She opened her eyes. Still dark out.

:Nearly dawn,: Elyth said, sensing her question.

Maglia uncurled, one tight limb at a time. Her muscles ached from the terrified ball she'd clenched them into.

Daytime was better than night. Light was better than dark.

Still, *safe*. She was safe in Elyth's stall, no matter what the time, no matter what the terror. She was protected here.

Only here.

The door between the stablehands' stairway and the main stable banged open, and upbeat whistling filled the silence between the rolls of thunder.

"Mornin', you beautiful creatures," a cheerful female voice

called. "Aye, it's early, but that's what my job's all about, the earliness, to make sure you're all well fed before the day breaks and you might be needed."

Usually the stablehands came in later, and Maglia had enough time to hide in the tack room until the hands chores were done. It wasn't exactly a secret that she was living here, but she didn't want to speak to anyone or to invite gossip. Out of sight, out of mind.

She should have had at least half an hour.

She rolled into a standing position, brushing hay from her Herald Whites, which were starting to look disturbingly more like Trainee Grays. Her hair . . . She reached up before remembering she'd shorn most of it off, not able to deal with braids or other styling, not after . . . after what happened. Last she'd seen a mirror, what was left had looked something akin to a spiky black hedgehog.

The owner of the cheerful voice was coming down the aisle between the stalls, greeting each Companion by name. Every Companion had an etched brass name plaque on their stall, but Maglia wasn't sure she'd ever heard a stablehand address them with such familiarity.

Or maybe she'd never paid much attention.

Companions didn't need quite the same close care as horses did. While their open stalls were still mucked out and fresh hay replaced, they generally went outside to do their business in Companions' Field. Grooming was done by their Heralds. Stablehands cleaned the stalls, provided food, and cleaned tack, often saddling a Companion when the Herald was in a hurry.

All Maglia knew was that her hair probably looked like a hedgehog had died on her head, and she smelled like someone who hadn't bathed in days, because she hadn't, not really, and—

"Hello, lovely Elyth, and how's your morning—oh! I didn't expect anyone to be here."

The stablehand had red hair in two plaits, bright blue eyes, and freckles dotting her nose and the arch of her cheeks. A pair of wire-rimmed spectacles perched on her nose. She was perhaps a few years younger than Maglia.

Those arresting eyes, even made smaller by the glasses' lenses, were wide with surprise.

"I'm sorry," Maglia said. "I didn't mean to startle you. I'm Maglia. Elyth is my Companion."

The redhead bobbed her head. "Pleased to meet you. I'm Zan. My younger brother, Joson, was recently Chosen, and I came along with him because, well, I'm good with horses and . . . I'm sorry, I probably shouldn't be bothering you."

"You're not," Maglia said. She must've hidden before Zan came through previously—and now she was sorry for that. Something about the young woman's cheerful energy spoke to her. Or maybe it was just because she hadn't spoken to anyone except Elyth for days, or that Zan was a stablehand she hadn't met before.

"Can I bring you anything? Food?"

Maglia's stomach clenched at the thought. The Healers, when they came to check on her, always brought some food, but mostly she'd been soaking some of Elyth's oats and snacking on his extra apples and carrots. She dreamed of so many meals . . . .

"Yes, if you could, that would be wonderful."

"Right, then," Zan said. "Once I'm finished with these lovely creatures, I'll see what I can gather up for you, yes?"

Maglia listened to Zan whistle and coo at the Companions as she fed and watered them. Through the windows, the sky reluctantly grew lighter, but only to storm-gray. Thankfully, the thunder had subsided and the rain was a distant patter, and Maglia's immediate terror had lessened with it.

Eventually the stables grew quiet again as the stablehands finished tending to their assigned Companions. Zan left, promising to return with food. Maglia hastily used the privy and washed her face in water from the tap in the kitchen. She had no other clothes, unfortunately, but she used a cloth to sponge herself off.

:This is the most you've taken care of yourself in a while,: Elyth noted.

"Hush, you," Maglia said affectionately.

It was true, though. Staying here with Elyth, apart from other people, meant she hadn't cared about her own grooming. She'd focused on Elyth's care, of course.

When Zan returned, she brought a covered wooden bowl of steaming lamb stew and a thick slab of buttered rosemary bread, and the very scents made Maglia's stomach clench with hunger. The stew, redolent with garlic and onions and stuffed with carrots and neeps along with a generous portion of lamb, was perfect, and the bread was the perfect companion.

Maglia tried not to shove the food in her mouth too fast, acutely aware of Zan's presence.

She stood in the open doorway to the stall, arms crossed across her chest. Her tunic and trews were both medium brown, useful for hiding dirt in a job like hers. The color shouldn't have been attractive on anyone, but Zan's red hair and blue eyes seemed to counteract the blandness of the hue.

"So you're a Herald," she said. "That must be exciting."

A bite of bread clogged Maglia's throat. She swallowed hard. "It can be," she said finally. "Other times it's boring, and other times it's frightening."

Zan nodded. "Like most of life, I suppose. It was kind of scary for me to leave home and come here with Joson, but it was also good because there wasn't much prospect for me at home." She lifted one shoulder in a shrug. "I figured I'd try my chances here, earn some money, get to spend time with these majestic creatures."

"Elyth says thank you," Maglia said.

Zan blushed. Her pale skin made a good canvas for that. "Augh, sometimes I forget how smart you are," she said, directing her words to Elyth. "Horses understand some things, but generally not human speech."

"It does take some getting used to," Maglia said dryly. "I had to kiss any idea of private thoughts away once I was Chosen."

Elyth leaned down and pushed against Maglia's shoulder. She laughed and rubbed the Companion's velvety white nose, then spooned up another bite of delicious stew.

Zan chuckled. "Our house isn't tiny, but with five children, it felt like there was nowhere to be alone. My da's the stablehand at the manor of Traynemarch Reach, and I'd go with him just to get away from the others and have some peace." She gave a wry, one-shouldered shrug, and pointed to her lenses. "Plus, without these early on, I couldn't see well far away—but horses were big enough that I could see them just fine! My da said they knew to be careful around me because I was little, and they were so gentle, so I just fell in love with 'em, and learned how to care for them."

"I can see why," Maglia said. "I started riding in front of my mother when my hands were barely big enough to grab the pommel."

Zan grinned, and Maglia liked the way the edges of her eyes creased.

"Well," Zan said, "I've got other chores to attend to."

"Thank you," Maglia said. "This was wonderful. I'm sorry I've kept you from your duties."

"No worries. I'll be back for the bowl in a bit."

Maglia found she was looking forward to that visit.

In the meantime, Maglia brooded.

She'd been here for nearly two weeks. After her return from the skirmish at the Border, she'd woken those first nights from horrific dreams to find herself trembling, panicked, drenched in sweat. And her screams had woken others.

Because the only time she felt truly safe was with Elyth, she'd started spending more and more time with her Companion, to the point that she'd found it safer to never leave the stables.

Now, the farthest she could go was to the tap by the trough outside the front doors, the porch area covered by a roof. Any time she tried to step farther, her diaphragm spasmed, not allowing her to breathe. Sweat dampened her clothes, her mouth dried up, and she lost her ability to hear except for the pounding of her heartbeat in her ears. Her limbs would go weak, and if she didn't back up, she'd fall on her backside, the stable spinning around in her sight.

It was embarrassing, really. Humiliating. She was a grown woman and a bloody Herald, for goodness sakes! And here she was, afraid of the sky.

The sky, so vast. Like a giant maw. It made her feel insignificant, helpless, even though she knew, logically, that she wasn't.

Anything could be lurking beyond her sight. Anything could come suddenly flying at her. The thought of being vulnerable made her want to crouch down and cover her head with her arms, like a child. Pull her tunic up over her head to hide beneath it like a little girl in a dress. She actually chuckled once at that mental image, and Elyth joined in, snorting.

Physically, she had no injuries.

But she had memories of the horror, and even though the recent thunderstorm had triggered her panic, she otherwise felt safe and free from nightmares as long as she was with Elyth, who had supported her decision to stay in the stables with patient reassurance. Even the distance from the stables to the Heralds' Quarters, despite their ability to communicate at that distance, was too, too far for Maglia.

Now she couldn't leave even if she wanted to. Since she felt safe, she didn't want to, and that was what it was.

And she didn't want the Healers in her head. Didn't want them probing her memories, seeing what she'd seen and feeling what she'd felt, and manipulating all that. Changing it. She hated feeling this way, but more than that, she hated the idea of someone mucking about in her head and making her believe she hadn't been there or seen what she'd seen or felt what she felt.

She didn't want to dishonor her Senior Herald by forgetting.

At the Collegium, all the teachers drummed into the Trainees, over and over again, that being a Herald was dangerous. Not just because of wearing bright "shoot me now" Whites, but because enemies of the country, bandits, and brigands were making constant forays over the borders.

Maglia had thought she had understood. Being a Herald was a double-edged sword: glorious and perilous. She'd thought she was brave, confident, strong.

But then she'd encountered real menace, and she realized how vulnerable she—and all the Heralds—really were.

They might be Chosen, they might be educated and trained, they might be the best of the best . . . but sometimes there were events they couldn't predict and anticipate. Sometimes there was an enemy stronger, faster, more prepared.

For the first time, she understood what it meant to be mortal.

In the end, Heralds were no better than anyone else. They were just as assailable as the next person.

At some point, everyone dies.

Zan brought her a wooden box to store food in. She also brought, over time, sausage rolls, cheese, apples, carrots, meat pies, and fruit pies, things that would keep for a day or two if necessary.

Maglia was grateful for the food, but she found herself even more grateful for Zan's visits. Always cheerful, the stablehand was happy to stop and chat, and their conversations were easy, sometimes spirited, as they learned about each other, agreeing on some things, debating on others.

Inevitably, though, the past would have to resurface. The question would have to be posed.

The Companions' stable had been modified and enlarged over the decades, from what Maglia understood. Originally an open space with stalls along the walls, it now had several aisles of stalls to accommodate more Companions. The stable might be only half full due to the number of Heralds riding Circuit, but each Companion still had their own home.

An open area in the middle provided a space for Companions to gather and converse if the weather urged them inside. Elyth was currently there.

"So, if I can ask . . ." Zan, sitting cross-legged across the stall, bit her lip. "Why are you here?"

Maglia frowned. "Because I was Chosen. Because I've trained to be a Herald."

"No." Zan waved her hand around the stables. "I mean in here."

Maglia tried to deflect, weakly. "Why do you ask?"

Zan leaned forward as if wanting to extend a hand. "Well, it doesn't make sense—given I'm told you Heralds have quite fine quarters elsewhere. Plus . . ." She drew her hand back, probably in response to the fact Maglia hadn't accepted the gesture—as much as Maglia wished she had and now regretted she hadn't. She wanted to feel those work-roughened fingers against her own.

She wasn't sure she dared to want that. Not as she was, broken, a shadow of herself.

But that was who Zan had come to see, had brought food to, again and again. Who now asked the question that was so, so very hard to answer.

"Plus what?" She heard the rasp in her voice and wanted water, but she didn't want to turn away to scoop some from the wooden bucket in the corner of Elyth's stall. She wanted to continue looking at Zan, at her freckles and her earnest expression, and hoped to hell Zan wasn't judging her for being weak and broken.

Zan shrank back, clearly uncomfortable. "There's gossip—which I try to ignore, mind you—but some say you're weak, your mind is touched somehow, that you can't go on Circuit any longer . . . ." She sucked in a deep breath. "That you're refusing the Healers' help and you don't want to . . . to continue everything that you do, to keep Valdemar peaceful and safe."

Maglia's stomach clenched, the pang not for lack of food but for lack of the truth she'd attempted, at all cost, to pretend hadn't happened.

She hadn't told anyone except the Queen, just after she'd returned.

No one else had asked, really, except the Healers, and she wanted nothing to do with them.

But Zan had asked. With kindness and concern in her cornflower eyes. And Maglia suddenly wanted to tell her story once more, to this woman who was, she hoped, starting to share her heart.

She reached out and grasped Zan's hands.

"The rumors are wrong, and they're right as well," she said. "You've heard about the Border War, yes?" At Zan's nod, she continued. "Copeland, my Senior Herald, and I were patrolling the Border along with another team. We'd heard rumors there might be an attack on a town that produces a great deal of lumber, thanks to its site in the mountain forest at the side of a waterfall, where they'd built a mill."

It had been a beautiful place at first. The air was crisp and laced with the scent of pine, the sky a perfect blue, the waterfall something of a wonder to behold.

Then everything changed.

"We were attacked, and they had a Fire Mage with them, who set fire to the mill. Copeland ran inside to help those trapped, and I managed to shoot the Mage."

An arrow through his heart couldn't change what happened next.

"Preen, Copland's Companion, went into the mill after him. I was fighting, didn't see exactly what happened, but Preen came out . . ." She choked, struggling to describe something so awful, words couldn't truly depict. "Preen came out on fire."

Zan gasped.

Maglia heard the sound, but she was too lost in her memory to react to it.

Still hearing Preen's screams.

"She must have panicked . . . she leaped into the gorge," she managed to say. "To extinguish the flames, but the rocks . . ."

Zan's hands squeezing hers was all that kept her from curling up and adding her screams to the memory of Preen's.

The boom of the firebomb. The anguished screams. The pounding roar of the waterfall, no longer breathtaking, but a scene of horror.

The smell . . . .

"Copeland came out of the mill with someone in his arms in time to see Preen go into the ravine. A moment later, he–he joined her. They were gone." She sucked in a shaky breath. "The other Heralds and Companions were also killed, but we took down the enemy. And Elyth got me home."

"Oh, Maglia." Zan wrapped her arms around Maglia—and Maglia accepted the support.

"As for the Healers," she said, her voice muffled in Zan's shoulder, "I don't want them in my head. I don't want them convincing me I'm okay, because I don't want to fall apart again and fail the other Heralds and maybe get them killed, too."

Zan rocked her, murmuring wordlessly, and Maglia just held on.

It wasn't until the next day that they touched on the subject again. After Zan had left, Maglia felt drained, empty, and she slept for longer than she normally did. She woke to find food in the basket and Elyth telling her that Zan hadn't wanted to wake her.

After Zan finished her afternoon rounds, she settled back into Elyth's stall with Maglia.

"I know it's not the same, but I got scared of horses early on," she said quietly. "It wasn't the horse's fault. It shied at a snake, and for good reason, but I was a new, small rider, and I fell. Broke my spectacles. The horse stomped the snake, but then she ran away, and I couldn't see well enough to figure out which direction was home."

"How did you get over it?" Maglia asked, her heart going out to the young, vulnerable Zan.

"Took me some time, both to get back on a horse and to feel brave enough to go so far away from a place I knew that I couldn't properly see it.

"I'm still afraid, but I do my best to not to let that fear stop me from doing what I want to do." She shook her head and huffed out a laugh. "Coming to Haven, a completely unfamiliar place, was rather terrifying, to be honest."

"I can't imagine what that's like," Maglia admitted.

"I don't think about it, but it's always there," Zan said. "The vulnerability. I could trip and fall down stairs, wander off a cliff, not see a danger coming. I can't express how grateful I am for these—" she touched her spectacles "—but I know they could break and I'd be . . . helpless again. Sometimes I wake up at night and can't find them, and I panic until I find them again."

"What do you do," Maglia whispered, "when you panic?"

"I remember that I'm not alone," Zan said, her own voice soft. "That I have Joson, and the other stablehands, and . . . maybe . . . you?"

"Yes," Maglia said, her heart leaping in her chest. "You . . . have me."

She couldn't say who leaned in first, only that they met in the middle, eyes fluttering shut as their lips met.

The kiss was gentle, questioning and then answering. *Yes.*

Oh, yes.

Maglia's hands were on Zan's waist, and Zan's hands were on Maglia's shoulders, and the intimacy of their touch along with the kiss sent a warmth of pure joy through her.

Her fears melted away. There was no space for worry, or panic, or even thinking. There was just this moment, and it was a moment to savor, and a moment she hoped would never end.

:Maglia!:

Maglia jumped at the sound of Elyth's voice in her head. Zan stepped back, startled, but also looking dazed and satisfied, her breathing faster than normal.

If it weren't for the urgency Elyth projected, Maglia would have been annoyed. Instead, she said, *:What is it?:*

:Zan's brother, Joson. He's been injured.:

Maglia grabbed Zan's hand and pulled her to the open area near the stable doors, where Elyth had been chatting with two other Companions. The stable doors were flung wide to let in the sweet spring breeze, which smelled of grass and sunshine.

"Where is he? How bad?" she demanded. At Elyth's response, she turned to Zan. "Elyth says Joson had an accident—fell off his Companion. Elyth's not clear on his injuries yet, but Healers are on their way."

The color drained from Zan's normally rosy cheeks. "What? Where?"

"The far end of Companion's Field. You—"

Zan flew out of the stable before Maglia could finish offering Elyth to carry her. Companion's Field was huge, and not a simple flat, grassy area. It was full of humps and hillocks, copses of trees, small streams bordered by slippery rocks. It could be an obstacle course—and indeed, was used as a course for a grueling foot race competition.

Maglia watched helplessly as Zan raced across the field, aching for her friend's panic and love for her brother. She wanted to follow her, be there for her, but . . . she couldn't.

But then, she saw Zan stumble and pitch forward, falling hard on the ground.

Then, worse, she didn't get up.

A different kind of fear rose up in Maglia—fear for her friend's well-being. A fear that drove all other thoughts from her head except her terrified concern. Had Zan hit her head on a rock? Such injuries could cause permanent damage. Worse, was she bleeding? Broken?

"Elyth," she choked out as she reached for her Companion's mane.

Then she backed away. "I . . . can't."

:You can. I believe in you. You can . . . with me. Trust me, my beloved.:

She wasn't alone, any more than Zan was.

Maglia pulled herself up onto his back; their bond was strong enough to not need any more words than that. As soon as she was settled, Elyth raced out of the stable, hooves banging on the wooden porch before he leaped off and galloped toward Zan's unmoving form.

He hadn't come to a full stop before Maglia was sliding off him, falling to her knees beside Zan.

Facedown, Zan was thankfully breathing, but not normally. Maglia could hear a harsh huffing coming from her, then she groaned, clearly in pain. She'd had the wind knocked out of her.

"Can you roll onto your side?" Maglia asked, and essentially hauled Zan over. She grabbed Zan's ankles and pressed her knees up toward her chest.

In a few moments, Zan gasped. She rolled over, sucking in great gulps of air as she reached out a hand. "Maglia? What are you—how are you *outside*?"

Her single-minded need to help Zan had driven everything else away. Now Maglia looked up. The sky was a pale blue bowl dotted with wispy clouds. To anyone else, beautiful. To her . . .

The sky started spinning, spiraling down to press against Maglia, and she tasted stinging bile. Quickly she looked down again, focusing her gaze and her thoughts on Zan's beautiful face.

Zan's eyes were a different blue than the sky. They were the blue of safety. She swallowed hard.

Something was different . . . "Your lenses!"

"Where—?" Zan sat up, squinting around her.

They weren't hard to spot—or, rather, the remains of them. The broken glass glinted among the blades of glass.

Maglia remembered what Zan said about when she'd been thrown from a horse as a child. How she couldn't see, didn't know the way home.

Maglia wasn't going to let that happen again.

"Look at me," she said. "Just look at me. You're safe. I'll get you to your brother." She stood, and held out her hand. Zan grasped her wrist, and she grasped Zan's and pulled her to her feet.

Elyth knelt, knowing before Maglia even said anything that it would be easier. Maglia boosted Zan onto Elyth's back and then mounted in front of her. Without suggestion, Zan wrapped her arms around Maglia's waist.

Magalia felt Zan rest her head against her back.

Elyth would get them where they needed to be.

:Thank you,: she said

:Always,: Elyth said.

Maglia closed her eyes, pretending the world around her didn't exist. She didn't need to see; she trusted Elyth more than anything. As they had during the kiss in the stable, her senses narrowed down, now to nothing more than the ripple of Elyth's warm, strong flanks as he galloped and the feel of Zan pressing against her back, her hands clutching around her waist.

Elyth bunched for a leap, probably over a stream, and Maglia leaned forward, bringing Zan with her. Elyth's landing was as gentle as he could make it, not as jarring as a horse's, as if floating to the other side.

And then they were at the far end of Companions' Field. Maglia dismounted, held out a hand to Zan, who easily slid off Elyth's back.

"How are you handling this?" Zan whispered.

"Never you mind that," Maglia said, not sure how to answer the question anyway. "Let's get you to Joson."

Her presence wasn't questioned, even if her Herald's Whites were a questionable shade. She drew Zan up to the Healers surrounding Joson, at which point Zan broke through their ring and knelt beside her brother.

:He'll be fine,: Elyth said. *:A blow to the head the Healers can tend to, and a broken leg that will just mean some resting time. As if Heralds ever rest.:*

Maglia grasped the closest Healer's arm. Allion, who'd come to see her only to be rebuffed by Elyth. "Her lenses," she said. "They broke. She can barely see beyond her own hand. Can you help her?"

Allion nodded. They had a close-cropped beard, kind brown

eyes behind their own spectacles, and long chestnut hair in two braids draping over their shoulders.

"Of course," they said, gently touching her shoulder. "I'm surprised to see you out. Are you . . . all right?"

Their words broke Maglia out of her focus on Zan again. The world spun around her. "Not really, but thank you," she said, and staggered to a nearby bush, fell to her knees, and vomited.

She felt Elyth beside her.

Her stomach still churned, her head pounded, and she was finding it hard to draw in a breath. Without looking up, she dragged herself to her feet and leaned against Elyth's warm side. "Please, take me home."

:Whatever you need.:

Elyth had brought her home safely from the battle, more than once forsaking his own needs and bypassing Waystations to continue on, until he absolutely had to eat and rest.

Maglia remembered little of the ride, although she knew she cared for Elyth at the Waystations they did stop at, removing his tack, grooming him, and ensuring he had food and water. The Waystations, although small, gave her a small sense of security that the open road and open sky did not.

The rest of the time, she lay forward along Elyth's neck, eyes closed.

When they had arrived at the Collegium, she carefully dismounted and staggered to the throne room, where she gave Selenay her report of the attack.

The Queen had thanked her, hugged her in sympathy for her loss of her Senior Herald, and encouraged her to take the time she needed.

Maglia had barely slept one night in her room. Although it was enclosed, she had thrashed through nightmares, and just before dawn, she'd gone to the Companions' stable.

Now, Elyth brought her to that safe space again. He said he

required nothing—she hadn't saddled him before their ride, and in truth they hadn't gone far. She slid off his back, curled into a corner of his stall, and breathed in the sweet scent of hay.

:Nothing can hurt you here,: Elyth said, nuzzling her.

"I know," Maglia murmured, breathing slowly and carefully. "I just . . . hope Zan is all right."

Somehow, she fell asleep. Not a deep sleep, but one troubled by memories, causing her to twitch and half-wake before slipping away again. She got up once to stagger to the kitchen for a glass of water, before sinking down in the hay again.

When she heard a noise close by, in the stall, a noise that wasn't Elyth, she jerked awake, panic sizzling through her limbs.

It was Zan.

Relief, and something more, coursed through her.

They embraced, but whether Zan gathered her in her arms or she gathered Zan in her arms, she couldn't say. Not that it mattered.

When they drew apart, she saw the slightly bent, unfamiliar frames perched on Zan's nose, and she touched them gently with one finger.

"They save old lenses for people who can't afford them or need them in an emergency, like I do," Zan said in response to her unspoken question. "These aren't perfect, but they help. They're grinding new glass for me. And they said it's possible they can heal my vision to a degree—not fully, but not as awful as it is now. At least so I can find my way to the privy at night. That would be nice."

Maglia laughed, for the first time in as long as she could remember. "I'm glad they allowed you to find *me*."

"I think . . . I think I could find you even if I was blindfolded," Zan said, her voice rough.

"But I would never want to make things that difficult for you," Maglia said softly, resting her forehead against Zan's.

* * *

Maglia agreed to let Allion work with her. She was a Herald; she had responsibilities. She couldn't hide in the stables forever.

Coming to Zan's aid had reminded her of that.

She knew she still had the Queen's work to do.

She was a Herald.

And when she finally felt safe stepping out the stable doors into the light, she had Zan's hand in hers.

"My quarters are much more comfortable than Elyth's stall," she said. "I hope you'll visit?"

Zan laughed. "I can't wait to see them."

Together, they stepped out into the sun.

A Gift of Courage

Anthea Sharp

"*Will you stay, love, and go with me?*" The poignant lyrics echoed down the stone stairwell of the Bardic Collegium, accompanied by the sweet notes of a harp.

Tarek Strand smiled as he stepped into the hall leading to the Bards' quarters. There was no mistaking the lilt of Shandara Tem's voice, the sound of her intricate chords plucking a backdrop to the melody. He thought he'd never tire of hearing her music. It was one of the many things he loved about her.

And he was finally ready to tell her how he felt—even though the prospect made his throat tighten with apprehension. It was weakness to show emotion, his father had rebuked him time and again. Lords weren't weak, and no son of his should even *think* about admitting his feelings out loud.

But Tarek wasn't a lord. Not anymore. He'd denied his birthright as the heir to Strand Keep only a few short weeks before, to firmly embrace his path as a Healer. His feelings for Shandara had played no small part in that decision, of course. Everything important in his life was here in Haven, sheltered within the walls of the Collegium.

A sense of purpose. A place for his Healing Gift. And Shandara, the woman who'd seen him through so much turmoil as his life turned upside-down.

She's everything to me. Will I be enough for her?

The question had hovered over him like a shadow as he'd ridden back to the capital, dogged his footsteps as the life of the Collegium swirled about him.

He hadn't planned on this, after all—hadn't spent his life dreaming of mastering his Gift and dwelling happily in Haven. Nor had he bonded with his fellow Trainees throughout years of schooling. Being a late bloomer meant he was always a little self-conscious, a little on the edges of a world where everyone else seemed to know exactly where they belonged.

Shan, especially. She was lovely, and generous, and music was her heart's blood. At his lowest, Tarek worried that a minor lordling's son from a keep near the border of Hardorn had nothing to offer one of the brightest Bards in the Collegium.

But she'd welcomed him back with smiles and sweet kisses, and he'd begun to believe that maybe he was good enough, after all.

Humming softly under his breath, Tarek strode down the patterned rug carpeting the hall. Halfway to Shandara's door, the sound of another voice joining with hers brought him to an abrupt halt. A rich baritone sang in harmony with Shan, the sound of a gittern melding with the harp's notes.

"*Together dwell in unity . . .*" The two voices blended perfectly.

Tarek blinked. He didn't recognize that voice. Who was visiting her?

There had been an influx of new instructors recently as the Collegium prepared for classes to resume after the summer break. Bardic, especially, had seen the need to add more teachers. Maybe this was one of Shandara's old Masters, stepping in to fill one of the temporary vacancies.

Tarek hesitated before the door and waited for the final chorus to end before knocking.

"Come in," Shandara called.

He stepped into the sitting area of her small suite, noting how happy she looked. Her harp was resting against her shoulder, her honey-brown hair braided out of the way. She wore the usual Scarlets of a Bard—as did the man seated beside her.

The fellow holding the gittern wasn't a grizzled old Master Bard summoned out of retirement, however, but a good-looking bearded man about the same age as Shan. They sat with their knees almost touching, and he was gazing at her with an admiration that Tarek recognized all too well, since he felt the same.

A small knot of coldness settled in his belly, as though he'd swallowed a stone fresh from the River Terilee.

"Tarek!" Shandara smiled at him. Her hazel eyes were alight with pleasure, and she seemed not to notice his reticence. "Meet my old friend Rykallo Tayard. Ryk and I were Trainees together, years ago."

"Nice to meet you," Tarek said with a stiff nod.

"Years ago?" Ryk laughed and ran a hand through his wavy brown hair. "You make us sound positively ancient. Surely it wasn't *that* long ago—it feels like only yesterday."

"Well." Shandara played a quiet chord with her right hand, the notes ringing. "A lot has happened since then."

Ryk strummed an echo on his gittern, then nodded to Tarek. "A pleasure to meet you, Healer Tarek. Shan told me she's made some good friends in my absence."

Good friends. The words echoed inside Tarek. Was that how she saw him—as nothing more than a good friend? The confidence that had brought him to her door slipped another notch.

"Are you just visiting the Collegium?" he asked, hoping Ryk was simply passing through.

"No." the Bard glanced at Shandara. "I'm happy to say I'll be rejoining Bardic as a temporary gittern instructor."

The stone in Tarek's belly grew heavier. Here was a man who was everything he was not—charming, polished, and clearly a fine musician—and who shared a long history with Shandara.

"It was good of Lord Wendin to let you go," she said to Ryk. "I've barely seen you since you took your position there. We have so much catching up to do."

"That we do," the Bard said. "Not to mention many more duets in our future. I'm looking forward to playing with you again." He grinned at her, and Tarek tried not to gnash his teeth.

She nodded. "I'd love that. I can't believe you remembered the harmony to this one so quickly."

"I remember all of our arrangements. Even the ridiculous descant for that love song you made me learn."

Tarek shifted from foot to foot, feeling as relegated to the background as the woven hangings decking Shandara's walls.

Then she turned to him, her expression open and warm, and he pulled in a deep breath. He shouldn't let his worries get the better of him. He loved Shan, and he was fairly sure she returned his feelings. Just because Bard Ryk had arrived, that didn't mean anything else had changed.

Two nights later, Tarek wasn't so sure.

Despite his intentions, he hadn't been able to catch Shandara alone. Ryk was always there—rehearsing with her, discussing teaching strategies, even whisking her off to the tavern the Bards favored outside the Collegium's gates.

Finally, Tarek had given up—at least for the time being. Maybe after that evening's concert he'd finally have a chance to speak with her.

He and Lyssa Varcourt, the young Healer Trainee he'd been mentoring, sat together in the audience watching the Bards perform. The Bardic Collegium's concert space was smaller than the grand hall at the nearby Palace, but the evening's performance was mostly meant for the Bardic Trainees, so they could hear their new instructors play. Tarek had always preferred the more intimate setting, where he could watch the skilled musicians at close range, their fingers flashing over the strings as the air vibrated with song. For a short time, he even forgot the anxiety that had twisted through him for the past few days.

Until Bard Rykallo took the stage. Then all of Tarek's doubts came rushing back.

Beside him, Lyssa shot him a look. The young Mindhealer had clearly sensed his distress, but he resolutely kept his gaze on the stage—even when the group of fifth-year Trainees seated in the row behind them started whispering about how handsome and brilliant Ryk was and how much they hoped to be assigned to his gittern classes.

The Bard opened with an original piece he'd composed during his time as a Trainee, dedicated to the Companions. As he played, Tarek had to grudgingly admit the man was very talented. He could almost see the graceful white creatures in Companion's Field—the flash of silvery hooves and blue eyes, the soft whinnies of joy as they cantered through the summer grasses.

When the music ended, the audience let out a collective sigh. The Bard had captured the beauty of the Companions and also the yearning every non-Herald had felt at times, seeing the white creatures and the deep bond they shared with their Heralds.

"I know," Ryk said, after the applause faded, "it would be grand to be Chosen—except for the fact that one has to then become a Herald."

His worlds drew the intended laughter, and he grinned.

"There have been Heralds with Bardic power," said Master Bard Tangeli dryly from the front row.

"Always the teacher." Ryk winked at him. "I'm sure you can cover that in your lecture tomorrow."

Another spate of amusement ruffled the audience. Tarek turned, looking for Shandara. She'd been seated off to the side earlier, but now her chair was empty.

"While I retune, let me tell you about when I was a student here," Ryk said, tweaking the pegs of his gittern. "You might have heard the story about a Trainee who inadvertently put the audience to sleep during a performance—including the Queen and most of the Heralds."

Tarek knew the tale and who it was about. He'd been at the Collegium then, albeit not as a Healer Trainee but as a Blue—a lordling receiving an education that didn't include training in any

Gifts. In fact, he'd been openly disdainful of the Gifts, thinking the Heralds, Bards, and Healers little more than charlatans. He squirmed a little in his chair at the reminder of his own arrogance, even though it was what he'd learned from his father.

A father, he reminded himself, *who'd finally come to accept, if not fully embrace, the fact that his son is now a Healer.* Funny how a brush with death could do that.

It had taken a similar life and death situation to unlock Tarek's Gift—and Shan had been at his side ever since, steady and supportive as he'd stumbled forward onto the new path of a Healer.

"What you might not know," Ryk said, continuing his story, "at least not you younger Trainees, is that the student who accidentally knocked out her audience is here, under this very roof. Please welcome the beautiful and talented Bard Shandara Tem to the stage!"

Hearty applause broke out as Shandara emerged from the wings, her harp cradled in her arms. She looked luminous, her silk Scarlets setting off her light brown hair, a smile brightening her hazel-green eyes.

A stagehand, dressed in black, hurried to set a chair for her and a low stool for her instrument.

"Thank you," Shandara said to the audience before settling herself gracefully next to Ryk and positioning her harp on its perch. "And this is why you never let your friends rope you into a joint performance before you know what tales they're planning to tell."

She was so at ease onstage, so confident and lovely. And there beside her was the personification of everything Tarek was not.

He pulled in a sharp breath, and Lyssa turned to him, concern on her pale face. "Are you all right?"

"Fine," he said, making himself smile back at her and trying to settle his thoughts.

She pursed her lips, clearly unconvinced.

"What shall we play?" Onstage, Ryk leaned forward, giving Shandara an intent look. "The lullaby that put everyone to sleep?"

She rolled her eyes at him. "Are you *trying* to get me into trouble?"

"Always was a mischief maker," Master Tangeli remarked from the front.

Ryk let the comment pass and nodded at Shan. "How about one of your originals?"

The warmth of their friendship was undeniable, no matter how many years had passed since they'd seen one another. Tarek tried to shake off the creeping realization that he could never fit so easily into the world of a Master Bard. Maybe he shouldn't even embarrass himself by trying. Maybe he should give up on the idea that he and Shan—

Lyssa nudged him with a sharp elbow, and he glanced down at her.

"Tell her," the girl said.

Dratted empath. He frowned at her. "Maybe."

Lyssa frowned back. "You've both been dancing around the subject for ages. When you were gone this summer, Shan moped around as though the sun had gone out of her world. You have to tell her how you feel."

"Why does it have to be me?" he asked with an edge of irritation.

"*Shh,*" the Trainees in the row behind them said.

"Sorry," he said softly, then folded his arms and slumped back in his chair.

To be honest, though, he knew why he had to be the one to speak first.

He'd never planned to live in Haven, let alone become a Healer and stay at the Collegium. Until that summer, he hadn't been absolutely sure he'd be ready—or even able—to give up his expected role as the heir of Strand Keep.

And Shandara hadn't forced him to make that choice. She'd stood patiently by while he navigated the uncertain pathway under his feet.

"I've been practicing your composition 'Valor,'" Bard Ryk

said, giving Shandara a sly look. "I wonder if you can keep up with me?"

"Let's find out." Grinning, she pulled her harp back against her shoulder and struck a bright chord.

Ryk followed with a cascading arpeggio, and the two of them were off. After a stirring instrumental prelude, Shandara began to sing. Her clear soprano rose above the interweaving chords, telling of the Bards of yore and their service to Valdemar.

The connection between the two Gifted musicians was unmistakable, evident in the improvisational back-and-forth between the verses, the intent looks they shared as they played. Even if Tarek couldn't hear all the nuances, the indrawn breaths and soft chuckles of the audience of Bards and Trainees told him the two performers were having a deep, melodic conversation. The gittern player was communicating with Shandara in a way Tarek never could, and that knowledge twisted inside him.

At the chorus, Ryk's voice joined hers in harmony. She looked at him with such approval that Tarek felt suddenly invisible, as if he'd somehow evaporated into the air. As if he were nothing more than a fog made of yearning and doubt.

"Stop it," Lyssa said quietly, swatting his arm.

He frowned, but not at the young Mindhealer. Her admonishment had been well timed. No, his irritation was directed at himself. Why hadn't he said anything to Shan when he'd had a chance?

Maybe he'd been a fool to think someone like her could find happiness with him, when there were so many talented—and, unfortunately, handsome—Bards in Valdemar. When there were so many others who'd love to sit beside her and play music and make her laugh.

Shandara's voice soared triumphantly through the closing chorus, Ryk played an impressive run on the gittern, and the song was finally over. The audience members jumped to their feet, clapping and yelling approval. Tarek stood, too.

Onstage, Shandara and Ryk took several bows. She was

glowing, her cheeks flushed, her smile as bright as a hundred candles.

The air was suddenly stifling.

"I'll be right back," Tarek said to Lyssa.

She gave him a worried look but let him go without a word. He wended his way out of the row and then hurried up the short aisle to the door. He needed some fresh air—out of earshot of each beautiful, bittersweet note the Bards played.

In the light of the setting sun, Tarek left the Bardic Collegium and crossed the cobbled square toward the Palace and Herald's wing. The evening was quiet—most of the Bards were at the concert, the Healers in general didn't tend to rowdiness, and the few Heralds and Trainees he encountered simply nodded in greeting as they passed. Maybe they could tell he wanted to be alone.

He skirted the corner of the Palace and took a deep breath. The air smelled of meadow grasses and dusty late-summer flowers—the same yellow ones that bloomed around Strand Keep. The keep he'd gladly handed over to his sister, once their father had finally—grudgingly—agreed to release Tarek from his role as heir.

The stones underfoot gave way to grass as he headed to the fence surrounding Companion's Field. Once before, facing another difficult choice, he'd found peace here, and a bit of welcome clarity.

As he'd recalled, the top rail was the perfect height to lean his folded arms on. The fence wasn't there to keep the Companions in, of course, but simply to mark the boundary of their space.

A few white forms browsed on the other side of the Field, but none of the Companions seemed interested in his presence, and he was glad. It was further proof he was an unremarkable part of the Collegium: not an interloper, or a threat, or even an arrogant lordling.

He was a Healer. A little unsure, maybe, but still valuable. Still needed.

And he loved Shandara Tem with all his heart.

Twilight shaded the sky overhead to silver-burnished purple, and a few bats flitted, swerving and darting over the Field. He watched them for a while, trying to guess where their unpredictable, sudden turns might take them. They never ended up quite where he expected. *Much like my own life.*

He thought he'd crossed the biggest hurdle last month, when he'd ridden away from Strand Keep. He'd been wrong.

How strange that leaving the past behind had turned out to be easier than reaching for a future he dreamed of. A future with Shandara. But as the stars brightened overhead, he realized his dream wasn't entirely out of reach—unless he never tried to grasp it at all.

He owed it to her, to both of them, to take the next step forward. To stop assuming things about his place in the world, and hers, and do the hardest thing.

Ask.

The constellations were visible, the half-moon a silver boat sailing the sky, when Tarek stepped back into the lantern-lit halls of Bardic. He walked straight to Shandara's door and knocked. Softly at first, then a little louder when no reply came.

His heard thudded in his chest as he waited, but after a few moments it was clear she wasn't within. Maybe she'd gone with Ryk to celebrate their successful performance. With effort, Tarek took his disappointment and breathed it away. It took several long exhalations, but he felt better for having done so.

Shan belonged to herself. If she wanted to celebrate with friends other than Tarek, he wouldn't begrudge her. And he'd do his best not to jump to conclusions. He hadn't been anywhere to be found after the concert, after all. When he showed up to toast her—and Ryk too, he supposed—he hoped she'd be glad to see him.

To his surprise, he didn't need to go in search of Shandara after all. She was seated on the small bench partway down the corridor to his rooms. Seeing him, she stood.

"There you are!" she said, a hint of worry in her voice. "Is everything all right? I asked Lyssa, but she went all enigmatic and wouldn't answer."

Shandara had been waiting for him.

She hadn't gone off with Ryk and the other Bards but had come to find him, Tarek. And when he wasn't there, she'd waited. The knowledge made all his self-doubt, all his fear blaze away in a flare of pure joy.

Lighthearted, he strode forward. "There's something I wanted to ask you. I just needed a little time to figure out how."

"Ah." She raised one brow, a speculative smile flitting over her lips. "And did you?"

"Yes." He glanced about the hall, suddenly realizing it wasn't, perhaps, the best setting for what he was about to do. He offered his hand. "Come outside with me."

"So mysterious." Her smile deepened as she set her hand in his. Their gazes met, and he glimpsed the trace of a blush on her cheeks before he led her into the night.

They went to the small garden set between the Bardic and Healers' Collegia—a grassy square edged with flowerbeds and a few scattered benches. They'd spent hours there, talking, when they'd first been getting to know one another, and there was a particular bench near the wall he hoped was currently unoccupied.

"That was a wonderful performance," he said as they stepped over the grass. "I always love hearing you play. But I thought you'd be off celebrating with the others."

She waved a graceful hand. "I told Ryk we might join him later. He had plenty of admirers ready to accompany him to The Gilded Harp."

The smell of lilies perfumed the air, and the nearby lanterns were lit, illuminating the bench—fortunately empty—nestled among the flowers. He settled on it, and Shan sat beside him, close enough that their shoulders touched.

"Now, why did you bring me here, again?" she asked, a teasing note in her voice.

"Shan . . ." He swiveled and took both her hands in his.

She turned to him, a sudden stillness falling over her. For an instant, all Tarek could hear was his own heartbeat. All he could see was her face, the trust in her clear eyes, the beloved features he'd dreamed about for countless nights.

Memories of their times together flashed through him—all the moments she'd laughed with him, shared his sorrow, encouraged him to follow his heart.

As he was doing now. The last doorway was open. All he had to do was step through.

"Shandara Tem." His fingers tightened over hers. "Will you marry me?"

She smiled, slowly, the way dawn fills the sky with imperceptible light until suddenly the whole world is ablaze.

"Yes." She said the word softly, then louder. "Yes. I thought you'd never ask."

"I wasn't sure . . ."

"I know. But I was. I am."

"So am I." The words vibrated through him, resonant with certainty. "I love you."

If he hadn't found his courage, he might have missed the chance. Missed all the sweetness the future held—at least until he'd finally mustered up the nerve to act. Far better that he'd done it now, rather than later. Or not at all.

"I love you, too," she said softly. "I have, for a long while—I just didn't want that love to force you onto a path you weren't ready to walk."

"I know." He gazed into her eyes so she could see the truth in his heart. "But I've finally found my way."

He drew her toward him, and their lips met. Gently at first, as though it was the first time they'd ever kissed—then more fiercely as the reality of their promises took hold.

Finally, Shan pulled back, laughing. "We'd best stop, or we'll provide a spectacle I'm not sure the Trainees need to see."

He chuckled, his ears heating slightly with embarrassment. "You're right."

They would have time, and privacy, later.

She stood and straightened her Scarlets. "Now, however, I believe we have an appearance to make. With news that will outshine even Ryk's performance."

"Indeed, we do." Tarek rose. He had to admit he wouldn't mind stealing the spotlight from the handsome Bard.

But better by far was the knowledge that, at last, he was precisely where he ought to be—with the person he'd come to love best in the whole world at his side.

He'd asked. And her answer had made him the happiest man in all of Valdemar.

Sacrifices of the Heart

Michele Lang

Sparrow craved just a little more time. Time to rest, and to dream . . . and to think.

But the crow blocking her path, its bright eye fixed desperately on her, clearly had other plans.

Not two weeks before the crow's visitation, Sparrow and her heartmate, the Herald Cloudbrother, had said goodbye to their son Tis, who had just entered the Collegium as a Trainee.

Sparrow was ready to let him go . . . it was never a good time for a mother to say goodbye to her only baby, but he needed to face his own destiny.

She gladly let him go, but deep down the Choosing had broken her heart. Cloudbrother and she had decamped to a vineyard near the Iftel Border, alone together for the first time in years. Sparrow fully expected a week or two of ease as a kind of compensation, lost among the vines and fruit orchards, before taking up the mantle of their Herald's life once again.

The owner of the farmhouse in the Vineyard Hills, a Healer and the wife of a wealthy winemaker, made the heartmates welcome, and except for lush dinners and plenty of scones and tea for breakfast, Lady Belamane kept away and let them enjoy the voluptuous glory of the rolling, fertile hills.

In the early mornings, dew clung to each budding grape, and the mists rose all along the rows of gnarled, ancient vines.

Despite the Tis-shaped hole in her heart, Sparrow surrendered to the delicious beauty of their surroundings, and she and her heartmate Cloudbrother took long walks, many naps, and had long conversations about everything and nothing, reminding her of their love before their son had been born.

She and Cloudbrother slept and slept, and they healed. Bit by bit, Sparrow had finally let Tis go in her heart. He was young, but he had been Chosen, and now he was in Grays at Haven, a new Trainee. Tis had his path to travel, and Sparrow had hers.

Their Companion, Abilard, stayed with them at the vineyard, but he kept a respectful distance too, giving them time alone. Even in Abilard's silence the great, magnificent Companion demonstrated his profound love and respect for them. Her heartmate remained a Herald, Sparrow remained his heartmate, and in this time before their new adventures, they simply rested.

After a week of this, Sparrow woke uncharacteristically early, surely a sign that she was rested for the first time in years. She slipped away from her warm and inviting bed, leaving Cloudbrother to sleep and to dream on his own. She planned to watch the sun climb into the sky, maybe sneak a scone freshly baked from the oven, and then slip back into bed in time to greet her heartmate when he awoke.

Instead, the crow surprised her on her walk and upended all her plans. But Sparrow was ready. Such was the challenge, and the unexpectedness, of the Herald's way. You always had to be ready.

She was no Herald, but Sparrow stood on the edge of a new life, one where she would serve Valdemar in a new way. The Council had chosen her to serve as a bridge between Heralds and the loved ones they had to leave behind.

Now that her son was gone and her beloved had served, it was Sparrow's turn to ride Circuit. To help the people who lost their way when their beloveds became Heralds. And now that she had accepted this new mission, Cloudbrother and his Companion, Abilard, stood by to help her.

It was strange to think of herself as the one in the lead. But life was often quite strange.

For example, this crow.

Sparrow had fully expected to rest her fill in the wine country, and then report back to the Council to receive her first assignment. But the crow now blocking her path would have none of this. Like it or not, Sparrow was already on duty.

The blue-black bird had alighted on the muddy dirt path directly in front of her, tilted its head, and regarded her quizzically with one milky-blue eye. Its feathers shimmered iridescent in the morning sunshine.

"Mama!" the crow cawed.

Sparrow froze, all of her senses suddenly on high alert.

Behind them, the lands near the Iftel Border rolled gently downhill and up again, rounded shoulders of tilled vineyards and fields of wild heal-all. Bees buzzed patiently as they flew from flower to flower in the orchards, and a clean, herbal scent rose as the sun grew hotter.

Every sensory impression only raised the level of Sparrow's alarm.

Sparrow knew crows. They had appeared to her in years before as a susurrating flock, bearing messages of danger and of hope. But this time, only one crow sought her out, one crow far away from the northern lands and the Forest of Sorrows, where she had seen them every time before.

This crow was lost, alone.

"Mama!" the crow cried again, hoarse with a wild despair.

Sparrow's blood turned to ice.

Her son.

Tis had disappeared into the Collegium not two weeks before, and he was already adept beyond his years. He had the gift of Mindspeech, his reach already formidable.

But Sparrow doubted he could reach her mind from so far. Could he have sent this crow in a bid for her help?

"Mama!"

Sparrow crossed, then uncrossed, her arms, utterly at a loss. What was she to do with this creature? She had no Gift of Mindspeech, no magery to work. She had common sense, and a mother's experience, and long years of traveling with her beloved on urgent missions. That would have to be enough.

"Hello there, crow," she said, feeling strangely ordinary, speaking to the bird. "You are looking for me, I can see. I am no Herald, but I have a heart, and I am listening to you. I am a mama, but not yours. You seem lost, I'd say. Can you speak more than the one word?"

The crow hopped impatiently closer to her, staring up at her now, and then in a sudden burst of flight, it alighted on her shoulder, its blue inquiring eyes only inches from her face now. Its beak, sharp as a dagger, hovered near her ear, and Sparrow tensed.

If this bird was bent on evil, it was close enough to do serious physical harm. But still she waited, holding her breath now, listening. In her years, she had learned that listening was the first and best step, in just about any trouble.

The crow rested its head against the side of Sparrow's head, and faintly she could sense its heart beating rapidly, fear-filled. "Mama," the bird whispered now, in a deep mire of misery.

It was clear they were at an impasse. Sparrow was sure now the crow meant her no harm. It had come to her for help, but she could not divine the details.

So she took the crow home. Love, patience, and her friends would help her find the way.

Lady Belamane herself was bustling in the kitchen when Sparrow returned from her morning walk. Her head wrapped in a kerchief and her sleeves pushed up to her elbows, Belamane looked like a country cook or a farmer's wife.

Sparrow knew better. Belamane lived Healing, it radiated from her like music. And cooking was an expression of her art. She had staff for the farmhouse, hands for the fields. But Belamane poured her Gift into her hands, and the herbs and fresh fruit mingled in her baking to form their own healing magic.

The tense, solid body of the crow relaxed as they drew inside, and Sparrow cleared her throat to warn Belamane of her presence. "It's me, lurking," Sparrow began.

"Why, hello there," Belamane said, not turning around. "I'm working on a meringue, and time is of the essence. Do take your rest at the kitchen table, love . . . look in the basket, under the dishcloth."

Sparrow couldn't restrain a grin. Even without peeking, the glorious scent of moonberry scones greeted her and beckoned her closer. She slid gratefully into one of the wooden kitchen chairs, reached under the clean white cloth, and closed her fingers around a still-hot scone.

"I have good timing," Sparrow said with a little laugh. "Your baking called me home."

Belamane snorted, her arms working as she beat the egg whites into stiff peaks. "I can't help it, baking is my sickness. Good thing you are here to provide the cure. Without you, I would be in here nevertheless each morning, baking in vain. You've saved me, sister."

The crow hopped onto the table and regarded Belamane's back, then the whole of the kitchen in one wild glance. "Sister," the crow croaked, "sister, sister, sister."

Belamane froze. Before she could say anything, Sparrow murmured, "Peace, my friend. It's only a crow, who found me outside and wouldn't let me alone. No fear."

The Healer half-turned to take in the sight of the crow on her kitchen table. For a long moment, bird and cook regarded each other. The color drained from Belamane's face.

"I know her," Belamane finally said, her voice flat. "I would know her anywhere."

"Her?" Sparrow asked. "The crow? Who is she?"

"She is my sister," Belamane replied.

And then she fainted dead away.

* * *

Sparrow rushed to her side and cradled her head in her arms. Belamane hadn't hit her head, and in a few moments she began to return to consciousness.

"Easy, now," Sparrow said. In the past, she had fainted herself and knew how awful it felt. "Give yourself a chance to come back in your own time. Easy."

Belamane groaned. She was the color of a bay leaf. "I just had a shock," she replied. "Never . . . never fainted away like this before."

"It's rotten, isn't it? And Healers make the worst patients . . . please don't ask how I know." Sparrow allowed herself a little laugh, and she hid from her worry inside it. "Rest here, the floor is nice and cool, and I saw, you went down easy, not hard. You didn't bang your head a bit."

"I just had a shock," Belamane said again.

Together, they looked up from the floor at the edge of the table. In the silence, the crow hopped onto the back of the wooden kitchen chair and looked down at the two of them.

"Mara," Belamane whispered. "What are you doing way out here?"

"Sister," the crow replied.

Sparrow studied Mara, the crow who was a sister. And then she began to understand, the knot began to unravel. "You need help, my friend. I am here to help. By the Mother, who must have traced my path to you. To help."

She hugged Belamane closer, whispered, gently so as not to frighten her host. "Mara is here for your mother. She was calling for her. Where is your mother?"

Belamane paled again, closed her eyes for so long that Sparrow feared she would faint again. "My mother, my poor mother. It hurts to even speak about her. But it's all starting to make sense now."

"It does? What I see is a crow in your kitchen, you on the floor, and me very confused. How is your sister a crow?"

Belamane sighed, a low soft shudder. "No, my sister is a

Herald, not a crow. But she can make a Sending of herself with crows, birds, small animals. She hasn't done it in years. But here she is. Maybe she got stuck this way, I don't know. Ah, Mara . . ." Belamane sighed again, and a single tear traced the edge of her cheek and dropped gently onto Sparrow's forearm. "I don't know what to do. Please help me know what to do."

Sparrow looked from crow to Healer and back again. "Well, do we need to do anything? Mara's just doing what she does, from what you say."

"But here's the thing. I first heard it, what a shock, from the Guard's Border Station down the road to Norflam . . . Mara. Well, how shall I say this . . . Mara's dead. She's dead and gone, but here she is. We put her in the ground not a month past, but here she is. My poor mother. Oh, Mara."

A hot flash worked its way through Sparrow's body like a bolt of white lightning. The quick heat, a body memory of the tropical Vale, brought her back for a second into her little ground-level *ekele*, her past life as a mother bringing up a child in a lush jungle.

Mara's mother had lived to see her child buried. Sparrow shied away from imagining what it must have been like.

Before granting them this leave, the Council had called Sparrow a bridge, a link between Herald and family left behind. But she had never expected to reach across the world's boundaries, to serve as a bridge from this one to the next.

This was past her level of ability, Sparrow was sure. But here Mara was. She was going to have to figure something out.

"Tell me what makes sense now, my friend. Why has your sister come?"

Belamane could not explain in words, could only shake her head no. But her tears, streaming steadily down her cheeks, told Sparrow that the answer would have to reveal itself one step at a time.

The mother in her took charge, took the lead in setting things to rights. "Well, never mind the explanations for now. Let's get you settled in a better place to rest. Can't do a thing if you aren't feeling better. I will get my heartmate, and we will call for Abilard. Together we will make this right."

"I'm not so sure," Belamane replied, but she let Sparrow help her up. With a loud rustle of wings, the crow, Mara, flew to Sparrow's shoulder once again. The firm, cool claws found their purchase in Sparrow's cloak, and she tried to relax into the business of taking care of what was right in front of them.

When Herald business was afoot, Sparrow had learned the key to keeping her head was to keep her feet on the ground and her hands moving, doing useful things. The mystery of the crow, her name revealed, her sister, all of it tumbled madly in her head, a wild circle dance that left her dizzy. Sparrow didn't know how she would make things come right, but at least she knew how she would try.

Once Belamane was settled on the lovely settee by the open windows in the covered verandah overlooking the vines, Sparrow hurried to her heartmate. Mara clung to her shoulder with a vise-like grip.

"It's going to be okay, Herald," Sparrow muttered as she shot down the hallway to the rooms where she and Cloudbrother had come to rest.

Cloudbrother was awake when she came in. All rumpled in the bed, with silver hair tousled, relaxed and full of smiles. Sparrow's heart leaped to see him like this, rested and happy. His lean, muscular body shifted under the sheets, and a sunbeam slanted fully onto his face. Given his sightlessness, the glare didn't bother him in the least.

"Hello there, Spark," he said, his voice ordinary and cheerful. "You're full of bustle for a sleepy, sunny morning."

But his eyes, sealed shut forever due to a childhood fever, still saw far and deep. His expression changed as he sensed Sparrow's agitation. "What's wrong?"

"Mama!" the crow called, and she leaped into the air and beat her wings against the window casements. "Mama!"

Cloudbrother leaped out of bed and to Sparrow's side in a

moment. "Are you hurt?" he asked, in a low, firm tone. His fingers, knowing and sure, searched her face then body for injury. He was ready to do battle, wearing only a linen nightshift, anything to protect her.

"I am safe," Sparrow replied, her heart pounding with worry, but also with her love for him. "But we have a situation here, and I don't know what to do."

She recounted the morning's events as he felt around for his trews and day tunic. The tale was short, and once she was done, he raked his fingers through his hair, then stood suddenly silent in the middle of the room, so still that he seemed to disappear.

It was merely the cessation of movement. But it was also magic.

The energy of the room changed, the world changed, and the crow landed on the bed, her beak open, panting. She looked again at Sparrow, her expression incredulous—*you married a Herald! What were you thinking!*—and then the crow Mara sat down on the bed, closed her beak, and also ceased her frantic flight.

All was stillness in the room.

"I'm sorry," Cloudbrother said, so quietly Sparrow had to strain to hear him. "It is the way of things. We all take these chances, you see. But you did your best."

It took her a minute for Sparrow to realize he was speaking to Mara.

He grew silent again, and Sparrow remembered to breathe. "Did you divine her fate?" she finally asked. "What magery did you just do, my love?"

"No, I did no sorcery. I just remembered her name, and the tale matches. We heard it at the tavern when we were traveling down to Haven with Tis. Remember? It was at the village of Brach . . . we stopped there for a meal and provisions. There was a Herald who had died breaking up a fight on the road to Karse."

All at once, Sparrow remembered. The tavern was rowdy, and it was still early while they had made their meal there. It was this noisy tavern that had convinced their party to stick with Waystations on the way to Haven after that.

And it was the story of the doomed Herald Mara that had tinged their meal in Brach with sadness and the desire to draw away from village folk.

The merchant telling the tale had traveled from far away, and Sparrow figured his tale had grown in the telling. But the basic facts were clear. The Herald was alone with her Companion on a wild and little-traveled road. In a wood, she had come across two robbers, fighting over the money and precious stones they had stolen.

Mara had ridden and dismounted into their midst, and they acknowledged her Whites, bowed and scraped and made up some kind of story. But when she had begun to ask questions they didn't like, with a flash of a knife she was cut down before she could defend herself.

Uneasily, Sparrow had wondered how the merchant had come to know so much about the murder. But at the time, burdened by her own cares, she had only just listened.

Characteristically, Cloudbrother had remembered the tale and kept it in his mind, and he found out more than Sparrow had. And this knowledge filled in Mara's side of the story.

Now, apparently, Mara nestled on their warm bed, watching them intently. Had she returned to find her revenge? Sparrow wasn't sure.

"Shall we take you to the Council?" Sparrow asked the crow. "Surely your teachers and mates will help you to reach the Havens. And demand justice for you."

"Mama!" the crow insisted. Agitated again, it flapped its wings and left a beautiful blue-black tailfeather behind on Sparrow's pillow. "Mama, Mama!"

Sparrow sighed. "Well, that's plain. Maybe Haven is where you go after, but we will surely take you to Mama first. So you know, my dear, Herald Mara is the sister of our host, Belamane, and her mama must be near to hand. So we will go to her today."

Cloudbrother nodded, and then he smiled the brilliant, open smile that had captured Sparrow's heart years and years ago, when she was just a little girl. "Lead the way, Bridge. Abilard and I are at your service."

It was a humbling thing, to know she led a Herald and his Companion forward. But it was what Sparrow was meant to do. She reached for the crow, and Mara alighted on her wrist like a hawk. The crow was at peace again. Sparrow knew she was on the right path.

Strangely, Belamane refused to join them on that path to her mother.

"I would only cause Mama more pain," Belamane said, with so much pain in her own voice that Sparrow feared to press the issue. "She's been through enough. The sight of me only hurts her more."

Belamane did give them detailed instructions to where her mother lived, close to the Border, so close that on the hill behind their house you could see the flat, shimmering lands of Iftel beckoning. And she took the basket of scones, wrapped them in her best tablecloth, and gave it to them for her mother.

"She won't eat them, I fear. But perhaps . . . she is the one who taught me to bake, maybe she will recognize these. But she bakes no more. All my Healing arts have only caused her pain. But maybe you, Sparrow . . ." and there she broke off, and spoke no further.

Maybe. Sparrow had only heart and her gumption. Still, she would do her best.

Abilard waited for her and Cloudbrother on the paved path leading from the kitchen to the road reaching down the hill, winding north to the Iftel Border. His brilliant white coat caught the sunshine, glowed silver, and his silver hooves danced in the dust, so bright Sparrow had to squint to see them.

Abilard was in fine fettle, eager to be off. *:Lead the way, dear Sparrow:* he Spoke, and his warm encouragement filled her with strength and courage. It was not a small thing, to win the support and the friendship of a Companion, if you were not yourself a Herald.

But Abilard believed in her unique mission, and in that way he was her Companion too. Sparrow was awed by the privilege and the honor of it. But more than this, more than anything, Abilard was her dear, magnificent friend.

Mara roosted in a cedar tree and cawed a greeting when Sparrow reached Abilard's side. Now that she knew they were off to see her mother, she had calmed tremendously. But still, her dark, nervous presence was like a shadow in the sunshine, an ever-present reminder of the gravity of their visit.

Cloudbrother mounted first, his long, lean legs swinging easily into place. He reached down to help Sparrow, and she used the mounting block with more need than in years past. Years of scones had added some padding to her frame, but she could still hike and ride like a Herald.

She looked down from her mount, her arms wrapped around Cloudbrother's waist. They had tied Belamane's basket to the back of the saddle, and Belamane patted it now, to make sure it was securely strapped in place.

"Farewell," she said. "May you ride easy and well, and may you bring peace and healing with you. Thank you!"

She paused then, and looked up into the cedar tree where her sister waited impatiently to go. "Goodbye, Mara," she said, her voice hoarse. "Help Mama if you can."

Help Mama? Sparrow hadn't thought of Belamane's mother as the one in need of help, only Mara. It put their journey into a new and more complicated light.

Sparrow reached down as far as she could and took Belamane's hand. She squeezed her fingers gently, as if she could convey strength, healing, and love through her fingers and into her friend's heart. "We will get things sorted out. I'm sure of it! Never fear, my friend. Love is greater than fear."

Belamane nodded, clearly choked up. "I hope grief is not greater than love. Alas, sometimes it is. You will see. But thank you again."

And with these cryptic words, they were off, on the road

together again. The morning was glorious, and they knew their way. This was much more than they could have said on many other Herald's quests.

Still, secretly Sparrow questioned her ability to set this muddle to rights. But, as always, she would try.

The road was easy and wide, and they had traveled it once before, all the way to Iftel. This day was sunny and breezy, scented with lavender and sandalwood, and the countryside all around was lush and opulent, growing things everywhere, filled with life. Years before, they had ridden through in a drought, and it filled Sparrow with joy now to see all the tender green growing things, the bumblebees, the darting sparrows.

After drought, the rain, then the spring. Sparrow hoped the weather was an omen of good tidings, of healing and peace.

Mara flew from tree to bush to hedgerow, waiting for them to catch up, then flying ahead again, guiding them even though the way was clear and there was only the one main road through the wine country.

Sparrow, watching her fly overhead, wondered at her presence. "What do you think, my love?" she asked her heartmate. "Why do you think Mara is still here? Why does she not just fly away, into the next world where she belongs?"

Cloudbrother bowed his head, and from long experience Sparrow knew he was looking deep inside, seeing from his inner sense.

"She is like to Lord Vanyel, who would not pass until his mission was complete." His voice was a low, dull murmur, different from his ordinary voice. It startled Sparrow . . . he had not traveled into his clouds, the borderlands of the esoteric realms, since they last had come to Iftel.

Sparrow squinted up into the brilliant blue sky to pick out the fleck of blackness that was Mara, beautiful, darting restlessly from tree to hedge, waiting impatiently for them to reach her.

"Even death will not end a Herald's mission," she replied.

In that way, Heralds are like mothers, she thought. A mother's love reached from before to after, from the boundary of birth to well beyond the veil of death. Love didn't fade with distance, time, or tragedy. It didn't fade from hate or indifference.

She was beginning to suspect that Mara and her mother had many attributes in common.

They arrived in the heat of the afternoon, at a time where the local folk often rested and napped until the sun began to sink in the sky. The house where Mara and Belamane had grown up was much smaller than Belamane's vineyard house. It stood proudly on a hill, rising above the road, half-hidden by a grove of cedar trees. It was trim and lovely, and by a trick of the light it seemed to float above the earth.

As they drew closer, Mara became agitated again. "Mama!" she called, her voice so hoarse now Sparrow could hardly make out the word. And despite the lovely, bright afternoon, Sparrow's heart became shadowed with a strange, static dread.

A sense of hopelessness washed over her, a sense of fatality and apathy. It disturbed her, this house all alone at the edge of nowhere. It was so pretty, and yet it emanated abandonment, desolation.

Abruptly, Mara landed on Sparrow's shoulder, as if the crow also sensed the air of menace, and needed her mundane support.

She stroked the bird's back, muttered, "We are close now, my dear; we will set things to rights for sure." But to reassure herself she leaned against Cloudbrother's strong, slightly sweaty back, and inhaled his singular musky, cinnamon scent.

As long as they were together, they could face what they would find inside.

But what they did find inside would stay with Sparrow for the rest of her life.

All of the shutters were closed. The sight was so incongruous for the Vineyard Hills, and for such a perfect, breezy day, that it startled Sparrow as the little band arrived at the front door.

The front door, too, was sealed up tight. It was painted sky blue after the manner of the local houses, but it was firmly jammed shut, and it occurred to Sparrow that she had never seen a closed door in her travels through this plentiful, peaceful region.

"You've grown up in a peaceful land, Mara, but this house looks like a place in war," Sparrow said, surprising herself as she spoke.

Mara croaked, without words this time, a mournful, desolate sound.

Abilard drew close to the door. Sparrow looked for a mounting block, but there was none. She slid ungracefully down Abilard's side to the ground, not caring how awkward she looked. Cloudbrother dismounted as gracefully as ever, needing only the gentlest of Sparrow's touches to find the ground safely.

Sparrow reached up to untie the basket of scones from the saddle and tucked it securely under her left arm. She took a deep breath and stepped to the front door. "Abilard, I don't think you will be able to come in here, the doorway looks too small. Are you all right, waiting here? There isn't much shade except behind the house."

:*No trouble, dear one*: Abilard replied. :*I will wait in the shade, and will be with you in Spirit at all times.*:

Just the knowledge that he waited close by gave Sparrow a measure of peace and strength. She stroked his flank in thanks and watched him amble around the corner and into the cool of the shade.

Cloudbrother's fingers brushed her own, and he squeezed her hand tight.

"Time to go in," he said, his voice gentle.

Yes. Sparrow took a long, slow breath, felt her feet on the ground, and started walking. When she reached the threshold, Mara swooped down and landed on her shoulder once again.

She reached for the door handle, tried the door, and with a single push it swung open.

Darkness, complete darkness.

And then the smell hit her, and she took a half-step back.

It was not the smell of death, which Sparrow had secretly feared to find. No, the place reminded her of a tomb, fetid and sour and closed, however, the smell of death had not yet permeated this place.

But death stalked this once-happy place, she knew to a certainty.

Sparrow forced herself forward, clutching Cloudbrother's hand with her own, and the bundle of scones under her other arm.

"Hello?" she asked, her voice gentle and tentative.

"Go away!"

The force of the reply made Sparrow, paradoxically, smile. Mara's mother was most emphatically alive. She was not especially wanting to be alive, clearly, but she was alive.

And where there was life, there was still hope.

Sparrow ignored the command and followed the voice to a kitchen in the center of the house, with lovely blue fieldstone flooring and long low wooden benches, a kitchen for a baker.

But the hearth was cold, and the kitchen no longer yielded health and healing.

Sitting at the low wooden table near the back door hunched a low, huddled form.

The face that peered out at her from the shadows looked less than human. It was a face distorted with anger and hatred and wild despair. "Go away, you miserable slut, you and your foul carrion and your man worm! Leave me alone, that's all I want, to be left alone!"

This was a creature in terrible pain. "Your daughter Belamane told me the way—" Sparrow began.

"Her? She is not *my* daughter! I threw her out and told her never to come back. She and her sister, both traitors. Traitors! They abandoned their mother here, alone, alone, alone . . ." Tears half-strangled the woman's voice, but her eyes were dry. Pure rage burned off the honest grief that hid within her heart.

"I see, you are alone," Sparrow said. "Please, tell me your name. I come from the Council in Haven. I was sent on this mission to help you."

"The Council . . ." The woman sneered, and her smile was more terrifying than anything else about her. "The Council of the Crown ruined me. To the bottom of Evendim with the lot of them." And she spat at the ground with such vehemence that Sparrow half-expected the stone to dissolve with the venom from her mouth.

"You never told me your name," Sparrow said, her voice quiet.

"Iris," the woman said, and for the first time, her voice softened, cracked.

"Well, Iris, I can't say as I blame you for your saltiness. To give not one but two girls to Haven, it looks like you gave everything you had . . . no wonder you curse the Crown and Council."

And Sparrow meant what she said. The sacrifices of Heralds were deep and hard, and Valdemar could not exist without their heroism. But what of the mothers left behind? The heartmates that would never form a lifebond with another?

"Look at this place, abandoned to the four winds of the past," Sparrow said. "You live barricaded in the battlements of memory, Iris, and more's the pity. Without your armor, how could you have borne it all?"

Iris's face twisted. "Don't you start with your clever words," she said, but the tears were closer to the surface now. "When the younger one, my Mara, was killed, I had half the duchy here, filing through, clucking and bowing and telling me I should be proud—proud!—that my girl was dead. 'Proud' of her 'sacrifice.'" She spat again. "Such a pretty one, such a one that should have had a passel full of children, and all of them here. *Here!* After her da was gone, I'd promised this place to her."

Sparrow's own tears threatened now. "And now you live in this castle of lost grandbabies, lost dreams, love that should have been but can never be. Nobody ever asked you to choose, Iris. And yet here you are."

"Yes!" Iris buried her face in her clawed hands. "How could they take both those girls from me? The older one still lives, but she's just as bad. The Healer, living in that vineyard, traveling Circuit whenever the Council demands it. Her husband hardly sees her, and I can't bear her face anymore."

Sparrow drew near to her, leaving Cloudbrother standing behind her in the shadows. "I can understand you, Iris. My name is Sparrow, and I'm from the Northern country, a little village called Longfall. My son and my heartmate are both Heralds, Chosen, both. I don't Heal, and I am no Bard, and I can't Artifice to save my life. I like to cook and keep a little house, and I like to sit with friends of a morning and talk and dream. But none of this is my fate."

"So why are you here?"

"Because," and here Sparrow had to take a deep breath and gather her courage to speak the truth. "Mothers sacrifice, fathers and sisters too. In quiet ways, ways that don't win fame or save the world. But without the sacrifices of the heart, none of the great ones can save Valdemar. You have made a great sacrifice of the heart. But you still live."

"What kind of life is *this*?"

"Not much of one," Sparrow admitted. "But you can *choose* to live again. You just have to let go of those unrealized dreams, let them go."

"I can't. I *can't*!"

"Yes, you can," Sparrow said. "I've brought you a visitor, dear Iris. She is your daughter, who can't fly into the next world because she is tangled up in your pain on this one. She is a Herald who is on her last mission . . . to save you."

Mara flew to the table, alighted a few inches from her mother's face. "Mama," she croaked, sadly, gently. "Mama . . ."

The tears came, they finally came. Iris bent her head all the way down to the table, sobbing, her fingers reaching out to caress the blue-black feathers, the neat little head, the graphite-gray beak. "Why . . ." Iris managed to say, "why you too, Mara girl?"

Mara reached out, stroked her mother's tangled hair with her beak, gently ruffled it, tucked her beak into the strands.

"You have to let her fly free," Sparrow said. "Mara needs to go, and this world still needs you. Your girls have met their destiny, but you still have yours ahead of you."

An idea seized her. "Please . . . come with me."

"Me? Come with you where?"

"To Haven," Sparrow said, shocking herself again as she spoke. "I want you to come to the Council, to tell them what you've told me. About the price you and your family have paid. I think you can help other mothers, other daughters, other sisters. The world is full of hurting people, Iris. Please come with me, let's help them together."

Iris looked away. "I'm just a used-up old woman."

Sparrow shook her head. "Not at all. You are the mother of a Herald and a Healer. Your hands are gifted, and you can help other mothers, other Healers, other Heralds. Come with me now. But first, say goodbye."

Iris raised her head to look at Sparrow for a long moment . . . then slowly nodded—and Sparrow couldn't believe her words had actually worked their necessary magic.

Years later, Sparrow asked Iris what had moved her, what magic was in her words that had convinced her. Iris said actually it wasn't anything Sparrow had said (and that put paid to any glimmers of pride that Sparrow might have entertained). It was her daughter's gentle touch, still loving her mother, despite her rage. A rage so bitter it held Mara prisoner between Valdemar and the next world.

That gentle touch was asking her mother for another sacrifice. And somehow, Iris had found the strength to make it.

She drew the crow close to her, kissed the quick, neat head goodbye. "I will go," she said. "Mara, my girl, you need to go, too. Fly, be free. I promise I will let go."

And with a final grateful caw, "Mama! Sister!" Mara lifted out of her mother's arms to flutter along the edge of the kitchen walls.

Sparrow rushed to throw the shutters open and Mara shot into the air, free in the sky, a small speck that soared into the sunlight and was gone.

:*Farewell, brave Herald!*: Abilard Spoke into Sparrow's mind, Cloudbrother's mind, and Mara's mind all at once. :*Fly across the borderland, to the Havens, brave Spirit!*:

They Don't Burn Children

Louisa Swann

Riann knew she was dying. She was colder than a dead chicken, clothes sodden from an eternity of drenching rain, boots squelching with every step. The baby swaddled snug against her chest was the only warmth she'd felt since leaving the village what had to be a sennight, or maybe even a fortnight ago.

Miz Goat—her only companion besides Lil Beebee—bleated a sneeze, summing up her feelings about the weather with a single sound.

A corner of Riann's winter cloak flapped free as the chill wind drove stinging rain into her face and eyes. She tugged the cloak over Lil Beebee's head in an attempt to keep the wet off the baby's young, tender skin and struggled to remember why she was carrying a baby through the rain and why a goat was following them and why she was wrapped in wet, stinky wool when she could be safe in the chicken coop. The coop wasn't warm, but it was dry, albeit a bit smelly.

If you'd stayed, you'd be in the Cleansing Fires right now, with Sunpriests laughing as you burned.

Ah, yes. The visions. In Karse, Sunpriests burned children who had visions—or any other form of what they called "magic."

Not that she'd had a choice in the matter. The visions had chosen her. She would have been happy to live her life without strange dreams-that-weren't-dreams tearing her life to shreds like a cat eating a mouse.

The baby hiccupped and seemed to fall asleep.

Sleep.

Riann wasn't sure she even remembered what sleep felt like. Her head was as soggy as the leaves around her and the mud they were slogging through. She couldn't think straight. Couldn't keep her thoughts focused . . .

Everywhere she looked, eyes stared back. Blood-red eyes. The eyes of a demon . . .

Only the eyes weren't really there.

Only the visions. Visions that had grown more and more frequent the farther she got from home.

The visions weren't the only things that had changed.

The familiar woods surrounding Brinleville thinned as she walked, tall, slender trees with shimmering needles giving way to heavy forest where leaf-filled trees broad as a barn loomed overhead like gnarled giants while brush and brambles climbed their trunks. The brush was particularly nasty, with hidden thorns snatching and tearing at her cloak like Miz Burdock's fingers whenever she slapped Riann for doing something wrong.

Simpleton. Dolt. Cain't ya get anything right?

She shook the old woman's voice from her head and squinted through the rain streaming off her eyelashes and hair, struggling to see past the watery gray curtain draped across the land.

Would this Vkandis-forsaken rain ever stop?

No one ever talked about weather when they talked about other lands, not that she'd ever heard. She just figured other places were the same as Brinleville, with warm springs and hot summers and wintery winters.

No one ever mentioned rain beyond what was needed to bring in the crops.

She never *dreamed* the sky could keep emptying its bladder like Miz Burdock after too much brinlewine.

Riann bit the inside of her cheek, forcing herself to stop

thinking about bladders—another need that would have to be seen to—and focus on what she was doing. Ignore, or *try* to ignore, the itchy feeling that someone—some*thing*—watched her, knew what she was going to do before she did it.

She closed her eyes, pretending they were walking down a sunny path, warm and dry, stomachs full, surrounded by chirping birds and chittering squirrels all minding their own business.

Warm. Dry.

The rain blurred into a swirling melee of sparkling colors, and faster than a falling raindrop, she was in a different time, different place . . . falling into another vision . . .

At first, Riann thought she was in the place she'd been thinking about, but she quickly realized this place was different. The rain had stopped, and it was night instead of day, no sun warming the top of her head. The scent of wet earth and growing things filled the air. She stood at the edge of a clearing with gray-and-black boulders the size of Miz Burdock's cottage dominating the far end. Rugged stone silhouettes rose into the dark beyond those reflecting the light of a fire . . .

The world swirled again, transforming fiery sparks into gleaming red eyes and dripping fangs—

An abrupt shove jolted Riann back into the land of rain. She stumbled forward, mud sucking at her boots. Mouth gone dry, she clutched the baby protectively and peered about, certain she would find fiery eyes glaring back, searching for *her.*

Something glowed further down the road, and she almost choked on her breath.

There are no eyes, she scolded herself. *Only the rain.*

She glared down at the goat near her heels, blinking both vision and rain from her bleary eyes. "What's gotten inta ya? Why ya getting all pushy like?"

Riann drew in a deep breath, head still swirling. She missed the sweet spring smell of brinle flowers in full bloom back home. Instead of sweetness and light, the air stank of wet wool, wetter baby, and the muck they'd been slogging through for far too long, topped off by a whiff of sodden goat when the breeze shifted now and again.

Sweet or stinky, the air cleared her brain.

For a breath—maybe two.

She used to have visions once every fortnight or so; now they struck every hour, or so it seemed. For the past few days, the visions had been focused on the same things: strangers and crackling fires, demons and more demons.

None of the visions made sense, not in Riann's current state. She could barely tell what was up and what was down. Visions would lead the Sunpriests to her; draw the demons of the night. Since she couldn't understand the visions, couldn't use them, she'd tried to control them, slapping her face, pinching her skin; she'd even tried knocking her head against a tree when she could feel a vision coming on.

Nothing worked.

Now she felt watched every moment of every day.

The farther she went from Brinleville, the more the sensation grew, until she swore every villager throughout Karse was somehow watching her.

The goat—mouthy thing—uttered an irritated bleat. She glared at Riann, light amber eyes with their flat, black pupils filled with reproach. Rain beaded and ran off Miz Goat's rough coat as if someone had greased every strand of the long brown-and-gold hair.

Thoughts of red demon eyes melted into the rain as Riann shivered, studying the goat. *Need ta make a cloak from that goat hair.* Wool was *supposed* to stay warm when it got wet. Whoever had made that claim hadn't lived for days—and nights—in soaking wet wool.

If they didn't find some type of shelter—*and food*—soon, she should probably butcher Miz Goat. Not only could she use the skin and hair for various items, they—*she*—needed the meat . . .

She glanced down at the goat, heart twisting in her chest. Miz Burdock wouldn't hesitate to do whatever was necessary, no matter how cruel.

But Riann wasn't Miz Burdock, thank Vkandis. One look at Miz Goat's eyes and Riann knew she'd never be able to take the goat's life. She'd never killed *anything*, not even a fly.

What in Vkandis' name would she do with a dead goat? Yes, she'd seen the butcher cut up a wide variety of meats, but the meat had always been . . . meat. Even if she'd had a knife, there was no way to cook the meat.

As if reading her thoughts, Lil Beebee hiccupped and moaned softly. She'd be wanting to eat soon and likely needed changing.

Without Miz Goat, Lil Beebee wouldn't have milk, and that was not acceptable. Far as Riann knew, Lil Beebee was no more than a couple months old, far too young to eat food meant for chewing. No matter how hungry Riann was, they would live on goat milk and water.

After all, it had gotten them this far.

She readjusted the cloak in another attempt to direct the rain away from the baby. She should've brought more supplies from the wagon where she'd found Lil Beebee, but she'd gotten the heebie-jeebies just thinking about using the dead folks' things.

"Yer gonna be jus' fine," she whispered to the cloak-covered baby. "We'll be findin' help soon. Jus' gotta hole on a bit longer."

It had been a vision that sent her searching for the wagon and the family Riann *thought* was going to kill her entire village. Instead, she'd found the family dead—all except Lil Beebee . . . and the goat.

Returning to Brinleville with the baby wasn't an option. Riann's visions had sentenced her to death in the Sunpriests' eyes. Just the thought of those Cleansing Fires set her heart skittering like a frightened bird.

She'd decided to head to Valdemar. They didn't burn children in Valdemar—or so she'd heard. Since there was only one road out of Brinleville, she'd kept walking, trusting to the visions that told her safety was out there. Somewhere.

But after several days on the road, she realized she had no idea where Valdemar was.

Miz Goat butted her hand, gently this time as if sensing the distress pouring off Riann like the rain.

"Don't suppose ya kin find us a way outta this?" she asked the goat, the skin on the back of her neck prickling as the "being watched" sensation returned.

To her surprise, Miz Goat moved ahead, traveling straight as though following a path. The goat had always grazed as they walked, never traveling in a straight line. Riann hurried after her, neck hunched against rain and eyes. She darted quick glances to either side as they went, struggling to catch sight of red eyes or dripping fangs.

Would their hurrying draw the demons closer, like wolves after a deer?

And what would they do—what would *she* do—if the demons attacked?

She shoved the thought from her mind, keeping her gaze on the road as the coming night darkened both sky and world around her. The world soon looked as gray as the storm, eventide turned to soggy gloom. Rain made the road appear smooth as Lil Beebee's behind, gloom and water hiding rough depressions and toe-catching stones.

And everything smelled . . . wet.

Miz Goat could likely see better in the dimming light, she reasoned, trying to keep the goat's hind end in sight. They needed to find a place to settle down for the night, one as far out of the rain as possible.

As far from watching eyes as possible.

Then she could tend to all their needs, including milking Miz Goat.

How do babies survive on all that milk? Just the thought of drinking more goat milk made her stomach flipflop. But she'd choked down the last of her moldy bread and leather-hard sausage days ago. If not for Miz Goat and her mostly reliable milk supply, both Riann and Lil Beebee would have starved.

Miz Goat ate anything and everything and was the only one

who seemed to thrive, her udder straining with milk at the end of each day. Lil Beebee seemed to like goat milk, eagerly attacking the makeshift teat Riann had made out of an old leather glove.

Living on goat milk and water had kept Riann going, but it was far from satisfying. The milk nearly turned her inside out, causing her guts to tumble and twist like a river gone wild in spring. Her knees were as weak as a newborn filly's while her head refused to stay attached . . .

The world spun, almost sending Riann to her knees as the rain became crowds of glowing red eyes and dripping fangs. Her stomach tightened as though she'd eaten rotten meat, worms and all.

She clutched the baby tight, closed her eyes tighter, torn between a world of eyes and fangs and reality, trapped with the eyes, sliding in mud and rain, trapped again with the fangs . . .

A scream rent the air, tearing through raindrops, blood-red eyes, and dripping fangs alike. Riann shuddered and pulled herself together, feeling as though bits and pieces of her had been scattered throughout both the real world and the vision world.

Miz Goat screamed, the sound harsh and almost metallic. A real-world sound, different from what had come before.

Something small and furry leaped from the brush, bouncing on Miz Goat's back, then to Riann's shoulder. Needle-sharp claws pierced her skin through the sodden wool before the creature leaped back into the night, vanishing amid the raindrops.

Demons!

The practical side of her brain reminded her there had been one creature, a small one at that. The panicked side dwelled on the red, glowing eyes and dripping white fangs.

Demons are real!

Scanning the darkness, Riann moved up beside the goat, rubbing her burning shoulder and talking nonsense as she hurried them both along. Should they duck into the trees, try to hide in the bushes?

Where had the demon come from?

Where had it gone?

Are the demon's claws poisonous?

She sniffed at the air, expecting to find the sting of sulphur or the stench of death the tales said always accompanied a demon.

Instead, a sweet, musky smell tickled her nose for the blink of an eye, then was gone.

Demons are real, she told herself over and over.

She'd known this, down deep in her heart. That was why she'd been unable to sleep after dark, why she kept walking, taking advantage of the full moon until it slipped from the sky, napping during the day when the baby slept and she could no longer go on.

All because of demons. Demons watching. Demons waiting . . .

Now that the full moon was gone, traveling at night had become difficult. She'd reluctantly decided finding a relatively safe place—often at the base of an enormous tree surrounded by dropping branches—was wiser than risking the chance of injuring herself or the baby stumbling around in the dark.

The pain in her shoulder faded to a dull ache as exhaustion once again set in. The sound of rain on leaves became whispers that spoke of boggles and basilisks lurking in the dark . . .

Riann closed her ears to the whispers, set her jaw, and forced herself to keep moving, following Miz Goat, boots softly slurping with each step. Fear was replaced with determination. Whatever that *thing* had been, they were all still alive—scared but alive.

Her mother had never tried to frighten Riann with tales of vicious demons and Sunpriests who set children on fire. Her mother's mind was more child than adult, though Riann didn't know if she'd been born that way or been left addlepated by an accident. No matter how she came that way, Mother had believed—and feared—the tales as much as the village children. Their not-so-beneficent benefactress (as Miz Podahl, the seamstress called her) had delighted in filling the heads of anyone who'd listen with tales of demons and monsters, both human and not.

Even though she was now fourteen and *knew* demon tales were meant to scare children into behaving, darkness always brought night-frights boiling with razor-sharp teeth, blood-red eyes, and child-eating flames.

And after the sickness that had brought her visions, Riann *knew* the night-frights were real.

On the road, far from everything familiar, every cracking stick, rustling branch, or unexplained thump sent her heart skittering like a stone down a slope, confident they were about to become demon snacks.

So she kept watch every night while Lil Beebee and Miz Goat slept. Sleep could be had when they reached someplace safe, she reminded herself over and over and over.

She was already exhausted when the rain had started . . . and never stopped.

Numb from lack of sleep and the constant wet, Riann squished along, one foot after another, not realizing Miz Goat had stopped until she bumped into her. The goat didn't even bleat, standing frozen in place like a tree stump.

"What . . . ?"

Maybe it was the rain or the fact she was so numb she couldn't feel her feet, but she'd somehow missed the acrid smell of woodsmoke and the glow a stone's throw from the goat.

It all seemed so unreal, like a vision, only not a vision.

Lil Beebee let out a goatlike bleat and wiggled restlessly against Riann's chest. "Ya smell it too?"

The baby couldn't know what she was smelling, could she?

Then again, she had been born to a traveling family, a family Riann had found dead around a firepit. Perhaps she recognized the smell as something familiar.

Likely just hungry and needing a change.

She also needed to get warm, really warm. And dry. They all did.

Holding that thought tight in her mind, Riann inched around Miz Goat, who still refused to move . . .

An arm's length past Miz Goat, she felt it. A tingling that

tightened her skin, creeping across her body and lifting her rain-plastered hair from her scalp. Lil Beebee shifted again, her soft cry adding to the "don't go any closer" sensation.

A soft melody drifted through the air, weaving through the raindrops, dancing away until barely a trace remained, then dancing its way back again.

Music that sweet has ta be from Vkandis himself.

Her body stayed frozen, desperately not wanting to move, to go any closer. *Run*, her body whispered.

Her mind didn't agree. "*Stay*," her mind whispered in return. "*Yer safe now. Welcome.*"

The rain lightened, the downpour slowing enough to reveal a fire burning at the base of an enormous boulder . . .

Just like her vision.

Riann's heart caught in her throat. Was she caught in another vision?

Or were the fire and boulders real?

The thought barely tickled her mind as darkness fell.

And the world went crazy.

Miz Goat screamed again and bolted *toward* the fire. Lil Beebee screeched like a wounded cat, little body twisting so fiercely Riann feared the baby would wind herself right out of the swaddling.

Riann's feet still refused to move. Whatever was happening? Confusion mingled with the fog numbing her from the inside out.

As far as she could see, there was nothing—*nothing*—around.

Riann squinted through the rain, peering at the trees, the bushes.

Then she glanced at the fire.

This was part of the *real* world, not a vision, she decided.

Why did the scene before her seem impossible, then?

Shadows danced across the boulder on the far side of the fire, tall black figures with hunched backs and clawlike fingers.

Transfixed by the dancing shadows, it took several heartbeats—or perhaps several hours—before Riann's fog-ridden mind realized there nothing around the fire to create shadows, big or small, clawed or not.

A heartbeat later, she realized she was wrong. There *was* someone—some*thing*—small and scrawny and more than a little furry.

A rat then. Or perhaps a weasel. The way the shadows and firelight shifted and played, she couldn't decide which.

Miz Goat trotted right up to the fire . . . and lay down.

The goat is crazy, Riann decided, returning her attention to the fire. The flames flickered and beckoned, warm. Dry . . .

The rat-weasel glanced her way, and she found herself staring into blood-red eyes—above glistening fangs.

Her vision—tied in a bundle and dropped right in front of her.

And she still didn't know what—if anything—it meant.

Was this tiny creature a demon? If so, why was it ignoring Miz Goat? Didn't demons eat everything?

Curious, Riann slid closer to the fire . . .

And stopped as the tingling grew into a sting.

Out of the darkness slipped a second figure, a man wrapped in a brown cloak. He nodded at Miz Goat and perched on a nearby rock. The rat-weasel chittered—at least she thought it was a chitter—and scampered up the man's leg, then his arm, and stretched out on his shoulder.

A Sunpriest?

The only Sunpriest she'd ever met was Tondjen, their village priest. He looked nothing like this man.

The lower half of the man's face was covered in a braided beard of near black. The braids were impossibly thin and had evidently been oiled, judging by the way they glistened in the firelight. Each narrow braid sported a bead of a different color. A mustache drooped to either side of the man's mouth and had been braided as well.

The man's hair . . . was totally missing.

He'd evidently spent a lot of time in the sun, his bald head appearing almost as dark as his beard.

She couldn't tell what his cloak was made of, but it didn't look soaked like Riann's. Could be he'd dried off by the fire . . .

That's when she noticed the ground around the fire was dry.

She peered through the rain, looking up, up, up, straining to see what might be protecting the space.

No tree, no roof, nothing but sky . . . and clouds . . . and rain . . .

Rain that never reached that little piece of ground.

While Riann struggled to solve this newest puzzle, the man slid what looked like a stick from beneath the cloak and held it to his lips.

Once again, music filled the air. The fire snapped and crackled, smoke—and the aroma of cooking food—swirling through the air, dancing with the music.

The music teased, gently calling her to come closer, then just as gently pushing her away. Riann had never heard anything so beautiful, like a sunset after a storm, something that couldn't be held, yet would never be forgotten.

The soft kiss of a kitten. Lil Beebee's sweet breath. The innocent smile that used to light her mother's face.

The tiny rat-weasel—it couldn't be much bigger than a half-grown kitten, she decided—scampered back down to the fire, twisting and turning in time with the music, playing as the music played.

With a start, she realized *this* was the creature that had attacked them. Riann rubbed her shoulder where the claws had dug in. It had likely drawn blood.

The creature didn't seem so fearsome now.

Once again, she stepped forward, drawn by the music, lured by the warmth . . .

And again froze as the stinging sensation sharpened. She startled, feeling like someone had just slapped her awake.

What in Vkandis' name was she doing?

Could be a trap. She'd seen animals trapped by the villagers, lured by enticing bait to their deaths.

This man could be a Sunpriest come after her. Drawn by the visions she couldn't control.

Or he could be just a man. Perhaps a peddler or . . . or a Bard . . .

Riann was fairly certain she wasn't in Karse anymore, though there'd been no sign she'd crossed any borders. She couldn't even say how long she'd been following the road—could be a fortnight or two months.

Easy enough to approach the man, beg a moment or two by his fire. He'd likely tell her where they were.

If he didn't cast her into the fire . . .

The world shifted, and she was standing *in* the flames, surrounded by burning logs, smelling her flesh burn . . .

Just as quickly, she was back in place, mouth watering at the smells tickling her nose.

Ya'll never know unless ya have faith, faith in yerself, faith in yer fellows.

That voice—her mother's voice—had never sounded that way. This version of her mother's voice was filled with confidence . . . and . . . sorrow?

Mother had never given her advice. Riann had been the one pulling Mother from in front of a galloping horse or away from Miz Burdock in one of her rages.

Ya'll never know unless ya have faith . . .

Clenching her teeth, Riann took a step, then two, biting her lip as pain racked her body. The pain of fire, she realized. This was how it felt to burn. Lil Beebee squeaked a protest at being held so tight and Riann forced her grip to loosen slightly.

. . . faith in yerself . . .

She almost stopped. Almost gave in. All this pain could be a warning, couldn't it? Whatever caused her visions could be telling her she was walking into a trap.

. . . faith in yer fellows . . .

Faith that *this* man didn't burn children?

Did that mean she should show him her true self?

Ever since Riann had found herself on her own after her mother's death, she had played her mother's simpleton role. Often, she'd been teased and bullied by children and grownups alike. To show her true self meant revealing her visions (how else to explain the way she stumbled and often fell when a vision struck her, generally at the most inopportune times). Revealing her true self meant sure death.

She'd be burned in the Cleansing Fires.

But this was Valdemar, wasn't it?

They don't burn children . . .

Another step . . . the world spun and darkened, and for a moment Riann thought she'd lost consciousness.

But she stayed in the real world.

One. More. Step.

A tearing sensation ripped through her, leaving her feeling disoriented, as though she'd been split in two. Each half wandered in a different direction—one back along the road, the other drifting toward the fire.

No.

Riann reached out, taking hold of her retreating self with one hand, her advancing self with the other . . .

And pulled.

The world snapped back together, leaving her in a heap on the ground. Lil Beebee squeaked again and Riann uncurled, keeping her arms protectively around the baby. She glanced up at a silent tableau.

The music stopped, the fire seemed to pause. Man and creature stared at her as though she might be a . . . demon?

Miz Goat let out a bleat, sounding both exasperated and relieved. The man jumped up and hurried toward Riann, concern in his emerald-green eyes.

"Here now, little miss. Come sit by the fire."

She let him help her up, shocked at how warm and . . . safe . . . the simple touch of his hand beneath her arm made her feel.

The pain was gone.

"Much thanks," Riann murmured, so soft she could barely hear herself. She raised her voice—and her head. "Much thanks."

"No thanks needed, little miss. Helping's what we do out here on the road."

She stumbled a bit as they drew near the fire. Her numb feet refused to support her. The man swept her into his arms as though she were Lil Beebee's size.

Lil Beebee decided all the commotion wasn't to her liking—or she was hungry. Likely both. She let out a screech that nearly topped Miz Goat's bleat. The man glanced at Riann, eyes wide with wonder.

"I been keeping her safe," Riann said. Her face flushed with heat that had nothing to do with the fire.

The man nodded, setting his beard braids and beads bobbing. He carried her to the rock he'd just left and carefully set her down, stepped away and then back, a steaming mug in his hand.

"Drink this. It'll help." He paused for a breath, then nodded at her cloak. "Ya don't look old enough . . ."

"I found her," Riann said, opening her cloak and fumbling the baby free of the swaddling wrap. She wrinkled her nose. Lil Beebee definitely needed changing. "Her parents—all her folks—was dead. Poison, far as I kin figure."

She hesitated, swallowed hard. "We be from Karse. I get visions, ya know. Don't want ta burn. So we headed north. Ta Valdemar."

She glanced around, then nodded at Miz Goat. "Need some milk from that 'un. I've a change here somewheres . . ."

Still fumbling—why didn't her hands want to work?—she found the small pouch used to carry the teat and several cloths. Took her twice as long as it normally did just to change the baby's cloth.

"Name's Darl, and that be Gnash," the man nodded at the ratweasel. "Found him near dead a year or so back. Caught in a Change Circle, poor thing. Folks what found him near beat the little guy ta death. Not his fault, all that changing. I took him in, cleaned him up, been with me ever since."

Riann shivered and reached for the mug, taking a tentative sip of what turned out to be some sort of stew broth. She took a bigger sip, feeling warmth spread from her stomach to her hands and feet.

A shudder raced through her, accompanied by a strong sense of "being watched."

Demons!

"They're here." Her voice, ragged and hoarse, caught the man's attention. Darl took the teat from her hand and gave her a long look.

"No one's here but us. Folks tend to fear what they don't understand. Sounds like the things ya do—that what happened to ya?" he interrupted himself, nodding at the place she'd split in two. "A vision?"

She started to nod, then shook her head, glancing at the shadows dancing around the fire. Were those demon eyes in that nook? She bit her lip and sipped at the stew, trying not to show . . . what? Her fear? Her . . . curse?

"Yer thinking someone's after ya?" He glanced where she'd been looking, bushy brows raised in question.

"Sunpriests. They send their demons ta find children with a touch a magic and burn 'em." She could barely get the words past the lump in her throat. *Have faith* . . .

"Rest easy on that count. Ya made it ta Valdemar, little miss. I'm thinking yer feeling the little magics set about ta keep track of just that—magic. Valdemarans don't think much of magic."

Riann's heart sank. "I've no place ta go, then."

Lil Beebee quieted after her cloth was secured. She pursed her tiny lips and made sucking motions. Darl chuckled and went to Miz Goat.

Miz Goat, bless Vkandis, stood without prompting, waiting patiently while the man drew enough milk to fill the teat. He patted her rump before bringing the teat to Riann.

"No need ta worry your lil head. They take care of folks like us here." He grinned. "From Karse meself, as ya kin likely tell. Wandered inta Valdemar when I was still young enough ta know I needed something, just not what that something was. Got a bit of the magic, in a healing sorta way. Do a bit with the music as well."

Gnash must've decided he was missing out on . . . something. The rat-weasel darted over from the fire, clambered up to Darl's shoulder, and peered down at Lil Beebee. Riann's heart stuck in her throat, remembering the claws sunk into her shoulder.

"Don't worry 'bout him." Darl shook a finger at the rat-weasel. "You leave the little one be. She's not big enough to play yet."

The rat-weasel chittered at Darl, then settled down, front paws crossed, and simply . . . watched.

His eyes *were* red. And he definitely had sharp fangs.

Gnash cocked his head and gave her a quizzical look. Could he read her mind?

"This 'un be sensitive to moods 'n such. Never seen a critter quite like him. Seems ta know what I'm feeling afore I even know myself."

Gnash laid his head on his paws. Trying to show his innocence?

Riann grinned, something she hadn't done in far too long. "What say we be friends?" she asked the rat-weasel.

Gnash sprang from Darl's shoulder and began to dance.

Before she knew it, Riann was on her feet, feet she could once again feel. Had Darl put some of his magic healing in that stew? She hadn't felt this good since leaving Brinleville.

She paused for a moment, holding the teat while Lil Beebee sucked. Then she made sure the baby was snug.

And began to dance.

Out of Bounds
Charlotte E. English

Mariana's eighteenth birthday was, of necessity, to be a grand affair. It loomed a scant week away, and nothing was *ready*. Which was odd, perhaps; the date could hardly come as a surprise to anyone, after all.

"We must have a Bard to play for all the guests," Mother had proclaimed some time ago. Nobody had acted upon it, however; not even Mother.

"You must *of course* have a new gown," she had also decreed. "Something befitting a Longdown, and as you're to be of marriageable age—" This sentence tended to be left unfinished, but the rest of it unfurled in Mariana's own mind without needing to hear the words aloud. *Since you're to be of marriageable age, and you're still here, and there is nothing else to be done with you . . .*

The gown, at least, she was to have, if not the Bard. She would be clad in sapphire silk and lace, and all of Mother's finest jewels. Her hair would be curled and perfumed and woven with ribbon (it was a fine, bright blond, Mariana's hair, and though Mother had never cared much for the color before, *now* she was pleased). And by the end of the evening, Mariana's fate would be decided.

Father would arrange the engagement. He had humored Mother's wishes for the past eighteen years, and all for nothing, but Mariana was the pride of the Longdowns still. She could serve her family in the simpler, time-honored fashion of marrying the son of some trading partner of Father's; such an alliance was *easy* to arrange, Father could make it happen overnight, and he would, and then at last everyone could be satisfied.

Father had the elder son of his old friend Everard in mind.

One week to go, and Mother had stopped talking about the Bard (except to say, from time to time, "It *is* a pity about that, I do not know what I shall do about the music *now*."). Mariana spent each day at her needlework, seated at Mother's right hand in the handsome solar abovestairs. The leaded windows were south facing, and the sunlight that poured into the room on finer days shone golden upon heavy, carved oak furniture and fine tapestries.

Mother preferred the solar, but it was neither the sumptuary nor the sun that enjoyed her favour. The grand, glittering windows overlooked the road to Haven—or, rather, the road *from* Haven, and Mother had been watching for many years now.

Just in case.

"The dress is to be in pink," Mother remarked on that morning, quite early, for she kept early hours. The leaves were all but gone from the trees lining the city road, and the gray light filtering through the large, mullioned windows was as wan as Mariana's mood. "I had thought the blue, but it would not become you so well as I had imagined," Mother went on, drawing a length of rose-colored silk through the square of white linen she was improving. Perhaps it had given her the idea.

Since the color of her birthday gown was a matter of utter indifference to her, Mariana agreed to this without comment.

"Don't slouch, dear," Mother added. "A Longdown never slouches."

Mariana straightened her shoulders, stifling a sigh. A *lady* was it, now? She had never been obliged to be ladylike before, not until recently.

Mother's tone never varied. She spoke with modulation always, every syllable just *so*, for it did not do to make a display of one's feelings. That was the way to make a spectacle of oneself. Still,

Mariana could read her displeasure lacing every word. She felt the full weight of Mother's gaze, heavy with disappointment, and submitted in silence, for it didn't *do* to argue with Mother. Besides, what would she say? She had failed, and nothing could ever change that now.

A distant *thud, thud* of hoofbeats caught Mariana's ear. They were coming down the Haven road. Reflexively, she straightened, her face turned to the window. Mother sat tall, too, and watched, *stared,* the hope in her iron-gray eyes painfully bright.

The hoofbeats came nearer, and some traitorous corner of Mariana's heart flared with hope. Was there a *ring* to those hooves that spoke of some special promise? There was. She was almost sure of it, here came the animal now, surely there would be the pristine white coat, the azure eyes—

A bay stallion thundered past. Mariana had turned away already, did not watch it pass; the moment her gaze had registered *dark coat* instead of *brilliant white*, she'd turned back to her needlework.

She'd forgotten what she was supposed to be making.

"Certainly pink," said Mother after a time, perfectly serene, and Mariana had no difficulty in reading the thoughts behind those two words. *Really, any color will do, any at all, if you couldn't have Whites.*

Why couldn't you have Whites?

It took two days for the pink gown to arrive, attended by a harassed tailor from Haven. Mother did not trouble to preside over the fitting; the woman must know her business, and Mariana certainly knew hers.

"It seems a little large?" Mariana observed, standing in the midst of Mother's favourite solar all draped in silk. Too much silk. There wasn't time for a new gown now, only an altered one.

"It was . . . made for a larger lady," admitted the tailor, on her knees before Mariana and fussing with the hem. "But don't you worry, miss. We'll have it fitting right before your party."

Of course she would, she was being paid well to fit the silk to Mariana's slender figure. Mariana did not trouble herself to reply, merely stood, turned as she was bid, and waited. Her mind had wandered ahead to the party in question and what lay beyond it. She knew Everard's son a little; Rogert was comely enough, and she'd never taken a dislike to him. Doubtless all would be well. Of course it would. If her heart suffered a twinge of disappointment—there would be no more galloping over the hills to practice her riding, no more archery training with Amfrid—well, what of that? She would be mistress of her own manor, and if she wanted sometimes to gallop about as a Herald did, why, she would.

So lost was she in these thoughts, she barely felt it when the tailor's fingers slipped, and something sharp pricked her leg. She did not hear the tailor's gasp, nor her harried apologies; she did not even hear the distant thunder of hoofbeats, not until they became a loud, insistent clatter.

Then Mariana looked up. Her heart gave a thud, and began to pound; even though she was almost eighteen, and there was scant chance a Companion could have come for her *now*, even Mother had given up—

The hoofbeats came to an abrupt halt.

They'd stopped. Stopped at *her* house.

Mariana hardly dared move. She stood, paralyzed, unwilling to step forward to the window. Because if she *did,* and discovered it to be yet another horse—another messenger from Haven with an urgent missive for Father—she believed she might actually expire of the disappointment.

So she stood with her birthday silks pinned about her and waited for the horse to move on. Some time passed; the tailor went on with her work.

Then a shout went up somewhere in the house, and there came the thunder of feet on the stairs.

The door to Mother's favorite room flew open, and there was Mother herself, ashen-faced and out of breath. Had *she* galloped up the stairs, like a common messenger?

"Mariana," she gasped. "It's happened. It's here, *she* is here, and she's so beautiful, and they are asking for you."

Mother was crying. Great, gulping sobs of relief, and those hard eyes shone with a pride and a joy Mariana had never inspired in them before.

Mariana found she couldn't speak.

"*Go*, child!" cried Mother impatiently.

"But I'm—" began Mariana, gesturing at her silks. She couldn't have said what caused her to hesitate, only an odd sensation of discomfort, of disbelief. When at last she had resigned herself to her future as a merchant's wife, *now* her Mother's prayers were answered?

She was interrupted. "Never mind that, you may change on the road. Your things are being packed and brought to the gate, they will be ready any moment. Go!"

"To be sure," said Mariana. "If I don't show myself at once, my Companion will grow impatient, and Choose someone else." She spoke calmly, though her heart pounded and her hands trembled and she had trouble drawing breath.

She left the room with all the dignity Mother had instilled in her. Only once she reached the stairs did her resolve crumble, and she tore down them at a reckless pace.

Mother had been right. A Companion waited at the gate, there was no mistaking this magnificent creature for a mere horse. For though her tack was splashed with all the mud of the road, her coat shone dazzling white, and those eyes, a penetrating blue . . .

Mariana threw herself upon her Companion, her arms around the mare's neck, and covered the long nose in kisses.

"Excuse me," someone said. "Are you Mariana of Longdown?" The voice was male and adult, and the words emerged clipped and tense.

Only then did it occur to Mariana that the Companion, *her* Companion, was backing up, head tossing. Impatient.

"I am," she said, releasing her Companion. She turned to find a Herald standing there, a real Herald in Herald's Whites. Her first, horrified thought was that this must be *his* Companion, but no; another trotted behind him, mane rippling in the wind.

Two Companions, and a Herald? Why had her Companion arrived with an escort?

The Herald did not wait for pleasantries to be performed. "They tell me you may know where to find Sela." He waited, watching her with an odd intensity. He looked tired, she realized, his Whites mud-splattered, his face drawn with tension and weariness.

She'd hesitated too long. "It is urgent," he said. "Do you know where she is?"

"Sely?" said Mariana. The situation was changing too fast for her to comprehend; she felt as though her brain were stuffed with wool. "She isn't in the kitchens?"

No, of course she wasn't. If Sely were in the kitchens, where she was supposed to be, this tall and stern Herald wouldn't be asking her, would he? She didn't blame him for the impatience that crossed his face as he shook his head. "She isn't there. Elys says she is in some kind of trouble, but she can't determine exactly *where—*"

"Elys?" interrupted Mariana.

The Herald gestured to the Companion Mariana had so thoughtlessly hurled herself upon. "Elys is Sela's Companion. She's looking for her. They say in the kitchen that Sela's been gone for some hours, nobody knows where, but Libet says you may know."

Mariana felt the Companion's—Elys's—nose shove her from behind. She shook her head, collecting her scattered wits. This Companion was here for Sely, not for her. Sela, the cook's daughter.

Libet had not erred when she'd sent the Herald to Mariana. Unbeknownst to most—certainly to Mother—Mariana and Sely had been fast friends as children. Less so in recent years, for Mariana's time had become less and less her own, and Sely's duties had kept her busier than before. But there'd been a time when merchant's daughter and cook's brat had roamed the woods together, never at a loss for an adventure, and if anybody could guess where Sely might have got to, perhaps it was Mariana, after all.

Mother had appeared at the door. The smile had gone from her face. She may not yet have understood the full horror of the situation, but the truth was dawning on her, for there stood Mariana at a distance from the dazzling Companion, talking to a grown Herald, and nobody was being whisked away to the Collegium for a life of noble duty.

Mariana felt sick. She'd been so good, for so long; so *good*, she'd done everything right, she'd done everything she was told, and this, this *humiliation,* was her reward?

She took a deep breath. "I'm afraid Sely and I haven't been friends for years," she said, and felt some pride at the way her voice didn't shake. "I no longer know where she goes."

Mariana turned, and walked back to the house with her head held high. She'd done well, she knew she had done well. She had proved herself Mother's daughter, after all. It was Mother who came tripping to the gate, desperation and rage warring for dominance, and begged, actually *begged*, the Herald to take Mariana to the Collegium.

"This is not Mariana's Companion," said the Herald, and that was all he said. He was mounting up again, he and his two Companions were leaving, streaming out of the gate into the cold wind, and there was nothing Mother could do to prevent them.

This, Mariana thought, *is why one does not make a spectacle of one's feelings*. It took Mother some time to collect herself, and once she had, her eyes were angrier than ever.

"She's for Sela," said Mariana. Might as well get the worst over all at once.

"Sela," repeated Mother. "And who, pray, is that?"

"Libet's daughter. You know, the cook?"

The full weight of the truth sank in, and Mother crumbled under it. She withdrew in silence, her back very straight, and left

Mariana standing at the gate alone, the muddied silks of her pink party gown trailing in the dirt.

Mariana went inside. The hall stood empty and silent. Even the servants had gone elsewhere, the spectacle over. She turned her steps back toward the stairs, and up to the chamber where her tailor waited. She'd ruined the dress, of course, but perhaps something could be salvaged.

She paused halfway up, and sank against the panelled wall.

She'd still hoped . . . that was the problem.

She wasn't surprised about Sela, not really. The little kitchen girl had always been rather serious-minded, and sharp as a tack. She was wasted on the scullery, and everyone knew it. A surge of resentment came up—it wasn't as though Mariana wasn't dutiful, after all, and she wasn't stupid either—but she pushed it down. You were either Chosen or you weren't, and that was that. Worthy or unworthy. There was no use in repining.

Sela. Mariana hadn't spoken to her in months, really, and it *had* been true; she didn't know what Sely got up to these days. Still, it wasn't like her to vacate the kitchen when there was work to be done. She wasn't the type to shirk. What could have happened?

She is in some kind of trouble. Hadn't the Herald said that? She had barely heard the words at the time, but now . . .

She stood up quickly and trotted back down the stairs. Through the hall and down again and into the kitchens. Libet was there, her graying hair tied up on her head and her sleeves up to her elbows, rolling pastry. Two kitchen maids were at the great, scrubbed-oak table, preparing vegetables, but Sely wasn't there.

"Sela's not here?" she said.

Libet looked up. It wasn't usual to see worry on that placid face, but Mariana read it in her dark eyes today. A flicker of anxiety began, somewhere near her heart.

"She's not here," said Libet. "Like I told the man." She looked away from Mariana, went on with the pastry.

She knew, Mariana thought. She knew the Herald had gone to

Mariana; probably she'd sent him. And she knew Mariana had refused to help. Word traveled fast.

Shame joined the anxiety. Mariana fought with a brief impulse to withdraw to the top of the house and never come down again.

"Did she say—" began Mariana. "Does no one have any idea what's become of her?"

"If we knew, we'd have told the Herald."

"He's here for her, Libet. She's been Chosen. That was *her* Companion."

"I know," said Libet, and that was all, and then Mariana knew how worried she was.

"I'll find her," she promised.

Libet looked up again, at last. "She was troubled last night, my Sely. Went out early this morning—"I need to get out for a bit, Ma," she said, "I'll be back to do the pies"—and that were three hours ago now. Like as not she's well enough, or so I thought, but then that Herald—"

Mariana's thoughts whirled. Sela liked to ramble, she knew that, especially when she had something on her mind. She and Mariana used to ramble the woods together, once upon a time; Libet didn't mind, even if Mother did, provided they didn't stray too far from home.

And they didn't, as a rule. There'd been only the one time they'd got into any trouble.

"I think I might know where she is," gasped Mariana.

She was gone before Libet could answer, running up the stairs in her too-large dress. She wouldn't have time to change it now. If Sely had been gone for hours already, there was no time to waste, and she'd have to catch up with the Herald—

Mariana ran straight for the stables, her heart pounding. She'd never ridden out alone before, but she didn't have time to find someone to go with her. She was calling for the stableboys before she got through the door—she couldn't saddle the horse herself, Mother thought it beneath her; Heralds were important people, they'd have servants to do that sort of thing for them, and how *foolish* that seemed to Mariana now—

"Saddle Jumble!" she cried, "Quickly!" And, bless them, they did, rushing to drop her saddle and bridle onto the faithful old gelding, and within minutes Mariana was up—without even using the mounting block, what would Mother say about *that*—and galloping out of the gate.

Rafe's Foresight wasn't up to much, but it had certainly got him into a mess this time.

He'd woken with that vague but powerful sense that today *needed* him, somehow. He and Orella would be doing something important.

It was the reason that he'd chosen to ride down that one particular road this morning, where he'd encountered Elys half an hour later. It was the reason why he'd led the two Companions to the Longdown mansion shortly thereafter. Somebody there could help, he'd felt that to be true.

When he'd seen Mariana, he'd known he had found the right person and had felt . . . relief. The problem would soon be solved; Sela and Elys would be united, and he and Orella could go about their regular business.

And then she'd *refused*.

Rafe left the Longdown house in a mood of suppressed fury. He'd wanted to box the girl's ears. Standing there on her dignity, in a dress that must have cost a fortune, and utterly indifferent to the possible fate of a mere cook's daughter. And the cook had said they were friends.

She wasn't the sort to have friends, he thought savagely.

:You are upset,: observed Orella, his Companion.

"I'm worried," he told her. "That's probably what it is."

And it was, to a point. Rafe had been worried ever since Elys had come tearing up, mud-spattered and weary, and had gone into urgent conference with Orella. He'd been worried since he'd known they had a missing Chosen and even her Companion couldn't track her down.

That wasn't usual.

And it didn't help that he and Orella had been on the road a bit too long, and he was running on too little sleep.

His Companion wasn't buying it, however.

:You are angry,: Orella disagreed. *:With that girl.:*

"All right, yes. I am angry. The only person who could help us, and she just said *no.* How could she refuse?"

:It's my belief she was scared.:

"Scared," scoffed Rafe. "What she could have to be scared of, I've no idea." The way she'd thrown her arms around Elys, then looked so *offended* when she'd understood the Companion wasn't for her. Spoiled since birth, probably. She didn't understand why she couldn't have whatever she wanted.

Neither did her Mother. The woman had practically ordered him to take her daughter to the Collegium! As though that was how it should work, when you were rich.

:I don't know, exactly,: said Orella. *:But she looked awfully alone to me.:*

Rafe sighed. They were heading back into the oak trees again, Elys in the lead. He had no idea where they were going, and he feared that the Companion didn't, either.

"What does Elys say?" he tried. He didn't have Animal Mind-speech himself, and he couldn't hear the other Companion. It was Orella's job to relay Elys's ideas to Rafe—and his job to relay them to others, like the Longdown girl.

Perhaps he'd made a mess of it. Had he made the situation clear?

Did he even understand the situation himself? Elys wasn't frantic, but she was visibly troubled, and though she'd spent the past two hours going in circles around this wretched wood, she hadn't been able to find Sela. He didn't perfectly understand why; something about *confusion,* though whether it was the direction itself that was somehow confused or whether Elys was, he hadn't grasped. He hadn't heard of a Companion unable to find her

Chosen before, but what did he know? He wasn't an expert at this. He'd just happened to be the only Herald nearby.

:Elys is doing her best,: came Orella's reply, which meant Elys had no information. She was barely more than a filly herself, of course. She *was* doing her best.

Frustration surged up again, and he had to take a few calming breaths. He was supposed to fix this, that was the problem, and he didn't know how. Beleaguered youngsters in need of help, and only he and Orella were around to provide it.

:I'm not angry, really,: he told Orella. Or if he was, it was the kind of anger that came from stirrings of alarm.

:Someone's coming,: was all that Orella said.

Rafe heard nothing at first, but the rapid, dull thud of hoofbeats on the forest floor reached his ears before long. A rider approached.

:It's my belief it's that girl,: said Orella.

She came into view moments later, still wearing that abominable dress. She was mounted on a nice bay gelding, and she had a good seat on her. Someone had taught her to ride.

If it weren't for the dress, though, he would scarcely have recognised her as the same girl. Gone was her haughty dignity. This girl was a mess. A few low-hanging branches had done terrible things to her perfectly arranged hair, she and her horse were all over mud, and as she drew level with him, she turned on him a face transformed by–worry? Terror?

For whom?

"I'm sorry," she gasped.

He shook his head. There wasn't time for apologies, not now. "Where's Sela?"

"I don't know for sure, but I think–if her Companion can't find her, then it has to be something unusual, and there's only one place I can think of."

He didn't like the sound of that. His Foresight twinged again. "Is there some kind of Change Circle around here? Something like that?"

"Yes. At least, I think so. We found it a few years ago, Sely and I, and we knew it was dangerous, but we were—it was mesmerising; we kept going back just to look at it until one day she almost fell in, and we got scared, and we haven't been back since—"

"You never told anybody else it was there?"

"Of course not! Even Libet wouldn't have stood for nonsense like that."

Rafe suppressed a sigh. He'd caught only a brief impression of this girl's mother, but he could read between the lines well enough.

This was what came of terrorizing children. When they misbehaved—and all children would, sooner or later, even a girl like this one—well, they didn't dare tell you about it, and then dangerous places like Change Circles—or, as he suspected, some kind of active rift lingering after the Mage Storms—well, they went untended to.

Rafe didn't waste any time expressing any of this. "Lead on," he said, and Mariana took off into the trees.

The ride wasn't an especially long one, but the route was winding, turning in ever-tightening circles, and he no longer wondered that Elys had grown confused. Or that nobody else had stumbled upon the Change Circle since the two girls had stopped going there.

Or, at least, nobody who'd got out again to talk about it.

Mariana brought her horse to a stop at last and slithered out of her saddle in the same motion. She was on her knees in the earth of the forest floor by the time Rafe levered himself off Orella's back and contrived to join her.

"I don't know why she'd come here today," said Mariana, speaking very rapidly. "But she was here. Look." She held up a scrap of blue linen. It would pass for a hair ribbon with a kitchen girl, Rafe supposed, and he accepted without question that it was Sela's. Mariana seemed certain.

If Elys hadn't seemed frantic before, now she certainly was. She was trotting around and around in distracted circles, her head tossing, her blue eyes wide and frightened.

:She says her Chosen is here but also not here,: Orella translated. *:Or she* was *here and she should be still, but Elys can hardly sense her at all.:*

A confused report, thought Rafe, but today was a confusing day.

He had heard of rifts left behind by the Magic Storms, but he'd never seen one himself. This one wasn't so impressive. If he had passed by this spot alone, he might have noticed that the light seemed odd but thought nothing of it.

The light was more than odd, in truth. They had fetched up in a darkened glade, so shrouded in old oak trees that little sunlight could penetrate the canopy. Nothing much grew on the forest floor—it was largely bare earth and leaf mold—and yet, there was a silvery glow, as though a ray of moonlight shone on this spot alone, even in the middle of the day.

There was also a faint glitter in the earth, like moonlight on water.

:See if you can calm Elys,: he asked Orella. *:We're going to need her if we're to get Sela out of there.:*

"She's gone through," said Mariana. "She must have, but I don't know how to get her out. We never went through before."

Rafe squatted down on his haunches beside her, keeping a wary distance from the rift. "Do you know much about Companions and their Chosen? How they communicate?" he asked.

"Yes," she said firmly. "They can talk to each other in silence, I mean without talking out loud."

"There's a special bond," he said, nodding. "Elys can sense Sela, and perhaps Sela can sense Elys, too. I don't know if that holds true when the two haven't met yet, and Sela hasn't formally been Chosen, but—I'm hoping it's true. It may be that Sela can find her way out, using Elys as a kind of lodestar."

But Mariana shook her head. "So we just sit here with her Companion and wait? She doesn't even know she *has* a Companion. She's lost, and she must be frightened, and whatever is on the other side of that light must be confusing. Sely can't try for something if she doesn't even know it exists."

She was right, of course, but Rafe was out of ideas. He couldn't send Elys in after her, or they'd likely both be lost. And how else could her Companion's presence be communicated to her?

Could he go through himself? Maybe Orella could get him out again; they had an established bond, but it was risky—

"I'll have to go in," said Mariana.

"Wait!" Rafe cried. "You can't just go in there. How are we supposed to get *two* of you out? It's not—"

"Sela will bring me out," she said. "With Elys's help."

Rafe had no more time to remonstrate with her or to come up with a better plan. She took a step and was gone, and that was that.

He cursed.

:*Steady, my Chosen,*: said Orella. She radiated serenity, and he calmed a little.

Elys had stopped running rings around the glade, and stood, tense and alert, on the edge of the rift. "Can she still sense Sela?" asked Rafe.

:*She is doing her best,*: said Orella, and Rafe had to be satisfied with that.

Hopefully her best would be enough.

The other side of the rift was mostly light, as far as Mariana could tell. Odd, shifting light that bedazzled her senses and half blinded her eyes; she couldn't see through it, and she soon ceased to try.

"Sely!" she shouted, for the place wasn't only light, it was *sound*, a confused mess of both. "It's Mariana! Come to me."

A reply came at once, or she *thought* it did; but there were several unearthly voices mixed up in the cacophony, a relentless jabber of nonsense Mariana's ears could make no sense of. She concentrated, sifting through layers of the shrieking din, until—

"I'm hearing voices," sobbed somebody, a disembodied voice its own self, but this was *real*, a true, earthy, *human* voice.

Sely.

She followed the sound of sobbing, and quickly encountered a form as warm and flesh-made as her own.

Sela turned, stumbled, and all but fell into Mariana's arms. "I can't see," she was babbling. "All I can hear are *voices*—"

"This voice is real enough," Mariana assured her, quite calmly, though her own heart was pounding fit to burst, and the hands that clutched Sela were shaking with fright. If poor Sely had been trapped in here for hours, no wonder she was losing her wits.

"Mari?" Sela's fists closed on Mariana's reviled dress, and clung. "Is that you? Really?"

"Really. Steady, now. What voices are you hearing?"

"Somebody keeps saying, over and over, *where are you where are you I can't find you I need you,* it's like that, and I don't know where it's coming from, but it feels like it's inside my mind—"

"It is," said Mariana. "It belongs to a Companion called Elys, and you're Chosen to be a Herald, Sely. But first you have to get us out of this madness."

"*I'm* going mad," sobbed Sela.

"You aren't going mad," said Mariana firmly. "Can you feel where the voice is coming from?"

"I—don't know."

"Try, Sely. It's important." Mariana half wanted to laugh at the extent of the understatement, a laugh tinged with hysteria. Here she was, stuck in a magic rift with Sely, and it was down to *her* to talk her friend through the process of getting out again. So she could go to the Collegium with her Companion—and leave Mariana behind.

Enough, she told herself sternly. She could grieve later.

"I can," said Sela. "I think."

"Then that's where we need to go. That direction." Mariana didn't know if Sely would feel it as a direction, but she had no better words to use; she didn't know what she was talking about.

But Sely seemed to. She straightened, ceased to cling to Mariana, and began to move. It was Mariana's turn to clutch at Sela, so she wouldn't be left behind in this nightmare of a place.

What happened next went by too fast for Mariana's comprehension. There came a surge of *something*; she thought she saw a hand reaching out of nowhere, a man's hand; was it Rafe's or was she seeing things now? Could you put just a hand into the rift without falling all the way in? Or without losing the *hand*? Wouldn't your hand just be spirited someplace else without the rest of you? She was definitely losing her senses, so it was lucky that Sela and Elys knew what they were about, or they'd figured it out, because the *surge* grew stronger, and brought a fair bit of agony with it, and then—

Then the horrible light was gone, and Mariana lay prone in the earth of a forest glade. She couldn't see with her dazzled eyes, but she heard Rafe's voice saying, "That's it, very good, steady, you're safe now, is Mariana with you?"

"I'm here," croaked Mariana. And then she felt a soft, velvety nose shoving itself against her torso, her face, and knew it for gratitude.

She lay still a while yet, unsure of the point in getting up again. Sela would be fine, that was the important thing. Sela and Elys would both be fine.

When her vision finally began to clear, she saw Rafe seated nearby, watching her.

"I'm alive," said Mariana. "I think." She sat up a bit, caught a glimpse of Sely and her Companion becoming joyously acquainted with one another, and averted her gaze.

"You did well," said Rafe. "Extremely well."

Mariana frowned. She didn't feel like a person who'd done well. "Sela could hear Elys," she said. "But she didn't know what she was hearing. She thought she was going mad."

"I can see how she would, at that," Rafe nodded.

"Did you . . . pull us out?"

"Something like that. Orella anchored me so I could try to reach you. Elys was reaching for Sela, and somehow . . ." He shrugged.

It didn't matter. The important thing was that everybody would be well.

Rafe said nothing more for a little while, and neither did Mariana.

At length, though, the Herald spoke again. "People are sometimes Chosen later in life, you know."

Mariana shook her head. "I don't understand."

"You wanted to be Chosen, didn't you?"

Remembering her embarrassing display over Elys, Mariana felt her cheeks warm. "Mother wanted it," she said. "More than anything."

"I see."

Mariana sighed and sat up carefully. "There are three Heralds on her side of the family. Mother's own sister is one of them. Her portrait hangs in the hall."

"And your father's side?"

"One." She smiled faintly. "Mother would never have married anybody without that bloodline."

"It isn't a bloodline," said Rafe. "Though that's not an uncommon misconception. You aren't any more likely to become a Herald just because you're related to a few."

"Don't tell Mother that. It's all she lives for."

She saw understanding in Rafe's face. "After everything you just did, I think you could make a wonderful Herald," he said. "And I wouldn't be surprised if someday you're Chosen after all. But if it isn't what you've wanted . . . what *do* you want?"

Mariana thought about it. She knew what she was supposed to do: marry and produce a few children herself, so that perhaps the next generation might produce another Chosen.

But the prospect held no appeal for her. But what did she want instead?

She didn't know.

"No one's ever asked before," she said, apologetic, obscurely ashamed at being unable to answer so simple a question.

"Well, I'm asking now," said Rafe patiently. "I've got to go to Haven next. I can't close that rift, but somebody needs to, and I'll need to report it. So I'll be attending Sela and Elys on their journey into the city." He paused, and looked keenly at her. "Would you like to come along?"

Mariana froze. "Come along? To *Haven*? To do what?"

"Well, to begin with, we'll need you to find this rift again, once I've tracked down someone who can do something about it. That's important. After that? I don't know. But perhaps we can figure it out along the way."

Mariana felt a spasm of something like terror just thinking about it. She sat here at the farthest edge of her known world; she'd never passed beyond it before, save for scant occasions when the family traveled into Haven for business and shopping. To go there alone? With no notion of what she was to do once she got there?

She looked down at the pink dress she wore, ragged now and spoiled, and thought of Everard's son.

"Please," she said. "I'd love to go."

Rafe smiled, the first smile she'd seen on him. "You'll need some new attire, I'd think."

An answering grin rose to her face, and she shrugged. "No problem there. Mother had my bags packed the moment she caught sight of Elys. They're probably still waiting for me. And Libet needs to know her daughter's safe."

"Back to Longdown, then," said Rafe. "And thereafter, who knows?"

Mariana nodded, the smile fading from her face, but a glow of hope radiant within. "Who knows?"

A Clutter of Cats

Elisabeth Waters

She was drowning. It was cold, wet, and dark, and she kept bumping into other bodies as she struggled to find air. Then someone was shaking her.

"Lena, wake up!" her husband said urgently. "You're having a nightmare. Wake up!"

Lena sat up in bed, still gasping for air. The moonlight shining through the window let her see Keven's concerned face. He wasn't the only one worried; her dog was practically having convulsions at the foot of the bed.

"It's not a nightmare, damn it," she said, rolling out of bed and grabbing her novice's robe. She always kept it by her bed because if she had to throw on the nearest garment and run out into the night, this was decent clothing. Fancy nightshifts bought to amuse her husband were not. "Look at Orson. Someone is drowning baby animals—kittens, I think." She grabbed her boots and shoved her feet into them. "Where around here is someone likely to do that?"

"Nearby?" Keven asked as he threw on an identical robe. Both of them were novices of the Temple of Thenoth, Lord of the Beasts; they had met at the main Temple in Haven. That was also where they had acquired Orson. He had been one of a litter of puppies tied in a sack and thrown in the river but rescued and brought to the Temple. "The lake where the godwits nest, perhaps?"

"We'll try there first," Lena agreed. She ran out the door, trusting him to follow. He didn't have Animal Mindspeech, but it didn't help her much in this case, because it wasn't directional. The best she could tell was louder or softer, which she prayed indicated distance and not imminent death. There was a daughter house of Thenoth's order on a part of her estate she had given to the Temple, and several of the novices there also had Animal Mindspeech. If the god willed it, they would find the animals in time.

She quickly discovered she had not been the only one wakened. Maja, head of the daughter house, also had strong Animal Mindspeech, but it looked as if most of the population of their little temple had followed her. "It's this way, I think" Maja told her. "It seems louder, at least."

"All I hear is a child screaming," said Stina, one of the novices who did not share their Gift. "And that's this way." She darted ahead, and the rest followed.

As they headed toward the lake, Keven joined them. He was carrying Orson and trying to soothe him, but the dog wriggled frantically in his arms.

As they drew closer, two figures were illuminated by the torches several of the novices—ones without Animal Mindspeech—had had enough presence of mind to grab on their way out. One was a grown man, and the other was a small girl who appeared to be trying to attack him. Given that she was unarmed and a third his size, she wasn't doing much damage, but the man looked nervous. Of course, that might have been because the godwits were gathering near them. The birds were several feet tall and had very long, sharp beaks. One of them had a bit of sacking in her beak and was dragging it toward the shore.

Orson twisted himself out of Keven's arm and ran to help. In less than a minute the sack was out of the water, but everyone with Animal Mindspeech could tell the animals were in trouble.

"Knife!" Maja gasped, and one of the male novices produced

one and cut the sack open. Hands reached out and grabbed the kittens, including, Lena dimly noted, the little girl, who had left off screaming and fighting to save the kittens.

"Do you know how to revive a drowned kitten?" Maja asked gently. She was still struggling a bit for breath, along with Lena, Nalini, Britta, and, oddly enough, the child. The child shook her head, looking hopeless. "Give the kitten to—" Maja looked around at her novices.

"I'll take it," one of the boys said. There were more people than kittens, so he didn't have one yet.

"—to Anders," Maja finished. "Thank you, Anders."

Lena didn't have a kitten, either, so she decided to tackle the humans. *After all, it's my estate, and they're presumably my tenants, which make them my job. Still, I think I'll start with the girl.* She sat down next to the child, who was still gasping and looking about anxiously.

"What's your name, child?" she asked quietly.

"Tansy."

"Tansy, can you tell me which of the kittens is worst off?"

"That one," Tansy pointed with a shaking hand at the one Britta was working on. "His lungs have the most water in them."

"Britta?" Lena called.

"He's in bad shape," Britta replied, as the kitten finally started to cough up water, "but I think he'll pull through. He's really not happy, though."

"And he's broadcasting," Lena said wryly. "I think most of us know how unhappy he is."

"He's not gonna die?" Tansy said hopefully.

"Probably not," Lena replied. She looked around. "I think all of them are going to pull through." She noticed Orson had decided to help, and was going from kitten to kitten, giving each one a good lick. "Can you tell me what happened?"

"They're just babies!" Tansy said indignantly. "They were with their mother in a box by the kitchen hearth, and I woke up when my father started grabbing them and stuffing them in that awful sack. I followed him and tried to take them back, but he threw them really far into the lake, and then the birds came . . ."

"Followed by most of the people from the Temple of Thenoth," Lena said.

"I'm sorry my daughter woke up the whole Temple," the man said, "but I am *not* taking those damned cats back!"

Maja eyed him coldly. "Nobody would give the cats back to you if you begged for them," she snapped, "and it wasn't just the Temple you woke up. Lady Magdalena and Lord Keven were at the manor house."

The man looked around with a mixture of nervousness and bewilderment. "How could the Lord and Lady hear Tansy all the way over there?"

Lena rose to her feet. "We didn't hear Tansy until we got here. What woke us up was the kittens. Have you not heard that I have Animal Mindspeech?"

The man gaped at her, obviously having trouble recognizing the lady who owned the estate in a muddy novice's robe. "I'd heard it," he admitted, "but I don't know what it means aside from if somebody tries to hurt you, all the animals will come and hurt them."

Lena sighed. "That's true, but what it really means is that animals can hear me, and *I can hear them*." She found she was still shivering a bit. "It means that when you crowd kittens into a sack and throw them in the lake, I can hear each and every one of them—and kittens who are being drowned are *loud*. Very loud. I was asleep when you threw them in the water, and how long did it take for me to get here?"

"Not long," the man replied in a small voice. "But it's not illegal to drown kittens."

"It is now," Lena said grimly. "Within the boundaries of my estate it is illegal from this moment on to drown kittens, puppies, or any other unwanted animal. Unwanted animals are to be taken to the Temple of Thenoth."

"It is what we're here for," Maja added. "Thenoth is Lord of the Beasts, and all animals ultimately belong to him." She smiled at Tansy and added, "and you can visit your kittens any time you want to."

"Can I come live there?" Tansy asked.

"No, you can't," her father said firmly. "You are coming home where you belong."

Lena decided that arguing about his parental rights could wait, especially because it was an argument she would lose. At the moment there was a more pressing concern. "What about the mother cat?" she asked. "She's been nursing the kittens, right?"

"She has to have been," Maja pointed out. "They're nowhere near old enough to be weaned."

"She's a good mouser," the man said, "when she's not burdened with kittens."

"So, you want to keep her?" Lena asked, and the man nodded. "Would you be willing to let her stay at the Temple until the kittens are weaned? If we have to hand-feed the entire litter it will be a lot of extra work for us. And if you don't want her to have any more kittens, we can arrange for that."

"There's a magic that can keep a cat from having kittens?" the man said in surprise. "I didn't know Healers could to that."

"Healers can do it," Lena replied. "There are techniques that will stop female animals from bearing young and male animals from engendering them. That's why Haven is not knee-deep in unwanted animals."

"You can have the cat then, but I want her back as soon as you can fix her."

Lena glanced at Maja, who nodded. "Agreed."

Lena had duties around the estate that kept her busy for the next few weeks, although she did make time to tell Algott to arrange for an Animal Healer to come to the Temple and to make certain that everyone on the estate knew they could get their animals neutered.

"I don't think this is one of the traditional duties of a Game Warden," Algott remarked lightly. Despite a somewhat strained beginning, he and Lena had developed a good working relationship.

"After all this time," Lena teased, "surely you're still not suffering from the delusion that this is a traditional estate."

"Not at all," he replied calmly. "I'll take care of it." He bowed slightly and left her. Lena mentally crossed that job off her unending list of things to do and moved on to the next item.

When she next visited the Temple, the kittens were starting to be weaned, and the Animal Healer was there. "I'd like to wait another week before I do the surgery on the mother," he said. "As long as she's nursing, she's using energy that would otherwise be used for healing. Also, I've seen a copy of the proclamation you issued . . ." Lena vaguely recalled signing it when Algott shoved it into her pile of papers to be read and signed.

"Do you have questions about it?" she asked encouragingly.

"It says 'within the boundaries of this estate'," he said, "but a few people who live just outside your lands have asked if I can neuter their animals. As you are the one paying for this, I told them I would have to get your consent."

"You have it," Lena said instantly. "I can enforce policies only on my estate, but I wouldn't bet that I can't hear drowning animal beyond its boundaries."

"Hear drowning animals?" he repeated, obviously puzzled.

"Animal Mindspeech. I have it, and so do several people here at the Temple. This all started when the owner of that cat tried to drown the kittens." She shuddered. "It was a very unpleasant experience. By all means, neuter any animal whose owner wants it done, as long as it's safe for the animal."

He nodded. "I hadn't realized you were Gifted. I was wondering why you were being so generous with your tenants."

Lena smiled tightly. "That's why. I hope I'm not *un*generous with my tenants, but this is in partly self-interest. I really dislike being wakened in the middle of the night by drowning kittens, and animals in that much distress are very loud."

"Do you plan to force your tenants to become vegetarian?"

Lena laughed. "That's a path to open revolt! No, I have no plans in that direction. People here who kill animals for food do it quickly and skillfully, so the animal doesn't have time to feel much, if anything. There is a big difference between quickly wringing one chicken's neck and killing an entire litter of kittens by slow torture. Kittens don't drown as quickly as people who put them in a sack and toss them into the nearest body of water think they do."

"People who do that confuse living things with garbage," he said disapprovingly. "They're not going to stand there and keep track of the time."

Their discussion was abruptly interrupted by a shout from the Temple's gate. "Tansy, you get out here right now!"

Lena drifted in the direction of the gate. Normally the Peace of the God prevented major displays of anger in the Temple, but she noticed Tansy's father was standing with his feet just outside the gate.

He saw her and glared at her. "Thing were just fine here before you started meddling. Then you not only saved those damned kittens, you told Tansy she could visit them here any time she wanted."

"Actually, it was Maja who told her that. She's the Head of the Temple here."

"Bunch of meddling women who think they can tell my daughter she can shirk her chores and play with useless kittens."

Lena saw Maja approaching, escorting a foot-dragging Tansy. "Neither of us said Tansy should shirk her chores."

"You think you can tell my daughter what to do!"

I wish I could drag him across the threshold so we could discuss this calmly. "What I think I can tell your daughter is that parents have rights and that she should obey you and make sure her chores are done."

His mouth fell open. Obviously this was not the response he expected.

"What I think I can tell *you* is that if she does her chores *first*, it would be a kindness for you to let her visit the kittens."

She ignored his mumbled, "If I'd managed to drown them, we wouldn't have this problem."

As Tansy reluctantly accompanied her father home, Maja led Lena to her office.

She poured out two cups of water from a covered pitcher on a shelf near her desk, and both of them collapsed into chairs and drank.

"Does that happen often?" Lena asked.

Maja groaned. "I still don't know why the Prior thought I was up to this job."

"Probably because you are."

Maja ignored that. Possibly she would never feel ready for the job she was doing. "Unfortunately, that happens nearly every day. I wish he'd let her become a Novice here . . ."

"I noticed that night that she has Animal Mindspeech," Lena remarked. "That brings the total here on my estate to five of us: you, me, Britta, Nalini, and now Tansy. That's a lot for a Gift that's supposed to be rare. Do you think we're contagious?"

Maja chuckled. "Maybe we are. Or perhaps the god calls us to where he wants to use us. There's also Arvid and Bram back in Haven. That brings the count to seven."

"Mostly among the Novices." Lena thought about it for a moment. "Can you see Arvid as the next Prior?"

"No. The problem with having our Gift from childhood—as you may have noticed—is that it doesn't teach you how to talk to people or do human politics. I'm so thankful you're the only highborn I have to deal with. I'm afraid, however, that Tansy's father will be hard to cope with no matter what we do."

"I told him we acknowledged his parental rights but that it would be kind of him if he allowed Tansy to visit after her chores were done."

"Well, at least that doesn't make things worse. I suspect that he views Tansy in the same light he views his animals—a combination of property and worker—except he knows it's illegal for him to kill her."

"He won't kill her as long as he thinks she's useful," Lena pointed out. "Galling as it may be, remind her that she owes him her obedience, and tell her she needs to finish her chores before she comes here."

"I'm pretty sure she has more 'chores' than can be done in a day," Maja said grimly. "She sneaks out after dark and comes here to sleep with the cats. Nobody here has been hard-hearted enough to kick her awake and send her home when we wake up."

"Aside from the kicking part, it might be a good idea to make sure she's home in the mornings. Perhaps assign 'wake Tansy and walk her home' to the Novices on a rotating basis? Not that I'm telling you how to run your Temple."

"Please do," Maja said fervently. "I can use all the help I can get."

"I noticed he called her from just outside the gate. Has he ever come inside?"

Maja snickered. "Just the first time. He doesn't seem to appreciate the Peace of the God."

"That's a shame."

"Yes. It really is. Any other advice?"

"Pray. I will too. Perhaps Thenoth will provide a solution beyond what we can think of."

Lena was in her study, working her way through a pile of paperwork that had been brought from Haven. The messenger was in her kitchen, refueling for the trip back with the papers that were urgent instead of merely tedious.

Keven walked in with an odd look on his face. "I hate to say this, but there's a Companion looking for you."

It took Lena a moment to change her focus from her paperwork to her husband and realize what was bothering him. "If you're afraid I'm about to be Chosen, don't worry. I'm not. Companions do not Choose people who are needed elsewhere."

"Are you sure?" Keven looked nervous. "Conceivably I could take over the estate if I had to . . ."

"We don't have children yet," Lena pointed out practically. "And once we do, neither of us is going to be Chosen." She scrawled her signature on the last of the urgent papers and rose to her feet. "Front courtyard?"

She followed Keven out the front door. There was a Companion there, and it was one she knew well. She and Meri had been though a lot together including a "trained animal" (more like "trained humans") act, and the middle-of-the-night flight from court to the Temple where she first met Keven.

"Hello, Meri," she said. "What can I do for you?" *I don't think she came down here to visit me.*

:I need your help,: Meri replied. *:One of your tenants is denying me access to my Chosen.:*

"You're Choosing someone?" Lena smiled. "That's great news! I'm happy for you, and your Chosen is a lucky . . . girl? Would this be Tansy, by any chance?"

:Yes. You probably even know why she's being Chosen.:

"Aside from its being the answer to Maja's and my prayers? And the Animal Mindspeech? Yes, I do know. I wish you both joy." She squared her shoulders. "Let's go tackle her father."

Tansy's father stood firmly in front of his closed—and possibly locked—front door. "Lady, you yourself told me that parents have rights. I don't have to let my daughter make a fool of herself over a pretty horse!"

:At least he thinks I'm pretty: Meri thought archly.

"This is not a horse," Lena explained. "Note the white coat, blue eyes, and sliver hooves. This is a Companion. If you could hear her, she would explain the difference at length."

:Hey!:

:Well, you would.: "Please fetch Tansy. Companion's Choice

overrides your parental rights, but you will be paid a stipend so you can hire someone to take over her work."

"They'd better pay well. She does a lot of work." He grudgingly opened the door a crack, and Tansy slid through it, took two steps, and froze, looking into Meri's eyes.

Neither of them moved for several minutes, and then Tansy said, almost dreamily, "Her name is Meri."

I know that, and I know her better than you do, though that's changing now. Lena refrained from saying that. What she did say was, "Congratulations. Did she tell you what happens next?"

"I'm to go to Haven and learn to be a Herald." The dreamy look slid away as Tansy remembered the only thing she didn't want to leave behind. "Can I take the kittens?"

Lena choked back laughter at the sight of Meri's face. "I have no objection, and I don't think Maja will, but is your Companion willing to carry a clutter of cats to Haven with you?"

"Oh, please, please, please!" Tansy clung to Meri's neck. Meri looked pointedly at Lena.

"There are six of them, they're weaned, they'll fit in a pair of saddlebags, and she can manage them with her Gift," Lena said helpfully.

She didn't hear what Meri said to Tansy, but apparently it was affirmative, for Tansy started babbling thank yous and took off at a run, leaving her new Companion and Lena to follow her.

"Don't worry," Lena said cheerfully as they walked side by side to the Temple. "I'm sure you'll have her properly trained in no time."

Ghost Cider

Brigid Collins

Silence hung like a bead of water on a spider's silk while Simen's rapt audience let his final notes ring through the tavern. That moment of silence was a transient passage, the ephemeral place between the held breath and the gasp of joy, the quivering stillness between every song and the audience's appreciative response.

Like every such moment, the fleeting silence burst, the bead of water fell from the spider's silk, and Simen's audience broke into applause.

"Not bad for a warm-up, eh?" he quipped, grinning at those sitting nearest. They laughed, as they were meant to.

Simen twiddled with his harp's tuning, letting the gathered people of Orchard Lake pepper him with requests and giving his fingers a subtle stretch. The tavern was like many others, warm and crowded, boisterous yet cozy. The scent of woodsmoke and fresh cider mingled with the savory aroma of day-long simmered stew from the kitchen. Bursts of laughter lent percussive accents to the swell of conversation.

What made this tavern stand out among all the others Simen had played in was the décor: Everywhere one looked, one found the pleasingly round forms of apples—red, yellow, and green. They were arranged artfully as centerpieces on the tables, dried and strung on garlands dangling from the rafters or bundled into wreaths on the walls, even replicated in the forms of the cups, pitchers, and other utensils.

The place was clean, the customers were happy, and Simen was feeling confident, both of singing for his supper and of his real purpose in coming to this small lakeside community.

Shipments of Orchard Lake cider, always excellent beyond compare, had recently arrived in Haven stamped with a mark from a new mill: Ghost Cider, home to more than one kind of spirit, according to the rumors.

A haunted cider mill! The thought had a boyish giggle bubbling up in his throat. Supposedly, according to the drovers who'd brought the cider to Haven, the place had been the site of a terrible tragedy many years ago and had fallen out of operation until very recently, when a strange new owner had set up shop selling his ghostly wares.

Mysteriouser and mysteriouser.

How could Simen, a Bard whose specialty extended to cover all things spooky, occult, ghostly—anything associated with Sovvan Night festivities—possibly resist? He was so known for his Sovvan songs, his reputation would take a hit if he *didn't* make the trek out here.

Plus, his Herald friend Marli had asked him for a favor.

"I heard a rumor while I was on Circuit there that a young girl went missing some weeks prior," she'd said when they'd passed each other coming and going from Haven. "But the locals didn't want to open up to me about it."

Because she was Marli, ultimate compassion in Herald form, she didn't sound bitter about being snubbed, only confused.

"And you think a Bard will have a better chance of getting folk to talk? Dreyvin, oh man of my heart that he is, says I'm a touch too garrulous to allow anyone else to get a word in edgewise."

"Just keep your ears open, Bard, and I'll keep an eye on you now and then with my Farsight," Marli had said with a humor that hadn't quite touched the melancholy lingering about her ever since her winter Circuit.

Simen would do a lot to cheer his best friend up. Hence, he'd begun an investigation, though thus far he'd got nothing but a handful of oft-repeated complaints, mostly about the family that had taken over the old mill. The big man was too disrespectful of the history of Orchard Lake, and he hired such disreputable sorts as to make any good man worry for his family's safety at night. The older son was a no-good drunk who never settled up at the tavern. The daughter hadn't been seen in a while, but that could be chalked up to her being a haughty miss who considered herself too good to play with the other children.

Any attempt to turn the conversation toward the history of the mill resulted in doors firmly shut in Simen's face.

The folk of Orchard Lake liked to keep their secrets close to the chest, it seemed.

But he wouldn't let an initial failure send him packing. Bard Simen was too optimistic a man to abandon the trail of a good story, or so Dreyvin would say.

He'd never seen a real ghost before, but something about the taste of that cider, the ring of those rumors, and the closed-mouthed nature of the locals . . .

This is going to be it!

Still, he kept a tight rein on his giddiness. Work came before play, even if his work *was* play. His harp was in tune, and his audience was clamoring for another song.

Casting another charming smile about, he placed his fingers upon the strings. Any good Bard could loosen lips with the right ditty. He needed a song that would get folks in the right mindset for chattering about local legends.

"How about one of my own compositions? This one's about a vengeful spirit returning from beyond the veil of death to protect his family from bandits. Might want to order a round of that Ghost Cider to go with it!"

The silence that plummeted over him did not ring or vibrate or anticipate. It utterly stifled. Simen's smile faltered. His fingers twitched discordantly against the strings.

His jolly audience had turned dour and, dare he say, angry. Their cheeks no longer rounded like plump apples, but instead hung slack and gray with—yes, that was fury right there, right in the tavern keeper's flinty eyes as he approached Simen where he sat before the fire.

"Uh," Simen said. "Have I done aught to offend?"

"If ye kin't respec' th' dead, ye kin fin' sommer else t' sing."

The tavern keeper didn't give Simen a bare moment to consider this ultimatum before grabbing a fistful of Simen's scarlet sleeve and lifting him from the stool.

"Wait, wait! My good man, what about my room?"

"Ye kin fin' sommer else t' sleep, too. Sure ye'll fin' like-minded folk down yon *spook mill.*"

And thus, stammering like a child before a solo performance, Simen found himself deposited outside in the dark of night and the rising wind of an oncoming storm, clutching his harp to his chest.

The tavern door closed with a sharp thud.

"Hey!" Simen called, spinning to pound at the door. "My harp case! I won't have you damaging—"

The door opened, and the harp case tumbled out to bang against Simen's shins. Before he could utter a sound, either of pain or of indignation, the door snapped closed again.

"Well!" Simen huffed, bending to pick up the case. He brushed a bit of dirt off it, then swiftly detuned his harp strings and slipped the instrument inside. At least *that* was still safe and sheltered.

The wind ruffled his hair as he straightened his shirt. A hint of dampness in the air underlined the certainty of stormy weather.

Simen let a wide smile spread over his face. How exciting! He'd never been bodily tossed from a tavern before. And though he would prefer a happy audience to an irate one, any reaction was better than indifference for an entertainer.

Oh, there was *definitely* a story to sniff out here in Orchard Lake.

And where there's a story . . .

Lightning flashed on the horizon, drawing his eye toward the hulking buildings at the lake, the acres of trees bearing valuable fruit, and the light and activity still blazing down at the cider mill.

Where there's a story, there might be a ghost!

Simen hitched his harp case over his shoulder and started down the road.

A tang of inclement weather hung in the night air, and flickers of distant lightning lit the clouds along the horizon.

Inevitably, irritatingly, Kimfer's mind jumped from lightning to Herald Marli, then from Herald Marli to the firm, unbreachable barrier that stood between his way of life and hers.

Not for the first time, he wondered what she would think of his employment here, driving wagon tours at the Ghost Mill. He didn't *want* to wonder, but his traitorous brain supplied the thought anyway. It must be part and parcel with their . . . *situation* as an unwillingly lifebonded pair, along with his undeniable need to be with her, which had driven him to quit the bandit life and find gainful employment in return for a chit of recommendation.

That, or it was some witch-power spell she'd set upon him before they'd parted ways last winter.

Was she thinking about him as often and as unwillingly as he was thinking about her? He didn't like the tingle that accompanied the thought: half-fearful, half-wishing. And every time it happened, he could swear he heard the faint chiming of the stupid little bell he'd taken from her witch horse's bridle.

Idiotic thing to have done, that.

Kimfer was no stranger to death, having lived as a bandit after losing his holderkin family to fire. Nor was he unfamiliar with those who wouldn't show proper respect for the dead. He'd bitten his tongue a time or three while the big men he had followed cackled over screams, then he'd simply packed his meager things and left in the night. Easy enough to move on when you lived outside the law. He worked better alone, anyhow.

But things were different when you were living straight. A job was not a thing to abandon on a whim, especially for someone with his unsavory history, no matter how cheeky the boss's mockery of death became.

It doesn't get much cheekier than turning a tragedy into a pile of coin.

He twitched the wagon team's ribbons to turn them along the path through the orchard. As the sleepy pair of horses pulled the wagon out of the closeness of the trees, his passengers chattered amongst themselves, recounting the eerie sights and sounds they'd witnessed on the Ghost Ride.

Kimfer did his best to shut his ears against them. At least in his role as "Demonic Wagon Driver" he wasn't expected to speak, merely to point ominously to where each batch of fright-seeking fancy folk ought to look. He wasn't expected to tromp around on the supposedly haunted ground of the old mill, either, which was fine with him. His cartloads of guests might whine at being forced to remain in the wagon, but Kimfer had grown up with enough stories about spooks and haunts to keep him happily on this side of the veil. If there *were* true ghosts here at the Ghost Mill—not that he necessarily believed that, given his employer's showmanship—Kimfer wanted nothing to do with them.

Most nights, he kept himself distracted from such thoughts by envisioning how—if he were working as a bandit still—he would relieve these silly rich idiots of their valuable trinkets while they were distracted by the Ghost Ride.

But tonight's crop of passengers and their city-sharp accents pierced through his usual feigned deafness.

"D'you think the Sovvan Bard will turn up tonight? I heard he's been seen in town."

"Ooh, *that's* what we need to finish a perfect evening! A glass of Ghost Cider and the Sovvan Bard himself singing us to sleep."

"If we *can* sleep after that shriek from the mill. My skin is still crawling." The speaker rubbed his velvet-clad arms and gave an exaggerated shiver.

Kimfer ground his teeth out of reflex, but truly he couldn't deny that tonight's ghostly shriek as he'd driven his wagon around the base of the old mill house had been *piercing*, at the least. That part of the show had received some extra fine-tuning, it seemed of late. If it kept up, even a hardened man like himself would be hard-pressed to keep childhood stories from the forefront of his mind. Not to mention how, lately, driving past the old mill had brought on an uncomfortable sensation of being *looked at*.

Even he, hardened man that he was, was having trouble sleeping through the night.

For now, though, the evening's show was over. He directed the team to the new mill house and its brightly lit yard. There was activity about the place, though that wasn't unusual for the Ghost Mill at this time of night. Were those people clustered together hoping for their turn at the wagon ride? Or were they hounding a newly arrived Bard for other entertainment?

In answer, the *plink plink plink* of some stringed instrument rang out, the notes clashing in an eerie way.

Kimfer's passengers whooped and hollered to those waiting.

The wagon rattled to a halt, and the passengers spilled out. They and the other gathered thrill seekers grasped fresh mugs of cider and warm, apple-scented pastries, and generally made a nuisance of themselves.

Kimfer's stomach growled at the smells as he secured the wagon team, but his eye fell upon his employer.

Gaspard Heilin stood just on the edge of the pool of light, exuding both hospitable welcome and enigmatic otherworldliness. His old-fashioned dress hinted at an ability to commune with the past. His dark eyes glinted.

A curt movement of his head called his employee over for a private conference.

Kimfer slunk through the shadows toward Gaspard. Easy enough for a former bandit, as was the ability to quash his hunger and silence his empty stomach's grumbles.

By the time he reached Gaspard's side, the plinking notes had become a song, and the Bard's voice had lifted in a strong tenor. The listeners stomped along with the eerie rhythm.

Kimfer did his best to ignore the fanciful song. "Sir?"

"The Sovvan Bard has honored our little mill with his presence and has even suggested he might consider joining our merry band of entertainers! He must be given a behind-the-scenes tour tonight. I'd send my son out to do the honors, but he is indisposed. You'll oblige, won't you? There's money to be made from even a single Sovvan song inspired by our mill."

Special consideration for a like-minded artist, I guess.

Kimfer glanced at the sky, breathed in the growing scent of rain and lightning. Another stray thought for his bonded witch-woman tried to caress his mind like a gentle mist, but he shoved it away.

"Storm's comin' in."

Gaspard clapped a hand on Kimfer's shoulder. "All the more for atmosphere, yes?"

The hand on Kimfer's back became a gripping vice, and Gaspard's glinting eyes pinned him with obligation. Kimfer resisted the urge to squirm under that knowing look.

No one else will give a former bandit a chance, Gaspard had said when he'd hired Kimfer on. *I'm your only ticket to a life of respectability.*

A few raindrops flicked at Kimfer's face, and the unwanted yearning for Herald Marli grew stronger.

"Sir," Kimfer said.

"Good man. Show him all the little tricks we employ. He's sure to appreciate our theatricality. Perhaps he'll even have some pointers for improvement! Oh, but Kimfer," Gaspard said as Kimfer started toward the wagon.

Kimfer turned only his head to show he was listening.

"Don't let him poke around in the old mill. The place is quite dangerous for those not trained to work there, falling apart like it is. I'd have it fixed up, of course, except a repaired mill doesn't exactly look haunted. I'm sure he'll understand."

Gaspard's bright smile invited Kimfer to smile along, but Kimfer simply held his gaze a moment before nodding sharply. He didn't want to consider how one artist or another turned death and loss into coin, particularly.

He was glad of an excuse not to poke his nose into the old mill. He came from good holderkin stock. With those screams lately, good theater or not, here in this land of white-clad witch riders and demon horses, this was one line he was perfectly happy to keep his wagon wheels from crossing.

Simen's reception at the Ghost Mill's lantern-lit yard was much more the thing.

Though none of the patrons of the place—obviously wealthy, obviously not local—knew anything about any currently missing girl, they had plenty of theories to offer on the mysterious tragedy at the original mill. Sadly, theories were all they had, and quite fanciful ones, at that. As if Herald-Mage Vanyel had ever even heard of Orchard Lake, let alone rained his displeasure down on Karsite invaders at the site of the old mill!

Even mysterious Ghost Mill owner Gaspard Heilin had laughed at that one.

At least he'd gotten a delicious apple pastry and another mug of Ghost Cider out of his schmoozing. He'd done his duty toward Marli's request, was pleasantly full, had a cozy bed lined up in the new mill house, and was now ready to go on his own private Ghost Ride.

Of course, for the candlemark since Gaspard had introduced him to the exceedingly unfriendly driver Kimfer, Simen had also been nurturing a superb sense of mischief. Here he'd come looking for ghosts, and what did he stumble upon but the very man responsible for the haunted look poor Marli had sported since winter!

Oh, he hoped she chose to peek in on him during this wagon ride.

Rain fell in drips and drops, and the wagon lurched through

squelching patches of mud and sodden leaves, but Simen's pulse still beat an excited tempo. A grin stretched his cheeks so wide they ached.

Ghost time! Ghost time!

As if Kimfer knew Simen's sing-song thoughts, he scowled from under his soggy black hood as though he thought he could call lightning bolts down on Simen. He probably thought he was intimidating, and there was a certain roughness to his scruffy jawline and the angle of a nose that had clearly been broken in the past. But those eyes were too bright, even narrowed in distaste, to be anything other than handsome.

That handsomeness along with the grouchy glare reminded Simen of Dreyvin, and he felt the curve of his lips turn gentle. Simen certainly did have a type.

Too bad they were both spoken for.

"So," he said through his smile, "what do *you* know about the tragedy at the old mill?"

Kimfer's voice rumbled ominously. "I reckon you'll find out what's to know when we get there."

Simen tipped his harp case toward Kimfer. "Have you ever considered training as a minstrel? You've got a certain knack for showmanship."

Kimfer's face twisted as if a wave of indigestion had gripped his innards, but any answer was cut off by a lightning bolt crackling across the sky.

The purplish light flashed over the silhouette of the old mill just ahead of them, giving Simen a glimpse of dilapidated wood siding, sagging beams, broken bits of shale roofing, and the skeletal remains of the old waterwheel gaping like the slack mouth of a corpse.

"Wow," Simen said, breathlessly giddy. How spooky! Was it his imagination, or were there . . . *echoes* of that lightning flashing in the broken-out windows of the mill?

Kimfer made a throaty, dismissive sound.

Simen blinked furiously to bring his night vision back. But the flashes he thought he'd seen in the windows made no reappearance. Faintly, under the shush of the rain, came the creaking of old wood.

A line of lyric twirled about his brain like a vine searching for a trellis to latch onto.

The lightning flares, the timbers moan,

A spirit cries from time unknown . . .

Hmm. Something like that, anyway. It needed work.

"Nothing for it," he said. "Tie up the horses. Let's flush the ghosts out from hiding!"

Even before they approached the haunted mill, Kimfer felt exceedingly uncomfortable. The Bard was eye-catching in the way that would have prompted Kimfer to take him to bed—in the days before Kimfer had fallen under the witch-Herald's spell and thus lost all interest in such things with anyone other than *her*. The Bard—Simen—was also annoyingly giddy at the prospect of trespassing beyond the boundary between life and death. But worst of all, he had an unnerving way of staring at Kimfer, as if he *knew something* he shouldn't.

Then, the moment the wagon's wheels trundled onto the grounds of the old mill, the sensation of being *looked at* covered Kimfer like a shroud. His shoulder blades itched under his black cloak. He was inclined to have the team cart him and the irritating songster straight back to the yard.

"We're not leaving the wagon," Kimfer said instead of shaking the Bard by his flamboyant scarlet frills.

"Don't you want to know what happened here?"

"I know enough."

"*Do* you?" Simen's voice tilted up along with his eyebrows. "Then you've had more success than I in getting the locals to spill their secrets. I think a couple of outsiders like you and me ought to pool our knowledge."

Kimfer clamped down on a splutter. It didn't matter how the Bard knew he wasn't from Orchard Lake, despite Kimfer's best efforts to blend in. He squelched the desire to accept the *us* Simen had so easily offered. He didn't need anyone except his witch-woman, and even that was on sufferance.

"My knowledge is that we're staying in the wagon." Even if he wasn't uncomfortable with getting closer to the source of that *looked at* feeling, it was more than his job was worth to break Gaspard's rule.

"*You* can stay," the Bard was saying as he gripped the sides of the wagon. "I will be investigating."

Horror mounted as Kimfer watched his charge scramble over the side, harp case bouncing against his bony back. In a few rabbitlike bounds, Simen was well on his way toward ruining everything for Kimfer.

"Stop," he called. "Come back!"

But nature chose that moment to drown his voice out with a torrential sheet of rain and another crash of thunder. Kimfer's hood was plastered to his head in moments, and the horses shied nervously, making the wagon creak as they tried to back up.

Instantly, Kimfer's attention locked to the horses. If he couldn't soothe them, they were liable to bolt at the next crash of thunder. He clambered down from the bench, ran both hands along their steaming flanks, and reached for their bridles. Mud slopped over his boots.

Still, he couldn't ignore Simen. The prancing idiot was poking around the old waterwheel now as if it weren't a death trap waiting to collapse on the first hapless fool who stumbled into it. Gaspard might be willing to cross lines to make coin, but he was right enough to insist they keep away from the old mill.

The horses weren't calming. More lightning pulsed across the sky, and the horses reared, their eyes round and white in fear. The scent of fire and cold mud mingled into an odor ripe for frenzy.

And then the scream rent the air.

Kimfer's neck prickled. His muscles froze. Nobody was supposed to be working the old mill haunting at this time of night. The place was supposed to be empty.

He, so used to being predator, had never felt more like prey.

The horses broke from his hold. They disappeared into the orchard, screaming as well. The wagon crashed along behind them.

Fear coated Kimfer from head to toe. Losing the horses would mean getting the sack. Getting the sack meant no chit of recommendation for other jobs.

No chance at meeting his witch-woman as a man worthy of her company.

He lurched forward after the horses.

A third scream joined the others, sharp with pain. On reflex Kimfer turned.

The Bard was down in the mud, clutching his ankle. His mouth was no longer wide with excitement but drawn and gray in agony.

Kimfer's fear dissipated into fury, but he was already slogging along the thin track to reach the injured idiot before he had time to think.

So much for the horses.

Fury melted into crude determination as he set his shoulder beneath Simen's. Better to feel nothing, same as he'd done while watching other bandits give in to needless murder. He'd move on from the Ghost Mill just as he'd moved on from everything else.

Even the feeling of being *looked at* couldn't penetrate his numbness as he half-dragged the Bard over the threshold of the old mill. They could use the bare shelter the rotting pile of sticks provided. So long as they didn't breathe the wrong way, the place should stay standing.

Did he feel a tingle down his spine as he crossed that line? He didn't know. He was too numb to care.

"I'm okay, I'm okay," Simen panted. He swatted Kimfer's hands away, but Kimfer settled him against a leaning support beam before releasing him. He glanced into Simen's face, expecting to find it etched with lines of pain.

Instead, his eyes shone with boyish wonder. Kimfer watched in disbelief as his charge took in the dilapidated beams, the moldering machinery of the mill and the cider press, the curtains of cobwebs hanging from creaking rafters, the streaks of rust staining the stone floor. It was blacker in here than even the dark of night could account for. Something filmy coated what remained of the walls. It reeked of fire.

Simen brought his gaze back around to meet Kimfer's. He had the audacity to wink.

"Got you in here after all, didn't I?"

Anger flaring, Kimfer tugged the bottom of the Bard's trews up roughly, certain he'd find that ankle as pristine as a newborn babe's. Simen's pained yelp assured him the injury, at least, was real.

"Bright Lady, you're a rough healer," Simen said.

"Better rough than none at all."

"An idiom for life if I ever heard one. Say, do you hear that?"

Kimfer paused in his haphazard ministrations, fully alert as if he were back in the woods preparing to rob an unsuspecting traveler. The dull pound of rain and frequent growls of thunder reverberated incessantly. Underneath that came the soft groans and moans of an ancient building about to fall down around their ears.

"I don't hear anything," he said. But he felt that sense again, those phantom eyes staring at him.

Except, this time it wasn't a feeling of being looked *at* so much as being looked *past*. As if a conversation partner were staring hard at something just over his shoulder.

He resisted the urge to glance back himself.

Satisfied that the Bard's ankle was in as good shape as he could get it, he rose to his feet. Hopefully the Bard could manage to stay put while Kimfer slogged through the storm to reach the new mill and get help.

Quick as lightning the Bard wrapped his fingers around Kimfer's own ankle tight enough to leave marks.

"Listen!"

Kimfer listened. From somewhere overhead came a snuffling,

sniffing sound, then a metallic clink like a chain being disturbed. Kimfer wanted to believe it belonged to some animal seeking shelter from the storm.

The pounding of his heart told him differently. He managed, with effort, to tear his gaze away from the sagging loft.

A high moan—it couldn't be mistaken for the groaning of ancient wood or the cries of some critter—set the cobwebs swaying.

Now the Bard's strong tenor voice became a thin whisper. "There's someone . . . some*thing* in here!"

Oh ho, so now *you've got a healthy fear of ghosts.*

"Whatever it is, we don't mean it no harm." Thankfully, Kimfer's voice came out steady despite the tightness of his throat. "If we just keep to ourselves and don't bother it, we should—"

"Burrrniiiiing! Daddy, noooo!"

A cold deeper than that of the storm-drenched clothes on Simen's back turned his normally limber muscles as stiff as drying clay. The disintegrating timbers reverberated in heart-sickening harmonics, until the entire building throbbed in time with the spirit's anguish. The throbbing in the beam he leaned against pulsed into his body horrifically, but he was powerless to move away, let alone to stop it.

A child's scream, and one that went on and on as if an entire choir were staggering their breathing to sustain the single, fearful note. It made Simen speed up his own breaths to compensate, until his head felt light and sparks flew at the edges of his vision. That voice couldn't belong to a living child, not with that rippling, pain-rent quality to it.

Simen knew he'd found a real ghost this time.

Bright Lady, I wish I hadn't!

Standing at Simen's side, Kimfer shouted, "Don't look at it! It'll pull us across to its side of death."

Funny, Simen had never believed such superstition before. Now he wanted to lift his hands to his eyes, but his arms wouldn't work. He could only hum in dissonance with the throb of the building.

If they didn't get out of there fast, the entire place would collapse upon them.

Kimfer, at least, retained his motor functions. He grabbed Simen roughly and lifted him. Simen felt muscles like overtuned harp strings coil around his shoulders. His ankle hurt, but he barely noticed.

Together, they hobbled fast toward the sheet of rain beyond the open door.

The door slammed closed as they approached.

Simen's heart seized hard as a rock.

Maybe the spirit knew about all his irreverent ghost songs. Maybe it was his own father, furious at Simen for using his death to entertain strangers.

I'll never write another!

The childlike screaming rose in pitch. It was behind them, chasing them, coming to boil their blood. An acrid smell of smoke curled under Simen's nose.

Kimfer, rigid as iron, turned them to face the ghost.

Simen clapped both hands over his eyes. "*What are you doing?*"

"I'm not afraid of death. If this ghost pulls me over, I swear I'll cross right back. I've got a more important boundary to jump than this flimsy thing, and I'll jump it if it takes a hundred jobs in a hundred haunted mills, and—"

As if he'd suddenly realized he'd forgotten something, he stilled, his arms slipping away from Simen.

Simen peered up at Kimfer, sure he'd find the man drooling from ghostly possession.

Instead, Kimfer wore a serene expression as he stared into his open hand.

A tiny silver bell lay on his palm.

Marli.

Her eyes were on him. He responded to that look and strained to look back. He couldn't quite see her. The brief contact was like a trickle of water to a parched man: tantalizing and sweet and too soon dried up. But the taste lingered, and he could breathe again. He could act on practical thought rather than terrified reflex.

He'd never expected *she* would be the first one to reach across the barrier between their worlds. Or was it that, in defying his fear of crossing into death, he'd managed to reach out to meet her halfway?

Either way, she'd used her witch powers to move his stolen bell from his belongings in the new house straight into his hand. However briefly, she'd touched his mind with hers. He grasped the message immediately.

This was no ghost.

The child was still screaming. The heat inside the mill had grown to an unbearable swelter. Out of the corners of his eyes Kimfer kept catching flickers of a fire he knew wasn't there.

The Bard clung to him, trying to favor his ankle. Fear still shone in his youthful face. "Come on! Before the ghost—before it—before—"

Kimfer swallowed the urge to smile. He wasn't ready to get that friendly yet.

"It's not a ghost," he said. "It's someone with witch powers. One of your Herald types."

And despite everything my folk taught me, a Herald's powers are nothing to be afraid of.

"It's not? I mean, it is?" Simen glanced around with his eyes wide. Comprehension dawned.

"Projected Mind-magic. None of this is really happening. This poor kid can't control her gift."

Kimfer didn't know what that meant other than a kid was in trouble.

In a slick maneuver that would put many a light-fingered bandit to shame, Simen whipped his harp out of its case and set his fingers to the strings.

"Hold me up while I play," he said, leaning on Kimfer's shoulder.

At first, Kimfer didn't see how a song could help, especially from the Sovvan Bard. Wouldn't a song about ghosts only distress the child more?

But the song that flowed from Simen's fingers was happy and bright rather than dark and eerie, and the words came in the cadence of nursery tunes.

"Ground and center, my love, center and ground.
Then your place in this world you'll have felt and
have found . . ."

The notes floated through the heated darkness, smothering the images of flames and shushing the child's screaming, until finally the snuffling, sniffing sound Kimfer had heard earlier returned. Hearing it now, it was obvious it belonged to a frightened child.

He eased Simen to the floor, then pointed at the loft. Simen nodded, but didn't stop his song.

It took some upper body strength and some light steps up a ladder that had more empty spaces than rungs, but Kimfer soon reached the top. The spiderwebs were thick as cotton here, and the dark streaks of ancient soot blackened his hands and knees.

Gaspard Heilin's small daughter lay on the loft floor, her legs chained to the wall where a gut-twisting soot-shadow of a burned child was all she could look at.

She trembled with sobs as Kimfer pulled the rusting chains free of the rotted wall. "Did Daddy say I don't have to play with the burning children anymore?" she hiccupped.

Outside, the pounding storm had become a soft, steady hiss of rain.

With the girl cradled in one arm, Kimfer brought the both of them back across to the world of the living.

"She has a kind of Foresight, but more like . . . Pastsight. She looks into the past of a location rather than the future," said Herald Pell after examining little Lillia Heilin. He'd arrived mere moments after the storm had broken, riding on an urgent call for aid from Herald Marli. His Companion had been so coated in mud it took several poundings on the door to convince the Heilin family that a Herald truly had come to call.

Bard Simen, his wrapped ankle propped on a pillow before the fireplace, nodded. "And because she's had no training, she couldn't stop herself from projecting what she saw onto others. Hence, everyone who came close enough got a glimpse of the fire that gutted the old mill and of the child who—"

His boyish face hardened as he looked to where Gaspard, his wife, and his older son stood trussed and quivering under Herald Pell's watchful gaze.

Kimfer tightened his arms around Lillia, who snuggled against his shoulder as if she'd known him all her short life. She'd become quite attached to him, literally.

Herald Pell made a sound of disgust at Gaspard and took his arm none too gently. "We'll get you nice and settled in the town's lockup, then deal with your trial in the morning. I'll be back to discuss Lillia's education."

He marched out, shoving the Heilin family ahead of him.

A moment passed, then Simen let out a theatrical sigh.

"So much for my ghost hunt. I thought I'd found a real one this time."

Kimfer stroked Lillia's hair. "That depends on your definition of real. And of ghost."

"At least it'll make for a great song!"

Lillia smiled. Kimfer felt it against his collarbone.

She'd have to go to Haven, his little boundary crosser. She needed to learn to protect herself from her own witch powers. Maybe one day she'd even bond with her own demon horse, just like Marli.

And perhaps, he was ready to cross into that world with her.

The Beating the Bounds

Fiona Patton

"Sort it out, son."

"Right, Da."

"Da?"

"Sort it out, Lance Constable."

"Right, Sarge."

"Wha . . . ?"

"Sort it out . . ."

Bells.

Bells?

Bells. Dawn. Bed. Dream. Only a dream.

Corporal Aiden Dann of the Haven City Watch awoke, the sound of his father's voice fading with the sound of the capital's call to the new day. He lay still, using the deep, even breathing of his wife, Sulia, asleep beside him, to unloose the tendrils of the past and anchor him in the present.

At the foot of the bed, their twin sons, Thomar and Preston, twitched and snuffled in their sleep, their tiny movements rocking the cradle he'd built for them back and forth with a faint crick, crick. There was nothing else to be heard; outside, the capital was only beginning to stir and inside . . .

Only a dream.

Rising, he pulled on his blue and gray uniform before slipping from the room.

In the tiny, second bedroom, their eldest son, five-and-a-half-year-old Egan, and two-and-a-half-year-old daughter, Leila, sprawled across rather than lay in their beds. He retrieved Leila's blanket and Egan's stuffed dog from the floor, tucked them back where they belonged, pressed a kiss to each forehead, then closed the door softly behind him. Everything was well. Everyone was safe.

Always the watchman.

Well, yeah. So why . . . ?

"Sort it out, son."

The third bedroom was empty. His younger brothers, Jakon and Raik, both night constables, wouldn't be home for at least an hour. By then, the noise and clamour of four littles greeting the day with enough energy to deafen the neighborhood would have died down sufficiently for them to get some sleep. And by then, Aiden himself would be well into his own shift, waiting impatiently, if he were honest, for Sulia to bring him his noon meal, littles in tow, as his mother had done for his father, and his granny for his granther, inserting a moment of family into the workday, reminding them why they did it and why they should do it well.

He stared past the shuttered window to the pale strip of sunlight beyond.

Do it well? The beating of the bounds was tomorrow, and how was he supposed to do that well now that Egan, so like his mother, kind and cheerful, was old enough to be there to see him do it?

He glanced down the hall at his son's door.

The beating of the bounds was a ceremony almost as old as the city of Haven itself. Every five years, the watchmen of each jurisdiction marched in procession along their ancient boundaries, a crowd of littles, usually their own, trotting along behind them, chattering, laughing, and learning about the city, their city, and the small part of it that their fathers, uncles, and brothers were responsible for, the part they too would be responsible for in the future. A festive day; one to look forward to, or most of it, anyway.

"Sort, it out, son."

Aiden's father had died in a fire two years ago; gone so suddenly that it had left the family reeling. Sergeant Egan Dann had been a taciturn man with a legendary temper. Aiden was the same. But he'd sworn that day he was not going to be like that with his own littles. When he died, there wasn't going to be any words left unsaid. They were going to be the right words, and his actions were going to be the right actions.

But how he was going to manage that, he had no idea.

Turning, he heard Thomar and Preston greeting the day with their customary screaming, and he headed back up the hall to help Sulia.

An hour later, whistling a nonsense song Leila had sung to the twins to get them to eat breakfast, he took the steps of the Iron Street Watch House two at a time.

Usually filled with gossiping Watchmen, the main hall was surprisingly hushed this morning, and his mood grew serious as he spotted Corporal Hydd Thacker holding court at the Duty Officer's desk instead of Night Sergeant Jons. The older man looked haggard.

"Broke his foot late last night," he explained to Aiden's silent question. "Jaz Poll came in on his usual drunk an' disorderly and had some kinda fit halfway down the stairs. Took the Sarge to the bottom with 'im. Jons says he'll only be off a day or two . . ."

Both Hydd and Aiden shared a snort.

"Doc says it'll be more like a week or two," Hydd continued. "His missus says he oughta retire."

"Oughta?"

Hydd shrugged, but allowed a slight smile to lighten his usually scowling countenance. "Her words were a touch more definite and a lot spicier when she came to collect him, I'll grant you. Much like mine were when I was roused from my bed to take 'is place."

"I'll bet."

"Doc had a look at Jaz, too. He reckons he had a stroke."

Hydd's voice quieted. "He's in a bad way, Aiden. He's really weak and can't hardly talk. Doc figures he's gonna die. Probably some time this mornin'. Sarge wanted to send for Holly, but Jaz said no. Just about blew 'is top when Jons pressed 'im. Still has some life in him, I guess, the stubborn old fool."

Hydd sniffed, not unkindly, and Aiden echoed it. Most of the Iron Street Watchmen had known Jaz Poll their entire working lives. His drunken brawls were the stuff of legend, as were his wife's reactions.

"Nessa took 'im some porridge earlier, but he can't eat," Hydd continued. "The night shift's been down to pay their respects. I reckon the day shift'll wanna do the same. You're the first in." He jerked his head towards the stairs. "See if you can get 'im to send for Holly. I wouldn't wanna do it behind 'is back, but . . ."

"On it."

As cells went, Iron Street's were neither the best nor the worse in Haven, but the Night Watch had clearly done what they could to make their old guest more comfortable. Jaz lay in the center cell, wrapped in a cocoon of blankets and shawls, two pillows under his head and one under his feet. A lantern had been set just outside the open door, casting a warm light across the cell, revealing a number of cups and earthenware bottles lined up like tributes beside the uneaten porridge. His face was ghastly pale, the right side drooping as though it were made of melted candle wax. His eyes were closed, but they fluttered open when Aiden approached.

"Hey, Jaz."

The left side of the old man's face turned up in a familiar grimace. "S'mister Poll, ta you . . . rozer," he whispered.

Aiden gave a soft snort of laughter, then sobered. "You sure we can't send for Holly? Don't you think you oughta have your wife with you?"

Jaz shook his head. "Don . . . wan . . . 'er ta see me like this," he struggled. "Wan' 'er to remember me . . . strong."

Aiden shook his head. "How could she remember you as anything else?" he asked. "But still, don't you think she's gonna want to say . . . I dunno, goodbye or somethin'?"

Jaz smiled faintly. "Been 'spectin' this awhile. Won' come as no surprise . . . Let 'er sleep."

He beckoned the younger man over with a weak jerk of his head. "Gotta give you somethin'," he wheezed. "Was gonna give it to Cal Jons, but . . . the fool got hisself injured tryin' ta . . . fall on me." He fumbled through the layers, then gave up, his face twisted in pain. "Fetch it."

Aiden moved the blankets and shawls as gently as he could, then reached into Jaz's pocket, pulling out a thin strip of faded burgundy cloth.

"Gotta go back . . ." the old man whispered. "Back ta hang with the rest . . . You take it."

"Take it where?"

Annoyance crossed the older man's face but then he sighed. "Old . . . Clock . . ."

"Old Clock? The pub?"

Out of breath with the effort those few words had taken, Jaz just nodded.

Aiden frowned. "You know I can't go in there. No one goes in there. No one who isn't . . . old, anyway."

Jaz's brows drew down, too weak to take full umbrage at this disrespectful comment. "Ribbon'll . . . get you in," he grated. "Give ta . . . the barman." He let out a ragged breath, his eyelids closed, fluttered, then opened again with obvious difficulty.

"Gotta go back," he muttered. "Always goes back . . ."

He let out another ragged breath. His eyes closed again. Aiden waited but then, as the old man's face slowly took on the waxy pallor he'd seen far too many times on the faces of the dead, he nodded.

"The street won't be the same without you," he said quietly. Stuffing the ribbon into his pocket, he headed back upstairs.

His youngest brother, Padriec, the watch house's Chief Runner, hovered by the Duty Officer's desk. Aiden gestured him over. "Fetch Holly Poll, Paddy," he told him. "Tell her her man's passed."

The boy nodded and darted off.

Hydd gave a deep sigh. "Well, that's it then," he said. "I'd say that's how he mighta wanted to go out, but more likely he'd of rather died in a punch up."

He turned back to the desk, straightening the night's reports. "An' there's business to attend to. Always business, no matter who leaves us. Speakin' of that, the beatin' of the bounds is tomorrow. With yer da gone, an' me stuck here for who knows how long, that leaves you in charge of it."

Aiden blinked. "Why me?"

"You're the senior Corporal next to me."

"Really. How'd that happen?"

Hydd snorted. "No idea. I look at you an' all I see is a snot-nosed Sweeper fallin' over 'is own feet. Still, I guess everyone grows up eventually. You know where all the markers are. You oughta, you've been out four times now. Just lead the procession, point 'em out to the littles, make a note if any need to be repaired, and carry on. It's not hard."

"And the ones that aren't there?"

Hydd shrugged. "They always turn up. Just sort it out. And try not to break any heads doin' it," he added darkly. "The patch knows what to expect. They just like to pull our chains from time to time. It's not a crime; it's just a nuisance."

"Right."

"Sort it out, son."

"Oh, an' yer brother wants a word."

"Right."

Aiden's younger brother, Hektor, the Watch House Day Sergeant, stood by the door of his office. He caught Aiden's eye, pulled out his pipe, and gestured toward the main doors. Assuming he wanted to talk about Jaz, Aiden nodded.

Outside, the two men leaned against the wall at the top of the steps where hundreds of watchmen had leaned before them where they could be both on duty and off at the same time.

"So," Hektor began, gazing up the street, "Hydd says you're in charge of the beatin' of the bounds this year."

Aiden shrugged. "'Parently. Unless you want it."

"Nope."

"Figures."

"I was thinkin' about the markers, though. How not all of 'em are always where they're s'posed to be."

Aiden gave a snort of derisive laughter.

"An' how that usually slows us down on procession day."

"That's one way of puttin' it."

"So, I thought," Hektor continued, "why don't you go round an' check on 'em today."

Aiden gave him a puzzled look. "Today?"

"Yeah. That way, if there's a problem, like one's missin' or blocked, you can sort it out today instead of tomorrow."

"But . . . the procession's still tomorrow, right?"

"Right. But this way there won't be any surprises or violence tomorrow."

"Hm." Aiden took a drag on his pipe, filling the air between them with a cloud of aromatic smoke. "This come from you or the Captain?" he asked. Iron Street's new commander had originally come from the Breakneedle Street Watch House, an entire social stratum away, where things were likely *sorted out* in a more . . . genteel manner than was common on Iron Street.

"From me."

Aiden considered the idea, trying to give his admittedly far more diplomatic brother the benefit of the doubt. "I could," he began. "We jus' . . . never have before. We jus' proceeded an' dealt with any trouble at the time."

"I remember. But there's no real reason why it has to be that way every year, is there?"

"No . . . I suppose not. Huh. I wonder why no one's ever tried that before."

"Maybe 'cause folks like seein' a punch up in the middle of the street," Hektor answered dryly.

Aiden gave his brother a shrewd look. "You're thinkin' about Ned Carter, aren't you?"

"Partly."

Ned's family were costermongers, running a barrow at the corner of Chandler's Row and Cutler Street. Ned's granther had set up shop directly on the boundary marker between the Iron Street and Water Street jurisdictions, and he would not be moved, not for one hour, not for five minutes. Neither would his son, neither would his grandson. From the time he'd been a brand-new Lance Constable. Aiden had been called on to sort it out on procession day the way his father and his father before him had, with his fists; three generations of Carters and Danns punching it up in the street like a couple of gangs.

"Mostly I was thinkin' you'll be bringin' Egan this year, yeah?"

"I was thinkin' about it. He's been after me for a week now to let 'im come. He is old enough."

"And I hear Ned's got a little of his own too, almost the same age, named Gus . . ."

Hektor let the sentence hang.

Aiden stared into the past for a long moment. *Three generations of Carters and Danns.* Three not four. Not yet. And maybe not ever, if Hektor's idea worked. He nodded. "I'll get on it."

Tapping his pipe clean against the wall, he headed down the steps. "*Besides,*" he thought, his fingers brushing against the burgundy ribbon in his pocket as he put his pipe away, "*I've got something to do up the street, anyway.*"

He nearly walked right past his destination a few moments later, deep in thought. The Old Clock Tavern, or The Old Coot Pub, as the younger denizens of Iron Street had always called it, was a narrow establishment squeezed between a pie shop and a locksmith in what had once been the entrance to Clock Close. Entry was by membership and invitation only, and it seemed mostly to be restricted to persons at least forty years old. It had a painted frieze over the thick wooden door, so faded now that no one knew what it had once depicted, and a small recess in the right side of the jamb containing a carved stone clock, a gift, it was said, from one of the founding members.

Most people ignored it. Goods went in the back, and members came and went through the front. It was quiet and private. The Watch had never been called in to mediate so much as an argument. Aiden had to assume that since obviously Jaz Poll had been a member, they must have had a pretty stern method of keeping order. Jaz could've started a brawl in an empty street at midnight.

He took a step forward, then hesitated. As he'd told Jaz, no one went in the Old Coot Pub unless you were . . . *an old coot*, his ten-year-old self pronounced, *not even on a dare.* As littles, he and his friends had speculated on the decor: shawls, canes, the smell of camphor and fish oil. As youths, they'd speculated on the fare: mushy vegetables, weak soup, and weaker beer. And later, they hadn't speculated at all. Families, work, weather, and too many other things had taken over their adult lives. The Old Coot Pub had faded into the background along with all the other things they no longer had time for. Now . . .

Now a belligerent old man had asked him to go in there. Asked him to sort it out.

Aiden turned away. Later. He'd go later. For now, other things were still more important.

Running along Harp Way, which paralleled Iron Street to the north, the first eight markers were exactly as they should be, set into the cobblestones at each intersecting corner. The ninth . . .

Jay and Annie Dell ran a tiny apothecary shop just up from the Iron Market grounds in Grass Court. Their marker had been one of the few officially relocated half a century ago when a royal surveyor had determined that its actual site should be two feet to the west, from just below their main window to directly in front of their shop door. After three customers had tripped over it, Jay had received permission to dig it up provided it *never left the premises* and *was replaced for the beating of the bounds.* Neither Jay nor Annie were one of those who *just liked to rattle our chain* as Hydd had put it. On the contrary, they took their duty to keep it safe very seriously. The problem was that it tended to move. Some years it would be found under the bed, other years in the pantry ,and once in the cellar, so buried under decades of old furniture and miscellaneous trunks and boxes that it had taken nearly an hour to dig it out.

And the Dells liked to *visit.* That took even longer.

Bracing himself for the flood of words to come, Aiden pushed the door open, the tiny jingle of bells above his head betraying his presence.

"Why, Corporal Dann, what a pleasant surprise!" Jay Dell bustled out from behind the overflowing counter, his thin face beaming. "We weren't expecting you until tomorrow. This isn't anything too official, I hope. Nothing wrong? Of course, we heard about Jaz Poll. Sad that. Poor Holly."

"No, it's just—"

"Because Annie hasn't even begun the tarts yet, you see, and you know how much the littles look forward to Annie's tarts. What can I do for you today?"

"About the marker—"

"Why, Aiden Dann don't you look handsome." Annie joined her husband, her expression as pleased as his. "How are the family? Everyone well? And two new babies last year, Sulia must have her hands full, but such a joyous handful, of course. We've had a new grandbaby ourselves this spring, you know."

"Yes . . ."

"Corporal Dann's come about the marker, my dear."

"The marker? That's not today, is it?"

"No, ma'am, it's—" Aiden started.

"Oh, that's a relief. I thought I'd gotten the days all muddled up. I do now and again. Not as young as I once was."

"Nonsense, my love, you're as young as the day I met you."

"It's tomorrow," Aiden managed to squeeze in when both

husband and wife paused to smile at each other. "I just thought we might find it today. That would save, uh . . . all of us tramping through your house . . . tomorrow."

"Oh, we don't mind, do we, Jay?"

"Not at all. Anything to oblige the Watch, but we can dig it up today, certainly. Now . . ." The apothecary turned in a slow circle in the center of the crowded room. "Where did it go?"

"In the workshop dear? Under the heal-all plant?"

"No, no. I moved it last week when Dirk Bakker came in with a toothache, remember?"

"Oh, yes . . ."

"Never fret. You just take the Corporal back to the kitchen and make him a cuppa while I conduct a search. Won't be a tick."

As it turned out, it was closer to hand than expected, propping up a set of shelves, piled high with ceramic jars, behind the counter. After helping Jay replace the leg, Aiden set the marker just inside the door, elicited a promise from the couple that they wouldn't move it again until after tomorrow, and made his escape.

Four markers at each corner of the Iron Market were easily accessible, a bit dusty. The fifth . . .

"So, you built a chicken coop on it?"

Brody Drove owned one of the largest and oldest shops on Poultry Row, which ran along beside the market grounds to the south. The marker had decorated the wall surrounded his pens out back for as long as the family business had been there. This year, however . . .

The shopkeeper scratched his head. "Well, no, not exactly on it, more like alongside it. We wanted to go into eggs as well as meat this year, and while my youngest was fixin' the coop to the stone, the marker kinda jus' . . . fell out."

"Fell out?"

"Well, the mortar has to be a couple of centuries old, if not older. We were going to reset it, but we haven't had the time, and now . . ."

The two men stared at the very large blue and green cockerel standing sentinel on the marker in the middle of the coop, giving each man a baleful glare of warning. "He's powerful protective of 'is hens," Brody explained. "Only the wife can get around him to collect the eggs, you see. Anyone else and he goes right for 'em. Better'n a guard dog. Anyway, she's not here. She's at her auntie's for the day."

Aiden returned the bird's dark gaze with one of his own and could have sworn the creature's eyes narrowed. "She gonna be back tomorrow?" he asked, watching one huge, spurred foot scuff the marker in obvious challenge.

"Should be." The briefest hint of a smile flashed across Brody's face. "You want us to bring the marker out to you tomorrow, or just have the missus hold the beast at bay while you go inside?"

"I'd like you to reset it in the wall by then," Aiden answered, wondering how Hektor would have handled this. "As long as we can see it, we won't need to . . . trespass on His Lordship's territory."

The smile became a full out grin. "I'll get my boys on it as soon as she gets back, Corporal."

"Thank you, sir."

Two more markers along Poultry Row, then down Measure Street and . . .

"Are you certain it isn't next door?"

Aiden sighed. "No, Missus Grey. It was right here where this board is coverin' up the hole." He glanced over at the line of traders coming and going through the front door of the large Lorimer shop. "Movin?" he asked as pleasantly as he could.

"No," she answered, her tone distinctly frosty. "My brother and I are cleaning out some of our mother's old things. She passed last year, as you might remember."

"Yes, ma'am. Problem is, five years ago it *accidentally* got sold to Martin Chambers down the street when your father passed, and five years before that, to Carrie Tanner when you were enacting repairs."

"Your point?"

"It's a royal boundary marker, ma'am. It's supposed to stay put."

She gave him a belligerent look but turned. "Wes, you got that hunk of stone? The Watch is here for it."

There was a scuffle from inside the shop, and after a few moments her brother appeared with it in his arms, two traders trailing after him looking decidedly put out.

"Right here," he said sullenly. "T'was in the way, that's all."

Aiden pointed at the hole. Once Wes had replaced the marker, he made a note to have someone come back and mortar it properly into place and left, Missus Grey's eyes boring a hole in the back of his head.

Two more markers, then Chandler's Row and Ned Carter's barrow.

Aiden had known Ned his whole life. They'd been to the temple school together when they were littles. They hadn't been friends, but they hadn't been enemies either. Not then. The two five-year-olds had been wildly excited about the upcoming beating of the bounds. Aiden was going to be in the procession for the first time, Ned was going to be helping with his granther's barrow. The day had started with all the pomp and ceremony Aiden had expected, and it had ended with his father and his Uncle Daz mixing it up in the street with Roy and Gus Carter, Ned's father and granther. The next week, both boys had been sent home from school three times for fighting. Five years later, the two ten-year-olds had taken one look at each other and started the brawl their fathers had ended up finishing. Five years after that . . .

"Sort it out, Lance Constable."

And five years again . . .

"Sort it out, Corporal."

And now . . .

"It's not a crime; it's just a nuisance."

Ned saw him coming and came out from behind his barrow, arms crossed.

"Dann."

"Carter."

"You come to dance?" Ned asked.

"Nope, just to talk."

"Doesn't sound like you. Why?"

Aiden glanced down the street, ignoring the line of costermongers to either side making no pretense of minding their own business.

"I figure it's about time."

"I figure it's about twenty years past time."

"Maybe, but there's nothing we can do about that. I've come to ask you to set up your barrow to one side tomorrow so we can come and check the marker and move on."

Ned blinked in surprise. "Wha . . ." He opened his mouth two or three times, narrowed his eyes, then cocked his head to one side. "Why the sudden change?"

Aiden sighed. He'd spent the entire day trying to come up with the right words, now he settled on honesty. "I got a son, Egan. He's five. He'll be with me tomorrow. He looks up to me to do the right thing, an' the right thing ain't using yer fists when it ain't called for. I want 'im to learn that."

"An' it ain't called for here?" Ned's voice dripped with sarcasm, but Aiden just shook his head.

"No. You're a businessman. I'm a Watchman. If you got robbed, I'd come when you called. So would a Water Street watchman, for that matter," he added dryly. "You're in both jurisdictions."

"Water Street sends a runner crawlin' under the cart to check the marker," Ned pointed out.

"Yeah, that's not gonna happen."

"Too good to get a little dust on your fancy uniforms?"

"Somethin' like that. Too good to let your neighbors see you do as yer told?"

Ned's eyes narrowed again. "Something very much like that, yeah."

"An' that's why I'm askin'—not tellin'—you to set up different in the mornin', not to move in front of everyone."

"An' that wouldn't be the same thing?"

"No. Askin' ain't tellin'. It's askin'."

"And if I don't, what happens then?"

Aiden met his eyes. "I've honestly got no idea, Ned. But I've got a son. I hear you've got one too. I don't want have to go to their school tomorrow 'cause they took up a fight their fathers didn't even start. I want to show my boy the boundaries of his patch, then take him for sweets before givin' 'im back to his ma. I want 'im to grow up to be 'is own man."

Ned stared out at the street for a long time. "Gus's been after me for a month to let 'im come watch the procession tomorrow," he allowed after a while. "His ma doesn't want 'im to. Can't hardly blame 'er, really. Now my da's dead. Granther, too."

"So're mine."

Ned turned back to Aiden. "All right," he said finally. "I set up to one side of the marker tomorrow, you come, an' you go. That's all. Anything's said, all bets are off."

"Fair enough."

"Now, if you don't mind, Watchman, you're drivin' away trade."

Aiden turned, and after nodding darkly to the growing crowd of onlookers, he left.

That was all he could do. The rest would be up to Ned.

At the steps to his family's tenement house, he glanced down the street. He couldn't see The Old Clock Tavern from here, but he could feel it . . . waiting.

"Tomorrow. I'll do it tomorrow."

That evening, he sat in his chair after supper with Egan tucked up beside him and Leila bouncing on his lap as she sang a long and complicated song of her own devising about mice. When she finished, she accepted their applause before raising her arms to her mother, who'd just appeared in the doorway.

"The twins are down," Sulia said, taking her up. "You're next, little sparrow. And you, young man," she added, fixing Egan with a stern eye. "Ten minutes. No more."

"Yes, Ma. Da, what's that?"

"Hm?" Aiden started, realizing he'd been absently rubbing Jaz's ribbon between finger and thumb. "Jus' somethin' someone gave to me for safe keepin' today." He held it up for the boy's inspection.

"I've gots one of those too," Egan declared.

Aiden looked down at him in surprise. "You do?"

"Uh-huh. In my box. You wanna see it?"

"I do. Um . . ." Aiden glanced up at Sulia. She returned father and son's equally hopeful looks with a frown of her own, then, as their expressions became plaintive, she relented. "All right, go and fetch it. But quickly, mind. And quietly."

Egan leaped from the chair, evoking a grunt from his father as one pointy fist pushed off from his lap.

"He's getting big," he noted. Sulia chuckled.

Egan was back almost at once, cradling a small wooden box in his hands. Aiden glanced at the painted label. Salt. He vaguely remembered seeing this sitting on the top shelf of his mother's pantry. "Yer granny give you that?" he asked.

"Great-granther. The day . . ." Egan trailed off. "You know."

"Yeah, I know." The day Egan's great-granther, Aiden's granther, Thomar, had died. The family had taken it in turn to sit by the end of his narrow cot all through the night, each one getting a chance to talk quietly to him one last time, each one getting a chance to say goodbye, I love you, I'll miss you. Don't go. You didn't always get that chance.

"It's for me to keep stuff in," Egan said, breaking into his thoughts.

"Stuff? Like treasure?"

His son's dark eyes, so like his own, widened in surprise. "Yeah." He caught Aiden's hand. "I gotta show you in the kitchen," he declared.

"Why the kitchen?"

"'Cause I need the table." Egan turned. "It's all right, Ma. We won't be long. You can take Leila to bed now."

She bent to kiss him, giving Aiden a warning look over his tousled head. "See that you aren't."

"Leila has her own stuff," Egan explained, leading the way into the kitchen. "But she'll still want mine."

He climbed up onto a chair, sitting on his knees so he could reach the tabletop, then lifted the box lid with all the reverence and solemnity of a priest to reveal a trove of objects any city child would envy.

"I got lots of feathers," he began, bringing them up as a single handful and fanning them out for his father's inspection. "Most are from Aunt Kassie's pigeons. Some're brown, some're gray, an' some're white, but these two are kinda blueish, an' these little yellow an' black ones are from Daedrus' finches."

Aiden nodded. His granther had kept pigeons on the roof, and his sister Kassiath had been obsessed with them from a very early age. Now she looked after them as well as the Watch House messenger birds and their elderly friend Daedrus' houseful of songbirds.

"An' this one here . . ." Egan continued, holding up a longer, stiffer feather with layers of brown and white striping, "I found it at the Iron Market. I figure it's from a hawk. Or maybe a goose. It's real big. Maybe I'll make a pen out of it. That's called a quill.

"I got four beads, three buttons, an' one, two, three nails," he continued once Aiden had examined each feather. "The nails prob'ly came offa cart. I got a broken spindle whorl that Missus Poll said I could keep, an' two marbles I won offa Charlie Tyver." He held them up to the light. "This one's clay, but this one here's real red an' blue glass. It's really rare," he stated in the voice of a proud marble expert. "So I don't play with it anymore in case I lose it.

"This is some kinda bug's nest, see? Daedrus calls it a casin', an' we kept it at his house until we were sure there wasn't a bug still livin' in it afore I brought it home, 'cause Ma wouldda been mad if a bug had come out here."

"Very wise."

"An' I got eight different kinds of rocks." Egan set a handful of different colored pebbles on the table in a line from smallest to largest. "Most of 'em're from the Iron Market, too. Daedrus says that if I bring 'em over, he'll help me figure out their names." Egan turned a questioning look on his father. "Did you know that rocks got names?"

"What, like Toby or Jannie?"

Egan guffawed. "No, like iron or granite, cause iron's a kinda rock, Daedrus says. Or it's in a rock. I can't 'xactly remember. An' there's granite like I said, an' limestone, an' lots of others besides." He gathered them up.

"Hm." Aiden examined one covered in tiny metallic flecks that flashed in the pale sunlight. "What's this one called?"

"Dunno yet. I'll ask Daedrus." Egan lifted it from his father's fingers and returned it and the rest to their place in the box. "I've also got this coin here, see?" He held up a tiny copper. "Daedrus says it's from Hardorn, an' that we can't spend it here, so I should jus' keep it for when I grow up in case I ever go there. An' I got this bit of wire. I think it came off a gittern. An' this is a pick for one. Aunt Kassie's friend Laryn gave it to me when they looked after us last week. She says she'll teach me to play one day." He straightened. "That's near everything, 'cept . . ."

The boy's face lit up as he reached into the box once more. "This here. My very best treasure ever. Prob'ly the best for my whole life."

He opened his fist to reveal a small silver bell nestled in the center of his palm.

Aiden stared down at it. "Here. That's not . . ."

His son nodded. "I figure it is. I found it on the street that day Herald Tayn came to the Watch House, 'member?"

"I remember."

How could he forget? The street had been filled with battling night soil apprentices and angry townsfolk, and in the middle of it all a newly discovered Herald Trainee, no more than twelve years old, had appeared on his way to the Collegium. His Companion, Aislin, had been the most beautiful and ethereal being

Aiden had ever seen. The entire street had hushed. Most had never seen a real Companion up close. It was something they would be talking about for the rest of their lives.

"I figure it was offa Aislin's tack," Egan continued. "One day I'm gonna walk all the way up to Companion's Field and give it back, but for now I'll keep it safe."

He returned it to the box with a reverential air.

"I usually carry what I find around for a while, you know, for luck, an' then I put it in here."

He looked up at his father shyly. "You could, you know, have something, if you wanted, for you to carry for luck," he offered.

Aiden smiled. "I'd like that, son."

"What do you wanna take?"

"Hm." Aiden made a show of thinking it over. "I dunno, really, they all seem so precious, Maybe you should pick one for me. You know them best. What do you think I should take?"

"Hm." Egan rubbed his chin the way he'd seen his father do many times before. Finally, he reached inside and drew out the rock with the metallic flecks. "I think this one." He passed it over with an air of extreme gravity, and Aiden put it in his pocket with the same expression.

"That's everythin'," Egan said.

"Except your ribbon." Careful not to touch it, Aiden pointed to a thin strip of faded burgundy cloth tucked against one side of the box.

"Oh, yeah. That was in the box when Great-granther gave it to me," Egan pulled it out and together father and son compared their individual ribbons. "He'd had it a really long time," Egan continued. "He said it was important. That I had to keep it safe. He said that one day I'd know where to take it. He said: 'It's gotta go back, they always gotta go back, but it doesn't gotta go back right now.' I dunno where it goes, but Great-granther said I would know one day, so I jus' keep it safe next to the bell 'til then. Do you know where yours goes?"

Aiden nodded.

"You gonna take it there?"

"Yeah."

"Do you think mine goes there, too?"

"I do."

"Maybe we can take 'em together."

"That's a good idea."

Egan returned the ribbon to its place in the box, then closed the lid. "So, ah, Da . . . ?" he began.

"Hm?"

"The beatin' of the bounds is tomorrow."

"Mm-hm."

"An' you said you'd think about me comin' with you."

"I did."

"Granny says I'm real 'sponsible."

"I have heard her say that."

"An' she says you were five when you first went."

"I was."

"So, can I? Please?"

Aiden smiled. "Yeah. 'Course you can."

Egan threw himself into his father's arms.

"I was gonna tell you tomorrow," Aiden said with a grunt as he rose, the boy squirming around to catch up his box.

"Why tomorrow?"

"'Cause I wanted you to sleep tonight."

"I'll sleep."

"Yeah, sure."

The next morning dawned both sunny and warm. Aiden and Egan took their places at the front of the procession, and, after Egan had given the signal to begin with a solemn wave of one hand, they headed up Iron Street, shopkeepers and customers lined up to cheer them on.

One by one, they checked each marker, the Watchmen and their littles gathered around them.

Jay and Annie Dell were waiting with beaming smiles on their faces and trays of tarts in their arms, their marker proudly sitting in the middle of their front door stoop. Brody Drove had been as good as his word. The marker had been replaced in the wall, and the cockerel caught and held in Missus Drove's strong arms. Aiden handed Egan to Paddy, entered the chicken coop, checked the marker and returned, the skin between his shoulder blades tensing as he passed the creature whose eyes followed him knowingly.

The Greys' marker was in place—upside down, but in place. Aiden signalled to Paddy, who turned it right-side up, carefully cradling it into place as if it were a child, then pulled out a handkerchief and deliberately dusted it off with a reverent expression before calling the littles over so that each one of them might touch it. Aiden was pleased to see the look of awe on their faces and the look of discomfort on Wes's. Missus Grey was nowhere in sight. The procession moved on, and two stone masons moved in. With luck, it might still be there in five year's time.

As it turned onto Chandler's Row, the procession hushed. Oblivious, Egan maintained a chattering presence by Aiden's side. Paddy gave him a quick look. Aiden just shrugged.

Ned Carter stood with arms crossed, neighbors holding their breath. Beside him, a small boy with Ned's eyes and his grandfather's hair, looking as excited as Egan, proudly displayed the marker set in the cobblestone, to the right of his father's barrow.

Aiden let out a breath he didn't remember holding. He led Egan to the stone. Both Danns inspected it. Both Danns nodded to both Carters then, without a word, as agreed, they returned to the front of the procession and carried on up the street.

An hour later, it was all over. The littles had gone home, the Watchmen had returned to their beats, and Aiden and Egan Dann stood together in front of The Old Clock Tavern.

No one young ever went in, but, then, no one, young or old, had ever convinced a Carter to move their barrow either. If one boundary could be crossed today, then so could another.

"It looks kinda scary, Da," Egan noted, clutching his ribbon tightly in his hand.

"Yeah, an' it probably smells scary too," Aiden agreed. "But Jaz said these would get us in." He pulled the other ribbon from his pocket. "An' you know your great-granther would never ask you to do anything dangerous."

"Did they know Great-granther in there?"

"They must have. This was his local."

"His very own?"

"Well, not just his."

Egan cocked his head to one side. "Will they have sweets?"

"Probably. But hard ones, you know, the kind old people usually have."

"Oh." Egan sighed. "That's all right, I guess." He glanced up. "Could we get other sweets later?"

Aiden chuckled. "Yeah. I'll think there'll be time for that. You ready?"

"You still got my rock?"

"I've still got it."

"Then, yeah. I'm ready."

"Sort it out, son."

Aiden turned to the memory of his father, standing as he always was and always would be, right behind him, fronting a line of Danns in Watchman's uniforms, stretching into the past, and looking toward the future.

His future. His and Egan's.

It's sorted, Da, he thought. *But the right way this year. I wish you coulda been the one to do it, but there it is.*

Taking a deep breath, he caught up Eagan's hand, and together, father and son headed for The Old Clock Tavern.

Stepping Up

Angela Penrose

Bardic Trainee Bruny set a sturdy oaken trunk down on the floor of her room with a solid thump, then turned to steer Trainee Tessy, who was buried under mounds of bedding, toward the second bed. The arm-thick walls of the Bardic Collegium did a fine job of muffling the noise from room to room, and incidentally keeping heat and cold from ever being too terribly dire, but nights were still chillier than was comfortable for most of the year, and Trainees tended to accumulate blankets and quilts.

Tessy barked her shin on the low, wooden bedframe, yelped and dropped her armload, which fell onto the bed, more or less where it belonged.

"Be you fine?" asked Bruny. "Naught bleeding?"

"Ouch! No, I'm fine, it just hurts." Tessy flopped down onto the bed next to the fluffy pile, and reached down to rub her shin through rust-brown trousers. "I wish you'd let me take the trunk. Or we could've carried it together. It's heavy! I told my pa I didn't need such a large one, but he insisted."

"It's a fine trunk," said Bruny, "and will be serving you well for many years. Asides, you just wanted me to be carrying the bedding so I'd be the one with a sore shin."

"Bruny!" Tessy glared at her, then fell to laughing. "No, honestly, I just . . . it's heavy."

"And I be that much bigger and as much stronger than you. I

grew up wrestling with ornery sheep while you never lifted anything heavier nor a spool of thread in your pa's shop." Which was another tease, that. Bruny had grown up in the sheepherding Tolm Valley, while Tessy's parents had run a sewing shop, making all kinds of clothing, plain and fancy. Bruny could herd and shear and card and spin, but Tessy could embroider with threads so fine they seemed to be made of single hairs and make flowers that looked to be blooming right there on the cloth, then sew it all up into a gown fit for a lady at court.

"I'll have you know I could haul four bolts of fabric at once when I was just ten!" Tessy's glare at Bruny was clearly feigned, so she just grinned and shrugged.

"I'm sure you're being right strong for a tiny shoot of a girl, but I could be hauling you up a hill under my arm and not be noticing the burden."

"Well . . . well, fine—next time I have to go to Notation, you can carry me!"

Notation class was up at the top of an old tower, and they both laughed at the thought.

When they both huffed quiet once more, Bruny asked, "Did we be getting everything from your old room? Naught was being forgotten under the bed or behind the door?"

Tessy looked all around, her gaze pausing at the trunk on the floor, the leather case with her bone flute on the table beside her bed, the stack of books next to the flute case on the table, and the pile of bedding. "No, I'm pretty sure we got everything. My old room is between here and the choral hall, so I'll poke my head in and give it one last look-around on the way to class, but I'm sure it's empty."

Tessy was sixteen, a year younger than Bruny, but she'd been at Bardic since she was twelve and so was two years ahead of Bruny in the curriculum.

More like to three years, or even four, Bruny thought, given how little schooling she'd had in anything, much less music, before Herald Josswyn had sent her to Bardic. But the Masters were pleased with her progress and told her she'd graduate when she was ready. It was a glum thought and a hopeful one both.

"Have you signed up to mentor one of the newlings?" asked Tessy, who'd left off rubbing her leg and was straightening her bedding on the worn mattress.

"Ah, nay," said Bruny. "I'm only being here two years—I've naught to be teaching anyone. And aside that, I still be studying and practicing that hard. I'll never be catching up otherwise."

Tessy straightened her top quilt, a fine cream linen cover with tiny flowers embroidered all over, and she turned to Bruny with an odd look. "Nobody expects you to catch up, Bruny. You know that, right? You started so late, nobody expects you to master six years of learning in three years. That'd be horrible if they did! You work hard and you're doing great. You've learned a lot, and you could do a lot to help out a brand new student."

Bruny managed a smile and shook her head. "There are being plenty of others who are having more knowledge than I to pass."

Tessy shrugged but didn't press, which Bruny appreciated. Tessy was kind and encouraging, but Bruny had a hard enough time with her own studies. She'd noticed many of the new Trainees came to Bardic having had music lessons already, from their temple or sometimes their school, or private lessons if their parents had the coin. To say nothing of the rest of it, the education that seemed to be standard everywhere in the kingdom outside the Tolm.

In her first year, some of the younger Trainees had sometimes come up to her in the hall or the garden to ask questions about musical *texture,* or Rethwellan verbs, or some sort of arithmetic that didn't even use numbers, and Bruny had stammered out apologies while imagining what the other Trainees around her were thinking of her ignorance.

That was near three years ago, though. Fourteen of the oldest Trainees had convinced the Bardic Council to let them go off on their Journeyman rounds with full Bards. They'd play market days and fairs and festivals and private parties, whatever they could find, through the spring and summer and into the autumn, with the experienced Bards showing them the way of it. They'd spend the months getting gigs and making contacts, meeting people, learning towns and villages and manors, to start them out on their Bardic lives.

That was the sort of mentor the newlings needed—someone who actually knew things to teach.

With the graduating herd departing, though, there was room for the standard intake—students who'd always wanted to come to Bardic, who'd planned and prepared, and all came in at once. That mid-springtime was when classes formally began, with instructors starting at the top of their lesson lists. Students came in at odd times of the year, as Bruny had, but it was more orderly for as many folk as possible to be on the same page of the book.

Bruny's old roommate, Seladine—who'd been a fine mentor to bewildered, fumbling Bruny for two years and a bit—was off into the world, as was Leoda, Tessy's roommate. Since there was a great shuffling of bodies anyway, Bruny and Tessy had decided to room together, rather than roll the bones and hope not to get someone too unbearable.

Thus, Tessy moved into Bruny's room.

With the incoming newlings, though, a call was put out for mentors among the older students. Bruny understood that didn't mean her, however kind everyone was.

"Well, I have a mentor meeting to go to, then," said Tessy. "I'll see you after lunch? Or after dinner, at least. I promise I'll get everything unpacked and put away before bed."

"Aye, don't be rushing," said Bruny. "So long as I be not tripping over your things, I'll not be grumping."

Tessy laughed, waved, and vanished out the door.

Bruny sat on her own bed and pulled her music theory book out of the stack on her side table. She knew what musical texture was now, anyroad, but there was always so much to learn!

That evening, the dining hall seemed even noisier than usual, despite the thick hangings on the walls. Shy, wide-eyed girls and weedy, awkward boys clumped together throughout the large room, shuffling little herds that wandered here and there like sheep searching for sweet grass in a dusty pasture, until finally settling down at a couple of tables.

Bruny was sitting with Delvan, a young man just a bit older than she was who played the double clarinet as if he had four hands. Across from Delvan was Calius, a short and wiry boy a year younger than Bruny, who was shy and halting in regular speech, but a master of the mandolin, with a deep, rich singing voice.

A clump of newlings ended up at their table, and Bruny smiled at a skinny slip of a boy who ended up next to her. "Ho, there, and welcome! I be Bruny. This be Delvan, and Calius."

"Umm, hello. I mean, hello!" The boy sat up stiff and straining, clearly trying to make himself look as tall as possible, which was futile since even drawn up as much as he could manage, the top of his head was barely level with the bridge of Bruny's nose. "This is Vella," he said, gesturing at a short but curvy red-haired girl sitting on his far side. "And Ambrian." Another gesture, this time to a taller but thinner newling one down from Vella. Bruny leaned forward to wave and try to memorize faces, but she couldn't quite tell if Ambrian was a girl or a boy. No matter.

"And what be *your* name?" she asked the boy next to her.

"What? Oh, umm, sorry!" He flushed red as an apple. "I'm Kay. Sorry!"

"Welcome to Bardic," said Bruny, pretending not to notice his embarassment. "I wager there be names and places and schedules and all manner of stuff leaking from your ears by now, nay?"

The three newlings grimaced, and Vella added a laugh. "I'll never remember everything, I swear! I'm going to need a dog to get me from here to class to my room to wherever else I'm supposed to be!"

"If you can find a dog that smart, you'll get rich off his stud fees," said Delvan with a chuckle.

"I had a dog that smart," said Vella. She looked away, her face taking on a sad slant. "I couldn't bring him to the Collegium, though, and I couldn't not come here. I'll visit him when I've a chance, and Mam said when they bring sheep to the city for slaughter, she'll bring Crook, and I can see him then."

"You be a herder?" asked Bruny, perking up a bit. "I be from the Tolm Valley, to the north. I did be keeping sheep all my life before I came to Bardic."

"Really?" Vella leaned out to beam at Bruny. "I thought I'd be the only shepherdess here!"

That was an odd word, and Bruny laughed. "Nay, now there be two of us!"

The kitchen helpers started carrying platters to the ends of the tables just then, and conversation focused on passing and serving, with the occasional exclamation of joy at a favorite or groan at the opposite.

Once the first push of hunger was satisfied, Delvan asked, "So what classes are you all in?"

Small slips of parchment came out of pockets, and the new Trainees read off their schedules.

Kay was in the same history class as Bruny, which made her flush, but she just smiled and said, "I be in that class too. I did study with Bard Tommis before—he do be interesting to listen to."

Kay stared and asked, "You are? Why?"

Bruny forced herself to sit up straight and kept her expression pleasant. "I did start late, and did get little schooling back in the Tolm. I do have some years to go still."

"Oh. Umm, sorry?"

Bruny shrugged. "It do be fine."

Calius looked back and forth between them, then said, "So do you all have mentors assigned?"

Ambrian piped up, "I do. Kindal is my mentor."

"We know Kindal," Delvan said with a nod. "He's wonderful on the oboe."

"Well, I play the harp, so I don't know if he'll be able to help me much with that," said Ambrian with a wry smile.

"Bruny plays the harp," said Delvan. "Maybe she can help you?" He looked over at Bruny with one eyebrow cocked.

Bruny leaned back, as if her body were trying to withdraw from the conversation. She said, "I do be a newling myself on the harp. May'p you could be giving *me* some help?" She made herself lean forward and gave Ambrian a quick smile, then took a big forkful of mashed redroots and focused on her plate.

She was better at the harp than she was a year ago, but still, she'd only been playing it for two years and a bit, which didn't make her fit to help anyone. If Ambrian played the harp already, he'd—she'd?—probably been playing for a while then and likely was much better than Bruny.

Conversation went on without her for a bit. Vella's mentor was Tessy, and Bruny was sure she'd be in good hands. Kay's mentor was Ethafrid; Bruny didn't know him very well, but he could play the tambour drum like a demon.

There was fizzberry cobbler for the sweet, which was likely to improve anyone's mood, and it did perk Bruny's up some. When everyone was done, they showed the newlings where to put their plates and cups and such. Vella said she was meeting Tessy in the garden, and Bruny offered to show her where Tessy usually went after dinner. Delvan and Calius waved goodbye, but Kay and Ambrian followed.

Bruny wasn't sure if they were that curious to find the garden—which wasn't exactly hidden—or whether they were just nervous to be left on their own in the middle of the Collegium. Either way, she didn't mind showing them around.

They'd just stepped outside when a rich, baritone voice said, "Now *that's* something worth leaving Penbrook for."

Bruny sent a hard stare at the young man who'd spoken. He was about her height, with thick, light brown hair and a full, thick mustache and beard. Which made him look as though he should be close to earning his Scarlets, but she'd never seen him before, which meant he was likely one of the newlings. Another late starter, like her?

He was handsome, but the smirk twisting his lips made him look ugly, and the way he let his gaze roam over Vella's curves—which made her look much older than her thirteen years—made Bruny step between the two of them.

He finally noticed Bruny and scowled, then put the smirk back on once more. "The little mink has a longshanked cow stumbling about her." The younger men he was standing with all laughed—some of them mean and some of them strained, though they wanted his approval but weren't quite sure why.

The bearded boy took a couple of steps to the side, then stood with one graceful hand on his canted hip, and gave Vella a hungry look. He likely thought it a compliment.

Bruny glanced at Vella. She was stock still and staring at the boy as though she couldn't figure out what to do or say. Bruny nudged her gently with an elbow and gave her a grin. She raised her voice and said, "If that one did be a spring ram, I'd be sharpening my gelding knife."

Vella giggled and nodded, her posture relaxing.

Kay was glowering at the bearded boy, as if he might go over and start something, but Bruny put a hand between his shoulderblades and said, "N'even such as that be worth explaining yourself if he do go missing, aye?"

It looked as though Kay wanted to disagree, but he was smart enough to keep his mouth shut and merely fume while Bruny steered him, with the others following, to where Tessy sat on a sun-warmed bench by the garden wall.

The tiny white honeystars that covered the wall wafted their perfume into the evening air, and a few birds in the thick-leaved trees squawked and quarreled over whatever it was birds had to argue about. Likely fighting over mates, like Beardboy, although birds had more excuse, having brains the size of a fingertip.

"Ho, Tessy! I did find your little lamb and some few others!"

Kindal was there too, so that was Vella and Ambrian sorted. Bruny stayed to chat with the group, making sure the newlings got the names of the other Trainees clustered around Tessy, and she kept an eye out for Ethafrid.

Beardboy didn't wander by, which was fine by her. The older Trainees told stories to make the newlings laugh, and they passed on a few lessons learned about getting along at the Collegium. Some of the stories weren't even that exaggerated, which was so much the better.

When they got back to their room that night, Bruny hardly let the door shut before she asked, "Are you knowing the new boy, the bearded one?"

"Who? Oh, yes. That's Helvan Redmount, Serissia Redmount's son." Tessy sat on her bed to undo her shoes. Her trunk was down at the foot of her bed, and her things were hung on pegs or lined up on shelves, so apparently she had indeed made it back some time that day.

"Serissia . . . Bard Serissia?" Bruny frowned, searching her brain. "I have done heard tell of her, I be thinking."

"I would think so! She's known all over the kingdom. She's the court Bard of the Duke of Highvale. Helvan is fifteen, but he's expected to graduate at eighteen because his mother's been teaching him since he was old enough to screech."

"Fifteen? I've not known any boy of that age who did have such a beard."

Tessy shrugged. "It happens sometimes." She lowered her voice and said, "Look at Vella. She has a bust like a mother with a new babe. Different folk are different."

"Oh, aye. But still it do be . . . awkward." She thought a few moments, then something popped out of the back of her mind. "Ah, Seladine did mention his mam. She did say Bard Serissia has a lovely voice."

"You could say that." Tessy tossed her shoes under her bed and leaned back on her hands, looking up at Bruny. "Why the interest?"

"I do be thinking may'p Bard Serissia did be convincing young Helvan that he does be that grand. She did teach him no manners, anyroad."

She told Tessy about the encounter with Helvan and his rude interest in Vella.

Tessy hopped to her feet, her fists clenched. "He said *what*? She's thirteen! I'll cut his balls off if he does any more than talk!"

Bruny laughed. "Aye, I did say to Vella that if that one did be a ram I'd be sharpening my gelding knife."

Tessy huffed. "I'll report this to Bard Ulfrid. Helvan said he didn't need a mentor, that he'd be fine on his own. Ulfrid might decide to overrule him. And if not, at least he'll be aware of the situation. And I'll pass the word among the other mentors, too. The more eyes on him, the less likely it is he'll try anything."

"He did have a little group of followers about him, other newling boys," said Bruny. "Likely he did be just talking big to impress them. He do be a new boy, and older. That be hard."

"If he's been in a ducal court all his life, he should know better how to make friends and impress people."

"I not be knowing, but may'p that do be how the menfolk of the duke's court do impress one another?"

"What a horrible thought." Tessy's mouth screwed up like she'd bitten into a berry with a bug in it. "Anyroad, I'll go speak with Bard Ulfrid before he's gone to bed."

Bruny nodded and sat to pull off her own shoes as the door closed with a crack behind Tessy.

The older Trainees chatted and gossiped about the newlings over the next couple of weeks. Some of the more ambitious went out of their way to get to know Helvan, calculating that he—or rather his mother—might be in a position to do them a favor later on if they became friends of his. Several didn't even deny it, speaking one-on-one or in a small group of friends. Being successful as a certain kind of Bard was as much about knowing people who could do you favors as it was about your talent—or Talent—and everyone knew it.

Bruny actually had some respect for those who owned their ambition.

The rest mostly ignored Helvan or stood back and watched, hoping for some amusement.

Not that his harassing young girls was amusing, but it was soon clear that his influence and his little herd was composed solely of younger boys. The older Trainees who cultivated him for the sake of ambition would speak with him briefly, praise his practice, share sweets with him—all brief interactions. None of the older Trainees cared to actually spend time with him. None joined his little herd.

"Of course not," said Tessy, when Bruny pointed it out one morning. "They all see how pathetic it would be. It's one thing for a twelve- or fourteen-year-old to suck up to someone like him, but at sixteen or eighteen, hanging about a younger boy and following his lead—which is the only way he accepts "friends"—would be laughable. Even another fifteen would look a fool. He's the only newling that age, and the other fifteens have been here for two or three years. Alden's been here four. Licking Helvan's boots would be idiotic."

Bruny saw her point, once she looked at it that way.

Helvan Redmount didn't actually have friends. He had some contacts who were smooth suck-ups and an audience of awkward suck-ups. If he hadn't been such a rotten little tick, she'd have felt sorry for him.

At least he hadn't repeated his vile behavior toward Vella, or any other woman around the Collegium so far as Bruny heard. She thought one of the Bards, likely Ulfrid, had set him straight about that.

She imagined his mother wouldn't be pleased if he got himself thrown out of Bardic. It'd likely be worse for him than for most others. Bruny hadn't thought on it, but starting out with borrowed fame from his mother lifted him up some, aye, but it gave him farther to fall as well.

She and Tessy finished dressing and hurried off to breakfast.

Bruny'd gotten into the habit of having breakfast with Tessy, Kindal, Ethafrid, and their newlings. Delvan joined them sometimes. The newlings stuffed themselves for the day, sorted homework, did last minute run-throughs of songs they were learning, and asked frantic questions about things they hadn't quite been able to piece together from the previous day's lessons.

Ambrian was the only Gifted among the three, and Bruny helped her plan how to use her Gift in a particular song, amplifying different emotions, and when *not* to use it, to make the times she let it out more impactful.

All three were in Ensemble together, and the mentors and Bruny listened to them play a piece they were presenting that day. It was a quiet song, but not a sad one, with a regular rhythm that should've been easy to coordinate.

"You're holding that note too long," Kindal said to Kay. Kindal hummed that measure, to show Kay what he meant. "It should be like this . . . and you're doing this . . ."

"But it sounds better that way," Kay muttered.

"Maybe it does," said Tessy. "But when you're playing with a group, you have to work together. If you think that sounds better, don't just play it—talk about it with the others, and see if they agree."

"Aye," said Bruny. "You'll be getting no credit with Bard Kole if you do go your own path in Ensemble class. It be for teaching you to play *together*."

Kay looked at the other two and argued his point, trying to get them to agree to hold the note longer. Bruny's attention wandered, and she noticed Helvan across the room.

He stood near a group of older Trainees. Two of the boys and one of the girls were his age, but the rest were older, up to eighteen and nineteen. Bruny knew them all to nod to and had spoken with, studied with, or played with all of them at least once. They were all talented and hard workers. None were particularly looking to get a court Bard position, and therefore none were among Helvan's smooth suck-ups.

Helvan edged closer to the group, until he was standing a hand's width away from one of the oldest boys. He stood as if relaxed and cocked his head as though he was listening to the conversation, a half-smile on his face. Anyone glancing over at them would assume he was part of the group.

Unless they watched for a few minutes and saw that none of them spoke to him, or even looked at him.

Bruny knew word of his behavior toward Vella had spread—any number of folk could've seen and heard it just outside the dining hall at that time. That was likely part of the problem.

The other part was likely these older Trainees not wanting to be thought suck-ups.

Helvan laughed at someone's joke and opened his mouth to add something, but they mustn't have made a place for him in the conversation because he closed his mouth again. A few minutes later, he looked up as thought he'd just remembered something and strode away.

The newling group broke up and headed off to their first class. The mentors waved to each other and Bruny, and they all vanished in different directions.

That afternoon, she and Kay headed out of the history classroom. They were the last to leave, since Kay had wanted to ask Bard Tommis a question after the lecture, and Bruny'd agreed to listen to a piece he was thinking of playing at the Midyear Recital. Which was months away, but she'd agreed it was never too early to begin preparing.

"So it's like a palindrome," Kay was saying. "It's the same backward and forward, but it sounds good both ways! I've been working on it for over two years, and I'm sure it's ready!"

"So you did *write* this song?" Bruny asked.

"Of course! Nobody else has written anything like it before!"

Kay bounced along, practically dancing down the corridor as they headed toward the practice rooms.

Bruny's first thought was that getting a solo spot in the Recital was hard enough—as she well knew—but getting a solo spot with a song written by a twelve-year-old newling, no matter how enthusiastic, was going to be near impossible. She'd wait to hear it before speaking, but was pretty sure she'd have to explain the realities of the situation to Kay at some point.

He babbled on about his song while she listened and nodded. Then, just as they rounded a corner, Kay bounced off someone and staggered back.

Helvan and his little herd were standing right there, taking up nearly the whole of the cross corridor.

Kay caught his balance while saying, "Hey, sorry—" then he saw who he'd run into and stopped. His jaw clenched, and he took a step back but didn't say anything.

Helvan looked him up and down and brushed imaginary dirt off his tunic. He glanced over at Bruny, then locked eyes on her and sneered. "The little yapping dog with the longshanked cow," he said to his milling herd. "Do you suppose he needs a step stool?"

The younger boys around him stared, and most of them giggled.

Kay spat out a word they weren't supposed to say, and before Bruny could stop him, threw himself at Helvan.

Helvan fended off the smaller boy easily, shoved him to the floor, then dove in, straddling Kay and pulling back a fist.

Bruny shot across the corridor and squatted down behind Helvan, straddling Kay's legs herself. She slid her right arm under his and across his chest, clamped down on his shoulder and stood, taking him with her.

Helvan was the same height she was, and he was cursing and squirming, but as she'd said a few times since coming to Bardic, Bruny had grown up wrestling ornery sheep. She gave a little toss, just enough to shift so the side of her hip was pressed against Helvan's backside, made sure of her grip, and *leaned*. His feet left the ground and he dangled from her arm, prisoner of the leverage she had with her hip, kicking and swearing.

"Let me down you gangly bitch! Let me—!"

"What's he done now?" The voice was rich and sharp and very obviously displeased.

Bruny turned her head and saw Bard Tommis striding down the corridor she and Kay had just come from.

Kay scrambled to his feet. "He threw me down and jumped on me! Bruny pulled him off!"

Tommis's expression went hard. "Helvan, I know Bard Ulfrid explained the kind of behavior that wouldn't be tolerated here."

Helvan, still dangling in Bruny's hold, cried, "But he—!"

Bruny ignored him and said, "Kay and I did come to the corner, and Kay did walk into Helvan. He wasn't meaning it, and he said sorry. Helvan did say something nasty about me and Kay, and Kay did go at him. Helvan did push him down, and then did go down to hit him."

Tommis sighed and pinched the bridge of his nose. Bruny was fairly sure at least half of it was an act, deliberately meant to let everyone present know just how annoyed he was.

"So Kay technically attacked him first?"

"Aye," said Bruny, her voice quiet. "But he do be half Helvan's size. And after he did fend him off with n'even a wrinkle to his tunic, Helvan did go after him and he would be doing real damage did I not be separating them."

Tommis sighed again. "Fine. I'll let Gaytha know she has two new helpers for the next month, then. And, Helvan, this is your second warning. One more such incident and we'll send you back to your mother."

Helvan made a huffing sound, and Tommis scowled.

"I'll be making sure he understands," said Bruny. She looked at the top of Helvan's messy brown head, and past, and saw his hands, fisted but dangling. No fight, just . . . what?

Before she could think on what she was doing, she said, "You can be telling Bard Ulfrid I'll be mentoring Helvan."

Helvan squawked at that, but Tommis nodded. "Thank you, Bruny. I'll let Ulrich know." He glared at everyone else, Kay and the boys of Helvan's little herd, then turned and strode off, making his exit like the Bard he was.

Bruny let Helvan down but kept a grip on him. She looked at the herd boys and said, "You all be having better things to do just now, aye?"

They turned and scrambled away in three different directions, vanishing in a moment.

"Kay, I be having to listen to your song tomorrow. Will you be letting the others know I'm being busy this evening?"

Kay nodded. He didn't say anything, and Bruny couldn't read his expression. He seemed almost disappointed in her—had he expected her to lie to keep him from getting into trouble?—but she could deal with that later.

When Kay turned and left, she stepped back from Helvan and said, "We do be needing to talk."

"I don't want to talk to you! You can hardly talk as it is! Where's that twisted accent of yours from, anyway? No, I don't care, and I don't want a damned mentor! I don't need advice, not from someone like you who can't even—"

Bruny clamped down on his upper arm and hauled him down the hall into an empty practice room, then closed and latched the door. They were *only* for practicing, but they were also soundproof, and they needed the privacy.

"I did be like you," she said. "Fifteen when I did come and knowing nobody—"

"I'm *nothing* like you! I don't even need this place to be a Bard! My mother's the finest Bard in the Kingdom, and she taught me everything!"

"Did that be true, she'd not have been sending you here, aye? But she *did* send you here. If you do want your Scarlets some day, you do need to be here—and get along here." Bruny leaned against the door and crossed her arms.

She let out her Gift, with just a bit of a hum under her breath. She let him feel her feeling for him, feeling sorry for him.

He blinked at her, his eyes round with shock, then glared. "How *dare* you feel sorry for me, you provincial cow!"

"I be thinking that I be the only one here who do feel sorry for you. I be thinking that everyone else do be hating you, or may'p be sneering at you behind your back while they be sucking up to your face. That do be hard, I be thinking."

"Like you'd know," he sneered.

"Nobody be hating me," she said. "But I did feel alone and like to being crushed by the strangeness of it all. I be Gifted, and that do be a thing. I be thinking you be not . . . ?"

Helvan just scowled and looked away.

Bruny nodded. "So, I did be having something special not many have, but so much else I did lack. Like you. You do be having the knowledge, and I did hear you playing your mandolin and singing that fine. But you'll not be making it through even three years of Bardic with the whole of the place hating on you."

She tipped her head and looked at him. He was turned away, his arms wrapped around his middle, looking down at the floor. His glare had deflated into a despairing stare.

Bruny remembered the fear and shame and loneliness of her first weeks, then hummed under her breath once more and let her Gift out.

He shifted his weight but didn't say anything.

"It do be up to you. I be heading to Bard Ulrich's office and telling him that I be willing to be mentor to you. If you not be wanting me, you be letting him know, and that'll be the end of it. I'll not be bothering you no more if you don't be brangling with the others. It be your choice. You do think on what you want to be making of your life and what road will be taking you there."

She waited a moment, but he didn't move, didn't say anything.

Fine.

Bruny unlatched the door and left the room.

She took a belly-deep breath while walking up the corridor, then let it out in a huff.

That hadn't gone as well as she'd have liked, but she'd done what she could. The rest was up to Helvan. She would let Ulrich know she was still willing to mentor Helvan. And if he wouldn't have her, she'd take on someone else, whoever she could help.

Because she *could* help. She'd learned a lot—through her whole life, not just at Bardic—and she'd share that with anyone who needed it.

The Measure of Imagination

Paige L. Christie

Teig slammed the door as she stomped out of Belton's modest house. The accompanying bang, loud as last night's revelers at the inn, stopped her on the porch with a hitch in her heart. Biting her lip, she closed her eyes, then took a deep breath as hot shame swept up her face. The sound seemed to emphasize the message in the letter left on Belton's kitchen table. *See? This is exactly why they keep rejecting you.*

When she'd met the messenger on the road this morning—two days late he was!—hope had swelled warm in her heart. But no.

Once again, no.

The door creaked open behind her, and Belton's footfalls moved toward her over the planks. "All we can do is keep trying. You're young." The old man's voice was so carefully neutral that it sent a shot of anger through her belly.

She turned to face him. "They don't want me."

"Not yet," he agreed. He gestured to the pair of rocking chairs that offered a view down the valley to Sweet Springs. "Have a seat. We'll try again."

"I'll stand," she said, blinking back stubborn tears.

He sighed and settled himself in one of the chairs and reminded her gently. "You chose the harder way."

She shook her head, her throat too tight for an answer. In the eighteen months since she and Belton discovered the dangerous

Dream Eater, Hest, Teig spent part of each day with Belton, learning as much as she could about the blue-clad Guard and its work protecting every corner of Valdemar. She'd read every book in his collection on the history and threats that faced the Kingdom, memorized every strategy guide she could find. To what end? After so many years of imagining herself as a Herald, discovering the value and importance of the Guard had felt like opening a secret treasure box.

But just because she'd opened it didn't mean she could reach inside.

She sighed and folded her arms. Yes, she could wear the blue in some dreamless, rural town like Sweet Springs where few longed for more than what they already had. But the Palace—keeping the Queen and the most learned of the land safe and protected—that was a goal worth striving for. The catch was that she wasn't born to the role, as were most Royal Guards. That meant her only hope was a scholarship that recognized her potential. But despite Belton's recommendations and three attempts, the only response from the Collegium was carefully worded refusals. Was it her fault that she wanted what she wanted? Or that what was "available to anyone" wasn't as special as what she always dreamed for herself?

"We stopped Hest from feeding on people's dreams. We saved the inn and the whole village." Why wasn't that enough? Her future unfolded before her, shining and full of purpose. The spotless halls of the Palace, with her standing alert and proud on duty as the Queen and her Heralds swept past. The gentle smile and nod that acknowledged Teig's vital presence. The glory of—

"*Teig*!" Beldon's snap of her name yanked her back to the moment. "You've stopped telling your tall tales, but you still don't focus on the moment until it's almost too late to matter. Where were you just now? Anywhere but *here*, facing the hard thing in front of you."

She dropped her gaze, face burning. The boards beneath her feet, worn and gray, traced fine lines of direction. Rings sanded to grain marked intent, easy to trace, full of both history and meaning. Even things no longer living had more clear direction than she did.

"But I want—"

"Wanting a thing doesn't mean you've earned the right to it. Please sit, young miss."

Teig hesitated. Action without thought had driven her from the house. The very thing the letters of rejection found cause to accuse her of. She unfolded her arms and sat down hard enough to set the chair swaying violently.

Beside her, Belton chuckled. "Well, that took less persuading than I expected. Signs of progress."

The terrible knot of anger and humiliation that lodged in her chest loosened a little. She smiled the faintest bit as she planted her feet and stopped the rocking. "Maybe."

Belton settled back, his chair tipping back and forth in gentle motion to counter her deliberate stillness. "The Palace isn't a place of pure goodness and light any more than is anywhere else in Valdemar. Them rejecting you could be politics as much as anything else."

A dozen possible responses flooded her thoughts, but she bit them all back and made herself think about his words. Her brow furrowed. Even though what he said made sense, it did not change her situation. "How does that help me change into what they want me to be?"

Belton studied her, then shook his head. "Young miss, you need to stop thinking the road you want to take has a fork you need to navigate."

Teig entered the inn through the postern door and cringed as she met Mero's disappointed eyes across the kitchen. Warm smells of simmering stew and baking bread filled the space, but their familiar comfort dissipated as the inn mistress spoke. "Well done. Too bad Wilhem's not here to see your care in action." She punched down the ball of dough on the work counter.

Biting her lip, Teig nodded as she glanced back at the door. At least she'd made a small improvement just since the morning. Her fingers crushed the envelope in her hand. "Where is he?"

"Delivering post," Mero said with a knowing look. "It's two days late already, and he didn't want everyone's mail to be further delayed."

Teig bent her head, her cheeks flooding with heat. That was her job when the general messenger rode through. And she hadn't been here to do it.

Mero shook her head and spoke directly to Teig's shame. "A messenger arrives, and you're off who knows where. When you were gone so early, we assumed you'd walked to meet him but—" She stopped and glanced at the missive in Teig's hand. She gestured with a flour-coated hand. "Ahhh. Another rejection?"

Face pulled tight in an attempt to hold back tears, Teig nodded.

"I take it you went to Belton."

Where else would she go? Flights of fancy and dreams of greatness aside, she did have enough sense to seek advice from the person most likely to give it. Even if she was still trying to make sense of what he'd ended up offering. Change and roads and whatever that all meant. She sighed.

"Why this time?"

"No new reason," Teig murmured. Should she just give up? Was she just wrong for the Royal Guard?

"Well, then, no new reason for moping either." Mero tipped her graying head toward a basket warming on the rack above of the stove. "The messenger's still here and could likely use a fresh biscuit and more tea."

Trained by habit to respond quickly to Mero's requests, Teig stepped to the sink to wash her hands before she realized the strangeness in the older woman's words. "He's still here?"

"Indeed he is. Said he'd be staying some days before heading back to Haven."

Teig pumped water into a big bowl and used a bar of lye soap to scrub clean. Not since she was very small had a messenger done more than pass through after delivering light post. Most of the time they didn't even linger over a cup of tea after breakfast. Why would one stay longer, much less for days? "Why?"

"I suppose you can ask him," Mero said pointedly enough to again raise guilt at chores undone. The rest of the day would certainly be spent in the kitchen working extra-hard to make up Wilhem's absence—all too much her fault. No wonder the Palace had no use for her.

She gathered plate and biscuit, honey and jam, and the teapot onto a tray and headed to the common room before Mero could further take her to task.

Most of the seats in the big room were empty, though three souls slumped at the table nearest the hearth, their heads pillowed on their arms amid half-drunk mugs of last night's ale. She stepped over the sprawled legs of the youngest of them, a brown-headed young man in well-cut clothes, and she paused to use the toe of her shoe to nudge a fallen hat under the bench where it wouldn't get crushed.

At the next table the messenger nodded to her as she unloaded the tray. This morning, when she met him on the road, he'd been equally stoic, hearing her name and, without a word, handing her the letter from Haven.

She studied him as she poured his mug full. Blond hair and neat mustache, a firm face, well-scrubbed and proud. A narrow, shiny blade with a leather-wrapped handle on his hip. A uniform a bit too snug through the shoulders and two finger-widths short on the arms. He glared under her scrutiny.

"Is there anything else you need?" she asked, the questions she'd intended to ask quashed by his unfriendly gaze.

"Yes." The man pointed to the table draped with snoring patrons. "What rooms do they occupy? I hope nowhere near mine, as I need sleep for my journey."

Teig glanced back. The young man she'd stepped over was

waking, pulling himself straight and rubbing his eyes. "I'm not sure, sir," she said, returning her attention to the messenger. "Mistress Mero signed them in, but I can check."

"Do that," he said, paused and added, "If you please." He smiled for the first time, but somehow she liked that even less than his previously sour expression. She turned and headed back toward the kitchen.

"Miss—" The awakened man pulled his feet out of her way and blinked as he scrubbed at his face. He was younger than she'd thought, only a few years her senior. And his clothing more than just well made. It was *expensive*. Was he a noble? A scholar? A man of luck who'd done well in business and struck himself rich early in life? The possibilities tripped happily through her mind before she stopped them. No more time for such fancies!

She met the young man's gaze. "Yes, sir?"

"Is that tea?" he asked, eyeing the pot on her tray.

At her nod, he picked up his ale mug, dumped its dregs into that of his nearest companion and held the now empty cup out to her.

She gave a little laugh and poured it full. "This is going to taste terrible."

He tipped his head back and forth in amused agreement. "Most likely," he agreed as he took a swallow.

She shook her head as he flinched. "Let me clear the table and I'll bring you fresh mugs and some breakfast."

"Much appreciated," he said, and drank the mug of tea before setting it down, shaking his head in disgust. "I'm Delvin. And you are?"

"Teig." A brutal rejection, a grumpy courier, and a rich drunkard with no sense of self-preservation—what else would the day hold? It wasn't even halfway to noon. She balanced the tray with one hand while she reached around him to gather the rest of the crockery. "You paid for rooms you didn't use."

"*Teig?*" He brightened, but shifted his attention as his nearest companion stirred, lifting his head and blinking. "Hear that,

Shean?" Delvin asked. "We paid for beds. Remind Andin of that when he wakes." Delvin laughed, then put a hand to his head and offered a little groan. "Oh, and we should have used them. I've a feeling we'll be glad of them tonight." His voice defined regret.

Teig found herself smiling. So, he and his friends were staying as well. With the messenger lingering too, the inn would be far fuller than was usual this late in the fall. Maybe that information would ease the anger Wilhem must be feeling toward her. Maybe if they all stayed for several days they'd have tales of adventure to share and—

She jerked her thoughts to a halt once again, frowning, and forced herself to ask a normal question. "What brings you to Sweet Springs?"

He smiled at her, then groaned again and folded his arms on the table and dropped his head onto them without answering.

Teig raised both eyebrows, then glanced over her shoulder. The messenger was staring at her. How had both the guests she'd spoken to this morning turned out to be odder than most? What if . . . ? She shook her head. *Stop it, Teig!*

But as she returned to the kitchen, unease crept up her back like a clutter of spiders. "Mero, the messenger—he—" she said, as she carried the dirty dishes to the wash station. "His coat doesn't fit." The words surprised her as they left her mouth. She'd meant to pass on his request to know what rooms the noisy guests were in.

"Yes, I noticed." Mero nodded. Bending to add wood to the cookstove, she frowned a little. "Odd that, though he seems new. Being late on the route and all. Must be awaiting a proper fitting one." She straightened. "The other guests?"

Late. New. Ill-fitted. Teig shook herself. "They want breakfast and tea." She set to scrubbing as Mero nodded and bustled through the kitchen, preparing plates and boiling more water. As water puckered her fingers, Teig's thoughts skipped and fluttered. They'd had new messengers before, and the uniforms always fit properly. And . . . though most travelers carried knives for camping and eating, she'd never seen a dagger like the one this messenger carried, polished and long in the sheath.

"What if he's not a messenger?" she whispered.

"What?" Mero looked up, exasperation twisting her face as she carried the tray of breakfast plates out of the kitchen. "Oh, Teig, not *again*!"

Face flushed and heart pounding, Teig bent her head and kept washing. But the notion wouldn't let go, that once again something was *wrong* in the inn. Was it possible? The last thing she needed was to help earn her home a reputation for being unlucky! Wilhem would never forgive her if she managed that. She set the last of the dishes aside to dry and poured out the wash bucket.

"Well, that's solved!" Mero whisked through the door, her face bright and her eyes wide. Teig turned, startled as the older woman rushed up beside her. "You're right," Mero said, and stepped close. "He's *not* a messenger!"

Teig blanched. "You *asked* him?"

"'Course I did. Knew if I didn't, that idea would just keep roaming your head." She lowered her voice. "He's in disguise. He's been sent to protect that young man you spoke to. He couldn't tell me much, of course. Just that there's those who would do the young sir harm."

"And he's a protector." Teig managed her shock well enough that the words weren't even a question.

"Indeed he is. But we're not to say more to anyone. Otherwise his work could be in jeopardy."

Teig nodded as Mero moved away, humming happily in the wake of a mystery solved. But the unease tapping Teig's spine, if anything, increased. *Why would a protector travel in disguise? And an ill-fitting one at that?*

She stepped to the doorway and peered around the jamb into the common room. Delvin and his friends had perked up and were devouring Mero's breakfast.

Across the room, the man in disguise pretended not to watch them.

* * *

"Young miss, this has to be one of your stories!" Belton said as she finished telling him of the morning's encounters at the inn. Standing in the dooryard, he gave her his firmest look.

She shook her head. "No," she replied with equal intensity. "I told Mero something was wrong, and she *asked* him. *She's* the one who told me he's a protector on a secret assignment. And he's got this knife—"

"Everyone carries a knife." Belton folded his arms and shook his gray head. "But Mero misunderstood. Protectors only travel *with* their charges. They don't meet them on the road, and they certainly don't hide from them."

"Or maybe she's right and he isn't hiding from them—he's hiding from whoever wants to hurt them."

"Or maybe he's just a messenger who doesn't appreciate being accused of being something else and spun a story to ward off bothersome questions."

Teig winced. Now *that* made sense. More sense than anything either she or Mero had dreamed up or begged information about. After all, what business was it of theirs what he was doing? If Teig were him, she'd be just as irritated by the questioning as he seemed to be.

"I suppose," she agreed with a sigh. "Are you coming in for dinner?"

"No." Belton smiled. "I came with a letter for your messenger. A new recommendation for you."

Her stomach flipped a little at the thought of what the next rejection might say, but Belton's continuing generosity also sent warmth through her chest. If he wasn't going to give up, neither was she. Even if it took years. She smiled at him. "Thank you."

He pulled an envelope from his belt pouch and handed it to her. "Take it to the messenger and let him do his job."

"All right." She squeezed his fingers as she took the note.

"Sometimes, young miss, things just need to be left to being what they are."

* * *

She met the messenger at the bottom of the stairs as he descended to the take dinner in the common room, with Delvin's two companions right on his heels. No longer dressed in his uniform, the clothing he wore was plain and purely functional, a contrast to Sweet Springs' brighter tradition. It fit far better than his official garb. He stopped on the last step when he saw her, hand falling to his knife, then away as he recognized her.

"Sir—apologies—but I've a letter bound for Haven," she offered, raising the neatly addressed envelope.

He blinked as though surprised, then offered the same smile from the morning, the one that fit as poorly as his jacket and held out a hand. "Haven, is it? Who would you be writing to in Haven?"

"Oh, not me," she said quickly.

He looked down at the letter. "The Guard?" His lips twitched a little, as though something amused him. "No, I suppose that's not somewhere you would be writing."

A hard swallow kept her from announcing that the letter had been written on her behalf. After all, that was no business of his. And something about the ironic nature of his expression awoke the tingly-legged feeling on her back again. She simply shook her head.

He handed the envelope back to her. "Perhaps give it to me when I'm ready to leave. I've nowhere safe to put it this moment."

She blinked as she reclaimed it. Never had she seen a messenger refuse a missive, no matter when they were handed one. "All right," she said, managing to keep the surprise from her voice.

"Well, then," he said. "If you please." Looking over his shoulder, he shared a knowing glance with the men waiting behind him on the steps.

They were all late for dinner, thanks to her. Quickly, she stepped out of the way and let them pass.

Sliding the letter into the pocket of her skirt, she watched as the messenger wove between the polished tables. He passed up half a dozen choice spaces to settle himself at a corner seat. The other two men settled in with Delvin at a larger table in the center of the room. Now that they were no longer half-drunk and ridiculous, the messenger's interest in them seemed to have waned. He didn't even glance their way, nor they in his.

Teig frowned. Messenger. Protector. Which was he? Maybe both? Or something else entirely? She sighed and headed for the kitchen.

By the time she'd carried a round of stew to every table and returned to the kitchen for a pitcher of ale for Delvin and his companions, it occurred to her that she'd never answered the messenger's request from the morning. And that he hadn't mentioned it again. She paused in the doorway with jug in hand. "Mero, did you tell the messenger what rooms Mister Delvin and his friends are in?"

The inn mistress looked up from stirring the stew. "Of course I did. How else is he supposed to know what doors to keep an eye on?"

Teig's stomach flipped a little, and she frowned; then she shook herself and forced her attention back to the task at hand. Wilhem's anger had faded some since the morning, but she still had a lot of making up to do. Luckily, she'd long since learned how to work hard while her mind turned over wild ideas. If the one forming now made little sense to anyone but her, well, she'd become used to that too. She crossed the room, thoughts churning.

She should just go talk to Belton again, or the younger, active members of the Guard who were now on duty in Sweet Springs. But what if they didn't believe her? Or thought she was just trying to regain the praise that had showered her after her unmasking of Hest?

She bit her lip as she refilled Delvin's drink. "What if that *is* what I'm doing?"

"*What* are you doing?" Delvin asked, looking up at her with an intensity unwarranted by the situation.

She started. Had she slipped and spoken aloud? Well, clearly. "Nothing, sir." She stepped to his other side and filled the man called Andin's mug, then Shean's.

"You're the one who discovered that man Hest," Delvin said.

Teig's mouth fell open, and she turned to him and stared. "How did you know about that?"

"Oh, it was all the news in Haven when it happened. The Heralds have since discovered dozens of Dream Eaters and stopped them. Even the Guard is trained to look for them now."

Surprise could not have claimed her more thoroughly had he dumped a pail of ice water over her head. "I—How—"

He shrugged. "A thank you is in order," he said. "And a toast!" He lifted his mug. "To Teig of Sweet Springs. The girl with the wild imagination! The discoverer of hidden danger!" His companions joined him in drinking to her honor while she stared, face burning.

Danger. He was in danger. A messenger who was neither that nor a protector. A too comfortable look shared among the messenger and Shean and Andin on the staircase. A well-cleaned blade. She knew to her core that a threat loomed over Delvin, even if she couldn't prove it.

Still—if this moment wasn't an opportunity, nothing was. But how could she warn Delvin of something that she had no evidence of? *Wild imagination.* He'd think just what she feared—that she was trying to find advantage in past glory.

She made herself smile, offered vague thanks for his praise, and turned to flee back to safety of familiar chores. But Belton's words slipped through her mind. S*top thinking the road you want to take has a fork.*

She swallowed hard, turned back, and bent her head close to Delvin's and whispered her fears into his ear as his face went bright with shock.

Teig crept up the stairs, a length of lumber and a walking stick in hand and eased over the squeaky fourth step. In the darkness of the second-floor hallway, she wedged the shorter piece of wood under the doorknob of the room where Shean and Andin slept. It wouldn't stop them from exiting, but it would slow them down.

And that's all she could hope for tonight. At least if she was wrong, it would cost no one but herself.

Easing back, she took up her station in the recess that marked the turning of the stairs toward the next level. She smelled of horse and stale sweat, and if she was wrong, that alone would give Wilhem a reason to do more than scold her in the morning. As for the rest—oh, what would he do if he discovered what she'd talked Delvin into this night?

She had to be touched by madness, but she couldn't shake the idea that if she didn't act, something terrible would happen. Even as she had saddled Delvin's horse, her thoughts flipped between the idea that she was paranoid, and the image of the slender knife on the messenger's hip. It was the newness of the handle wrap that wouldn't leave her thoughts. That and the shape of the sheath—too narrow for a camp knife, too long for an eating blade—and the only item that fit the man, no matter how he dressed. It stuck in her thoughts as she packed provisions into saddlebags and tied them behind the cantel. Stuck as she carried the wood into the inn. Stuck like the recognition that Delvin's companions ignored the watchful stranger. *Protectors travel with the one they're protecting.*

A chance taken in the common room had led her to this moment. And the fate of her every dream might hang on that mad choice. But the horse waited outside the kitchen door, his breath puffing warm steam into the cool, moonlit air. And she waited here, ready with a sharp eye and a heavy pole and a heart trying to pound out of her chest.

She waited.

And waited.

Then the sound came, a slip and shift of old wood from above. Someone awakened and headed down to the privy? Perhaps . . . but what if? She bit her lip, eased deeper into the shadows and gripped the stick hard. Darkness moved within darkness, and a figure came down the stairs, slid past her. She smelled oil, the sign of a well-maintained blade.

The figure froze.

Smell. She smelled of horse.

As the man pivoted toward her, she swung low, swiped the back of his knees and sent him crashing to the floor. The tumbling thud shook through the hall, and she struck again, hard to the messenger's torso, heard a grunt as the air shot out of his lungs. Then she leaped over the fallen man and raced along the hall to thunder down the back staircase toward the one who waited there.

"Go!" she shouted to Delvin as she all but crashed into him at the base of the steps.

Above them, chaos erupted, shouts and pounding on doors, on stairs, and she grabbed his hand and dragged him through the kitchen and outside. The horse whinnied as she slid to a stop before it and caught the reins. She waited as Delvin climbed into the saddle, then tossed him the leads.

He caught them and held down a hand to her. "Come on!"

"I—"

"If you're right, they'll kill you!" he shouted.

She grabbed his hand and let him yank her into the saddle.

Teig wrapped her arms around Delvin's waist and hung on with all her strength as the horse surged into a gallop. Her hair whipped into her eyes, and she struggled to relax her enough to keep her seat and sway with the motion of the animal.

Hard over the road they pounded, faint moonlight lighting the way. She could wish the creature beneath them were more than an ordinary horse, but whatever Delvin's importance, he was not a Herald. It mattered little so long as they outpaced those soon to be in pursuit. But they had to dress, to saddle up, to gather supplies. This head start was a chance gained, and it would have to be enough.

"There!" She pointed to a faint break in the trees that marked a path only the local children would know, a route far shorter than the main road to the next town. She closed her eyes and tightened her grip as Delvin reined the horse into a hard turn and they raced into the night.

After the wild ride between the trees and dappled moonlight, the swaying walk of the stallion took on a sleepy, surreal quality. Teig's arms loosened around Delvin's waist, but she stayed close, seeking his warmth in the chill night air. Her plan had never included going with Delvin, and she wished for her coat even as she considered their situation.

Breakneck speed had cast them free of the trap in Sweet Springs, but such a pace could not long be maintained. What they could count on now was only the distance surprise action had gained them and Teig's knowledge of the land they traveled. With luck, both would be enough to make good their escape.

"How did you know?" Delvin asked, turning his head a little toward her.

How had she? "Little things," she said. "The messenger—he was two days late. Messengers are never late, and they never stay more than a few hours. And his coat didn't fit. He asked about your room—"

"And you put this all together to mean he wanted to kill me?"

She nodded, realized he couldn't see it, and told him the story the messenger had offered Mero, and Belton's reaction when she had shared the tale. "And then he wouldn't take Belton's letter to the Guard."

"Letter to the *Guard*?" Amazement tripped through Delvin's voice, and she heard the questions forming behind it.

She rushed on. "I'm sorry about your friends. But they didn't act right either. If they were there to protect you, they weren't paying attention. So, I wondered . . . when I saw them all together, and then how they ignored each other . . . What did you tell them I said to you?"

Delvin pulled the horse to a halt and shifted in the saddle to look at her. She got the impression that if she could see his face, he would be blushing. "I told them a lie," he said, paused. "You put this all together on your own? Why didn't you go to the Guard?"

"No one would have believed me. Why did you believe me?" She frowned. "And why didn't *you* go to the Guard when I warned you? Why'd you go along with my crazy idea?"

He hesitated, then smiled a little. "For the same reason my mother thought I needed protecting in the first place when she sent Andin and Shean as escorts. Politics."

Now what could that possibly mean? "What?"

"Tell me why your friend Belton was writing to the Guard."

"How did you know he's my friend?"

Delvin laughed a little and started the horse walking again. "His name was right alongside yours in the reports."

"Reports? What reports?"

"The Herald and Guard reports. Do you think I had us stop in Sweet Springs on a whim? I was hoping to meet you."

As baffling as the events of the last day had been, his words completely tumbled her thoughts, and she found herself speechless for several heartbeats. "Who *are* you?" she demanded at last.

He chuckled. "I've been touring the southern border for the month—gaining knowledge as my teachers suggested. But my mother is a captain in the Royal Guard, and she sent for me. I've mostly been a scholar, but she wants me to be officially invested as her successor and enter advanced training at the Collegium. She has a number of rivals who would prefer that *not* happen." He sighed and his voice shook as he said. "Shean's father among them. I never would have thought he—" Delvin shivered.

If she hadn't already been, in a way, hugging him, she might have offered the gesture as comfort for his distress. Instead, she just said, "I'm sorry."

Then all his words sunk in, and her heart started pounding as though it would break her ribs. "Royal Guard?" Could this really be happening? Was she really riding north toward Haven with a member of the group she so wanted to join? And an important one at that?

"Yes." He shook his head as though dismissing gray thoughts. "I suspect they'll find the real messenger trussed up somewhere along his route, his coat missing, along with all his letters." He paused. "What was Belton writing about?"

The letter her pocket. "Me," she whispered.

"You?" He paused. "You want to join the Guard?"

"The Royal Guard. On scholarship. It was a recommendation. Our fourth attempt. They keep rejecting me for being . . . too imaginative."

Silence fell for a long moment, broken only by the sound of the horse's hooves over fallen leaves and the rustle of wind through the branches overhead. Then his body began to shake with laughter, and soon she joined him, both of them giggling lightly despite the pressures of their situation.

At last they calmed. "Well, I for one am grateful that you're exactly who you are, Teig of Sweet Springs. And I think that if we're lucky enough to make it to Haven in one piece, I might be able to help you with that problem."

If they made it. Haven was a long way off. And they couldn't trust anyone along the way. Unless they were lucky enough to meet a Herald, they were on their own. But despite all that, Teig's heart lifted with hope. Perhaps she'd finally proved that her vivid imagination could be a resource, not just a distraction.

Belton had been right. She didn't have to pretend to be something else. She could be exactly who she was and exactly what was needed at the same time.

"I'll hold you to that," she said, and settled in for a long, long ride.

Puppies & Ponies

Phaedra Weldon

"I can't believe you found him so easily!"

The snap and pop of the hearth fire gave a comforting background to Harris Yerger's gentle smile as he faced the youth before him. "I just followed the sound of his cries." He placed his hand on the puppy's warm body, nestled happily in the boy's arms. "Now, what did I say about keeping an eye on him? He's just a baby, so he depends on you. I'd give him a warm bath before I'd bring him back in the house, though. Oh, and ask your mother first."

"I will," the boy said softly as he held the puppy close, grinning as it stretched up to nuzzle his face. "It's like how Mama's always watching me, isn't it? And Uncle Brent—he's the best when it comes to taking care of us."

"Yes." Harris tilted his head to his shoulder. "Remi, I do believe you're growing up."

The eleven-year-old puffed up and smiled at Harris. "Thank you again. You're not gonna let Mama know, are you?"

Harris sighed. The puppy had been a gift from Remi's father—his *real* father—a soldier in the Karse army. A man not entitled to have a family. Only officers could have families. But Remi's father had fallen in love at a young age, before he'd been taken into the army before Karse's war on Valdemar began, and he and Breeze had married in secret.

And in secret they had made a life together—what there was of it—for fifteen years. Harris had stumbled onto their secret marriage by accident and kept the truth for them, just as Brent—Remi's father—had kept Harris' secret about his strange ability to find things.

Being talented in finding lost things wouldn't seem too strange to most people. Everyone had talents. But Harris had escaped conscription into the army because he was, for all intents and purposes, blind. His vision had faded when he was in his teens after suffering a severe knock to the head. Harris could see shapes, light and dark, but no details. And so he was considered useless by most, until he met his own wife, Jasmin, who saw potential in Harris' talent to find things. The village had since supported Harris, his wife and daughter, and he, in turn, helped them find what they had lost.

Just as he kept the secret of Brent's family.

"Och, Remi, your mother's outside," came Jasmin's deep voice. "Is your puppy well?"

"Aye, ma'am. Harris found him for me! I don't know how to pay you—"

"Think nothing of it," Jasmin said. He felt her hand on his shoulder. "Now head out. I have to get supper started, and I need this fine husband of mine to check on Isabelle."

Remi squeezed Harris' hand, and he could hear the boy leave by following his footsteps. Harris knew the layout of their small house as well as he knew the paths in the village from shop to shop and house to house. These paths lived in his memories and his mind, where he could see as well as a sighted person. He didn't share this with Jasmin—this terrain his bright blue but useless eyes could see over the world. It was this map that showed him what he needed to find as the object he concentrated on would sparkle and shine in the distance, and he would just follow that path until he'd found it. Just as he followed it to find Remi's puppy that morning.

Harris stood and moved about the living area with an uncanny grace. But it was his wife's voice that stopped him. "How did you know the pup was missing? And how could you have found it? It was in a hole."

He turned to face her, his brows knitted over his eyes, but he said nothing because he wasn't sure he understood her question or the strange tone in her voice.

"Don't look at me with those eyes you claim you can't see me with." She was near him again. He could feel her warmth. It always surprised him that he couldn't see her in his mind the way he could see Isabelle, his own child, or even Remi and his mother. Could it be because in the past year or so he hadn't . . . wanted to find her? In the beginning, Jasmin never questioned what he could do, and in fact she charged for his services sometimes—though not always with his knowledge. But lately . . . ever since the Sunpriest Doswee had come to live in their small village, she questioned . . . everything. "You're looking at me."

"No," he said in as gentle a voice as he could. "I am looking in the direction of your voice. And as I have said many times during our marriage, I can see shapes, but I cannot see details."

"So, you do see me."

"I see . . ." he had to redirect his attention at that moment, from what his mind saw, to what his eyes saw. It was always an uncomfortable task, but one he'd had to do more often with Doswee now a part of their lives. "Colors. I can only say from memory, but you are wearing something brown . . . I believe. And white?"

Jasmin didn't respond at first. Then, "How did you know the puppy was missing?"

"I heard him, while I was out. It is a puppy, Jasmin. It cries."

"And the Coates' goat?"

"The same. Only they came to tell me their goat was missing, if you remember."

Silence.

Harris felt he should once again reassure her. He'd been reassuring her a lot these days. "Jasmin . . . is there something the matter?"

"I just . . . Doswee thinks it strange that you can find things but can't see."

Doswee.

Of course.

Harris sighed. "I use my ears, Jasmin. As I have done since I lost my ability to see. I can hear things." This wasn't exactly the truth, but once before, when he'd tried explaining what he saw in his mind's eye, her reaction troubled him. She'd called it a "witch power" only once, so he'd never spoken of that part himself again. He shared it with Brent and Breeze, and they seemed to understand. Especially Breeze, who on occasion, appeared to know about events before they happened.

"What about that thing?"

"Thing?"

"The thing you told me about when we were first married. That thing in your mind?"

Harris hadn't expected her to remember, but he also assumed she brought it up because she'd spoken with Doswee. He wanted nothing more than to tell her to stay away from that man—but he was also aware that when someone is told not to do a thing, they are more likely to do just that.

"Jasmin—" He held out his hands. "I don't know what you're talking about. Was it something I said in my sleep?"

Again she was quiet, and for the millionth time he wished he could see her face in detail to know her thoughts, to see her expression.

Several seconds stretched into what felt like years before, "It's nothing. Watch Isabelle for me. I'll make dinner."

He moved to her and held out his hands. She took his in hers, and he pulled her close to embrace her. "I don't know what's wrong, Jasmin. But I feel like I am losing you . . . to the Sunpriest . . . to worries I can't seem to quell. Talk to me."

"It's nothing." She held him close for a few seconds before she pulled away. "I need to get busy."

Harris shifted his sight to his mind and followed the path that lit up before him to his daughter, Isabelle. She played with her handmade dolls in her corner of their bedroom and yelled with excitement as he came into the room. She was small for a child of nine, but she was strong and filled with love.

"Papa!"

He knelt down, and she raced into his arms. He inhaled her sweet scent and held her close. "My little darling. What have you been doing?"

"I gave Ilythyrra a bath and just put new clothes on her," she said, very proud of herself. He knew she spoke about her doll because he felt the damp cloth of the toy between them. She pulled back and put her hand on his cheek. "I love Ilythyrra, Papa, but can I have a puppy like Remi? I promise I won't lose mine, Papa!"

The snow thickened as it melted during the day and refroze in the dead of night. Harris couldn't sleep. He couldn't get warm, not even an extra blanket or the presence of Jasmin beside him in their bed comforted him. He rose and rekindled the fire in the hearth, turning the wood. If a witness who did not know of Harris' disability watched him, they would not know he was blind. He moved as a sighted man would, hesitating only slightly when he turned, and his mind relayed the path of his intention.

This ability didn't appear after his accident—it had been there ever since he could remember. His mother had warned him to keep this knowledge to himself and to try not to find too many things for too many people. In their world, such an ability could rouse the curiosity of the Sunpriests.

Yet after he lost his sight, the power grew. It was as the Healer had told him. "Your other senses will grow stronger as they fill in your lack of sight."

Was it possible this . . . thing in his mind . . . this map of his surroundings, was one of his senses? And if so, wasn't it as natural as breathing, or hearing, or tasting, or smelling?

He wasn't so sure now. He was also unsure that confiding in Jasmin had been a wise decision.

Harris realized he wasn't alone. He turned to sense someone behind him, and when she touched his robe, he knelt down to his daughter. Placing his hands on her face, he read her emotion, though he already knew it as any father would. Her face had swelled from crying, and she knuckled her eyes as she moved into his arms and he held her by the fire. "What is it? Was it a bad dream?"

"No . . . maybe." Her voice was quiet as she sniffed between words. "It was the voice again, Papa."

Harris tried not to tense while he comforted her. It had been a few months since Isabelle had told him about the voice in her dreams. It was something she refused to tell her mother, especially now. Isabelle did not like the Sunpriest Doswee. "What did the voice say this time?"

He felt her hand on his face, her way of communicating with him. She spoke in a whisper, "It said he is in the mountain. That he will die if we do not save him. But I . . . I don't know who, Papa. The voice said it was nearly time, and I would need him."

The voice in Isabelle's dreams had sometimes told her things that had led to Harris finding objects, things no one knew were missing. One had been the wallet of a merchant found behind the tavern. Harris had wanted to turn it into the mayor, but Isabelle had been adamant that they would need it. So it had remained hidden, buried away from the house.

Thinking of who this person could be caused Harris to shiver. He set Isabelle down and rose from the fire, his skin hot to the touch from the heat, but his bones still cold. That was when he realized . . . *he* wasn't cold. Someone else was. Was it the person the voice warned Isabelle about?

This cold . . . this individual had to be family, and if not family, someone close to Harris. Was it Breeze? Or even Remi? Had he lost his puppy again and traveled out into the snow?

Isabelle yanked on his robe. "Can you see them now?"

"Yes, I can. Go back to bed and sleep, okay?"

She hugged his leg before she dashed back to the bedroom.

Checking on his wife once more, to assure himself she slept (he could tell from the sound of her breathing), Harris donned the layers of clothing he used to bring firewood into the house at night. He took his stick, a knife, and the flint he used to make fire and placed them into a bag that hung from his waist.

Stepping outside, he closed his eyes and succumbed to the thing . . . the map . . . the guide . . .

He didn't have the identity of this missing person, but their location was there, just off from the mountain pass. And they weren't moving. The pulse of the path was steady as it worked its way back from the feeling of intense cold and misery to where Harris stood. He had only to traverse it to find his target.

A sane man would go back to the warmth of his house and ignore the feeling. Perhaps even dismiss the voice his child had periodically heard since she turned seven.

But Harris had never been called a sane man, and the village forgave him much for being blind. But would whatever was at the end of his path forgive him if he did not at least try to find them?

One inexplicable thing about his map was that he knew it would lead him down paths less traveled, yet safer than the main road up the mountain. He could "see" brush and trees, rocks and holes, and he steadily, if slowly, made his way to the end.

The path took him down a ravine, along a trail eyes could not see. Using his walking stick for balance, Harris slowly, carefully maneuvered around jagged rocks until an all too familiar smell came to him.

The scent of death. Had he arrived too late? No . . . the feel of cold and misery was still . . .

"Who's there?"

Harris froze. He hadn't expected to hear a voice.

"If . . . you're a wolf come to finish me off . . ."

Harris *knew* the voice, and it wasn't one he imagined hearing. Not out here! "I am not a wolf, Brent."

"Harris!"

It was his friend, the soldier, and once Harris was near, he almost stumbled on what he discovered by using his hands and feeling it: his friend's horse. It was dead, and this was the smell that overwhelmed him. "Tell me where you are. Guide me." Now that he had found his target, the map vanished, though he knew it would come again when he wanted to go home.

With some direction under the moonlit night, Harris found Brent. He lay several feet away from his horse, but his leg was broken and he had pain in his arm, though could still use it.

"I'm afraid it was wolves," Brent said as Harris touched his friend and took his own assessment of his injuries. "I was able to kill two, maybe three, before another dove after Birch. She spooked and all three of us went over the side of the road. We're at mini-valley, aren't we?"

"Yes," Harris said, smiling at his friend's use of their childhood name of the ravine. Because when you are small, a ravine seems as big as a valley. "I'll need to set that leg. There are no bones protruding, but I'm not sure you can walk on it."

"I'll walk you through a field dressing, if you can get to my bags on Birch." He sighed. "I'm gonna miss that horse. Breeze is going to be upset with me."

"Breeze and Remi are going to be happy to know you are alive and not dead down here," Harris found the bags and unbuckled them. He dragged them to Harris and mentioned building a fire.

"No . . . it will draw more wolves. I'm fine enough, and I've endured harsher winters on the front lines. Let's get this leg into a condition I can walk on."

"Is that a good idea?"

"It's . . . all right."

Something in Brent's voice bothered Harris, but he remained silent as his old friend directed him on what to do. Using nearby wood and leather straps in Brent's bag, not to mention clean wrappings for open wounds, Harris was able to fashion a neat and tidy splint on his friend's leg.

Night slipped away while they worked. Harris knew this because the cold had lessened and he felt warmth on his face. With his walking stick under one of Brent's shoulders and his own under the other, Harris guided them around to the side path and up to the road.

"I never knew that . . . .path was there . . ." Brent said in a voice filled with pain. "I see your little . . . map . . . is still working."

"Hush. It brought me to you. Do not speak of it in the village."

"Ah . . . that new priest being . . . nosey?"

"Jasmin . . ."

"Ah. Say . . . no more."

They moved in silence as the sun rose even higher, and Harris could see the village in his mind. Finally, "Brent, why are you here? And you are not in uniform?"

Brent was silent for an uncomfortable length of time. Harris felt a rock settle in his stomach, knowing something bad had happened. And he thought he knew what. "You . . . didn't get the promotion."

A sigh. "No. I was passed over for another. As a consolation, I was given a week's leave to return home."

And tell Breeze . . . Harris felt that rock become a boulder. He felt for his old friend—to be a soldier was to be without family. Brent's only hope of openly sharing Breeze and Remi with everyone was for him to become an officer. Twice he had requested the promotion, worked hard for it, and now twice he had been denied, and Breeze would continue to live as a single mother, out of wedlock, in a village that barely tolerated her and her son. When in truth, she was married to a wonderful man who deserved happiness . . . and a family.

Harris felt guilty that he had those things . . . and his best friend didn't. *I cannot see my daughter's face, but I can be with her, and yet he can see and beholds only bloodshed and carnage . . . and can rarely spend time with his son.*

"I . . . couldn't in good conscience . . . wear the trappings of an army that I no longer believe in."

"Brent!" Harris hissed. "Don't say those things." He could hear the cries and voices of people coming as they entered the village, and he heard the shouting of his own wife and daughter.

Hands, voices, smells—it was all overwhelming, and it destroyed the map in his mind as they took Brent from him. Terrence, the village's elected mayor among the five village Elders, took charge and set everyone a task. He patted Harris on the back and thanked him for finding their village hero. The only one who had survived the army and returned home periodically to visit his family's resting place.

Brent's family—his mother and sister—were long dead. One by age and the other from illness. So often, Brent would stay with Harris. And this time was no different. Jasmin rearranged the living area and converted the couch into a bed. The Healers were called in, and she invited Doswee there to pray for Brent when he told the story of what happened.

Others retrieved Brent's things, and Harris sat by the fire, listening. He was tired but happy, and once everyone was gone he would slip away and fill Breeze in. And, hopefully, find a way the two could visit before Brent had to leave again.

"Harris."

A bit startled at the harsh tone in the voice, Harris looked away from the fire and focused on the origin of the sound. Brent still had a few visitors, and he could hear his daughter laughing. "Yes?"

"I am Sunpriest Doswee."

Harris nodded. "My wife talks about you frequently."

"She talks about you as well." There was another tone to the Priest's voice that Harris didn't like. "Mostly about how you find things."

Harris didn't say anything. He knew his icy stare was enough to put people off. Most of the time they would excuse themselves and leave in peace.

Doswee did not. "There is a witch power the Mages have in Valdemar. It gives their white devils the ability to find things no one else can find."

Harris didn't react. Mostly because he didn't know this. He knew very little about Valdemar . . . only that there were magical ponies, as his daughter called them, and they had magic and were permitted, and even trained, to do this. Of course, these weren't the teachings of the Sunpriests—their stories of Valdemar were much more . . . horrific. Demons, witches, powers, and other murderous things. Things Vkandis did not approve of.

Harris gave little thought of Vkandis. Or the priests. He only wanted happiness and peace.

"Why do you not answer?"

"I didn't know there was a question." Harris was tired, and he wanted this man out of his house.

"How do you find these things?"

Harris shrugged. "I listen."

"You can hear a yappy dog or a mewing kitten, but you cannot hear a man shouting from a mountain ravine, Harris Yerger. No one knew this soldier was on his way home. No one knew he was wounded on that pass." There was a pause, and though Doswee had been talking in whispers, his voice rose just a little now. "But *you* did."

"Come now," Brent said from where he sat on the couch, his leg, mended and thickly bandaged, propped on a chair. "Sunpriest—I thank Vkandis, who sent such a kind and caring man as Harris out to find me. Isn't it through the weak and invalid that He speaks? Had He not, I would have died alone, by an infection or been eaten by wolves. Can we not have a peaceful night?"

Everyone looked at Doswee, and though he couldn't see it, Harris was pretty sure the priest was blushing red. He heard the stool the priest had been seated on creak as he stood. "I must agree. Praise Vkandis and the Son of the Sun. I leave you in the Yerger's good hands."

There were footsteps, and then a shutting door.

"Was he accusing Harris of something?"

"I don't know. I've seen Jasmin with him a lot this past month."

"Well, it is a bit odd that Harris found him like that, isn't it?"

"Harris has always been able to find things. It's a gift."

"Maybe . . . but from where?"

Whispers. Innuendos. They troubled Harris now that a Sunpriest was here . . . and taking an interest in *him*.

"It's coming," Isabelle said the next afternoon as she helped Harris move snow from the back of their house. It covered the firewood, making it wet. He wanted to build a shelter for the wood, but he needed the material itself to burn to keep them warm. There had been a buzz in the village all morning. Harris had heard it when he'd made his daily trip to the village well, and no one returned his good mornings.

So he assumed Isabelle's statement meant something terrible was coming.

"Harris?"

He straightened and stood at the sound of his friend's voice. "You shouldn't be up and around yet. If Jasmin catches you up—"

"She left some time ago, after you came out here. Harris," Brent hobbled closer. Harris had fashioned a crutch from strong oak, and the leg had been recast into a stronger splint. "I think it would be best if you took Isabelle and left."

"Left? And go where?"

"Away from here. Menmellith would be a good start, and then get yourself into Valdemar."

"Valdemar? Why?" The two men kept their voices soft, but Harris knew Isabelle was listening to everything.

"Because it's not safe, Papa," Isabelle whispered.

"She's right," Brent said. He put his hand on Harris' arm. "You have to know you have a magic power, Harris. Your ability to find . . . me." He glanced down at Isabelle. "The fact she's hearing voices . . . the Sunpriests can't discover this."

"How did you—?"

"I—I told Remi." Isabelle whispered. "I'm sorry, Papa. I know I shouldn't have, but we were fighting, and he said I wasn't as special as you."

"Isabelle—"

"Harris Yerger?" This voice was different and full of authority.

Harris motioned for Brent to take Isabelle and put his finger to his lips before he stepped out from the side of the house, his boots crunching in the snow. "Yes? Can you identify yourselves? I am blind."

There was an awkward pause and a few whispers.

"This is the one with the witch power?"

"Is Doswee mad?"

The first voice cleared their throat. "I am Maxis Chever of the Karse army. I hear you rescued one of my own soldiers."

"Word travels fast," Harris said. "Your soldier is well and fine. He was attacked by wolves and fell into a ravine."

"And it was you . . . a blind man . . . who found him?"

Harris hesitated. He heard the tone in the man's voice. He already knew what was about to happen. Isabelle had been right. *It's coming.* "Yes."

"Then I must place you under arrest, Harris Yerger, for the suspected practice of witch power. You are to be held for the Sunpriests arrival tomorrow and tested. If you are found guilty—"

Harris held up his hand. "I am a man of thirty," he said. "And I have lived in this village all of my life. I know what the punishment is. Though I cannot protest my innocence enough."

"Sir, I am Brent Wressler, the soldier this man found—"

"Ah, yes. You look very much improved from the reports I received."

Brent came from behind the house and stood beside Harris. Harris didn't know if Isabelle was with him. "Thank you, sir, and I owe it to his man and his family. This man saved my life—"

"You know him well?" Maxis said.

"He is my childhood friend, sir. He and his wife allow me to stay with them when I am home, since my own family has long since passed." He paused. "I was on my way home for leave when I was attacked."

"Yes . . . I heard about the promotion . . . and I am sorry. But there has been an accuser, and the Sunpriest of this village says it is credible."

"Who has accused me?" Harris asked. He was aware of other voices now, as villagers passing by their home overheard the loud voices.

There was another awkward pause. "Jasmin Yerger," Maxis said. "Your wife."

Harris was surprised, and then he wasn't. What did shock him was the way he was treated by the priests. The soldiers had been respectful and descent. But the priests . . .

He'd been chained to a wall and stripped of his clothing down to his trousers. The room had been cold, with no fire, and he'd been questioned endlessly. *Where did you get the power? How did you find him on the mountain? How could you see your way to him?*

On and on their questions came at him, and every time he answered, he was struck in the torso. He assumed this way, when he was clothed again, no one could see the torture. He didn't know if this was the means by which those with witch powers were tested—but it was how they chose to test him. He didn't understand it.

Until finally he was left alone, hanging from the wall, shivering. He heard a bell ringing, but it meant nothing to him. All he knew was a respite from the pain and the incessant questions he couldn't answer.

The screech of the door being opened roused him, and he was unchained and allowed to fall to the ground. He was given water and dressed in a rough-hewn smock of some kind. No one said anything or answered his questions until he smelled something. It reminded him of the incense burned by the Sunpriests outside their temple.

"Harris Yerger," came Doswee's voice, and Harris knew where the smell came from. "You have been found guilty of using witch power for personal gain against the people of this village. You will burn first thing in the morning for your crimes." A pause. "Do you have anything to say for yourself?"

"I am . . . innocent."

"You all say that."

"You never tested me . . ."

A boot struck his side, and he doubled over as the pain enveloped him.

"Make sure he is gagged when he is brought for the burning," Doswee said, and then the smell vanished, and the door was locked once again.

His thoughts went to Isabelle. *What will happen to her? What if she told her mother about the voice? Would the Sunpriest burn her as well?* He wanted to stop them . . . but he couldn't. He'd never even learned how to master a weapon, never had the chance. And his daughter . . .

Voices roused him and he swallowed hard, knowing it must be time for his death. He didn't want to think about it, especially if Isabelle was forced to watch.

The door opened, and he was instantly brought to his feet. "What . . . what did they do to you?"

Brent? Harris reached out to touch his friend's face. "Why . . . why are you here?"

"Because I told you you need to leave. Can you walk?"

Leave? Harris coughed. "A might better than you, I would guess."

Brent kept his hand wrapped tightly around Harris' wrist to guide him. The escape was slow going, since Brent was still walking on his crutch. The night breeze caressed Harris' face, and he tried to pause to take in the fresh air.

"Not now," Brent hissed and pulled him along.

The smock they'd given him to wear—probably a better kindling for burning—wasn't much protection against the cold ,and Harris started trembling. His feet were wrapped in the same material, and the wet from the snow and mud soaked through. He was turned around and had no idea where he was until he smelled a stable and horses and a small child grabbed his leg.

"Daddy!" Isabelle whispered.

"Shush, child," Breeze's voice was beside him and a heavy covering placed over his shoulders. "This should do until we get to Menmellith. You can get us there, can't you Harris?"

"I—" He swallowed and blinked several times. If only he could see their faces. "Tell me . . . what is happening?"

"The wallet, papa," Isabelle said. "The voice told me to give it to Uncle Brent, that he'd know what to do with it."

"She's a brilliant child," Brent said as Harris heard the sound of horses' hooves on the snow, cracking the refrozen ice. "She had this plan in her head, and she and Remi worked everything out. You're going to Menmellith now. You can use your power to get your daughter and my family there safely."

"Wait," Harris reached out. "What about you?"

"I—" Brent hesitated. "I made sure Doswee never wrongly accused another innocent man, woman, or child. I tried begging for your release, and he threatened—" He took in a deep breath. "He knew about Remi and Breeze, and he threatened to tell the army about my little family if I didn't do exactly as he said."

"Oh, Brent . . ."

"I freed you on the condition that you get them out of here," Brent said.

"Come with us," Harris insisted.

"Papa, the voice said we have to go *now*!" Isabelle said in a voice a little too loud.

"Listen to her, Harris. I don't know what or who this voice is, but it's guided her and us so far. So has your witch power. I don't understand it, but I can believe in it, more than I can believe in what the Sunpriests say. I am already a dead man—Doswee wasn't a man to keep secrets like this to himself. The other priests will come looking for me when they find his body. It's best if I stay here."

"But—"

"Get on that horse. Now!"

A horse's hide bumped against Harris, and he found the stirrup and put his foot in it. With a pull and a push from Brent, he threw his leg around and settled into the saddle. "This is—"

"The mayor's horse," Brent finished. "He likes money too. Look for your path, Harris, and get them safely to Menmellith." Isabelle was placed in front of him in the saddle and the reins in his hands. "Go!"

Harris closed his eyes and sought out the way to Menmillith. The safest way. The way the others would not follow. Abruptly the way lit up for him on the map in his mind, and he turned the horse in that direction. He didn't look back because he had to keep going forward.

He and Brent both had made decisions in that instant, decisions that would change their lives forever. For him there could be a future, but for the man who had always sought a way to be with his family . . .

That man had chosen freedom for them by his own sacrifice.

Their journey was uneventful, almost anticlimactic in a way. The snow eased back, and the temperature rose a few degrees. He couldn't see Menmillith's structures, but he could hear their people. The joy in their voices and the play of children.

He led the way to something . . . something Isabelle said was up ahead and he could see in his mind. The two horses weren't out of place, according to Breeze, who gave him a play-by-play of what they passed as she pulled her horse along side his.

"She's here!" Isabelle started to squirm in her seat in front of him.

"Be still or you'll fall," Harris said.

"Sweet Lady," Breeze said. "I never thought I'd . . . they're beautiful!"

"Put me down!"

Harris stopped his horse, and Breeze said it was okay to dismount. They weren't in the way of anything. They were in fact, just entering the city gate.

And they were being met.

Isabelle couldn't contain her joy and ran off as soon as he got her to the ground.

"Isabelle!" he shouted.

But Breeze put a hand on his arm. "She's okay, Harris. She's . . ."

::She is Chosen, Harris Yerger.::

The voice wasn't in his ear but in his mind, and he staggered at the sound of it. It was beautiful music. Like soft bells.

"Heyla," said a female voice, and Harris felt a hand against his cheek. "I am Maelyn. I'm afraid Ilythyrra has taken me and my Companion on a merry chase to find you. All of you."

Ilythyrra? "I know that name. That was the name Isabelle gave her doll."

"That is the name of her Companion," Maelyn said.

"I . . . don't understand."

"It's all right," Breeze said beside him. "It's something Jasmin realized."

Harris turned to her beside him. "Jasmin?"

"It's time for some truths," Breeze said. "Jasmin realized your ability was a witch power early on, so she married you to protect you, because she loved you. But when the Sunpriest started taking an interest in Isabelle . . . and then you . . . she did the only thing she could."

"She told Isabelle to let the voice know what was happening," Maelyn said. "I'm not sure your wife knew she was talking to a Companion, but she knew she had to protect both of you."

"She tried to redirect Doswee's attention to herself," Breeze sighed. "But your finding Brent . . ." she sobbed.

Harris took her into his arms. "I'm so sorry, Breeze."

She put her head on his chest. "He might still be alive . . . I don't know . . . maybe one day . . . you can find him again."

Maybe, he thought. And he looked back the way they came to see the path was dark in his mind. Closed.

Gone.

"Let's get all of you into an inn, bathed and clothed. We'll start our journey to Valdemar tomorrow."

"Valdemar?" Harris said.

"Of course," Maelyn said. "To Haven. You and your daughter have a new home."

"What about Breeze and Remi?"

"They're included too. Let's go."

Breeze took his hand and led him as he held the reins on his horse. He thought he heard a puppy whining. "Remi . . . did you stuff your puppy in your bag?"

"Yeah," Remi said and then the puppy's cries turned into happy little barks.

"Why so sad sounding?"

"I got a puppy . . ." he said. "But Isabelle got a pony!"

The Gift of Twins

Brenda Cooper

Rhiannon balanced her gittern on her knee, the light wood bowl of the instrument a fine contrast to her bardic Scarlets. The crowd in the big barn moved restlessly. Late summer sunlight spilled in through the high windows, hot and bright enough to make people squint and mop their brows. Even though the animals had been sent out to pasture, the dirt-floored main room smelled of sheep droppings and dry hay. Faces looked pinched with worry, lips tight in anger, and individual voices, when she could make them out, sounded like desperate whispers. Not that Rhiannon could blame them.

Herald Moren stood on a ladder, head and shoulders above the crowd. He was classically beautiful, his dark hair and eyes and wide shoulders almost a cliché. He could have modeled for any sculpture that depicted Heralds if it weren't for the sweat beading his brow and the slight look of annoyance on his face. He had also been watching, but now he spoke again, his commanding voice drawing the crowd to quiet as he told them, "You will be expected to send up to a third of your able-bodied men and women to training. Send them with no more than one quarter of your weapons."

Valdemar had been sending capable soldiers to the Borders near here for a while. But Haven couldn't produce enough troops to patrol every mile. By next summer, the village would be expected to help guard themselves. Most of the men and women in this room would give up two seasons, winter and spring, to travel to a nearby large holding for training. While winter would become easier for it, with fewer mouths to feed, everyone left behind would have double the work in spring.

Rhiannon and her twin, Dionne, were along to make the Herald's message more palatable by offering people both song and surcease. There had been places where Rhiannon's singing and Dionne's gentle, effective Healing and advice had been enough. That wouldn't be true here. The angry and stubborn looks on people's faces convinced her she would need her secret weapon. She had a good dose of the Bardic Gift, and in the last few years she had gained a little more confidence in her skills.

She glanced around the room, quickly finding her twin's bright red hair and Healer Greens. Their twin bond always made it easy to find each other. The same bond meant it only took a breath for Dionne to look up in response to Rhiannon's gaze, nod and slip toward the door.

Rhiannon waited until she was outside.

Dionne was easily influenced by the Bardic Gift. That was Rhiannon's fault, and so was the way her twin hated that particular weakness. They had been twelve, not yet Chosen for the collegia. Rhiannon had delighted in discovering that her voice could call, or repel, dogs. She could sing her mother into giving them cookies. Dionne hadn't minded the cookies, but then Rhiannon had started played pranks on her sister, singing her into silly rages twice. The second time, Dionne was sent home from school for acting up, and she refused to talk to Rhiannon for two days.

With the cruel logic of a young girl, Rhiannon had found that hysterically funny. The next day, she sang her sister into an unfortunate crush on an older music teacher. He had, fortunately for them all, enough of an ear to catch Rhiannon at it and recognize the Gift. Right then and there, he forcibly pulled her into the back room of the music hall and gave her a lecture fit to blister her ears about what a treasure her Gift was and how horrible it was to misuse it. On anyone. Much less family.

Rhiannon had stumbled out to find her sister huddled at the end of the school hallway, tears dripping from her chin. Rhiannon had mumbled an apology and sworn on a cut lock of their mingled red hair that she would never influence Dionne with her Bardic Gift again. At least, not on purpose. In spite of that promise, she'd been forced to spend two weeks scrubbing floors in the music room after school. She had done the hard work gladly, and to this day the scent of soap mingled with hot water made her taste her young guilt.

Herald Moren drew her wandering attention as he wound down his speech with a request that almost always riled up larger gatherings like this. "Please make a list of names for the training. We will review it together to be sure it includes the right combination of strength and experience."

Faces soured even further as the crowd read his meaning: They needed to include some of their younger men and women in the trainee list. Parents would hate it, and so would young lovers or married couples.

She picked up her gittern. Almost time to work.

Herald Moren finished with, "While you discuss this among yourselves, Bard Rhiannon, one of Haven's finest young Bards, will delight us all with background music for your enjoyment."

Rhiannon blushed lightly and smiled, then took a deep belly-breath. The gittern's warmth tingled in her left hand. The instrument, gifted to her when she made full Bard, was a joy to hold, its smooth bole carved of a single branch of an oak that had once stood near the Bardic Collegium in Valdemar. She took another deep inward breath, centered, and reached for her Gift. Another glance at the crowded room full of unhappy farmers convinced her she would need to use most of her skill.

She decided to discard her first choice and start with "The Silver Brook"; it was long, low, and sweet, and probably known by everyone here. The quill in her right hand danced over the strings of the opening measure and she hummed the first few bars to warm up. Then she opened her mouth to sing, pouring a sense of calm into her heart to spill out through her voice.

"Dancing waters, silver bright, sparkle in the sun's fair light . . ." She kept her eyes open, her gaze level and even, and dropped her shoulders, trying to appear perfectly at ease. Nothing to see here. No one working extra hard. Sweat poured into her eyes and she blinked it away, both hands busy. The flow of effort overtook her, the raw power, the hope, the knowledge that her work mattered to Valdemar.

She continued for five songs. A long set with no break. By the time the crowd really calmed, her voice was barely able to hold high notes. She kept playing, with more breaks and less use of her Gift, relaxing into the beauty of the complex melodies.

Dust motes glittered in the softening afternoon by the time the town leaders came up with a list the Herald approved with only two changes: one to strike an older man and one to add two women.

She and Moren found Dionne outside with the twin's bays, Chocolate and Lily, saddled and ready. Moren's Companion, Fern, waited bedside them, her snow-white coat touched with gold evening light. As they started along the thin track that led to the same campsite they had used the night before, Moren turned to Rhiannon. "Thank you. That was very helpful."

She swallowed a slight burr of irritation that he seldom acknowledged Dionne, who looked almost as spent as she felt. "How many people came to you for Healing?" she asked her sister.

"Twenty. But only two were serious. An old woman with a twisted ankle that needed almost an hour of encouragement to knit back properly. Her bones were brittle."

Rhiannon smiled. That was one old woman whose bones had probably all been strengthened. Dionne had a soft spot for old women.

Her sister's voice changed tone as she added, "One young woman had a broken cheekbone. She said she fell, but I suspect someone hit her. Not that she'd admit it. But I know. It's harder to heal that kind of hurt."

"The kind that comes with a lie?" Rhiannon asked.

A frown broke across the handsome Herald's face and made him look almost like a normal human. "If only we could undo all of the ills of the world."

Rhiannon closed her eyes. "If only."

The White Stag Inn looked big enough to have twenty rooms. Rhiannon eyed it with weary approval as they pulled to a halt in front. Someone had applied a fresh coat of white paint to the doors and windows. White window boxes held purple and blue pansies. Lovers lace in full, pink bloom decorated the forward-facing fences on either side of the low-slung building.

She allowed a stableboy to take Chocolate, and, as soon as the others were off their mounts, she led the way inside. She uncurled her hands, flexing them, working out the stiffness from three nights of playing. The last night had been the hardest. The town's mayor had wanted nothing to do with Haven's plan, even though it would make them safer for years to come. Honor allowed Rhiannon to encourage things like group calm, but not to direct decisions or opinions. So, while Herald Moren had spoken to each person individually, she had sent waves of calm into the small crowd. It had taken a very long time. Dionne had taken one look at Rhiannon's hands and even as tired as she was from a day of Healing, she had held the swollen fingers and wrists and sent cooling energy into them.

The farther they got from Haven, the more pigheaded the farmers and millers and hedge-healers seemed to be—in spite of the fact that they were in more danger than those who lived closer to Haven. They *needed* special training in how to spot trouble and how to protect the town against roving bands of thieves. Whatever magic Vanyel had applied to the Borders when Rhiannon was young kept problem Mages out, but it did nothing to stop the thieves and brigands who came across the porous borders.

The common room had a stage and more than twenty tables, a sign that locals came here as well as travelers. The smell of roasting mutton, carrots, and bread fresh from the oven suffused the room and tickled Rhiannon's throat. She picked a table near the empty stage and sat with her back to it, letting Moren and Dionne slide into the two better seats. She lifted a hand for food and wine. Plates arrived almost instantly, the mutton decorated with fragrant sprigs of rosemary.

Half a candlemark and a glass of good, dark ale later, Rhiannon felt better.

A woman in a bright blue dress with white sleeves swept in the door, a lute strapped to her back and a small hand-drum tied to her side. When she spotted their table, she stopped and stared. Strangely, her gaze was fixed tightly on Rhiannon and Dionne rather than on Herald Moren. While Valdemarans appreciated Healers and Bards, they were usually most fascinated with anyone wearing Whites.

The singer offered a broad smile and held her hand out to Rhiannon. "I am so happy to see a Bard here. Will you play?"

Ah. Rhiannon shook her head. "I don't expect to offer you any competition this evening. I've been playing almost every night for a few weeks."

Someone at a nearby table said, "Not even a song or two?"

"'My Lady's Eyes'?" a plump woman asked.

Rhiannon laughed and shook her head. "Not likely. I am very tired." She smiled up at the pretty woman. "I'd like to hear you play. Do you sing as well?"

"I do."

Dionne smiled. "It will be good to hear a fresh voice."

Rhiannon kicked her gently under the table.

The woman flowed up onto a stage built against a brick wall hung with white curtains. She reached behind the curtain and brought out a folding stool and moved easily through what seemed to be a routine setup.

More people began drifting in, apparently expecting the show. In spite of how tired she was, Rhiannon accepted another ale. It didn't seem like a good idea, but the thin, sweet woman who ran the inn seemed to want her to have it. Besides, it would be very rude not to stay and listen to at least the first few songs. She turned in her seat to watch the woman start her set.

"Hello," the blue-garbed woman addressed the room in a silky, low voice. "I'm Lisue, and I'm happy to be performing tonight. Thank you to every one of my regulars in attendance and also to our distinguished travelers." She nodded at the Herald's table. "Thank you to other travelers who may be here and, as always, to the staff and proprietors of the White Stag Inn."

Standard patter, and polite. Rhiannon clapped lightly with the rest of the room, showing appreciation for the waitstaff.

When she started to sing, the woman's voice was not standard. It was deep, throaty, and really beautiful. Haunting. She sang a song about Vanyel's love for Stef that Rhiannon had never heard before. Rhiannon stared. The song was far too good not to be in the common repertoire.

She followed that with a comedic song about digging a hole in the ground to escape a deformed wolf in the Pelagir Hills, only to meet a rabbit with five ears who helped the protagonists escape. After that, a sea shanty and then a harvest song. The entire room sang along on the last two, first all sounding like rowdy sailors and then all swinging imaginary scythes together to bring in wheat. Feet stamped. Ale tankards slammed the tops of tables. Two teenaged girls in the back clapped a little out of rhythm, smiling and swaying.

The woman had range. Range in her voice, range in her set list. If she had written any of these songs—three of which were new to Rhiannon—she had at least the Creative Gift.

Rhiannon suddenly realized how much her neck hurt from being twisted so tightly. She turned back to her half-empty ale tankard and noticed Dionne looked at least as taken with the entertainment as she was. Her blue eyes were round and merry, and she swayed to the rhythm of the small drum tapping along with the harvest song.

As good as the music was, the days in the saddle, her sore hands, and her newly sore neck wore on Rhiannon. As soon as she finished her ale, she excused herself from the table. She managed to smile at Lisue to thank her, but exhaustion forced her to lean on the table for balance.

Herald Moren noticed, stood, and took her elbow. "Can I escort you to your room?"

"Please." She glanced at Dionne.

Her sister smiled and nodded toward the stage. "I'll stay."

"Remember we're leaving just after breakfast."

"I know. To go home." She smiled. "I'll be up soon."

Rhiannon sighed. Dionne always had more energy than she did at night, no matter what she had expended on Healing.

On the way up the stairs, Herald Moren whispered, "Lisue is good, but you are better."

She smiled. "Thank you. It's too bad no one spotted her for Bardic when she was younger."

"She doesn't feel like a candidate to me," he replied.

Rhiannon cocked her head as she mounted the last sturdy stair. "She's a little old, of course. But I've never heard some of her songs, and if she wrote them . . ."

"That's one Bardic Gift," he acknowledged, pausing at the top of the stairs with an absent frown, as if gathering his thoughts. "But I'm not sure she'd belong. I can't put my finger on it, but she has a fragility to her . . . or maybe a brittleness."

Rhiannon frowned. "I didn't sense that."

"You were busy listening to the music, and you only had a good view when you twisted your neck unreasonably." He resumed his measured pace down the hall, pulling her gently into motion again.

"I know. I should have sat next to you."

"I watched her face. She needed every bit of applause she got. Hungry for it in a way you never are. You do what you do because you love to sing, and to help, but she feeds her ego with her voice."

Rhiannon warmed at his compliment. "That's not uncommon for a performer."

"I suppose not." He stopped briefly at the door of the room she shared with Dionne, across the hall from his own. "Sleep well. I'll wake you early."

"Good night."

Just moments later, she was in bed, wrists still throbbing, her scattered thoughts telling her she was too tired to sleep easily. Bard Nickolas had taught her to use a bit of her own Gift on herself at night, but the best she could do was hum herself into a restless doze.

Rhiannon woke, startled. She felt groggy and . . . aroused? She blinked hard, stretching, wondering whatever had she been dreaming of?

"Dionne?"

No one answered. No one breathed.

Rhiannon rolled over. Starlight and a bit of moon threw just enough light to verify that not only was Dionne not here, but she hadn't been here. She struggled for her flint and lit a candle, pulling clothes back on by its flickering light. She could feel Dionne. And worse, *that was where she felt the arousal. Dionne felt it.* But she knew her sister. Strangers wouldn't do more than draw a raised appreciative eyebrow from her when they were working. Well, really, anytime. She was as happy as anyone in Haven to share physical play with close friends she loved. But unless one of Dionne's lovers from the Collegium had come here, this made no sense. Besides, why would Rhiannon feel it? They always closed the twin bond on dates.

Out of habit, Rhiannon grabbed her gittern case on the way out, careful not to drop it in her haste as she rushed down the stairs. She didn't think about Herald Moren until she was on the ground floor. Maybe she should have woken him. But what would she have said while pounding on his door in the middle of the night? "Dionne's *flirting*?"

They were thirty years old.

Rhiannon forced her feet to slow and stopped in the common room doorway. Nuts and bread crusts sat on the tables, scattered between empty tankards and clay pitchers. Everyone else was gone, except Dionne, Lisue, and two women working in the kitchen. They could be heard chattering and clanking silverware, but they hadn't started clearing tables yet.

Lisue stood near the front of the stage, singing *a capella* at the moment, something full of longing and remorse. She had removed her white sleeves and wore only the blue dress, now sleeveless, her dark hair failing down around her elbows. Rhiannon drew in a sharp breath at the curve of Lisue's partly bared breasts and the brightness of her smile. She inched farther into the room.

Lisue noticed, winked, lifted her voice a tiny bit.

Rhiannon glided forward, glad she'd brought her gittern. Maybe Lisue would play with her. She stopped halfway down the aisle and fumbled her instrument free of its case as her heart began searching for a perfect harmony.

Lisue kept watching her, her voice utterly stunning, so resonant it seemed to live in Rhiannon's very bones.

Dionne followed Lisue's gaze and turned around, noticing Rhiannon. Her eyes narrowed, her look decidedly unhappy at the interruption.

The look shocked Rhiannon back to herself. She gritted her teeth and closed her eyes. Lisue had more than the Creative Gift: S*he has the Bardic Gift.* She hadn't been using it earlier, but now? And it must be strong. While Dionne was highly susceptible, Rhiannon wasn't. And yet this woman had snared her completely. Her. Rhiannon. And she clearly still held Dionne inside a spell.

Well.

Dionne wasn't the least bit *shay'a'chern;*. All of her lovers were male. That didn't matter; they had *shay'ch* friends they'd kill for.

But it made the quickening of Dionne's breath and her fluttery hands all the more creepy.

Rhiannon slid next to Dionne and poked her.

Dionne slid sideways on the bench. Away from her.

Away. From. Her.

"Time to come to bed," Rhiannon hissed in her sister's ear. "We have to start back early."

"Maybe I'll stay here a few days," Dionne murmured. Her eyes, fastened on Lisue, were round, her lips parted lightly.

Rhiannon shivered. Lisue couldn't sing forever. If she sat here long enough, the woman would stop, and that would be that.

Lisue's song ended on a long, sweet note. She started another song.

Rhiannon felt her heart want to follow, noticed a slight sweat breaking across her palms. Staying wouldn't do. She dug her nails into her palms and tapped her feet, struggling not to listen until the song ended. When it did, she stood, stepped toward the stage.

Lisue cocked her head, opened her mouth.

Before she could say a thing, Rhiannon asked, "Duet?"

Lisue's smile looked part feral cat, part whore.

Rhiannon pulled a chair up on stage and looked directly at Lisue. The other singer's eyes were dark pools, impossible to read easily, but they felt hungry. "'Cat in a Summer Garden'?" she suggested.

Lisue raised an eyebrow. It was a sensual song but not bawdy. "Maybe 'Jeremy Locklear's Love'?"

Rhiannon swung into "Cat in a Summer Garden." It required a huge range, but both women could hit high and low notes with ease. Rhiannon had chosen it to turn down the heat, and she kept the energy low and sweet, in keeping with the soft and slightly silly song.

It should have brought down her own arousal and driven Dionne to sit back in her seat.

But she had to look away from Lisue and force her attention onto the notes from her own instrument and her own voice to avoid the slightly apprehensive, sweet buzz Lisue started in her heart, her body. In spite of her tight focus, she felt more beautiful, more desirable than she had since they had left Haven six months ago.

At the end of the song, Lisue nodded, clearly in high spirits. She flung her lightly booted feet up and starting into "Jeremy Locklear's Love."

Rhiannon knew it, but not as well. It took work to get the words and rhythm right. All the while her own attraction to Lisue made it harder to remember she was here to drown out what Lisue was doing to Dionne.

Dionne swayed with the music, her upturned face nearly glowing. Her gaze was so tightly fastened on Lisue that Rhiannon might as well not be in the room.

As the last notes of the song drifted away, Rhiannon felt for a third song to suggest, but fell behind as Lisue started right into "The Lady of Long Bear Island," which was worse than either of the other two. She should have started with a nursery rhyme.

The contest had changed from trying to best Lisue to trying to hold onto Rhiannon's very self. All the while, some part of her wanted to scream. She wasn't going to be able to sing Lisue down and away, to break her. Even untrained, the woman was too strong for Rhiannon to best her.

Rhiannon took a deep breath, looked directly into Dionne's eyes. Her sister was going to hate her. But if she couldn't sing Lisue into the ground, if her Gift wasn't enough, then she would use what she had. The bond between her and Dionne ran deeper than any bond between lovers. It ran deeper than any bond between normal sisters. It was stronger than Lisue. And so, even though she had promised on a twisted lock of red hair, she would do what she had to do and would find a way to make up for it afterward.

She should have started with a nursery rhyme. So she did. The one their mother used to sing, the song that sent her and Dionne easily to sleep on hot nights like this one.

My little ones, my best babies
There will be another day
This one is past like the last
It's time to sleep the night away.

Lisue looked confused. Good.

The night will let you dream
Each on your own winged pony
To lands you never saw before
That wait to catch your fancy

It wasn't even a very good song. Rhiannon had written better lullabies. But their mother had written this one, and as Rhiannon sang, she realized their mother must have had a touch of the Bardic Gift. Otherwise, how would this damned song have put them to sleep?

She smiled and poured more of her memories into the simple words.

Dionne's eyelids drooped, and she put her head on her hands.

The kitchen help began clearing the last tables.

Lisue stared. She couldn't know the song. It wasn't in the common repertoire. And she couldn't just sing over a full Bard like Rhiannon.

It wasn't done.

Rhiannon kept going, her fingers sliding the quill expertly among the strings in spite of the pain in her wrists and fingers.

Blankets tucked about your heads,
Like clouds to catch your dreams.

Hard to be tired and bothered all at once.

Rhiannon descended the two stairs from the stage carefully, still singing. She didn't so much as glance toward Lisue as she tucked her instrument back into its case, gathered Dionne in her arms, and carefully carried her drowsy sister to the edge of the stairs. There, she looked into Dionne's eyes.

Dionne whispered, "Thank you."

Rhiannon set her down and supported her elbow as they climbed up to bed together, Rhiannon continuing the lullaby all the way.

The next morning there was no sign of Lisue. The common room had been completely cleaned, and white dishes waited beside a buffet of fruit, bread, and rashers of fat, crisp bacon. As Rhiannon wound her hands around a cup of hot tea, she blinked tiredly, wondering how much of the night's events she even remembered correctly. To her surprise, Dionne wanted to talk about it.

"Lisue was using her Gift on me." She smiled. "I don't know if she really liked me or just wanted to show she had power over me. It was creepy. It was also working."

The Herald cocked his head, his face serious.

"They had a . . . song duel, I guess. Bardic Gift to Bardic Gift. It must have gone for at least an hour."

Rhiannon startled at that. "I don't think it was that long."

Herald Moren looked quite put out after more details emerged, although Rhiannon couldn't tell if it was because he hadn't even noticed or because it had happened at all. Maybe both. Even though she found him a little stuffy, he was a nice man and a good Herald. But he couldn't have helped. Rhiannon felt a little sorry for him over that. "I couldn't sing her down, and I don't like using my Gift that way. It feels like a desecration. Besides, it didn't work. I had to use it on Dionne instead."

Dionne glanced down at the top of the table.

Rhiannon took a deep breath. "I'll report Lisue as soon as we get home. I'd like to do more." She glanced at the Herald.

He shook his head. "We cannot fix it ourselves, not now. We have orders. Fern has relayed the story and promised that a delegation of strong Bards and a few Heralds will be sent to find her."

Relief flooded Rhiannon. Lisue needed to be brought to heel—and maybe even brought to Haven.

Dionne glanced toward Rhiannon, her eyes full of the complete understanding they so often shared. "If only we could undo all of the ills of the world."

Herald Moren laughed gently at having his own words sent back to him. He pushed himself up to standing. "I'll tell the stable boy to ready your horses."

After he left, Dionne reached across the table and took her hand. "It was an extraordinary circumstance. I forgive you."

"Thank you." Rhiannon could feel her shoulders relax.

Dionne squeezed her hand. "Maybe we should change the promise we swore on."

"To what?" Rhiannon asked.

"To promise not to use your Gifts on me unnecessarily."

Rhiannon leaned close and picked a bit of each of their hair between the same two fingers. "I promise."

They let go of each other, gathered their things, mounted, and turned the horses' noses toward Haven.

No Simple Kyree

Ron Collins

Once again, Nwah reached for a ley-line and hit a wall as hard as if it had been made of brick. A grumble escaped her throat before she could control it. The fur on her shoulders bristled as she took a stance in the middle of Darkwind's office, chest fully forward, muscles taut, jawline raised at the tilt that, in the wild, would let her opponent know this *kyree* was prepared to fight.

She had come to these offices in no little panic to report that her links had gone dead, only to hear from her mentor that it had been done on purpose, that Darkwind himself had administered the constraints that kept her from her Gift.

:No!: she said, pressing her front claws into the rug to contain her anger. *:You can't take the lines from me, too. I want them back. Now.:*

Darkwind sat passively in the recessed sill of the window, watching Vree, his bondbird soar gracefully in the currents above, the panes open to let in a chill breeze. The ugliness of the city sprawled outside the open frame. The odors of woodsmoke, earth, cattle, and horse mixed in ways so unnatural that they made Nwah's stomach curdle. It was near midday in early spring. The weather was growing warmer, the sounds of the city more fervent.

The Master Mage ran an implacable finger over the curve of his chin and simply nodded. The loose-fitting tunic he wore, pale gold and ephemeral green, with darker embroidery that spoke of something permanent, seemed to barely touch his thin frame. His eyes were distant, and for an instant their color faded from their usual cerulean toward the grayness of his bondbird's.

The passive nature of his response brought an impatient flick of Nwah's tail.

"I understand, pupling," he replied, his voice calmly modulated, as it always was. "But it is for the best. There are those who worry you cannot control yourself."

:Don't "pupling" me. I am no longer a child.:

"Being impetuous will serve only to prove them right."

:And just who are 'they?': Nwah asked, though she realized it didn't matter. *:I'm tired of this,:* she said before Darkwind could reply. *:Tired of the food and closed doors, the walls and the noise and the incessant chatter of people who never shut up—:*

"You're not doing yourself any favors, Nwah," Darkwind said, cutting her off as he slid from the sill and walked to his desk. He took a seat there, then gathered a calming breath. The lines in his cheeks caught the sunlight, and for just an instant, Darkwind looked old.

"I want you to perform a task," he said. "When it is finished, we can consider providing you access again."

:I will not be coerced.:

"I understand how you feel. But it's not like that."

But Darkwind was wrong. It was exactly like that.

In an instant of inspiration, Nwah knew who "they" were.

Elspeth.

Perhaps even the Queen herself.

From the moment Nwah had entered Haven, Elspeth and her cohorts had been concerned about her, even as Nwah had exposed the plot a small band of resistance fighters from old Hardorn made against the Queen herself. Nwah had used the power of ley-lines to call on her animal cohorts, and those cohorts had responded in ways both effective and horrifying. The public would need to be appeased, but, as it turned out, the down period Nwah had endured while making a full recovery from the wounds she'd suffered that first day had served to put events far enough into the past that she was not outwardly feared when she roamed the city.

Elspeth and the Collegium were another story. A simple *kyree* of the wild accessing the ley-lines was something stronger than a mere curiosity. They didn't fully understand her Gift, and that frightened them.

Elspeth, as Nwah had come to understand, was not one to hold opinions gently.

There would have to be boundaries. Nwah would have to be constrained.

Darkwind, as Nwah's mentor, was in this case Elspeth's mouthpiece.

Anger clotted Nwah's throat. Her gaze narrowed. An image of *kyree* in the forests came to her. The scent of pinewood and sycamore.

No, she thought. *I will not be shackled.*

:I'm leaving,: she said, fearing what she might do if she did not depart right now.

Nwah turned and stalked out of the office, into the wide corridors, and finally out of the building.

Darkwind, to his credit, did not attempt to stop her.

Sauntering through the streets outside the Collegium, Nwah watched as carriages and carts carried meats, breads, and crops, and patrons moved from one constructed building to another constructed building. The scents of cooking burned in her nostrils. The sound of a smith's cudgel against hot metal brought a blood taste to the back of her throat.

Nwah and Kade had come to Haven specifically for his studies at the Healer's Collegium, and he seemed ridiculously happy.

Having been Chosen by Companion Leena obviously hadn't hurt, either.

But Nwah hadn't considered the pure loneliness Kade's classwork would bring. He was so focused now, always fretting over some new method of using his Gift, which wasn't coming as freely as he thought it should. And if he wasn't focused on his schoolwork, he was training with Leena.

His lack of attention was bad enough that poor Winnie, who had been so smitten with Kade that she had followed them here, had finally gotten up the gumption to leave.

In some ways, Nwah was jealous of Winnie.

Nwah wished that she, too, had the strength to leave Haven—a place she hated more and more as each day passed.

She missed the woodlands. Missed the trees and the warmth of hard earth under her feet, the sound of leaves rustling, the scattering of jays prancing in the canopy, and the raspy rhythm the breeze played on the dry brambles.

Yes, she thought as her pace quickened into a run, *I am jealous of Winnie.*

She found herself running almost full speed, something she hadn't done since perhaps the days when she and Kade had lived in the Pelagirs. Moving like this—heart pounding, paws flying so fast they barely touched the ground—made her wonder whether this was how Winnie felt as she stepped away from Haven.

Yes, Nwah thought again as she ran.

Yes, this was how Winnie had felt.

And, yes, I am leaving.

Kade's mind was a tangled mess that night as he returned to his dormitory.

Bloodroot was a dangerous medicine. Too much, and a patient's innards would tie themselves in knots; too little, and their pain would still overwhelm them. He'd tried to make it work by using his Gift to augment the exercise, but that had just gotten him into deeper trouble.

"Learning medicine requires more than empathy," the headmaster had said, tutting at Kade and admonishing him to go back and do it again.

He threw himself onto the cot where he slept all too little these days. The joints of the bed squeaked as he let his arms drape over both sides.

"I don't understand why we can't just make it work," he said to no one. "What good is a Gift if we don't use it?"

He closed his eyes and tried to ignore the sounds of other students in their own quarters.

Fatigue was a blanket over his body, but his thoughts still raged.

There were new classes to register for, and if he didn't get the bloodroot exercise completed by tomorrow, he was going to be late on the assignment. He needed to work with Leena, too. They were still getting their differences sorted, and in the end that relationship was probably more important than any class he might take. An ignored Companion was an unhappy Companion, and an unhappy Companion was a real problem. Leena wanted to take him to see the tower—which is something he wanted to do, too, but the classwork here was intense. So much different from learning on his own out in the wilds.

A memory came.

The smell of soil. Grit between his fingers. Eyes closed. Hands on Nwah's pelt as he let his mind fall into her wounds. His breathing settling as he brushed away pain that he could not explain. Currents from a nearby brook babbled at the back of his mind, and the sweet scent of its water made him smile.

:Nwah,: he said.

He felt her in a copse of oak trees out past the walls of the city.

She was dozing, curled in the root nook of a tree, snout tucked under one foreleg to retain heat. The rhythm of her breathing was slow and steady.

He sat bolt upright.

"Nwah?" he said aloud.

She was outside Haven's walls. That was clear.

And something else was clear, too.

From the easy, unfettered sensation of her sleep, Kade understood that for the first time since well before they'd gotten to Haven, Nwah was content.

It was a sensation he'd forgotten existed until it suddenly arrived again, and now that he felt it, Kade was flooded with a barrage of emotions.

Anger.

How could Nwah leave Haven without telling him?

Rejection.

How could she care for him so little that she would just run off and leave like that, and how could she be so . . . comfortable . . . having done so?

Guilt.

I've ignored her. Taken her for granted. Kade had been so busy with his own struggles, he hadn't even noticed Nwah had grown despondent.

Stupidity.

How could I have been so blind?

Nwah was not of the city, and it wasn't like she hadn't talked about her disquiet. But he had listened to the Dean and to his instructors, and even to Leena as they all said that she would eventually adjust.

Kade knew her better, though.

He understood better than anyone that Nwah's Gift was as tied to the wilds as she was.

He should have seen this coming.

Fear.

What would happen if she got into trouble?

And she would, wouldn't she?

He remembered Leena's words about Blood Mages. Alone, Nwah would be a target. His veins turned cold. He couldn't bear the idea of her being out there, alone and vulnerable.

:Nwah?: he said, forcing himself into the essence of their lifebond.

:Nwah?: he said, feeling a sense of panic grow inside him as he called to her.

:Nwah!:

* * *

She was dreaming of her mother.

The black and brown of her pelt. The power in her being. The feeling of permanence in the den she kept, curled up so that the full litter fit into the curve of her body and hind legs, her head raised to be on the watch. The pups moved aside as Nwah lay in that curve and nuzzled against her mother's chest, the scent of the den washing over her.

Another image of her mother came then, standing proudly as Nwah was first pair-mated. A flash of her standing on a ridge then, pine trees behind as Nwah left the only woods she had known.

Nwah curled deeper into the warmth of her mother's belly.

:Where are you?: Nwah asked with a languid moan.

:I'm here,: her mother replied.

:No. I mean where are you right now?:

:I'm here, my child. I will always be here.:

Then came the taste of the ley-lines drifting on the waves of Nwah's perception, sweet and dry like peat in the depths of summer. She breathed the lines, and they tasted like the memory of her mother standing tall on that ridge.

Another voice came.

Or not a voice so much as a call.

She startled awake and felt the familiar sense of Kade's voice lingering in the dream space that still loomed in her mind. It was dark, and the songs of springtime insects were in full voice. Buoyed by the spirit of her adventure, she had ranged quite far in the half day and evening she had traveled. The land was sparsely populated here, the grounds filled with grasses growing tall enough around the scatterings of wooded areas that one could almost pretend to be the only creature on the ground.

Despite the distance of her travel, though, Nwah felt the power of Kade's call.

He was thinking of her.

She huffed, partially for the fact that he'd finally taken time to realize she was gone, and partially in the joy she felt to have him nearby again. That was the problem of being lifebonded to a person like Kade. It was hard to be angry and at the same time feel so . . . pleased.

She shifted to sit up.

A touch of desperation came on the wave of Kade's presence. He was worried.

Good for him, she supposed. It would do for him to worry for someone other than himself for a while. But then she felt the undertone of urgency and realized he was going to come for her.

She reached out to touch a nearby ley-line.

Either Darkwind had lifted her bindings, or those bonds had been tied to the boundaries of Haven itself. Either way, she'd been savoring the connection again throughout the day as she'd traveled, and simply touching them and feeling the rush that came from each contact had kept her happy.

:No,: she thought. *:Stay there. I'm fine where I am.:*

She felt the line's power again, but now she touched it only lightly, molding her thoughts in hopes they would keep Kade where he was. She was happy here. Happy to be in a place where she could be alone with her thoughts, to be sitting in the darkness under a clear sky of stars, listening to the sounds of a thin woods that was not really like her homelands, but close enough she could pretend they were. .

Nwah wanted this moment to last.

A wave of Kade's regret rolled over her, though, and she understood her arguments would not be enough.

Their bond was deep.

She understood that Kade loved her as she loved Kade, and she understood that Kade was not of the same mind as she was. Where she would have given him the space he needed to become himself, he would not sleep now until he knew she was safe.

That was who he was. It was why his Gift was so strong.

She gave a long huff and bristled the fur over her neck.

When they were in the wilds together, his approach to providing protection hadn't seemed so overbearing. Now, though, she just wished he would leave well enough alone. As much as she missed Kade, and as much as she loved him, she could handle herself.

:No,: she called through the ley-line, trying to settle him even though she knew it to be impossible—because *that* is who *she* was. *:I am fine.:*

Then she curled back into the tree root and tried to return to her dream.

Tomorrow would be a long day.

She needed her rest.

A *kyree*'s sleep is thin.

It floats in the gray spaces between conscious thought and oblivion, sliding sometimes into dream and others into a blanket of warm lucidity that feels like the sleeper is connected to everything around them at the same time. Movements are sensed. Smells grow into blooms of color that vibrate across every touch of skin along a *kyree*'s body. A breeze sighs. The song of a finch stretches to a string that loops an endless rope through time.

The sun had not quite crested the horizon when a sharp sound snapped Nwah back to her full senses. The sound of a heavy breath and the physical grunt of a leap had her standing before she could determine where it came from.

Weight fell over her.

A net.

Voices called out, sharp and male. Humans.

The dark shape of a man stood before her, but as she yowled the net gathered her up and her feet were swept away so abruptly she fell to the ground, one rib impacting a knob of root so hard her breath left her body.

:Kade!: She called an involuntary scream made in the still-gray fringes of a waking dream.

As she was dragged across the ground, however, her full senses returned.

Though Kade would be coming, even at full speed she knew he would not be here in time to save her.

Nwah extended her claws to rake at the net, but its twine was thick.

She reached for a ley-line, but found naught but a trickle—just enough to allow her to push the man dragging her netted body.

He stumbled, but he did not let go of the net.

A familiar sense of power raised hair on her spine.

Mages!

There were Mages among her assailants. That's why she couldn't touch the ley-line's full power.

She pushed a claw through a gap and caught enough thigh-flesh to draw a cry of pain.

It wasn't enough to do more, though.

The man doubled his efforts, limping forward to drag her away from the tree, through some brambles, and into a small clearing where three other assailants met him.

"Club her a good one," the man dragging her said.

"Shut up. You know the lady don't want her damaged."

"I got a bleeding leg that says if someone doesn't club this *kyree* a good one right now, we're not getting her back to the lady's place to begin with."

Nwah rolled to her belly and growled. With the exception of one forepaw, her legs were tangled. She missed as she swiped at another of her captors.

There were just the four of them, she realized, all dressed in dark, raggedy clothes.

One held the net, another a cudgel of some sort. The other two—the Mages—were both focused heavily on her.

If she could shut down one of the Mages, perhaps she could get to a ley-line, and if she could do that, perhaps she could call to the forest for help as she had done in the past. Without the ability to move, though, she couldn't really do anything.

She clawed gouges into the ground in hopes of throwing debris, but she accomplished nothing.

She rolled away in hopes of freeing another leg, but achieved even less.

The man with the cudgel came closer, and she spat, then lunged toward him to force his retreat.

He returned, this time holding the weapon higher in preparation.

She faced him as boldly as she could, but the second came in behind her, and the man with the cudgel tossed it to him too quickly for her to try to dodge.

There was a sharp crack to her skull.

Pain.

Then darkness.

The voice came through the fog of Nwah's consciousness returning. It was deep but smooth, alto more than bass.

"That was good work. I can use her."

As she came further around, Nwah saw the face of a woman, perhaps an arm's length from her own. She was bent to peer at Nwah, her jawline smooth, her lips wide, and eyes dark. As Nwah's eyes pried open, the woman smiled with an aura of satisfaction, then rose to her full height, revealing that she wore a pair of dark breeches and a thin white blouse that clung close to her body. A thin necklace held an amulet at the hollow of her throat. Her hair was a dark golden shade that would fade into the darkness, yet still catch the light of day.

Nwah tried to move but could not.

She was tied to a table, facedown, forelegs splayed to each side, hind legs stretched behind her. Her head was free to rotate from side to side, but that was the extent of her freedom. She was in a barn, or at least a building open to the air. It reminded her of the stalls where Kade's father had housed his horses and cattle and pigs. This was a single open area, though, probably more useful as storage than as stalls for livestock. Wagons and carts were parked to one side. What appeared to be an inactive smithy's station stood in one corner, though a fire burned there that brought Nwah a memory of another time she'd been in a smithy.

Double-wide doors were open to the air in front of her, and from the movement of currents over her fur, Nwah assumed there was another set behind her.

:Good morning, Nwah,: the woman said.

:Where am I?: Nwah replied.

The woman smiled again, and Nwah realized that by her response she'd provided the woman with what she wanted—confirmation of her identity. Nwah knit her eyebrows together as she considered what that meant.

"You can't get two of our people killed without us knowing who you are," the woman said as she pulled a hot iron from the smithy fire. Its end glowed orange and smelled thick with heat. The woman brought it back to Nwah, then squatted in front of her, her gaze focused on Nwah's as she brought the burning rod closer to Nwah's nose.

Nwah's entire body recoiled with the idea of what was coming.

A wave of fear took her.

She pulled her head back, and despite her every attempt to not show weakness, a thin whine escaped her lips.

The woman's grin this time was pure ecstasy. "Oh, yes," she said, standing again. She turned to the men in the barn. "She'll do well. I'll contact the others and tell them we can expand the approach."

She indicated the Mages. "Keep her off the ley-lines until I need her."

To the other two she said, "You two come with me."

The three of them left the barn.

Breath left Nwah's body in a single rush. She was safe. Or at least she wasn't going to be burned now, which she was ashamed to say meant the same thing at the moment.

She lay her head on the small section of the table before her.

What was happening?

By light of day, she could see the two Mages were young—the female wore a leather vest, the male was thinner and taller. They both stood in poses that seemed oddly rigid, both with palms cupped and concentration rapt.

Nwah hadn't had much time at the Collegium, but she had been there long enough to understand progressions and a bit of how magic came in different ways—that unlike for her, accessing the ley-lines wasn't a natural thing for all Mages. That was what had made Princess Elspeth and other Adepts of Haven so fearful of her to begin with. The idea was strange to her, though. How could magic come from anything but the lines?

Yet, apparently some mages—arguably, it seemed, most mages—brought the energy for their magics up from within themselves.

Could she do that?

The woman's words actually struck her then.

"You can't get two of our people killed without us knowing who you are."

The two people she was referring to had to be the acrobat and barker who had been performing at last year's Harvest Fair—the two Nwah had discovered hatching an assassination plot that was later revealed to be directed at the Queen herself.

The woman was a spy of sorts. A rebel from Hardorn.

If this was true, another mission against Haven was underway.

She had to do something.

Had to try.

She'd never made an attempt to bring magic up from within herself, but if there was ever a time to try something new, this was it.

Nwah closed her eyes and concentrated on herself only. Feeling the grain of the wood table against the length of her stretched body, the bit of ropes over her forelegs and paws. She sensed air flowing into and out of her body. Felt hair stand up. Claws flexing. The rough of her tongue against the roof of her mouth.

Beyond that, though, she felt nothing.

No magic. No flow.

And no sense of ley-lines.

Nwah had come up empty.

From a distance, Nwah felt a disturbance.

Her ears, attuned and more sensitive than her captors', heard a sound as familiar as time itself, one she'd heard since the days she'd been a young pup and her mother had warned her of falcons soaring overhead.

The whoosh of friction on feather.

:They're big enough to take a pup.: Her mother's voice came to her from nowhere. *:Keep your head down.:*

She dropped her head to the table and concentrated.

Waiting.

Vree's screech echoed through the hollow of the open building.

Massive gray wings beat the air as the forestgyre's claws gashed the nearest Mage, drawing a startled scream as her spell work failed.

A crack formed in the barrier between Nwah and the ley-lines, growing wider as the second Mage also turned his attention to Vree's surprise attack. The forestgyre's next attack didn't draw blood, but it was enough to take the barrier they were maintaining fully down.

Nwah was ready.

She reached for the ley-line and drank the sweet flow.

In one powerful burst she pulled the burning iron from the fire to slash at the ropes that held her. In a moment, she was standing free upon the table with only the scorched shards of her bonds dangling from her forelegs.

Vree took a second pass at his victim, so Nwah leaped onto the other Mage, impacting hard enough to spill them both onto the ground.

The man fought her, but he was obviously spent.

Nwah used her weight to pin him, then growled and snapped her jaws just over his face.

The Mage screamed.

Nwah narrowed her eyes and bared her teeth.

The Mage's throat was smooth and exposed.

The need for vengeance pounded at Nwah's temples. The memory of a burning rod waved so near her nose, the burn of rope bonds around her legs, and the taste of ley-lines denied gathered together to raise hackles across her neck. She could already taste the blood. Her nostrils widened, and her claws dug into flesh.

"Nwah!"

Kade's voice came from the open doorway, accompanied by the clomp of Leena's hooves.

Nwah turned to them, blood still pounding through her temples.

They filled the barn with their presence, the pale green of his Healer Trainee's blouse exposed under the darker riding cape on his shoulders, his dark hair windblown from what may well have been a full sprint from Haven, his soft fingers clenching the reins of his pristinely white Companion, Leena's chest heaving with exertion.

A moment later, Elspeth and Companion Gwena came through the open back doors.

The other Mage toppled to the ground.

Turning her gaze from Elspeth, Nwah saw Darkwind emerge from the farmhouse behind Kade.

Of course, Nwah thought. Vree would not be here without Darkwind.

"She's taken care of," he said as he came to the barn, clearly speaking of the Mage who had been here before.

:What are you doing here?: Nwah asked Kade.

:You saved my mother's life last year,: Elspeth replied. *:We couldn't very well leave you to a Blood Mage, now, could we?:*

All of her captors were under control. A patrol was being dispatched from Haven to collect them.

After a few questions, Nwah pieced together what had happened. Kade, worried about Nwah being alone, had told Darkwind he was going to get her. Darkwind sent word to Elspeth, who used her own magic to determine that Nwah was in danger—considerably more danger than Nwah had thought. Several hours of travel later, here they all were, Nwah, Elspeth, Darkwind, and Kade, standing in the farmhouse's open dining area, scanning the papers the Blood Mage had been working on when Darkwind had disrupted her.

"It's not good news," Elspeth said as she continued to scan the Blood Mage's notes. "We'll take them all back to Haven for real questioning, but from what I can tell, we've got a whole faction of rebels who still long for the days of Ancar. They're scattered around the open lands and across the Border, as well as embedded as lone spies in several cities."

"You're saying the assassination attack Nwah foiled last year was just the harbinger," Darkwind said.

"I'd say so. I think this means that Sia—the Blood Mage —was hoping to use the fact that they had captured Nwah as a leverage point to convince a collection of baronies they could be strong enough to band together and take Hardorn back sooner."

Nwah chuffed. *:I can't believe I'm that important.:*

"Don't underestimate yourself, pupling," Darkwind said. "Sia is a strong Mage. If I hadn't caught her in a distracted state, things could have gotten unpleasant quite quickly. You are young still. Your fear is pure, and your ability to access the lines could be turned in ways we don't yet understand."

"Besides," Elspeth added, scanning the notes further. "They wouldn't need to gain enough power to overrun Valdemar for this plan to succeed. Hardorn's new reign is tenuous in the way all new reigns are. Simply keeping Haven occupied long enough might allow them to take the land back."

She looked directly at Nwah then. *:You are no simple kyree, Nwah. Your magic is stronger than you understand.:*

Nwah lowered her head. *:I know that now,:* she replied.

And she did. She knew how truly little she understood. Her

failure to bring magic out of herself spoke to her lack of . . . something, and her utter despair and helplessness as the Blood Mage had threatened to brand her had filled in the rest. She needed to learn more. She needed to grow stronger.

She knew what was coming next, though. *:I can't go back to Haven.:*

:I thought you wanted to train in the city.: Elspeth replied.

Nwah grunted in reply and was suddenly very aware of Kade's nearness. Her admission would hurt him, but it was something she had to voice. *:I can't stay there.:*

"But . . ." Kade replied, "I'm in the middle of my studies."

:And you need to complete them,: Nwah said. *:But it's time I discover who I really am, too . . . I can't do that in Haven.:*

A lifetime of conversation passed in the gaze they shared. They were no longer the youthful adventurers who lived off the woodlands to the south. They could no longer pretend to ignore the fact they needed different things, that even when they were growing up together in the Pelagirs. Kade had been prepared to leave those woods forever, but Nwah had not. Their travels had been adventure for her, but that was all.

They also, however, could not deny their lifebond.

It would always be there. Kade's gaze said that in ways Nwah would never be able to explain.

That was love, after all. Deep and unexplainable.

:Where would you go?: Kade asked.

:I was considering returning to Oris.:

:You'll join Maakdal's pack?:

:If he would have me.:

Which, of course, Maakdal would. The playful grin that slanted Kade's lips let her know that even he understood the pairing had been clear from the moment they had met.

He turned to Elspeth.

"She's speaking the truth, Princess. Nwah cannot stay in Haven."

"That makes things complicated," Elspeth replied. "I'm not

excited about an untrained *kyree* with wild nature magic roaming on her own."

Nwah's stomach sank. That was Elspeth's answer to everything. Caution. Limits. The idea of returning to Haven hurt her head more than the bruise from her clubbing earlier in the day.

:I'll find a way,: she said, pleading to Elspeth. *:I understand how worried you might be about me. And I know you're right to worry. But there are schools in other places, and I understand now just how much I lack. I'll find a way to be trained properly. And I'll work hard. I promise you. It just can't be in Haven.:*

Elspeth grimaced.

"It's a high risk," she said. "There are more dangers in the wild than Blood Mages."

"I'll train her."

It was Darkwind.

"The journey to Oris—if that's where she's going—is long and fraught. She will need an escort. Vree and I should suffice. I am already her mentor. I know her powers. We can continue her lessons on the trip. Assuming she's true to her word and works hard at her Gift, I can linger if she has not managed proper control by the time we arrive, and I can arrange for more training before I depart.

"Besides," he said, leaning over the map on the table. "If these plans are true, I suspect Valdemar has enemies in the forests we will traverse. It might be good to have a spy of our own to set eyes on them. In addition to that," he slid a finger to land on Oris, "it would certainly be good to have such allies as Nwah can manage to the east."

Elspeth chuckled as she took in Darkwind's words. "Don't pretend you haven't wanted to get back to the woodlands anyway."

"Am I that transparent?"

Elspeth's eyebrows arched, and her head tilted with great animation. "Oh, no, my dear husband. You are always as thick as stew. That you've been restless for weeks has never crossed my mind."

Darkwind's answering shrug was subtle.

"It's settled, then," Elspeth said. "Darkwind and Vree will escort Nwah to Oris. The rest of us will return to Haven and get to the depths of these rebel plans."

The patrol had left, taking Elspeth and Kade and their captive Mages back to Haven and leaving provisions for the trip Nwah and Darkwind would be making.

Darkwind had made a fire in the farmhouse's hearth and now stood before a window to stare up into the blanket of stars.

Nwah lay before the fire, letting its warmth soak into her pelt.

She had reached out to Kade several times, and he to her. This would work, she knew now. Though separation would be painful at times, she need not have feared losing him.

Tomorrow she and Darkwind would set out eastward.

:I need to thank you: Nwah said.

:For what?: Darkwind replied.

:The Princess would have caged me if you had not agreed to come.:

:Elspeth is many things. But a jailor is not one of them.:

:I'm sorry. I didn't mean to offend.:

:It's all right,: Darkwind replied.

He turned from the window and took a seat before the fire.

:Why did you do it?: she asked.

:What do you mean?:

:All of the reasons you gave—they all make sense. But scouting the forests and finding spies could have been done from Haven. As could have been my teaching—despite my discomfort. And Haven has a collective of scouts. So why do this? Certainly your relationship with Elspeth is not so tenuous that you needed the cover of my trip to satisfy your restlessness?:

Darkwind's smile was a thin pursing of his lips, but it carried a hint that suggested he might be pleased with her.

"Let's just say that I know what it means to deny one's Gift," he said. "And I'm looking forward to seeing yours grow."

Nwah chuffed in acknowledgement.

The answer would do. For now, anyway. She sensed something more to his answer, too, something in the steadiness of his gaze. His demeanor, however, said that whatever else was crossing his mind tonight would have to wait.

She stretched her forepaws and laid her head over her legs.

:I'm looking forward to that, too,: she mumbled, drifting toward what she hoped would be a long and luxurious dream.

The Upper Air

Terry O'Brien

Tarresk's muscles hurt. His head hurt. Blazes, his *feathers* hurt. He felt like one gryfalcon-sized bruise that had been pummeled by a hurricane. Well, at least he was alive and suddenly conscious enough to feel it, and to *smell* it, too—the sharp, astringent smell of the all-too-familiar interior of the whitewashed Healers' Hall for the Silver Gryphon Training Academy.

Alive, but had he succeeded? Tarresk tried to remember, but his memories were blurry wisps and painful shadows. The harder he tried, the more painful, the more cloudy the memories, until he finally gave up. Had he succeeded? As far as he was concerned, not remembering was the same as not succeeding.

He must have groaned, because he could suddenly hear the unmistakable sounds of claws on stone moving toward him. Tarresk opened his eyes, and blazes, even *that* hurt, to see his fellow academy cadet Sheedrra and the lead academy *hertasi trondir'in* Sask looking at him, Sheedrra with mixed worry and relief and Sask with mixed approval and reproach.

Before Tarresk could say a word, Sask pointed an accusing claw at him. "Be s-s-silent! S-s-ave your s-s-strength for healing!"

Sheedrra, standing behind Sask, stifled a laugh she couldn't quite hide because it was shaking her wings. "Master Gerrin will be glad to see that you're awake. I'm sure she'll be by later to check on you."

Tarresk's wings would have drooped if he hadn't found they were lashed to the sturdy support frame. Facing the Silver Gryphon's new flight instructor was the last thing he wanted. Worse, it meant Gerrin's superior, the old Silver Gryphon Training Master Vellish, would also be in attendance.

Tarresk would have curled into a ball—if only he could move.

"You are very lucky to be alive."

It was the first thing the immaculately garbed Vellish said in his precise, Haighlei-accented, resonant baritone when he arrived, but he was the fourth person to say it to Tarresk in the past candlemark. Tarresk wished he himself were in the far-off Haighlei capital right now, rather than facing the Training Master.

Vellish nodded toward Sheedrra. "You should thank Sheedrra for saving your life."

Sheedrra laughed softly from the other end of the room. "He has, copiously." Only after considerable prodding by Sask.

Vellish folded his arms across his chest. "The Healers tell me you have stress fractures along the primary upper and lower bones of both wings, three torn tendons, and several strained muscles and ligaments, as well as scarred sinus and lung tissue. Sask says it will take a week of Healing and a week of rest, undisturbed, during the Winter Solstice Break festivities, before she will release you."

Tarresk's ear tufts perked up at the word 'undisturbed'; he hoped no one noticed.

Sask glared at Tarresk. "*If—if* he follows his Healer's instructions."

"He would not be a candidate for the Silvers if he did not."

Tarresk nodded, glumly: Silvers had the unfortunate but not unexpected habit of needing Healers on a more-or-less regular basis.

Sask turned to Vellish. "It will take that long just to repair all his feathers." Not actually; it was widely rumored that *hertasi trondir'in* overestimated their repair times to maintain their reputation as miracle workers.

Vellish nodded. "Then it will take another two weeks, possibly three, of training to fully recover your strength before Gerrin will release you."

Gerrin, standing next to Vellish, straightened her head, imperiously eyed Tarresk, and *tried* to look more serious than Vellish, which only prompted a stifled giggle from Sheedrra: Gerrin's official brass and leather pectoral was too shiny and new for her to be able to entirely pull that off.

"After you have proven yourself to Gerrin, *then* you will prove *to me* that you are fit to continue before *I* release you. Only then will you be permitted to make another attempt."

After that, Vellish allowed himself some time to be alone, so he went to his favorite solitary contemplation place, the isolated lookout over the city at the edge of the cliff at the far end of the Academy grounds.

Unfortunately for him, Gerrin accompanied him. "I see what you did, Vellish, but I am wondering . . . *why?*"

"Why am I letting him continue?" Vellish sighed. "Why am I willing to risk the finest flier I have seen in thirty years?" He rested his arms on the waist-high fitted stone wall, leaned forward and looked down toward the city, the busy harbor, and the lands beyond in the fading sunset glow. "You have not read the archives."

"Something to do in my copious spare time?"

"I found the time, starting the first day I became Assistant Training Master. There *is* something up there; what, we do not know, but we *need* to know. Five gryfalcons in the six generations since the Founding have attempted the exact same thing; five gryfalcons, each fully dedicated, fully prepared, fully equipped, have attempted to cross the sixth cloud-height layer and fly into the Upper Air. Tarresk is the first to survive the attempt. In addition, Sheedrra told me that after she alerted the Silverwings and used her lifting spell to arrest his fall, and she used her Mage Sight to examine the remains of Tarresk's flying spells. She said they looked *'deliberately sliced and shredded'*. I do not know of anything that could do that, and none of the Mages I asked did, either."

Gerrin rumbled an "Oh" deep within her throat.

"So, yes, I am willing to let him continue. That is a leadership lesson I had to learn, that sometimes you have consider the good of the whole instead of the one."

"I must have missed that day in leadership class." Not that there ever was one, officially, but it seemed that accompanying Vellish was going to be that class.

"Still, I will give him every resource at my disposal to continue, and I'll give him every opportunity and justification *and excuse* to decide *not* to continue. However, if—and I fully expect that to be *when*—he fully recovers *and* passes every trial we can think to throw at him, he will be at his utmost best flying form, more able to survive anything the Upper Air can throw at him than ever before. And he is likely to do so, with or without permission. That is another lesson in leadership I learned, much to my sorrow: the perception to recognize when an order won't be obeyed, and the wisdom never to give such an order." A lesson he learned far too early, one far too relevant—and far too costly. Best Gerrin learn it by example than firsthand.

"So, I hear you are being released today. Early."

Tarresk's ear tufts twitched, nervously. Vellish was quieter than a cat. He glanced away from Sask packing the rest of his books to Vellish standing inside the archway.

Sask was also surprised, although she hid it far better than Tarresk. "He listened to his Healers."

Vellish nodded to Sask. "A word with Tarresk? Alone?"

Sask nodded in return. "Done here." She picked up the book bag and scurried out the archway, no doubt to linger outside, just within earshot.

"How do you feel?"

"Fine." Tarresk flexed his shoulders and fluttered his wings. "At least that's what Sask wants me to say."

"And what do *you* want to say?"

"I'll get there."

Vellish nodded, then sat down on the chair next to Tarresk. "The Upper Air is another country, unknown and dangerous. You were more the head-in-a-book than the head-in-the-clouds type, so what made you think you wanted to fly there?"

"Valrusk. I read the report about Valrusk."

For the very first time, ever, Tarresk saw a look of surprise and possible reproach in Vellish's wide eyes. "That was in the restricted archives! How did you—?"

"The door wasn't locked! How was I supposed to know they were restricted?"

"So you just looked inside—"

"And saw books! Of course I had to investigate." Tarresk looked at Vellish's grim demeanor; there were reasons, *plenty* of reasons those books were restricted, especially from impetuous students—like him. "I only read the ones on flying, I swear by the Winged Ones!"

"And, of course, you found Valrusk's journals on flying, ending with the one about his attempts to reach the Upper Air. Including the notations at the end regarding his death." Some of which were Vellish's own.

"I read how you tried to stop him."

Vellish sighed. "It was Councilor Hessevaran who gave that order. I was merely the one he delegated to deliver it." Another leadership lesson for Gerrin: always give orders like that in person. "But it was a wise order: Valrusk was considerably more impetuous than he appeared in his journal." Much like other gryfalcons of his acquaintance. "What made you think you would succeed when he failed?"

"There was a flaw in his plans. I could see it; I couldn't see why he couldn't. I fixed it, then I tested it and tested it until I was sure I had fixed it."

"And did you?"

Tarresk hung his head. "I don't know."

"Valrusk described his preparations at length, yet there was one thing he never mentioned: why he did it. I always thought it was something only a gryfalcon would know.

"So, why did you do it?"

Tarresk looked away. "I don't know."

"Best answer that question before you make another attempt."

Gerrin did not expect that one of the requirements as the new flying instructor was to spend so much time in her drab, boring office, where the only color in the whitewashed-walled room was the long cherrywood plaque hung on the far wall, adorned with a row of bronze and gold feathers that surrounded the two silver feathers.

She set the leather-bound volume down on her desk and was *finally* going to call it a night when Sheedrra hesitantly rapped on the wall outside.

"Gerrin, are you available?"

Gerrin sighed and slumped back onto her couch. "Of course I am. Come in, come in."

Sheedrra ducked through the doorway and promptly *deflated* onto one of the woven reed mats on the floor with a loud sigh.

"It's about Tarresk, isn't it?"

Sheedrra nodded, slowly. "He's been avoiding me for almost two weeks. He's *sneaking.* He is so much more cat than bird I wonder how he can fly at all."

Gerrin glanced down at the sparse status reports on Tarresk on the low platform that served as her desk. "Sneaking?"

"Sask says he disappears for candlemarks at a time; even the *hertasi* can't find him. I don't know where or when or *if* he sleeps. I know he eats, because he does show up at the kitchens, at all hours, but he just bolts his food and fills his crop and rushes off again before anyone can get any answers out of him. And I just found out he's been sneaking out to the practice yard after dark, and he's been setting up the obstacle course at the highest difficulty level, *and* he's meeting or beating his best scores."

Gerrin's eyebrows twitched. She was quite familiar with the highest difficulty level obstacle course. Among other things, it required the flier to perform a full vertical wingtip-to-ground bank to catch a ribbon, then quickly invert to snatch the next ribbon, and then finish the course with a wing-over full roll to catch the last ribbon upside-down. Gerrin could still complete almost every training course at any level, but this was the only one she had never completed at that level, not even after twenty years of trying. Only a small number of gryphons ever did complete it. Tarresk did so regularly, before, but to do so now, so soon, was both encouraging and a little disturbing.

"Well, he certainly has met the appropriate standards for me to release him."

"I'm sure Vellish wouldn't."

"Vellish has different standards, and he has not seen fit to divulge them to me. However, the way Tarresk is acting right now, Vellish would certainly not approve his release."

"He's always been a bit of a loner, but this is *not good*."

"You're right, this *is* 'not good'. Something needs to be done."

"But what? I don't know what to do."

"I didn't know, either, so I took advantage of another of Vellish's leadership lessons: When you're not sure about what to do, talk to an expert."

"Who?" A famous mind-healing *kestra'chern*? Was there even one here?

"Vellish." Gerrin chuckled at Sheedrra's puzzled expression and tapped the short stack of books on her desk. "He recommended that I read the restricted archives. There are several accounts of similar situations, similar symptoms. The most recent was the aftermath of a pirate raid on an outpost more than twenty years ago. One of the survivors was severely traumatized, and the accounts included the details of his treatment. Very informative.

"In addition, these accounts are required reading for every senior *kestra'chern,* and every one of them I talked to agreed with me: what Tarresk needs right now is someone to talk to, someone he knows will listen to him, someone he can relate to, someone with common interests. A friend, a peer. And they all said that someone would best be you."

Sheedrra started and stared blankly at Gerrin. "M-m-m-m-me?"

"Of course. You're both not *quite* the smartest and most Gifted students in the Academy, but you're the most dedicated, most hard working, most determined." And her most favorite, but Gerrin wasn't going to admit that out loud.

Sheedrra smirked a little, then frowned. She knew the students Gerrin was talking about. One was a brilliant scholar yet meticulous to the point of indecisiveness, while the other was a natural Mage and could be a Master already if he only made the effort. She'd settle for determination, dedication, and hard work. "But, but, common interests?"

"Sheedrra, you hold the Academy endurance records in distance flying. Tarresk holds the endurance records in altitude flying. You two spend more time in the air than anyone else in the Academy. I think you have much more in common than you realize."

"You once held that endurance record."

"The one you beat, yes. We're more alike, too, than you realize. That's why I think you're the best person to reach Tarresk." She tapped the books on her desk. "You might want to take a look at these accounts, though, before you go looking for him, to see if anything might be useful.

"Then, when you're finished reading them, would you return them to the restricted archives?"

Sheedrra thanked the Spirits that it was Solstice Break so she could spend the following day reading through the accounts before returning the books to the restricted archives room after dinner. She stepped inside the door and froze at the sight of the immaculately organized rows of books on the bookshelves around the room and the precisely stacked books and neatly arranged papers on the table in the center in contrast with the chaotic pile of tumbled pillows and blankets next to the table and the huddled figure of Tarresk curled up on his makeshift bed, silently shivering and wordlessly whimpering.

While Sheedrra was still staring, before she could say a word, or even back out quietly, Tarresk gasped. He twisted his head over his shoulder and opened one bloodshot, bleary eye to stare at her. "Go . . . away."

Sheedrra started, then planted both claws and both paws, settled her wings, squared her shoulders and held her head proudly erect. "No."

Tarresk didn't reply, just closed his eye and rolled back into his bed.

Sheedrra carefully removed the accounts from her satchel and deposited them on the first table by the door, then carefully sat down next to Tarresk. "Did I ever tell you about my worst flight, ever?"

Tarresk sighed and half-opened both eyes to peer at her; he'd heard the rumors when he first arrived, but Sheedrra never talked about it.

"My first year. My first flight on the distance course. I missed the third turn marker. Kept going until I passed over one of the old boundary markers before I turned around. Was over two candlemarks late. They came looking for me, found me lying in a pile of downed branches, half-conscious, half a candlemark from the end. Flight instructor Shotoquan was most displeased with me. After I left the Healers, I spent a week hiding in my quarters. I know just how you're feeling."

Tarresk shook his head. "You didn't . . . nearly die!"

Sheedrra shook her head, too. "It was a hard landing: muscle cramps in my wings. I broke both my wings in three places: Shotoquan said I was very, *very* lucky I didn't break my neck."

"Ohhhh . . ."

"So, yes, I do know what you're going through. I survived and carried on, you survived, you can carry on, too."

"I didn't survive! You saved me!"

Wide-eyed, Sheedrra shifted back a step, almost knocking the table over.

"Maybe if you hadn't saved me, then maybe they'd stop trying, ever again." Tarresk sniffled. "That way my dying would make a difference."

"It didn't stop you, did it?"

"No . . . but maybe, for a generation? I could've lived with that. Well, I guess I am living with that, being the living failure, the living example?"

Sheedrra shook her head, slowly. "Not even a month. There's a group of hotheads in the Academy who want to 'show up' that 'stuck-up, skinny runt Tarresk,' and *soon*."

"I am *not* stuck-up!"

"I know that, but they don't. They want to do something that even the 'great flier Tarresk' couldn't do."

Tarresk hung his head. "So, when are they planning to try this?"

"The last day of Solstice Break."

Tarresk lurched to his feet. "A week? I spent *months* researching, experimenting, practicing. They think they can do this in a couple of weeks? *Blazes*!"

"So how did you do it? What were you using? A variation on the emergency lifting spell?" The one drilled into every Silver Gryphon Mage in their first year. "I couldn't tell."

Tarresk ruffled his neck feathers. "Lifting spell? That . . . would be *cheating*!" He was silent for a long moment. "Besides, lifting spells are *hard*."

Sheedrra shrugged, maybe for him. "So what were you using?"

Tarresk looked around at the close quarters within the restricted archives room. "I can't show you, not here, but I *make* a gryfalcon."

Sheedrra cocked her head and eyed Tarresk as if he had just grown a second pair of wings.

He ignored her gesture. "Do you remember your first flight class?"

"Not really." To be honest, Sheedrra was quite unimpressed with the instructor.

"Flying depends on wing surface area. Flight Master Hursq would describe the relationship between wing surface area and body weight with a series of pieces of paper and blocks of wood. When the paper got bigger in length and width by a certain amount, the block got bigger in length and width *and height and weight* by the same amount: when the wings grew in length and width for more lifting surface, not just the wings, but the whole body grew to support the wings. Ultimately, the block would get too big and too heavy for the paper to support it. That's why gryphons can't get any bigger, or else they can't fly."

Sheedrra barely hid her amused chuckle: there were more than a few overweight gryphons whose explanation of "wing pains" was barely an excuse for them not flying. "That's why gryfalcons like you can generally fly higher than other gryphons. Smaller body size, but relatively same wing size. But don't bigger wings mean more lifting magic?"

"Not really." Every gryphon instinctively knew that their wings gathered the ambient magic so necessary to sustain the lifting magic they needed for flight. "There, it's the *length* of the wing, well, the wing bones, that's important, and that doesn't change much; mine are almost as long as yours."

"I . . . see."

"That also means there are limits to how high any gryphon can fly. The higher you fly, the thinner the air gets, so you need bigger wings to counter the thinner air and sweep up more magic, but you'd just get too heavy. That's the limit." He sighed, but when he continued, his words started spilling out. "But! I know a way around that. I make a gryfalcon out of magic. A *bigger* gryfalcon with a *bigger* wing size, but no weight."

Sheedrra's eyes widened. She had the image of a gryphon with a wingspread wider than the bay. "You could make a *huge* gryphon out of magic!" In fact, she was already piecing together elements of her Mage training into a semblance of a spell to do exactly that.

Tarresk sighed again and shook his head. “If only it were that easy. I’m only a Journeyman, so there’s only so much magic I can use at any one time. But the higher I go and the thinner the air gets, the bigger the wing size, and that means even more magic. And worse, you start suffering from air starvation at those heights, and the air is so cold it burns, so I added a twist to the spell so that it draws in air and warms it. I think I can only hold the spells for maybe sixty breaths at my highest. That’s *my* limit.”

“Oh.” The spell she thought conceptually simple was quickly becoming a convoluted mess. “So, how do you do it?”

Tarresk lurched to his feet. “I got the idea from Valrusk; although he doesn’t say, he probably got the same idea from someone else.” He reached to one of the journals on the desk beside him, opened it to one of the many bookmarks, and pointed to the page. “Here’s his notes.”

And very detailed notes they were, in very precise script. As Sheedrra was reading, Tarresk opened another journal, this one in his distinctive, sloppy script that drew the ire of more than one of his instructors. “I made a few improvements, based on what we’ve learned from the Haighlei, but . . .”

Sheedrra noted the pause. “You don’t know if these changes worked.”

Tarresk closed his fist and barely restrained himself from sweeping the books off the table. “I don’t know! I don’t know why I failed. I’ve tried and tried, but I can’t figure out how I failed, and if I can’t, then how can I prepare to succeed?”

Sheedrra was silent for a long moment. “Maybe . . . maybe you *didn’t* fail. Maybe it was something external.”

“What!? How?”

“After I used my lifting spell to slow your descent, I Saw that you were still holding on to the remnants of your flying spells. I was surprised. But I also Saw that something had happened to them. They looked like someone took a knife to them.”

“A knife? Impossible!” Tarresk shook his head, then peered at Sheedrra. “Isn’t it?”

"They were shredded and not by accident. Directly across the spells. Several times."

"More like . . . claws, then?"

"But what could have done that? Do you remember?"

"I don't . . ." Then came the nightmares he was trying hard both to remember and forget: rainbows and noise and pain and the feeling of the wind rushing through his wings as he fell and . . .

Tarresk!

Sheedrra's *loud* Mindspeech shout dispelled the nightmares. He found himself curled into his blankets, clutching one of the pillows so tightly his meager claws were thrust completely through the feathered interior. "There's . . . something up there." Tarresk took a long, slow breath. "I have to go back up there and find out what."

"Well, not alone. You'll have help." Tarresk bristled at the word, so Sheedrra took a slight step back and a deep breath before continuing. "No, make that backup. After all, isn't that what Silvers are supposed to do for each other? Have each others' backs?" It wasn't the official Silver Gryphon motto, but it was certainly one of the unofficial ones. "If nothing else, you'll have a witness."

Tarresk's ear tufts perked ever so slightly at the last. "I'd . . . like that."

"So, when do we fly? You'll have to drill me on the spells."

"Tonight–it's a mostly cloudless night, and the moon is close to full and will rise soon."

"Tonight? Why tonight? Why not wait until morning and use the thermals over the bay?"

"The weather watchers posted a heavy cloud warning by sunrise and a heavy winter storm warning by noon, so we'd be stuck for days."

Sheedrra examined him with narrowed eyes. "You mean you'd lose your nerve if you waited."

Tarresk sighed heavily, then briefly nodded but held his shoulders high and firm. "Now, while you look over the notes and check my estimations and calculations, I'll tell Sask to ready our flight harnesses for a night flight."

In her ten years on the Silverwings, the elite Silver Gryphon rescue team, and her three years as the team commander, the operation to catch a falling gryphon was merely something the team practiced on a semi-regular basis. Now, for the second time in five weeks, but not so frantically as the last time, Gerrin observed the preparations from a respectful distance to do it again, and, for the second time in five weeks, resisted the urge to intervene. She had trained Kashatan, and she wouldn't have recommended him to command the Silverwings after her promotion if she didn't believe he could handle the position. Now she had to trust her decision and give him the space to *be* the commander without her hovering over him: another leadership lesson.

As she waited for the *hertasi* to lay out the rescue harnesses, she scanned the sky for the amber and red mage lights attached to Tarresk's and Sheedrra's flight harnesses without success. Instead, she noted movement out of the corner of her eye. The not-quite-immaculately-garbed Vellish was walking briskly up the ramp to the rescue platform, accompanied by Sask, who carried the teleson; she had forgotten he was on rotation as Silver Gryphon Watch Commander from dusk to dawn this week. Gerrin smiled inwardly: a leader never *ran*, it was a leadership lesson she had learned even before she assumed leadership.

Vellish was frowning, though, never a good sign. "Skandranon's tail!"

Gerrin looked at him with a slight smile. "What?!"

Vellish sighed. "One can gauge someone's years of leadership by the number of invectives they've learned."

"So. What are your plans regarding our two wayward students?"

"As Training Master, it is my duty to administer proper discipline to these students, which I will do only upon the completion of an investigation of their actions, which I leave in the hands of a capable expert—in this case, yourself. I recommend that you do as Urtho of legend did: he would not simply debrief them, but concisely and analytically critique them."

Gerrin shivered once in sympathy; she was the recipient of one such critique from a previous Watch Commander, and she remembered wanting to slouch out of the meeting on her belly when it was done. "Wouldn't he also promote them? Or, rather, here, graduate them?"

"I'll decide *that* later."

Vellish, Gerrin, and Sask stood patiently as the *hertasi* buckled the rescue harnesses on the dozen gryphons, while a squad of humans and gryphons laid out the rescue nets on the beach below the station above the high tide mark. When they finished, the gryphons lined up in a neat row awaiting Vellish's inspection, which he made with quick precision before nodding briskly to Kashatan. "Silverwings! Remember your training. Our brother and sister are depending on us!"

Kashatan turned to the rest of his team. "Height! Spot! Drop! Match! Snatch! Lift!"

Everyone in the team, gryphons, humans, and *hertasi* alike, shouted in reply. "*Height*! *Spot*! *Drop*! *Match*! *Snatch*! *Lift*!"

Kashatan turned back to Vellish. "Silverwings standing by!"

Vellish nodded. "Bring them home, rescue team leader. The sky is yours."

You're the expert here, Tarresk. How can we tell what cloud - height we're at if there are no clouds?

Accurately? You really can't, not by numbers, anyway. You have to go by feel.

Tarresk knew from the way the wind felt under his feathers and across his fur that they were at the third cloudheight. It was where most gryphons were most comfortable, where most gryphons flew for long distances.

Ready?

Tarresk watched Sheedrra take a long, slow breath. She was obviously *not* comfortable at higher cloud-heights; few gryphons were.

Fourth cloud-height definitely felt different, felt *papery.* Felt colder, too, just uncomfortable, not painful, not cloud breath, not yet.

Tarresk. My wings are starting to hurt. I'm going to use the flying spell.

Watch your energy. Remember, when we get there, sixty breaths, then descend.

Tarresk watched the translucent form of a gryphon manifest around her. Her enhanced wingbeats lifted her above Tarresk and broke into the fifth cloud-height.

Fifth cloud-height was home for gryfalcons like Tarresk. The air of the lower cloud-heights was thick, it weighed on them. He concentrated, and the translucent form of a sleek gryfalcon manifested around him. Now the world was quiet, the wind no longer whistled past his ear tufts. Now he could not feel the wind, but he also could not feel the cold. It was an acceptable compromise. He looked back to Sheedrra and nodded.

Time to cross the border.

The sixth cloud-height was the unpredictably dangerous border to the even more unpredictable and unknown Upper Air. No one really knew just how high it actually reached. Adventurous fliers flirted with it, crossed the border momentarily before dipping back or before being forced back down to the more comfortable lower cloud-heights. Skandranon himself, by some accounts, did exactly that, once, then swore never to do it again. Zhaneel, by all accounts, had better sense than to ever try.

Tarresk didn't know whether the violent crosswinds and the dangerous and unpredictable updrafts and downdrafts that marked the sixth cloud-height were local or everywhere. He argued that the extreme nature of the sixth-cloud height was the aftermath of the Cataclysm disrupting the world's weather patterns, and he hoped that someday it would return to a calmer state. Sheedrra never really thought about it; she just accepted it as it was, with no expectation of it ever changing.

Tarresk took the lead. It would take every trick he had learned at the Academy, and some he learned by necessity just recently, to navigate the unpredictable winds that threatened to send him tumbling uncontrollably head over tail back into the fifth cloud-height. Every wingspan of height, every claw length, was a battle he could not afford to lose, even once. The hazy clouds that blocked the view of the higher altitudes were liars and worse, worthless as measure of the winds as they should be, so he was forced to fly by feel. Worse, his "acceptable compromise" forced him to feel the direction and pressure of the winds second-hand, slowing his reactions just enough that the swiftly shifting and swirling winds treacherously forced him back more than once and nearly tumbled him at least once. Yet he continued upward. His belief that he had done this once before spurred him on as his pride conquered his doubts whether he could continue.

Tarresk glanced back toward his partner when he could spare the moment. Sheedrra was doing her best to follow him, using her greater strength and endurance and larger spell-wings to push through the winds that would suddenly shift directions in Tarresk's wake, and her best was just barely good enough. He slowed or sideslipped to keep from getting too far ahead of her, and he once dove into a downdraft when he was almost pushed back into a violent collision with her that would have sent them both tumbling out of the contrary winds in defeat.

They didn't know how long, nor did they even spare the time to think about how long, they were just too sore and tired and breathless, but suddenly the winds and clouds were gone, replaced by a cold, crystal, silent stillness, lit by the bright moon and the abundant stars. For Tarresk, who swore by the Winged Ones of legend, this was a sacred space, a place of magic, in truth because he could feel it prickling along his wings like Skandranon's Fire.

Tarresk slowly forced his clenched and cramped fists apart;

the red welts on his palms felt like fire, and they would remain for days.

Tarresk. We . . . did it?

He glanced at Sheedrra, who was shaking half-frozen sweat from her flanks. **We . . . did it. But . . .* *

I know. We can't descend until you—

Look around. Tarresk was already cupping his spell-wings to spin in place. **And Sheedrra, count.**

Three. You?

Four. No, five. He counted the fifth cloud breath that he exhaled, despite the warming spell. **Sound off, every tenth breath now.**

Sheedrra preferred to hold position, so, instead, she was turning her head. **What are those?**

Tarresk looked in the direction of Sheedrra's pointing claw. *Those* were a series of sinuous, shimmering, dancing ribbons of layers of iridescent blue and green and yellow light. Tarresk and Sheedrra couldn't tell whether they were miles high and miles away, or right before them, barely taller than themselves.

Are those moonbows?

No, moonbows are curved, like rainbows. Could they be starbows? Sailors told tales about the ribbons of light in the night sky. These, however, didn't quite match the descriptions he remembered, yet they looked and felt strangely, painfully *familiar.*

They do kind of look like them, but they're pretty rare this far South. Fifteen.

Could they be . . . ?

Maybe . . . ? Tarresk slid into position in front of Sheedrra. **Positions. Fifteen.**

Sheedrra shifted into the high guard position behind and above his left wing. Normally, their positions would be reversed, but was Tarresk's flight, so he was on point. **Tarresk . . . I think they've noticed us.**

That much was obvious. The ribbons halted their flowing, dancing movements and momentarily froze in place, their colors shifting up the rainbow into oranges and reds as they got larger and larger.

And I don't think they like us.

Tarresk could feel it now: a discordant, harmonic buzzing at the upper range of their Mindspeech. **Don't make any sudden moves, don't attack. Whatever they are, they're intelligent . . . I think.**

The ribbons continued to slither toward them through the air like sea eels caught on the beach at low tide. One in particular seemed to angle in his direction, until it completely disappeared from his vision. He blinked, glancing right and left to find it.

Tarresk! Dive! It's right in front of you!

He instinctively folded his wings into an emergency sideways dive, then looked back to see the side of the ribbon trailing across where he had just been. There was another ribbon right in front of Sheedrra, and she was quickly turning her head and glancing around as if she had lost sight of it, too. **Sheedrra, dive!**

Sheedrra ducked and dove, and the ribbon slid across her spell-crafted wings. Her Mindcall of pain lanced through his mind, and he could see the thin crimson mark where it sliced across her spell-crafted wings. **They're too thin—we can't see them edge on. We've got to watch out for each other.**

We've got to retreat!

Tarresk agreed; he wanted to dive back to the sixth cloud-height, but they were all around them, above and below. **We're trapped. Why are they attacking us? Are they protecting their territory?**

They're protecting themselves! We're predators! Change!

Two unknown, giant magical predatory raptors suddenly appearing among a flock of flying magical beings? Of *course* they'd be defensive. It was at least worth the try. Tarresk focused on his spells, and transformed the image of the giant gryfalcon into the image of one of the great sea albatrosses that soared above the bay. Sheedrra did the same, becoming the longfaring frigate bird.

The discordant buzzing feeling suddenly smoothed to a smooth hum as the ribbons returned to their cooler colors as they swirled and danced around Tarresk and Sheedrra, to their mingled surprise and suspicion.

*Sheedrra, you good?*

Sheedrra didn't answer immediately. _*I'm . . . good. I'm good.*_ She didn't look good, but the scars across her spell-wings were slowly regenerating.

*Count?*

*I lost count. Thirty? Thirty-five? You?*

*I think, maybe thirty. We should descend.*

*I want to talk to them.*

*How? Their Mindspeech isn't very talkative.*

*I think . . . I think they talk by flying.*

*Like that Haighlei kingdom, where they tell stories by dancing?*

*It's worth a try. Forty.* Sheedrra picked the one closest and mimicked its movement by slipping side-to-side alongside it. The ribbon paused, then ducked and turned a series of unseen corners. Sheedrra followed. The ribbon was joined by a second, performing a series of steep climbs and precipitous dives. Sheedrra followed, the mage lights on her harness leaving red and amber trails of light in her wake.

*What are they saying?*

_*I_ think _they're saying hello.*_

More and more of the ribbons started flying alongside her, and Sheedrra followed.

*You should join us. This is fun!*

Her enthusiasm was infectious, but Tarresk slowly shook his head. That was unlike the very serious Sheedrra he knew, watching her soar with a fluid grace that surpassed his own. He lost count of the number of times she passed by him . . .

Count?

Tarresk swore by the Winged Ones. He was so focused on watching Sheedrra that he'd forgotten his own counting. Was it fifty? Sixty? _*Sheedrra! Count!*_

*What?*

Count!

One, two, three . . .

Tarresk swore again. He felt light-headed, dizzy, confused, the subtle and often overlooked signs of air starvation. The same must be true with Sheedrra, maybe even more so. He was suddenly terrified of losing consciousness or losing his partner, or he'd never have seriously considered what he was about to do.

Tarresk waited until the moment when Sheedrra looped underneath him, then he pounced on her back. Her enthusiastic delight instantly became hysterical, instinctive panic, and she bucked and rolled forward to throw him off. He cupped the air to retain control, but Sheedrra continued to tumble tail over head. He was half afraid the ribbons would interfere, but they seemed to lose interest in Sheedrra the moment she stopped flying with them. He tried to disengage, to get a better angle, but his left rear paw was fouled in the straps of Sheedrra's rescue harness, and her tumble dragged him along and around and around helplessly, like a child's toy on a string, before he was able to cut himself free with a wild slash from the claws of his other paw.

Sheedrra continued to flail about more than uselessly, her flying spells decaying, transforming her tumble into an uncontrolled, spiraling, sideways fall. Tarresk tightened his wings and dived after her, pouring every bit of magic he still controlled to expand his flying spells. He lost precious moments trying to avoid her flailing wings until he could close and grab her harness before they dropped back into the sixth cloud-height, finally succeeding on the third attempt. Sheedrra screamed and flailed her wings defensively at the sudden jolt, and her wing struck the side of his face. He heard the distinct *crack* of a bone breaking and hoped without belief that it was his skull and not Sheedrra's wing bone; but then he could see shards of the lower wing bones jutting out between the bloody feathers near her elbow.

Sheedrra screamed again as her wing went limp. Then her whole body went limp, and there was nothing he could do for her except to hang on with every ounce of his strength through the sixth cloud-height layer. Not that he was in much better condition: He saw stars in his slowly narrowing field of vision, his wing joints were screaming in agony from fighting the savage winds, and his lungs were on fire from the frigid air.

Tarresk abandoned the now-flagging tatters of his flying spells and concentrated on the emergency lifting spell. It was even harder for him to cast in an emergency than in practice. His sole fading thought, as he descended into the fifth cloud-height, other than tenaciously holding the lifting spell, was that he hoped the rising specks of light from below were the Silverwing Gryphons with the nets ready to snatch them out of the air before they hit the water.

Tarresk's muscles hurt. His head hurt. Blazes, his *feathers* hurt. But nothing else hurt. He accepted that as an improvement. Well, at least he was alive and suddenly conscious enough to feel it, and to *smell* it, too, the familiar sharp, salty smell of the seashore at high tide.

Alive, but did he succeed? He remembered every moment of his flight with blue-water clarity, up to the moment he tumbled into unconsciousness as he tumbled into the waiting nets alongside Sheedrra. But he couldn't call his flight a success if it meant losing his partner . . .

"Sheedr-r-ra?" That was a mistake, for now his throat hurt.

"Her-r-re." The plaintive response came from somewhere beside him.

He opened his eyes, which, thankfully, did *not* hurt, and saw her laid out on the sand, wings spread, and a squad of Silver Gryphon *trondi'irn* and Healers hovering over her. "My head hur-r-rts-s-s." Probably because the Healers had already blocked the pain from her wing.

Tarresk nodded in sympathy. "Mine, too."

"Here." Sask knelt before him, holding a deep bowl of water with herbs floating in it. "Drink, drink."

Tarresk drank his fill, then suddenly noticed the torch-lit

silhouettes of Vellish and Gerrin behind Sask. Gerrin stepped into the torchlight. "Tell me what happened."

Tarresk's querying answer of "Now?" was drowned out by a chorus of "*Later*!" from Sask and the Healers surrounding Sheedrra.

"Now."

Sask and the other Healers and helpers looked to Vellish, who said nothing but said everything necessary by backing away, outside the circle of torchlight entirely.

"Initial report now. Debriefing later. Before you have an opportunity to forget anything."

"We did it. Seventh cloud-height layer." Sheedrra nodded, once. "Stayed ther-r-re. Stayed too long. Air starvation. Got to us. Didn't notice it, until . . . almost too late." His stomach rumbled, and not in a good way.

"Air s-s-spell . . . is les-s-s-s efficient . . . than our worst estimates-s-s . . . at greater heights-s-s." Sheedrra's stomach also rumbled.

"That's . . . where we found . . . *them*."

"*Them?*"

"Air-r-r-r elementals. Have to be."

"Like the *Vrondi*?"

Sask refilled the bowl, and Tarresk took another long drink before replying. "Like the *Vrondi* . . . as like me and a sparrow."

Vellish's voice rose quietly over the answering murmurs and mutterings of the nearby *hertasi*, humans, and gryphons tilting their heads to listen attentively. "Such elementals are very powerful, very unpredictable, and fortunately very rare. There are Haighlei sorcerers who specialize in dealing with elementals, and they rarely see one in their lifetimes."

"Indeed." Gerrin turned back to Tarresk. "Did you see any reason why they would be present?"

Tarresk looked up from the bowl. "Node up there, *way* up ther-r-re, high seventh cloud-height layer. Maybe higher-r-r, I think."

"You felt a node at that distance? That altitude?"

Tarresk nodded.

"Well, when you both finish your Mastery—and, I am told on the best authority that it is *when*, not *if*—I suspect you will be able to correct your spells and use that node to stay up there longer to communicate with them."

Both Tarresk and Sheedrra stared at Gerrin, wide-eyed, as did Sask.

"Just one final detail: I believe Vellish has something to say to you, Tarresk."

"And I have something . . . to say to him."

Vellish stepped forward into the light beside Gerrin, a questioning look in his eyes.

"Vellish? Know the answer. Know why I did it, why they did it. Needed to be done, the duty of the Silvers to do it, I was the best to do it."

"*We* were the best to do it."

Vellish smiled and nodded to both Tarresk and Sheedrra, then held out his fist to Tarresk. He opened it to reveal a brass feather, which he attached to the pectoral collar of Tarresk's flight harness. Tarresk's eyes widened. Vellish held out his other fist: inside was another brass feather, which he presented to a wide-eyed Sheedrra.

"Granting these awards for service above and beyond the call of duty to cadets is unusual, but you both deserve them. However, while I am not going to completely break tradition and graduate you both immediately, I have a feeling that *that* will be only a formality in the very near future."

Boundaries

Mercedes Lackey

Herald Lagan was not at all happy being where he was right now. Neither was his Companion, Hal. They were just across the Border inside Karse—although if he moved a little east or north, he'd be back in Valdemar. The Border here twisted and turned like a snake through wooded hills tall enough to be called mountains, and this was one of those pockets where Karse intruded into Valdemar like—like—

:A tumor,: suggested Hal.

:It's not a tumor,: he replied from his position, on his stomach, under an evergreen bush, which he fondly hoped (but was anything but sure of) would cloak his "Oh, shoot me now" Herald's Whites. If he'd had time to change—if he'd had time to smear Hal with a coating of red mud—

Well, he hadn't.

:It's not a tumor,: he repeated. *:This is what happens when you let cows and goats dictate your borders.:* It was more complicated than that, of course, but if you boiled down the Border-setting process to absolute basics, this came pretty close to the truth. At least this bush was pleasantly fragrant and *not* home to a million crawling critters.

The eight bandits he was after had completely relaxed their guard after crossing at the point where the bulge ventured farthest into Valdemar. They were plodding along a game trail below him with the air of men who know they hadn't anything to worry about. Because of course they didn't. What idiot would pursue them out of Valdemar into Karse?

:These idiots,: Hal supplied helpfully.

He'd been tracking this particular band of bandits since he arrived at the Border two moons ago. They'd been operating with virtual impunity for moons, which was why he'd been sent for. Herald Lagan was . . . not an ordinary Herald.

He'd always managed to be one step behind them until now, and once he realized the trail was finally hot instead of cold, he'd been adamant he was not going to let them get away this time. Small problem: The Border Guard here was—less than helpful, being pig-headed and stubborn about crossing into Karse.

:Boundaries are there for a reason. It's generally smart not to cross them.:

:Thank you, Captain Obvious.:

It wasn't as if he had a choice. These bastards were fast, clever, and ridiculously sneaky. This was quite literally the first time he'd set actual eyes on them. Until now, all he and the Guard had found were the remains of those they'd attacked. Traps and setups had been absolutely useless, according to the Guard Captain. Lagan suspected there was an informant somewhere in the Guard Post—or maybe the bandits had a Farseer among them.

Or perhaps one of the Karsite priests was helping them. Some Karsite priests certainly had powers, whether you called it Mind-magic or real magic. They certainly had ways of detecting children with Gifts, who were always taken from their parents and sometimes burned on the spot.

In light of that suspicion, Lagan had left the Guard Post, hadn't told anyone where he was going, and had spent the last fortnight moving around the arc of that Border bulge, looking for fresh signs of a crossing. Finally, fortune had been kind in the early dawn. *Or unkind, depending.* He'd found the signs—but they were going back into Karse.

But he was damned if he was going to expend all that effort for nothing. With Hal bitching the entire way, he'd crossed into enemy territory, and now he had his quarry in sight.

Now lead me to your camp, you bastards. If fortune is still with me, you'll take me to it, and my Gift and I will end you. If fortune is not with me, maybe I can find a way to slip aconite into your stew.

Fortune was not with him.

In the early afternoon, the demeanor of the entire band of eight bandits had changed. They went from having a leisurely stroll through the forest to *sneaking* through the forest, and if he hadn't been one of the best trackers in the Heraldic Circle, he'd have lost them. He'd had to move up on them a lot closer than he preferred, and now he watched from heavy cover—a cluster of bushes taller than a house—as they went over a ridge ahead, one by one. It was pretty obvious they had a goal in mind, and somehow he doubted it was their own camp. Oh, it could have been, but his instincts told him—based on the fact that none of them were in the least burdened by loot—that whatever target they'd had in Valdemar had been disappointing. So now they must have another victim in mind, in Karse.

And under any other circumstances, Lagan would just go back home and let them plague the Karsites . . . but . . . well, there were two things about that scenario he didn't like. The first was that he'd have to go through all of this again to find them coming into Valdemar, which would take time and luck, a lot of it. And the second was that the common farming and working folk of Karse weren't his enemies. The priests and their armies were.

:When nations war, it is always the common people who suffer, not the ones in high places.:

He snorted a little. *:Turning philosopher on me? Going to offer your services as a teacher at the Collegium?:*

:Mostly just talking to keep in contact with you. Just in case.:

Lagan didn't blame him. Oh, people said the Karsite demons only came out at night, but he knew from personal experience that it wasn't true. The priests could call them up at any time of the day or night; it was simply that they turned the creatures loose after dark every night as a way of controlling the masses. When you didn't dare leave your home after sunset, it was difficult to mount any sort of resistance movement.

:Keep well back,: Lagan advised, because the track led over that ridge ahead of him, and the last thing he needed was a bright white horse silhouetted against the blue sky. He got down on his belly and crawled up that ridge, wriggling under some faintly spicy brush to get there; and when he was able to get to where he could see below, he was glad he'd been that careful.

He'd found the bandits, all right. And he'd found their target.

It was a little village of about a dozen cottages, all surrounding a tiny Sun Temple in a pattern he was very familiar with. The bandits were spreading out on a second ridge below him. They'd probably attack at sunset, when everyone had gathered for the sundown ritual, and no one would have anything in their hands that could be used as a weapon.

He smiled grimly. They were about to have a very bad time.

Lagan had a very unique Gift, and he was about to make good use of it.

He backed out from under the bush and wriggled over until he had enough room to get his bow off his back and string it. It was one of the most powerful bows he had ever seen or heard of; certainly the most powerful any Herald used. And he was the most expert marksman in living memory, and that was no boast.

Nor was it his Gift . . . .

He could shoot from any position, including upside down. Shooting prone with the bow parallel to the ground was not a problem. And that wasn't his Gift, either.

He carefully put a murderous man-killing arrow to the string, sighted on his target, pulled, and—

And *now* he used his Gift. Or, rather, Gifts.

He concentrated with all his strength on the farthest man from him on the right, tightening his focus, until he saw the unprotected back of the man's neck as clearly as if he were standing mere inches from him. Some sort of Farsight, the experts at the Collegium thought, although he couldn't use it on anything that wasn't within his visual range.

Then he focused fiercely on the spot between the base of the skull and the spine, feeling tension building up inside him until it was nearly unbearable. And at that point, he released the tension and the bowstring.

He didn't even bother to wait to see if he'd hit, because he never missed. Instead, he put a new arrow to the string and sighted in on the farthest man from him on the left.

That was his second Gift. Some variation on Fetching, or so the mavens said. And—well, it was somewhat difficult for even the experts to tell what he was doing. It was as if he somehow connected the arrow *to* the target, and the arrow went straight to the spot he fixated on, like a bit of iron to a lodestone. He wasn't interested in the mechanics of it. He didn't care what it was, as long as it worked. And this was why he was no ordinary Herald and seldom rode Circuit.

:The Queen's Assassin,: mused Hal.

:Call it whatever you like. I've never eliminated anyone who didn't deserve it. You've seen what those bastards are doing.: It angered him a little that Hal should apply the term to him; his Companion should know better. He loosed the second arrow and nocked a third.

:I apologize, Chosen,: Hal said contritely.

He waited until he had nocked the fourth arrow before replying, letting his anger go with the arrow. *:You should. You know better. I am no more an "assassin" than the members of the Guard are.:* And since he had been a member of the Guard, an expert marksman at the young age of fifteen, before being Chosen, he felt doubly irritated. After all, this was most of his duty. But he was used to channeling his anger into his Gift, and he did so now, picking off his targets so precisely that they didn't utter a sound when he hit, and they didn't move afterward.

He searched the ledge below for the last of the eight bandits.

And his anger built again. He took care of problems like this. He was good at it. Thanks to his Gifts, he was *damn* good at it. He didn't boast about it; in fact, he'd wager no more than a double handful of people knew what he did, and most of those were in the Heralds' ranks. And he wasn't *proud* of it, any more than a Mindspeaker was proud of their Gift . . . .

. . . .and he realized too late that he'd let his anger overwhelm his vigilance when he heard the footsteps practically on top of him.

He wriggled around beneath the bush just in time to see that the last bandit was on top of him, and he nearly got his skull split by an axe.

In fact, it was only the bush that saved him. Thick, prolific branches protected him. At least for that moment.

He began trying to scramble out of that dubious cover as if the bush were on fire.

The bandit was a big, beefy man, and a lot faster than he had any right to be. As Lagan struggled to free himself of the now-imprisoning bush, twigs, leaves, and entire branches showered down around him while his attacker went at the unfortunate shrub with a hail of blows in order to get to him.

He scrabbled frantically out of the way, but he'd barely gotten free when the bandit managed to connect, right in the meat of his upper left arm. He screamed and lost his grip on his bow, his right hand clawing at his dagger because his sword was pinned beneath him.

The bandit wrenched the blade of the axe free and heaved it overhead—

—And was struck by a white bolt of screaming lightning in the shape of a horse.

No time to think; solve the next problem, which was that his arm was pouring blood. Lagan was too busy trying to get his belt off to tie around his arm to pay attention to what Hal was doing, but from the sound of it, there wasn't going to be anything left of the axe-wielding bandit but red mud.

And there won't be anything left of me if I can't get the blood cut off.

The pain was indescribable, but what had Lagan howling with fear inside was the amount of blood pouring out of his wound. If he didn't get a tourniquet around that arm—

It was taking too long. *It was taking too long.* He heard himself making an agonized whine between his clenched teeth as his vision narrowed, then began to gray out.

:Hang on, Chosen, help is coming!: he heard dimly.

Help? Help from where? *Karsites will just kill me faster.*

And the last thing he saw before he lost consciousness completely was a man in black robes dashing out of the trees, robes held above his skinny knees so he could run faster than a man of his apparent age had any right to do.

Long ago, Lagan had learned to keep his eyes shut and all his other senses open when he regained consciousness after passing out. If he was in friendly hands, that just allowed him to assess himself before he alerted whoever he was with that he was aware again. And if he was in unfriendly hands—

Had that been a Karsite priest?

He didn't know anyone else in Karse who would wear long black robes.

Surprisingly, his wounded arm didn't hurt as badly as it should have. It throbbed dully, but he should have been in agony from a wound that bad.

"You might as well open your eyes, Demon-Rider," said a matter-of-fact voice in Karsite, from very near his right side. "I've known you were awake for the last five or six breaths. And I need you awake for what I need to pour into you. I can't have you choking to death after all the work I just put into you."

Reluctantly he opened his eyes. He was lying on something soft and was covered with an old quilt. To his right was a middle-aged, hawk-faced man with a small beard, dressed in the black robes of a Karsite priest of Vkandis. Next to the priest was a large cat with the most peculiar markings Lagan had ever seen. It was mostly white, but its face, tail, and paws were marked like an orange tabby, and it had the bluest eyes he had ever seen outside of a Companion.

"Good," the priest said, before he could open his mouth to say anything at all. "Now, I beg your forgiveness, but shut the hell up, because I have a lot to tell you very quickly. I sent your demon-horse far enough away to be safe, but you two have definitely drawn attention, and that attention will be here very soon. You are Lagan."

How does he know my name? Lagan stared at him, numb.

"You are a woodcutter for this village, which is called Chert. You injured yourself when your axe rebounded from a tree limb. I found you; my name is Father Kefner. You were a bit feeble-minded before this happened, so act as stupid as you like when the Inquisitor shows up. I am going to give you a potion to drink that will block your Mind-magic for about half a day, so the Demon-Master won't detect it. If you refuse to drink it, I will just give you a dagger to kill yourself with, because that will be kinder than what the Demon-Masters will do to you when they haul you away."

Lagan obviously had mere heartbeats to determine what to do. He realized several things in that moment, but the primary one was that if the Karsite had wanted him dead, all the priest would have had to do was leave him where he'd fallen.

"Potion," he croaked, allowing that simple fact to determine what he was going to do.

"Good choice," said Father Kefner, and helped him to raise his head enough to drink, then held a bowl full of a bitter-tasting liquid to his lips. He drank it, slowly, as the priest went on. "This will also help some of your pain, but not so much your tongue will be loosened."

Almost immediately he felt something like wool fleece folding around his mind, muffling it. He didn't bother trying to speak to Hal; by now Hal would be out of range of his very limited

Mindspeech anyway, even without this "potion" to block it. The priest got up as soon as he'd drained the bowl and looked down at him with stern approval.

"Get a good look around; you may be the first of your kind to set eyes on the inside of a Temple of the Sunlord. This is where village priests bring our sick and injured so the priests can help them—if they know anything of Healing, that is—and rest."

"What, they don't pray to the Sunlord for healing?" he croaked in Karsite.

The priest had started to walk away, but he looked back, this time with an amused expression. "But the Sunlord would already know about their illness or injury, no? And if He feels they deserve Healing, they'll get it, without any begging involved."

The priest took the bowl over to the back of the structure, followed by the cat, leaving Lagan alone to take stock of his situation.

The arm wound throbbed dully, but the pain wasn't too bad, all things considered. He craned his head around to look at his arm, but he couldn't see anything because of the extremely professional-looking bandage around it.

And that was when he realized that under the quilt he was stark naked.

"My clothes!" he blurted.

"Burned," came the voice from the back of the building. "I told you, you and your demon-horse attracted attention, and I needed to erase all proof that you are a Demon-Rider before they get here. I put your bow and quiver on the demon-horse before I sent him away. We are not permitted such powerful weapons=nothing but light bows and hunting arrows that bring down small game. My plan is that the bandits you slew will be found, and the investigators will determine you killed them and then went back across the border to safety."

You could have put my uniform on Hal too, Lagan thought, although his thoughts seemed to be slow and hard to put together. But then again . . . the man must have sent Hal away long before undressing him. So, of course, the only thing he could do with the distinct uniform was burn it.

There were sounds as if Father Kefner was washing something. The bowl? His voice came from the back of the building. "I did not thank you for disposing of those murderous whoresons, so I will do so now. Why did you not leave them to attack us?"

The priest returned from the back of the room with a cup, which he set down beside Lagan as he resumed his seat on the stool next to the cot. The cat took up a position beside him, fixing its blue eyes on Lagan.

"The first reason is that I've been tracking them for moons, and I was damned if I was going to let them get away just because they'd crossed into Karse." Was that too much? Were the drugs affecting his judgment?

"And the second reason?" The priest asked mildly.

He wanted to shrug, but—bad idea, that would hurt a lot. "I didn't like the idea of them attacking a village full of farmers and children."

"Would you like to sit up and take some water?" the priest asked, with a measuring look at him—as if his answer had actually satisfied the man in some way. "You should. You lost a great deal of blood."

His mouth felt full of the same wool his brain was wrapped in. "Please."

Father Kefner helped him to sit up and packed some cushions behind him so he could stay that way. He needed them; when he tried to raise himself up on his elbows he realized he was as weak as a grass stem and just moving a little made him dizzy. Was that the potion too, or the blood loss? Probably both.

Father Kefner handed him the wooden cup, which was remarkably thin and made of a beautiful wood with a changing sheen not unlike the semiprecious gem called silkstone. He took it in his good hand, which shook with the effort.

"You lost a great deal of blood," the priest observed, dispassionately. "I hope you like spinach, lentils and liver, because you are going to be eating a lot of them until I can be rid of you. Mostly spinach and lentils," he added. "We are not a wealthy people."

Before he could reply, Lagan was distracted by the sound of many horses approaching; the thudding of hooves on dirt was unmistakable, although it did not sound as if they were in a hurry.

"And that is the attention you drew," said the priest calmly. "There will be at least one Inquisitor-priest among them. Remember, you are a woodcutter, you are somewhat simple, you hurt yourself when your axe rebounded on you, and most important of all, you were cutting wood here, down in the village, not up on that ridge. Slur your words at least a little. Being under the influence of a drug will allow you to say as little as you can get away with."

Then, before Lagan could reply, the priest got up and went to the door, leaving the cat behind. He closed it behind himself, giving Lagan a chance to think about his story—and get a better look at his surroundings.

He found himself in a small, neat building that consisted of a single room, perfectly square, made entirely of wood. Now that he was sitting up, he saw the rear third of the building was separated from the rest by a wooden wall with a single door in it. Presumably that was where the priest lived. In the middle of that dividing wall and pressed against it was something like an altar. Surmounting that altar was a statue. Both were made of the same silky-golden wood as the cup he was holding. He had been laid on a cot immediately in front of that altar, which had a Sun-In-Glory carved into its face.

As for the statue, which presumably was Vkandis Sunlord, it was exquisitely carved, but it was the most peculiar image of a god that Lagan had ever seen.

Every single bit of that statue had been sculpted with such exactitude that Lagan would not have been in the least surprised to see every single hair on the god's head depicted—but the face had barely been sketched in. It was just a suggestion of eyebrows, nose, a swelling where the lips would be.

And this was not a case of the carver leaving something half-finished; that much was obvious by the satin-sheen of the highly polished wood of this hint of a face. This was deliberate.

And it was astonishingly beautiful. So beautiful, in fact, that he found himself staring at it, mouth agape, lost in the wonder of it. The cat purred, as if it approved of his admiration.

The sound of approaching voices interrupted his slightly impaired thoughts. And before he could even do more than register the fact that there were at least two people approaching this building, the door opened, and Father Kefner gestured to his companion to come inside.

If Lagan had been thinking clearly, this was when he would have been terrified, because Kefner's associate was a red-robe priest. The demon-summoners wore red robes . . . .

But he wasn't thinking clearly, thanks to those drugs. Or was he? Because he remembered very distinctly what he was supposed to be and do. He was Lagan, a simple-minded woodcutter. As such, he was probably too dim to fear a priest, but he should also be very shy and self-abasing in the presence of not one but two of them. So he held his tongue, dropped his gaze to his cup, and just kept his ears open.

"—too busy tending poor Lagan to have noticed anything," Kefner was saying. "It was a very nasty cut, and he lost a great deal of blood. He's just lucky he was down here in the village instead of up in the hills."

"Well, my soldiers are looking in the hills overlooking Chert now," said the red-robe, glancing at Lagan. "If there is a Demon-Rider up there, we'll find him soon enough."

The new priest was cut from similar cloth to Kefner: lean, with a face like a bird of prey, though to Lagan he looked more like a falcon than a hawk. His dark eyes rested only a moment on the disguised Herald before rising to the statue he lay beneath.

"By the Great God, I had heard of the skill of the carvers of Chert, but I had no idea . . . ." His voice trailed away as his face took on an expression of wonder, one that significantly softened those harsh features. "This is amazing . . . ."

"Our carvers will be pleased to make you another for your own temple," Kefner said pleasantly. "But it will take a very long time. A year, at least."

"Red-robes are not associated with any temple," the other reminded him, with some regret in his voice.

"Then allow me to make you a personal gift from the village of Chert." Kefner went into his living quarters and returned with two small carvings, about as tall as a woman's forearm was long. "Do you prefer Vkandis Veiled or Unveiled?"

"Unveiled, please." The red-robe took the statue reverently from Kefner and examined it closely. "Incredible," he breathed.

"And now you know why Chert manages to survive despite living here in the hills where farming is . . . difficult." Kefner returned the other statue to wherever he had stored it and came back. "This is how we manage to bring in the money we need to buy all the many things we cannot grow for ourselves. Mind, it takes a very long time to make one of these, so it is not as if my villagers are ever going to see wealth. But nearly every household has a carver; the unskilled do the rough shaping and polishing, the skilled perform the actual carving, and the whole village shares in the profits these images bring."

"Clearly their wealth is in the blessing of the God on their hands," said the red-robe. Kefner handed him a piece of fabric that he took from the back of a chair, and the red-robe wrapped his statue in it with great care. "So one of these begins at the hands of your unfortunate woodcutter here?"

The red-robe turned his gaze on Lagan, and his expression grew inscrutable again.

But Kefner laughed gently. "Ah, no. Each branch that is made into a statue is carefully selected and culled from a living tree by its carver. Silk-oak is rare, and we do not cut down entire trees unless we get a commission for a temple-sized image. Instead, we have pollarded most of the trees nearest Chert, and we cull branches one at a time when they have reached sufficient girth. What is left of the branch that is not sufficient to carve amulets or statues is made into our cups and plates by laminating small pieces of wood together. Lagan is a good man, but he hasn't the wit to select and cut silk-oak. Have you, Lagan?"

"No, Father Kefner," Lagan said obediently. "My wood is for cooking, making charcoal, and keeping people warm." He tried to widen his eyes and make his expression innocent. "I should have known better than to cut that treacherous willow, but it makes such good charcoal! And the smith cannot make knives and chisels and hoes and horseshoes without charcoal."

The red-robe came closer to him. "So, Lagan, have you seen any Demon-Riders out in the hills when you were felling trees?"

Don't overplay this, Lagan. He shook his head and dropped his eyes, hoping he looked confused instead of suspicious. *What would a simpleton say? Probably nothing.*

The red-robe drew nearer and casually—too casually—put his hand on Lagan's head. Lagan held his breath. What had Kefner said about the other priests being able to detect Mind-magic? Did they have Mind-magic as well? The cat narrowed its eyes and stared at both of them, as if it were concentrating on the two of them. Or thinking about pouncing on something.

But before he could really begin to feel fear through the muffling effect of Kefner's drugs, the red-robe took his hand away and chuckled. "You are doubtless a good soul, Lagan, and as thick as two of your best planks. Be more careful about how you use your axe in the future—"

It sounded as if he was going to say more, but there was a knock at the door, and a Karsite soldier entered. "Your Grace! We found bandit bodies on the ridge above the village! Eight of them!"

The priest sprang to his feet and turned to face the soldier. "Report!" he snapped.

The soldier described the seven men Lagan had shot, then added, "And at the last body, which was on the next ridge up from the first, we found signs of a struggle—and the body was trampled, not shot."

"So," mused the priest aloud. "The Demon-Rider shot seven,

the eighth ambushed him, and was killed by the demon-horse. But why was he here in the first place?"

"We are not that far from the Border, and there has been a small band of bandits working here lately," Kefner said. "They had not troubled us until now, likely because we have no obvious signs of wealth or, indeed, anything much a bandit would want. But the other villages near us have been robbed, so I suppose after eliminating obvious targets, we were all that was left."

"But why did the Demon-Rider dare to—oh, of course." The red-robe nodded. "They have been working both sides of the Border, without a doubt, and the Demon-Rider followed them here."

"Strange that he would do that," Kefner observed in a neutral tone of voice.

The red-robe shrugged. "Perhaps we see the Will of Vkandis in this, to use the enemy to save those who create his image with such fidelity."

"If he is riding his demon-horse, he will be long gone across the Border again, your Grace," the soldier offered.

"If he has any sense, he will be." The red-robe snorted. Then he looked down at Lagan.

Lagan felt paralyzed under the red-robe's gaze. This priest was no fool. What if—

But before his thoughts could get any further than that, the cat sprang up and bounced to the priest's feet, light as a kitten, and began rubbing back and forth against the priest's legs, purring so loudly the sound filled the room.

Once again, the priest's sharp expression softened, and he bent down to pet the cat with his free hand, since the other still cradled the wrapped statue. "This is a handsome fellow," the priest said. "You are fortunate to have him. What is his name?"

Kefner chuckled. "I'm not certain what he calls himself, but I call him Petros, and he answers to it readily enough."

"Especially when fish or chicken is involved, hmm, Petros?" the red-robe laughed. "Well, under ordinary circumstances, I might have exercised my right to take hospitality of your village for myself and my men, but it is early enough for us to reach our garrison before nightfall, and this—" he lifted the swathed statue a little, "—has left me in your debt. So let me discharge that, and we'll be on our way."

He left off petting the cat and came back to Lagan's side, this time resting his hand on the bandage covering his shoulder. His eyes closed for a moment, and warmth spread from his hand all through Lagan's arm.

The Herald was quite familiar with being Healed, and this felt exactly like that. A moment later the priest removed his hand, and Lagan flexed the arm experimentally. It scarcely hurt at all.

"Your Grace!" he said, as if blurting it. "I—"

"Save your breath for recovering, Woodsman Lagan," the red-robe told him. "And remember that Vkandis chose to bless you because of your faith." He turned to Kefner. "Thanks for your gift, Father Kefner. All's well that ends well, eh?"

"Indeed," Kefner said. "Let me at least show you out and provide you and your men with a refreshing drink of birch beer to see you on the road."

"I certainly will not object to that."

The two priests left, followed by the soldier. The cat remained. Lagan let out his breath in a long sigh of relief as the cat jumped up on the cot and paraded up his legs to sit on his lap.

"Petros, your timing was impeccable, and I thank you," he told the cat gravely.

The cat just purred.

A little time passed, as the cat settled down on Lagan's lap, with Lagan petting him while the cat purred strongly enough to vibrate the entire cot. Finally, there was the sound of retreating hoofbeats, and Father Kefner returned.

"That went as well as I could have wished," the priest said mildly. "Petros, would you please tell the demon-horse that it will be safe to cross the Border at dawn to retrieve his rider?"

The cat looked up and mouthed a silent "meow" at the priest.

Lagan's jaw dropped. "What—"

"How do you think I knew you were up there on the ridge and what you were doing?" Father Kefner asked. "Petros told me and came to fetch me."

"But—"

"Petros is a Firecat, creatures beloved of the Sunlord and His faithful servants," Kefner continued, as if Lagan should have recognized this. "It has been many long years since Firecats walked among us, but if what I am hearing is true, they are appearing once again, even if far too many of the Sunlord's priests fail to recognize them for what they are. Those they choose to honor with their presence and aid are truly blessed."

Firecat? Is this something like—a Companion?

"Now, I am going to feed you lentil stew, you are going to sleep, and as soon as it is false dawn and safe to leave the village, I'll find something that doesn't leave you naked, and you can be on your way." Kefner didn't quite smile. "This situation is probably equally uncomfortable for both of us."

Lagan could only nod, as the cat smirked in a way that reminded him of Hal.

Early the next morning, Petros the cat led Lagan up a path to the ridge with the silence only a cat is capable of.

Kefner had been as good as his word; he'd seen that Lagan ate a full bowl of lentil stew, and Petros the cat had settled in with him—and as soon as the cat had started purring, he'd found himself unable to keep his eyes open.

He hadn't awakened until Kefner shook him awake, candle in one hand, and a set of well-worn breeches and a much-abused shirt in the other. He lost no time in getting dressed; bolted a rough meal of barley bread and a cold tea of some sort, and then tried to figure out a graceful way to say goodbye. Or even just a less-awkward way.

Kefner had beaten him to it. "Thank you for your service to my village, Demon-Rider, but the sooner I see the last of you, the better it will be for both of us. Perhaps someday—"

"But that day is not today." Lagan nodded. "Thank you for saving me instead of killing me, but for now, boundaries are meant to be kept."

"Indeed," Kefner agreed, and he extinguished the candle, letting Lagan out into the dim, gray morning. "Follow Petros."

And so he had, until the welcome bulk of Hal showed white against the darkness of some of that tall shrubbery. He would have run the last few steps, but the Healing the Karsite priest had done hadn't solved *all* his problems, and he'd had quite enough trouble getting up the ridge at a walk.

But Kefner hadn't lied; not only were his bow and quiver fastened to their proper places on Hal's saddle, but the belt holding his knife and sword had been slung around the saddle pommel. He looked around for the cat to thank it—but Petros was already gone.

With considerably more effort than he liked, Lagan got into Hal's saddle, and Hal launched himself off in the direction of the Valdemar Border, obviously just as eager to get out of there as Lagan was.

:That priest—and that cat—know more than they told you, Chosen,: came the welcome Mindvoice in his head. *:Something is happening here in Karse. They might not be our enemies for much longer.:*

He thought about that as Hal galloped across the hills, regardless of paths, taking the shortest way to safety.

:I—never thought I'd say this. But I wouldn't oppose that,: he replied at last. *:Though I would think it would take a miracle.:*

:Miracle? Well,: replied Hal. *:When the gods are involved . . . you never know.:*

He snorted, and he recognized with gratitude that they were nearly on top of the Border. *:That's past my pay grade.:*

:WE GET PAID?: Hal exclaimed.

Which left him laughing as they crossed the border and into the safety of home.

About the Authors

Dylan Birtolo resides in the Pacific Northwest, where he spends his time as a writer, a game designer, and a professional sword-swinger. He's published a few fantasy novels and several short stories. On the game side, he contributed to *Dragonfire* and designed both *Henchman* and *Shadowrun: Sprawl Ops*. He trains in Systema and with the Seattle Knights: an acting troop that focuses on stage combat. He jousts, and yes, the armor is real—it weighs over 100 pounds. You can read more about him and his works at dylanbirtolo.com or follow his Twitter @DylanBirtolo.

Jennifer Brozek is a multitalented, award-winning author, editor, and media tie-in writer. She is the author of *Never Let Me Sleep* and *The Last Days of Salton Academy*, both of which were nominated for the Bram Stoker Award. Her *BattleTech* tie-in novel, *The Nellus Academy Incident*, won a Scribe Award. Her editing work has earned her nominations for the British Fantasy Award, the Bram Stoker Award, and the Hugo Award. She won the Australian Shadows Award for the *Grants Pass* anthology, co-edited with Amanda Pillar. Jennifer's short- form work has appeared in Apex Publications, Uncanny Magazine, and in anthologies set in the worlds of Valdemar, *Shadowrun*, *V-Wars*, *Masters of Orion*, and *Predator*. Jennifer has been a freelance author and editor for over fifteen years after leaving a high-paying tech job, and she has never been happier. She keeps a tight schedule on her writing and editing projects and somehow manages to find time to volunteer for several professional writing organizations such as SFWA, HWA, and IAMTW. She shares her husband, Jeff, with several cats and often uses him as a sounding board for her story ideas. Visit Jennifer's worlds at jenniferbrozek.com.

Paige L. Christie is originally from Maine and now lives in the North Carolina mountains. While she is best known for her *Legacies of Arnan* fantasy series (#1 *Draigon Weather*), her work can also be found in several anthologies, including *Galactic Stew*, *Witches Warriors & Wise Women*, and *Passages*. When she isn't writing, Paige runs a nonprofit soup kitchen and food pantry, walks her dogs too early in the morning, and is teaching herself to crochet (badly). She is a proud founding member of the Blazing Lioness Writers. Find out what she's up to at PaigeLChristie.com.

Brigid Collins is a fantasy and science fiction writer living in Michigan. Her short stories have appeared in *Fiction River*, *Uncollected Anthology Volume 13: Mystical Melodies*, and Mercedes Lackey's Valdemar anthologies. Her fantasy series *Songbird River Chronicles* and her dark fairy tale novella *Thorn and Thimble* are available in print and electronic versions on Amazon and Kobo. You can sign up for her newsletter at tinyletter.com/HarmonicStories or check out her website at backwrites.wordpress.com.

Ron Collins is the bestselling Amazon Dark Fantasy author of *Saga of the God-Touched Mage* and *Stealing the Sun,* a series of space-based SF books. He has contributed 100 or so stories to premier science fiction and fantasy publications, including *Analog*, *Asimov's*, and several editions of the Valdemar anthology series. His work has garnered a *Writers of the Future* prize, and a CompuServe HOMer award. His short story "The White Game" was nominated for the Short Mystery Fiction Society's 2016 Derringer Award. Find current information about Ron at typosphere.com.

Brenda Cooper writes science fiction, fantasy, and the occasional poem. She also works in technology and writes and talks about the future. She has won multiple regional writing awards, and her stories have often appeared in Year's Best anthologies. Brenda lives and works in the Pacific Northwest with her wife and multiple border collies, and she can sometimes be found biking around Seattle.

Hailed as "one of the best writers working today" by bestselling author Dean Wesley Smith, **Dayle A. Dermatis** is the author or coauthor of many novels (including snarky urban fantasies *Ghosted*, *Shaded*, and *Spectered*) and more than a hundred short stories in multiple genres, appearing in such venues as *Fiction River*, *Alfred Hitchcock's Mystery Magazine*, and various anthologies from DAW Books. "Hearts Are Made for Mending" is her sixth story in a Valdemar anthology. She is the mastermind behind the Uncollected Anthology project, and her short fiction has been lauded in year's best anthologies in erotica, mystery, and horror. To find out where she's wandered off to (and to get free fiction!), check out DayleDermatis.com.

English both by name and nationality, **Charlotte E. English** hasn't permitted emigration to the Netherlands to change her essential Britishness (much). She writes colorful fantasy novels over copious quantities of tea, and rarely misses an opportunity to apologize for something. A lifelong history buff with a degree in Heritage, she loves dressing up, touring historical sites, and really good cake. Her whimsical works include the *House of Werth* series and *Modern Magick*. Her short fiction has also appeared in Mercedes Lackey's Valdemar anthologies.

Michele Lang is the author of the *Lady Lazarus* WWII historical fantasy series, and her fantasy, romance, crime, and science fiction short stories have been published by DAW, PM Press, WMG Publishing, and Running Press, among others. She is one of the original contributors to the Uncollected Anthology project, and is currently a Syndicate writer for the new quarterly magazine *Mysteries, Crime, and Mayhem* (MCM). Michele lives on Long Island with her family, and loves writing Valdemar and Elemental Masters stories for Mercedes Lackey anthologies! Learn more about Michele's writing at michelelang.com.

Terry O'Brien is a dual-classed bard/engineer who writes elegant software in several languages and crafts compelling stories and characters in several formats. He currently combines his creative and technical talents behind a camera, in the control room ,or at an edit station as a member of multiple audio and video production teams for several clients, employers and venues. His creative work can be viewed on his website: terryobrien.me.

Fiona Patton was born in Calgary, Alberta, and now lives in rural Ontario with her wife, Tanya Huff, an assortment of cats, and two wonderful dogs. She has written seven fantasy novels published by DAW Books and close to forty short stories. "The Beating of the Bounds" is her 14th story in the Valdemar anthologies, and the 12th to feature the Dann family.

Angela Penrose lives in Seattle with her husband, seven computers and about ten thousand books. She's been a Valdemar fan for decades and wrote her first Valdemar story for the "Modems of the Queen" area on the old GEnie network back in the 1980s. In addition to fantasy, she writes SF and mystery, sometimes in combinations. She's had stories published in *Loosed Upon the World, Fiction River, The Year's Best Crime and Mystery Stories 2016,* and of course the *Choices* Valdemar anthology. Find links to all her work at angelapenrosewriter.blogspot.com.

Kristin Schwengel lives near Milwaukee, Wisconsin, with her husband, along with the obligatory writer's cat (named Gandalf, of course), a Darwinian garden in which only the strong survive, and a growing collection of knitting and spinning supplies. Her writing has appeared in several previous Valdemar anthologies, among others. She was delighted to be able to work a quote from Julian of Norwich, a medieval mystic, into this exploration of the history of Mirideh, the young Karsite Mindhealer.

Anthea Sharp is a *USA Today* bestselling, award-winning author of fantasy and speculative fiction (not to mention a bestselling romance author under the pen name Anthea Lawson). In addition to her Feyland series, where an immersive game opens a gateway to Faerie, Anthea's newest novel, *White as Frost*, is the first in a trilogy retelling of the fairytale "Snow White & Rose Red." Her short fiction has appeared in numerous anthologies. She splits her time between the enchanted forests of the Pacific Northwest and the warm citrus of Southern California. Discover more at antheasharp.com

Stephanie Shaver lives in Washington state, where she is gainfully employed by Wizards of the Coast. Her previous stories have mostly followed Herald Wil and company, but she took a break in *Boundaries* to tell a slightly different tale. You can find more at sdshaver.com, along with the odd snapshots of life and way too many pictures of copper kettles full of jam.

A lover of local history and fantastical possibilities, **Louisa Swann** spins tales that span multiple genres, including historical fantasy, science fiction, mystery, and her newest love—steampunk. Her short stories have appeared in Mercedes Lackey's Elemental Masters and Valdemar anthologies (which she's thrilled to participate in!); Esther Friesner's *Chicks and Balances*; and several Fiction River anthologies, including *No Humans Allowed* and *Reader's Choice*. Her new steampunk/weird west series, The Peculiar Adventures of Miss Abigail Crumb, is available at your favorite etailer. Find out more at louisaswann.com or friend her on Facebook @SwannWriter.

Elizabeth Vaughan is the *USA Today*-bestselling author of fantasy romance novels. You can learn more about Elizabeth's books at writeandrepeat.com. Many, many thanks to Mercedes Lackey and John Helfers, for this opportunity to create in Valdemar. It has been an honor and a privilege.

Elisabeth Waters sold her first short story in 1980 to Marion Zimmer Bradley for *The Keeper's Price*. Her first novel, a fantasy called *Changing Fate*, was awarded the 1989 Gryphon Award. She also edited many of the *Sword & Sorceress* anthologies. Her favorite vacation place is an Episcopal convent.

Phaedra Weldon grew up in the thick, atmospheric land of South Georgia. Most nights, especially those in October, were spent on the back of pickup trucks in the center of cornfields, telling ghost stories, or in friends' homes playing RPGs. She got her start writing in shared worlds (*Eureka!*, *Star Trek*, *BattleTech*, *Shadowrun*), selling original short stories to DAW anthologies, and sold her first urban fantasy series to traditional publishing. Currently she is working on the paranormal women's fiction series *Ravenwood Hills*, as well as researching a new era in *BattleTech*. See more at phaedraweldon.com.

About the Editor

Mercedes Lackey is a full-time writer and has published numerous novels and works of short fiction, including the bestselling Heralds of Valdemar series. She is also a professional lyricist and a licensed wild bird rehabilitator. She lives in Oklahoma with her husband and collaborator, artist Larry Dixon, and their flock of parrots.